BIRTHRIGHT

— BOOK FIVE —

BIRTHRIGHT

The Adventures of Cassandra Rho

PHILLIP MARTIN

Published 2025

Printed in the United States of America

ISBN: 979-8-9913998-2-1 (Hardcover)
ISBN: 979-8-9913998-3-8 (Paperback)
ISBN: 979-8-9913998-4-5 (eBook)

Cover design by Daniela Ivanova
Map art by Shaun Carroll
Edited by Fabled Planet
Design and layout by Teddi Black Design

For information, address:
Phillip Martin
Phillip@cassandra-rho.com
www.cassandra-rho.com

BOOKS IN THE Adventures of Cassandra Rho Series:

I dedicate this book to my readers. Without your interest and support, writing wouldn't be nearly as rewarding. And a special thanks to Ben, Jenny, Shanna, and Trish who helped create four new characters found within these pages and/or in future books.

A special dedication to my sister in-law, Sally, who passed away just before this book was published: She fought cancer like a real-life Cassandra Rho, stubbornly, and maybe with a little magic. Like many warriors before her, she eventually lost her battle with the awful disease. This book is dedicated to you, Sally. You are a hero to many. We miss you.

Serpent
Tribe
Mateon
and
Sitra's
Cottage
Witch's
Rise
Prailic
Droflor
Sylor Woods
Swamp Ikma

Mayton
Tara
Attins
Castle
Denslock
Treesha's
Cottage
Sylor
Werewolf Den
Flig Cave
Flig Field
Nesin
Port Racip
N
W
E
S
100 MILES

Cassandra's World

The Allies:

Cassandra Rho—The main protagonist. Cassandra is born an orphan with strange, mystical powers and a bizarre ability to control ravens.

Kessi Rho—Cassandra's sister. Kessi is pure of heart and as close to her god, Adlesk, as she is to Cassandra.

Greyson Kavince—A prodigy of the god Plath. Greyson has a hard time putting his friends' interests above his insatiable sexual appetite.

Binta Mulay—Cassandra's best friend and love interest. Binta cares deeply for Cassandra and will do anything to protect her.

Baxter Von Glord—An instructor at Victoria's School of Magic. Baxter is a powerful wizard and is madly in love with Cassandra, who is half his age.

Kringus Brahmore—The king of Pelesea. Scarred by a duel with a red dragon, Kringus is a just leader who would do anything for his queen, Penelope.

Penelope Brahmore—The half-elven queen of Pelesea. Penelope's loyalty to Kringus and her city is unmatched.

Lady Victoria—The founder of the school of magic in Pelesea. Victoria is the most powerful wizard in her corner of the world, and Baxter Von Glord is her best friend.

Alleah Mansuell—An attractive priestess of Sinnis. She is as blessed by her god as she is by exquisite beauty.

Daro, the ranger—Keeper of the Woods south of Pelesea. Daro is an ally to Pelesea and an admirer of Sasha De'Formen.

Von and Lenore—The elven cousins to Penelope Brahmore. Von and Lenore are loyal to Pelesea and extremely dangerous when using a bow.

Arrin Malik—The captain of Pelesea's army. Arrin is best friends with Kringus Brahmore and would give his life for him.

Sasha De'Formen—An ice carofex who befriends Daro. Sasha is born with god-like beauty (to the human eye), but the ice carofex find her hideous.

Sabrina—Kessi Rho's best friend. The two grow close sharing a cell as virgin offerings to the demon lord, Marnelphion.

Chloe Fraland—A faithful priestess of Sinnis, and ally to Alleah and Greyson. Chloe is set on ensuring Alleah remains loyal to her goddess.

Jamison Oland—The steward of Pelesea when the royal couple leave the city to adventure. Jamison is madly in love with Binta Mulay and rescues her from servitude.

Breeston—The druid of Swamp Ikma. Breeston uses his power to summon powerful allies to defend the swamp and his friends.

Emiline—An elven vampire bride of Heinsvick. Despite her state of undeath, Emiline has a good heart and befriends Kessi Rho.

Mateon and Sitra—A married couple who befriend Cassandra. Sitra is a sleeth with snake-like hair and a gaze that can petrify. She and her blind husband, Mateon, live in the Yaddaton Desert.

Gophia—A culiem fairy. Gophia and Cassandra Rho become friends during their captivity in Yaddaton.

Spring Goodwright—The charismatic leader of the original New Order. Spring led the ill-advised charge to hell to destroy Marnelphion.

Leo—A member of the original New Order. Leo is known as the most powerful wizard ever to live and battled Marnelphion centuries ago.

The Villains:

Ronnis D'Breeth—The orphanage administrator where Cassandra and Kessi grew up. Ronnis blames Cassandra for all his woes and is intent on exacting revenge.

Cass Ruben—Cassandra's nemesis from Victoria's School of Magic. Cass is Cassandra's rival in every way and loves to humiliate and torture her whenever the opportunity arises.

Matilda—The high priestess of Marnelphion. She is determined to complete the prophecy that will summon Marnelphion back to the human world, requiring Cassandra's sacrifice.

Cerus the Grey—The demi-god son of Gorl. Cerus is Matilda's cruel, blood-thirsty husband who craves battle over anything life offers.

Heinsvick—The vampire lord of Novafontera. Heinsvick is a powerful sorcerer whose arcane abilities have carried over to his state of undeath.

Barktuck Misol—A high priest of Meshlor. Barktuck is good friends with Ronnis D'Breeth and assists him in his quest to capture and torture Cassandra Rho.

Vasheba—A mighty demon. Vasheba is Matilda's designated torturer and looks forward to spending an eternity in hell with her soul.

Marnelphion—The powerful demon lord. Marnelphion is a god-like demon who intends to return to the human world to finish what he started nearly seven hundred years ago.

OTHERS:

Kane, the lich-god—A powerful lich that discovered immortality. Rumored to be Cassandra's father, he seems to enjoy toying with her life.

Boz—A fire carofex mercenary. Boz is as dangerous as he is mysterious and hails from the monastery in Mecca-Loraine. He has never lost a fight or failed a mission.

Maltor—The vicious barbarian leader of the Serpent Tribe in the Yaddaton Desert. Maltor desires Cassandra Rho as a bride.

Jak—A barbarian warrior loyal to his king, Maltor. His unusually mild temperament for a barbarian has allowed him to befriend Cassandra Rho.

Inuentas the Indomitable—The half-demon messenger. Inuentas warns the current New Order of the prophecy centered around Cassandra Rho.

Franklin Ruben—Cass's father. Franklin is a wealthy citizen of Pelesea who serves as an advisor to Jamison Oland and blames Cassandra Rho for his daughter's problems.

Malikai—A demonic sorcerer. Malikai uses his unique powers to assist Matilda and anyone else who doesn't mind paying a steep price.

X'lor—The fallen god, also known as The Mystic, controls the plant life of the realm and possesses powers that could uniquely serve Cassandra and her friends.

Illa—The nepalin demon who serves X'lor and plays hard with intruders in their home of Vasym.

PLACES ON TORLIA:

Oldorburg—The small town where Cassandra and Kessi Rho grew up, located about eight hundred miles south of Pelesea.

Pelesea—A large city ruled by the just king and queen Kringus and Penelope Brahmore. Cassandra flees the evil of Oldorburg and begins life anew in Pelesea.

Novafontera—The dead city that Marnelphion cursed over six hundred years ago. It is located two hundred miles south of Pelesea and is the former home of the original New Order.

Godhomme—A small fortress of goblin hunters located near Pelesea.

Mecca-Loraine—A town located one hundred miles southwest of Oldorburg. Home to the fire carofex monastery and the priests of Meshlor who fled Oldorburg.

Farmer's Stop—A small farming community near Oldorburg.

Vasym—The desolate forest home of X'lor, the fallen god, where ash constantly rains at its core.

PLACES ON VARISH:

Port Racip—A large port city with two sets of leaders, one above ground, the other below ground. Neither vigorously enforce any laws.

Nesin—The mountain fortress home to Matilda and Cerus the Grey, near

Port Racip. The fortress is a base for the Marnelphion priests and Gorl warriors.

Tara—The small community of Plath priests where Greyson Kavince grew up.

Attins—A small farming town at the foot of the mountain where Tara is located.

Swamp Ikma—The home of the mighty dragon, Malebak, and the druid, Breeston.

Yaddaton Desert—Home to the desert barbarian tribes.

Contents

Prologue

Neclesious the imp flew through the tunnels of the mountain fortress of Nesin, striking and killing anyone in his way with his venomous tail. He had been the first imp freed from the magical sack the mercenaries opened. Matilda had ordered the summoning of the imps as a last resort to stop Kessi Rho and the other prisoners from escaping. Neclesious had purposely killed several mercenaries, giddy at the opportunity to punish those responsible for his summoning. He was created for such nefarious purposes and relished the act of murder. Like the other imps released into Nesin after him, Neclesious was born in the depths of hell. However, he was different—he was infused with the blood of his master, Marnelphion, the demon lord. All imps were born of the purest evil, but Neclesious more so, and his power far exceeded his brethren's. Neclesious was evil personified.

Once freed from the bag, he had one objective—to find Matilda, the high priestess in charge of the Great Summoning. She was tasked with that unholy ritual to return Marnelphion to the human world. Neclesious was unconcerned with the potential escapees. He was confident his fellow imps could kill them and, in truth, couldn't care less if they failed. He had a purpose far more important and exciting than babysitting a few worthless sacrificial virgins. And so he flew away from Nesin quickly, homing in on his target—Lady Matilda.

She was unique like Neclesious, her veins blessed with the master's blood. She had obtained that blessing on the streets of Novafontera months ago, where she lingered at death's door. She had been reckless and arrogant and had entered the dead city of Novafontera in search of Marnelphion's essence. The attempt had all but killed her until Marnelphion had decided to spare her life at the gates of hell. Instead, he blessed her with a slight kiss of the poisonous tar that plagued Novafontera. The tar had seeped into her body, into her blood, and mostly into her soul. Because of Marnelphion's blessing, Neclesious could sense her; he could find her and knew exactly where she lingered.

His master demanded that he seek her out and set her on the right course again. She had lost her way, slowly losing control of her charges. Her husband lay dead in Yaddaton's sands, Nesin's fortification was compromised, and the sacrificial lambs were lost. Worst of all, and most enraging to Marnelphion, her congregation dwindled. She had performed a ritual to turn the remaining priests of her cult into powerful undead to keep watch over what few sacrificial subjects she owned. She did so in desperation as she chased Cassandra Rho across the world. And after all her sacrifices, the Rho girl still eluded her. She had lost much and gained nothing. Marnelphion was most displeased!

Matilda was sloppy and needed direction. Marnelphion still deemed her the chosen one to perform the sacred ritual, but the imp would need to guide her to the destination. Neclesious beat his wings as quickly as he could and flew far away from Nesin and to the south, toward Faun's Swamp. Matilda was not there; she was at the edge of the Yaddaton Desert, still chasing after the Rho girl, the one sacrifice required to bring back Marnelphion. Without spilling Cassandra's blood, there was no hope of the Great Summoning occurring.

As crucial as the Rho girl was to everything, the imp knew he should seek another human to assist Matilda in her quest. Marnelphion had specifically imparted his wishes to Neclesious—seek out Bale Maflin to lead the charge to help Matilda. Bale was despicable, even by imp standards, and far more fanatical than Matilda. He would be an excellent companion to the lost priestess; he would see to the capture of Cassandra Rho, as Marnelphion had foreseen it.

So, instead of flying to Yaddaton, Neclesious flew toward the swamp, and the lair deep within that Bale called home. There, he would find Bale and his minions—hundreds of priests, all as passionate as their leader. Bale also had superior control over the undead, even more than Matilda, and his army of zombies numbered thousands. He was an asset that Marnelphion had kept close at hand. Now, it was time to use the man. Neclesious smiled mischievously and beat his wings harder; he could not wait to meet Marnelphion's most unusual priest.

BALE MAFLIN SMILED, SHOWING HIS SHARP, METAL TEETH, WHICH HE had had surgically installed as a young boy. Now in his fourth decade, he had learned to proficiently use the specially made teeth to chew without biting his lips or cheeks.

The pregnant woman screamed in pain, another contraction wracking her body. She lay on a rock slab Bale used for sacrificing to his demon lord, Marnelphion. The woman was bound to the slab, with her legs wide to help the inevitable birth.

Bale watched with great anticipation as one of his fellow priests encouraged her to push harder. He knew she didn't want to comply because doing so meant a cruel death for her newborn child. Its ending would be brutal and quick. The future mother knew it, and she tried hard not to push. In the end, her body betrayed her, and she had no choice.

Bale, a devout follower of Marnelphion, always enjoyed the third full moon of summer, a memorable holiday for his god. The woman and her husband were in a particular clearing in Faun's Swamp near Bale's lair. They had bound the husband similarly, and both were holiday sacrifices for Marnelphion. Bale enjoyed the screams of pain from the young couple, the woman nearing birth, and the man knowing life was at its end for him, his wife, and his unborn child. The desperation was a joy for Marnelphion, and Bale basked in the glory. He walked to the woman and gently touched her head, wiping the sweat from her drenched forehead.

"Please," the woman said, then grimaced during another contraction.

"You are blessed, dear woman. Your sacrifice is pleasing to Marnel-phion," Bale said, smiling peacefully.

"Please don't hurt my baby."

Bale bent low so he was eye level with her, and she turned her head to meet his gaze, pleading silently with her pain-filled eyes. He stroked her sweat-soaked hair that stuck to her face. They were outside, under the stars and the unholy moon. The air was thick and humid, which added to her discomfort. Giant bugs bit at them, and toads sang in the distance.

"Dear woman, I am going to boil your baby once you finally push it out of that nasty hole, then eat your placenta. Afterward, I will feast on your child's tender, cooked flesh."

Her eyes widened, and her sobbing intensified. Bale's smile grew, and he moved his hand slowly down her face, over her swollen breasts, and to her large belly.

"Now it's time to push, my dear," Bale said, and slowly he pressed on her abdomen.

She screamed as the pressure intensified. Bale placed a second hand on the frightened woman, adding his weight to his press. She could no longer delay the inevitable; a baby's cries soon echoed through the swamp.

"Leave them alone!" her husband screamed from the second slab, close enough for him to witness the birth of his doomed child but helpless to protect it.

Bale stood, his smile immediately fading, not pleased with the interruption. He held out his hand, and one of the priests handed him a utensil. It was a metal scoop-like device with razor-sharp edges. Bale walked to the man, who steeled his visage, but his lip quivered in fear, betraying his true feelings. To his credit, he did not scream until Bale scooped out one of his eyes. As Bale munched on the juicy eyeball, the screams of the newborn baby filled the heavy night air, joining her father's.

Bale walked calmly back to the woman as another priest drove a dagger through the man's heart, silencing his dying screams. The priests cut the mother's umbilical cord and gave it to Bale, who watched as they took the crying baby and dropped it into a nearby cauldron of boiling oil. The mother screamed and cried hysterically. Soon, the baby was quiet, and only the mother's sobbing remained. Bale took a dagger from a nearby priest as he chewed on the tasty umbilical cord.

"Who are you people?" the woman bravely asked between sobs.

"The future rulers of the world," Bale said.

The woman only sobbed, realizing her baby and her husband were dead and she had outlived her usefulness. Bale showed her the curved blade, drenched with her husband's blood. She closed her eyes at the sight of it, knowing she was all alone. Bale found her to be braver than her sniveling husband, and so he took his time bringing the dagger under her breast. He placed the tip there, and she let out a little yelp of fear and kept her eyes closed tight.

"There, there, you have done well. You should be proud of your efforts. Go now and join your family in the bowels of hell. Marnelphion awaits," Bale whispered.

Her eyes opened then, tears streaming down her cheeks. "I hope you get what you deserve one day. You are all monsters, and no god will show mercy on your—"

If there was one thing Bale couldn't stand, it was a loudmouthed woman. She had impressed him up to that point, but he drove the dagger home with one quick thrust. Her words stopped, and her mouth moved slowly. She was still trying to speak, but nothing escaped her lips. Bale watched gleefully, his metal teeth reflecting the flickering of flames from the nearby fire. Once her lips finally ceased and the light left her eyes, he tilted her head back and proficiently tore out her throat with those wicked teeth.

The gathering priests feasted on the flesh of all three victims, the tender meat of the newborn a delicacy to the fanatical group. They prayed after their meal, and their celebration lasted the rest of the night. As the hours ran together in the orgy of feasting and celebrating, some of the priests tore off their clothes and smeared the blood of their victims over their bodies. As tended to happen during rituals to Marnelphion, the excited priests eventually christened their sacrifices with sex. At first, it was just a few of the men who became overwhelmed and accepted the advances of their brothers. Soon, however, an orgy of men tangled together as their lust for their god took over the ceremony.

Bale watched it all unfold with a smile. His priests were the most devout to ever exist in the glory of their demon lord, and they took the vows of Marnelphion very seriously. Sex was a required component of every unholy night. Bale didn't participate in the sexual feast, for he preferred women.

But he was also their leader and had to set a good example. There was only one woman in the gathering, and so Bale began to undress; the half-eaten corpse of the woman would be an acceptable participant in the orgy. He mounted her and enjoyed defiling the corpse as his men writhed on the ground beside him. Once spent, he took the curved knife and cut out her liver, watching her face, or what was left of it, hoping there would be signs of life so he could enjoy her pain once more. Sadly, she was still.

"Not much of a sport about it, and a terrible lay, might I add," Bale said, smiling and taking a giant bite of her organ.

The blood ran down his chin, and he closed his eyes and savored the taste. He loved human liver almost as much as boiled fetuses. As he enjoyed the liver, he heard the unmistakable flapping of wings. His men must have heard it, too, because the grunts and groans of their tangled sexual rampage behind him slowly stopped, and all was quiet. It took Bale several moments to open his eyes, hoping to find a blessing from his god before him.

To his joy, standing on the woman's carcass just a few feet away was a special omen—an imp! The tiny creature, black-skinned with glowing red eyes and a venomous tail, paced impatiently on the woman's corpse, its clawed feet stabbing at the remaining flesh.

The naked and sweaty priests ceased their writhing and stared in awe at the creature's appearance. Some prostrated themselves before it while others gleefully prayed aloud to Marnelphion. The creature watched the spectacle, its eyes narrowing with hate, and waited for the commotion to subside. Bale approached it, his blood-covered chin and hands evidence of the fine feast he had just partaken of. He tossed the half-eaten liver to the ground and extended his hand toward the creature, palm up, awaiting its response. The imp eyed him menacingly and issued a low growl. Bale didn't flinch and kept his hand level and ready, waiting for the creature to make its move. Eventually, a wicked smile slowly spread across the imp's face, revealing large, pointed teeth. With blinding speed, it struck Bale's hand with its barbed, venomous tail.

All the priests watched and waited with anticipation. If Marnelphion blessed them, Bale would live; if not, the venom would kill him quickly, which would spell doom for them all. Bale turned and held his hand for the congregation to see. The garish wound dripped blood, but he didn't fall dead from the venom. Marnelphion had blessed them. The gathering men prayed and rejoiced at the fantastic sight.

Bale turned back to the imp and said, "We are blessed by your presence, dear minion of Marnelphion, especially on such an unholy night."

The imp wagged its tail and eventually impaled the woman's face, or what little remained of it, tearing the flesh and slinging it into the group of priests, who crawled over themselves to find the morsel and consume it.

"I am Neclesious, spawn of Marnelphion, and I bring tidings and news of utmost importance."

"We are here to serve our lord humbly. What is your message, Neclesious?" Bale asked.

The imp studied him for a while, its tail twitching menacingly. Finally, it spoke. "The chosen is failing."

"Matilda of Nesin?" Bale asked, puzzled.

"The same. I come from Nesin, and it is surrendered."

"The fortress city? How?"

"Yes, the sacrificial lambs have rebelled and escaped, and Matilda grows sloppy and careless with her obsession to find the Rho girl. Marnelphion wishes for your oversight in the matter. He is most displeased with Matilda's efforts, and you are ordered to seek her out and set her back on the righteous path from which she came."

"And blessed news it is. I am here to serve, and if the fool woman cannot complete the task, I am prepared to take over the sacrifice," Bale said, smiling and showing the imp his sharp, metal teeth. "I also have adequate sacrificial fodder to do so," he added excitedly.

"No," the imp responded. "Marnelphion doesn't desire that. You are to go to Matilda, protect her and the sacrifice. You are to help Matilda find her way and regain her control. Due to her obsession with the Rho girl, her empire is crumbling. Marnelphion still expects her to carry out all sacrifices, and you are to ensure it happens, nothing more."

Bale bowed low and said, "I serve as ordered."

"Excellent, he will be most pleased," Neclesious said with a wicked smile. "Enjoy your unholy night and prepare to depart when night falls again. I will lead you to Matilda."

"As he wishes."

The imp smiled mischievously and turned to fly off into the darkness, but Bale stopped it with a request. "A few questions for the messenger of his most powerful host."

"Ask," the imp said, turning back and folding its wings.

"First, how do we find Matilda? If Nesin is deserted, where can she be? Second, has Matilda found the Rho girl?"

"I came straight from Nesin's bowels, and I assure you it's quite deserted. However, the master attuned me to the powerful priestess, and I know she lingers at the edge of the Yaddaton Desert. She is close to finding the prized sacrifice, but whether the Rho girl has been obtained is unclear. You will ensure that she does indeed find the wretch."

"We are prepared to leave at tomorrow's nightfall. We are humbled to serve our lord." Bale bowed.

"Excellent," Neclesious said and flew off into the night.

Bale found himself deep in prayer, asking Marnelphion for guidance concerning the messenger. The appearance of an imp meant great things for Bale, and he wanted to know as much as possible before undertaking the quest to find Matilda. The sun was close to cresting the horizon, and dawn was the weakest part of the day to contact his god. But with the waning full moon holiday, Bale felt the communication was still possible. He hoped to gain some insight, possibly more knowledge that the imp hadn't relayed concerning Matilda. He found none.

And so, he understood that the imp's words were valid, and he would obediently carry out the orders his god demanded. Secretly, he hated Matilda, but he would protect her, even die for her because Marnelphion desired it. He would see it through, and then, once Marnelphion arrived with all his glory, Bale would be rewarded for his faith.

The next night, a contingent of one hundred fanatical priests of Marnelphion marched out of the swamp, taking two large wagons, one used for prisoner transport to hold Cassandra and Matilda if need be and the other loaded with supplies. They headed for the Yaddaton Desert and ultimately to Matilda. It would take nearly a month to reach the great desert, assuming the weather didn't slow them, as fall would surely set in before they reached their destination. Neclesious sat on Bale's shoulder, directing the small force of men. They left another one hundred followers behind to guard the underground lair filled with over a thousand sacrificial men and women. In support of the guards, Bale had his undead army. Thousands of zombies roamed the bowels of his fortress, ensuring there would be no escape attempt as there had been in Nesin.

Bale smiled, his teeth gleaming in the lantern light, confident that the Great Summoning would soon be a reality. He would collect Matilda, hold her hand the rest of the way, and gain all the glory of the summoning. Then, if things went well, Bale would kill her. He envisioned eating her liver, freshly plucked from her corpse. According to legend, the essence of Marnelphion filled her very being, and he would consume her and, in effect, consume him. He would become the most powerful mortal to rule by his god's side. He quietly followed Neclesious to find Matilda, pleased to serve and embrace his delusions of grandeur.

WITCH'S RISE

IT HAD BEEN THREE WEEKS SINCE MATILDA AND HER SMALL BAND of allies had lost their prey. Matilda, Cass, and Ronnis had chased Cassandra through the Yaddaton Desert and had nearly caught her before she mysteriously disappeared at the summit of a small mountain range called Witch's Rise. All three had witnessed her disappearance as the young woman stepped backward off a cliff face and vanished. It didn't appear to any of them that Cassandra had fallen from the cliff, but she had instead simply blinked out of existence. That was the disappointing conclusion to Matilda's chase of Cassandra Rho across the realm. There was no explanation for the girl's ability to elude her. Matilda had used all the skills and powers Marnelphion granted her to find the girl. She was nowhere to be seen, yet Matilda sensed she was near.

Cass had stolen a powerful medallion attuned to Cassandra's life force, which had allowed her to locate the troublesome girl just by concentrating on her. Matilda had used the device to track Cassandra to the Yaddaton Desert and the mountain range just south of the Yaddaton. According to Cass, Cassandra had met a crazed hermit in Pelesea named Cedric, who claimed the medallion was a creation of her father's, the lich-god Kane.

According to Cedric, the medallion existed to keep track of Cassandra and her whereabouts. Since Cedric's untimely death, or more accurately, his murder at the hands of Cass, the medallion's power had waned. Matilda had used every trick she knew to keep the magic alive in the device, but its effectiveness had returned as they came within proximity of Cassandra. Now, Matilda felt the energy in the necklace was greater than at any other point in their journey. It indicated that Cassandra was near, and Matilda refused to move from the spot for fear of Cassandra returning from some protective void if she did. Matilda didn't want to miss Cassandra's reappearance; she was too close to her prize and was not about to lose the trail.

Plus, Matilda had lost nearly everything trying to capture the elusive girl. Cerus, her husband, had been petrified by a nasty sleeth creature just moments before Ronnis had spotted Cassandra fleeing toward Witch's Rise. The sleeth, a hearty race of snake-like humanoids possessing incredible blessings and equally powerful curses, were common in the desert. That particular sleeth's blessing and curse were the same—her gaze caused anyone caught by it to turn to stone. Nothing should slow or hurt Cerus; he was the son of Gorl, the god of war. However, petrification was one way to harm him. Matilda missed her husband and felt alone without him beside her. It had all happened so fast, and she hadn't had time to mourn the loss or kill the sleeth responsible for his demise.

The loneliness within her as she waited for Cassandra to show herself nagged at her. She knew Cerus stood only a few miles away, a strange and beautiful statue adorning Yaddaton's sandy landscape. With Cerus gone, the men of Gorl would grow restless and probably abandon her cause. If they did, all her captives held at the conquered barbarian tribe would go free, and she would have no sacrifices for the Great Summoning, which was fast approaching. She did have a small group of slaves fit for the sacrifice back at her home in Nesin, as well as a few dozen virgins. She longed to be back there, relaxing in the natural spa in her room, melting into Cerus's strong arms. Before she could do that, she had to capture Cassandra Rho. The girl had been a bane to her for several years, always out of reach as Matilda had come frustratingly close to capturing her on several occasions. She was closer to the elusive girl now than ever, but her patience waned.

Matilda had met Cass in possession of the medallion while in Pelesea tracking Cassandra. The device was why Matilda had allowed Cass to travel with her. In exchange for using it, Matilda had promised Cass would be allowed to torture Cassandra in the months leading up to the Great Summoning. Cass's hatred for Cassandra was unmatched, and she greatly desired the chance to torment the young woman, both physically and emotionally.

Cass had also stolen another mighty artifact from Cedric's dying form—a magical cottage. The strange device was only about one inch in diameter, shaped like a small home. However, once the holder spoke the command word, it quickly grew, creating an extra-dimensional pocket large enough for half a dozen adults to sleep comfortably. Shutting the door hid its occupants from anyone outside. Inside, the magical pocket of space came complete with an ever-burning fire, several couches, and a table. It was another magnificent creation of the lich-god, Kane. Cass guarded it closely, as it was one of her prized possessions. In truth, Matilda entertained the idea of killing her and taking both the medallion and the cottage. But Cass had proven resourceful, and Matilda still needed her. She liked the feisty woman and fed off her hatred of Cassandra.

Ronnis had been another unlikely ally they'd met chasing Cassandra. He hated her nearly as much as Cass and had provided information to help find Cassandra once the trail had grown cold. Ronnis was quiet and calculating, and Matilda understood that the hunt for Cassandra was personal to him. Both allies had proven their worth over the last few months, and their assistance had Matilda close to realizing her goal of capturing Cassandra. Now, the three of them waited, not knowing how long it would take for Cassandra to reveal herself. For Matilda, the waiting had become a long, painful process.

So, as with the previous few nights, Matilda sat in the small cottage, holding the medallion and concentrating on Cassandra's location. The reading she received was the same as the other times since her disappearance—she was near, very near. Yet, she was concealed and undetectable. Matilda could only reason that Cassandra's father was assisting her. She just had to sit and wait for Cassandra to reappear. Her thoughts lingered on recent events as she clutched the necklace. She closed her eyes and thought of Cerus, her husband. She thought of him constantly and missed him more than she cared to admit. He should be safe in his current state of petrification, and she doubted any desert creatures would give him a second thought. However, she wanted him back, and she needed him beside her. For the first time since her rebirth in Novafontera, she was frightened.

Her thoughts were interrupted by moans of sensual pleasures. She cracked her eyes open and focused on Cass and Ronnis sprawled across the floor. Cass's new pet, Binta, delivered mysteriously and suddenly by a strange woman shortly after they'd lost Cassandra, was the focus of their pleasures. The poor girl was between the two, Cass holding her head tight between her legs and Ronnis having his way behind her. Matilda didn't understand the circumstances around the sexually charged girl. According to Cass, Binta had consumed demon milk at some point, and that, mixed with Cass's pheromones, had the girl hopelessly submissive to Cass and effectively a sex slave.

Matilda watched intently as the two mercilessly used the poor girl who, according to Cass, was ironically also Cassandra's lover. Matilda surmised that her closeness to Cassandra made Cass and Ronnis take out their frustrations on Binta more aggressively. Matilda looked to Cass, her head thrown back in ecstasy as Binta pleasured her. Cass appeared nothing more than a young, physically stunning woman, but Matilda knew otherwise. Demon blood coursed through Cass's veins, giving her the power over Binta she enjoyed. Cass was effectively a demon, not born as such but somehow transformed. Matilda didn't know her story but understood the girl was powerful and cruel. Currently, Binta was the subject of that cruelty. Matilda wondered if she could control the unpredictable demon without Cerus beside her.

Ronnis worked feverishly on the loveless act, seemingly trying to hurt Binta. His sweat-covered and slightly flabby body glistened in the firelight. He made Matilda more nervous than Cass did. He was quiet and calculating, and his mysterious black blade, the Black Adder, made him even more imposing. Ronnis wore his white porcelain mask as he forcefully took Binta, one that covered his face, which had been deformed in an attack from Cassandra Rho. Yes, it was personal for him, and Matilda wondered then if the two would kill Binta as part of their plans to torture Cassandra.

Matilda hoped they would kill her so she wouldn't have to watch any more of the sexual encounters in which the three regularly partook. It was always the same: Ronnis would have sex with Binta as she orally pleasured Cass. Ronnis and Cass would never have sex, and Cass would never reciprocate the act on Binta, who seemed perfectly happy with the arrangements and more than willing to participate. Cass and Ronnis abused the poor girl, but Binta seemed insatiable and glad to comply.

Binta's mysterious delivery into the hands of her tormentors had been a pleasant surprise for Cass, especially given that the strange woman who had delivered her was powerful. She claimed to be a nepalin demon and had tracked them down, using the powers of someone she called The Mystic. Nepalin demons were sexual creatures, cultivating nymphomaniacs among the humans who came into contact with them. The demon admitted to administering demon milk to Binta and supplied Cass with extra vials of the potent liquid. It was more than enough for Cass to maintain her control over the poor girl or kill her.

However, Matilda had the feeling there was more to Binta than just a simpleton hopelessly in need of sexual domination. Something about her seemed powerful to Matilda, but her actions didn't support that theory. She performed all Cass's demands without question, but Matilda wondered how submissive the girl would be if she hadn't consumed the demon milk.

The tryst was over, breaking Matilda from her contemplations. Cass led Binta by her leash to the corner of the cottage and had her lie on the floor, naked and far away from the fire. The young woman willingly obeyed and curled up to sleep. Cass and Ronnis then dressed and spoke casually. As usual, neither had touched each other during sex and weren't romantically involved, but both enjoyed the fruits of Binta.

Ronnis approached the couch on which Matilda lounged, buttoning his shirt and straightening his mask as Cass exited the cottage for fresh air. He made himself a drink and sat near Matilda. His breathing was hard, and behind his porcelain mask, he sounded inhuman. He wore the cover often, hiding the hole that Cassandra had made in his right cheek. He had provoked her wrath at some point during their tenuous relationship while he was the administrator of the orphanage where Cassandra lived in Oldorburg. His pride was wounded as much as his face that day, and an ugly scar ran from his eye to his jawline, with a hole large enough to see his teeth. Rumor had it that Cassandra's attack had even dislodged a few of his molars, though Matilda refused to look that closely at the grotesque wound.

"Satisfied?" Matilda asked with a snort of derision.

"Very much," Ronnis said, removing his mask to reveal his sweat-covered face and taking a large draw of his drink. "She is insatiable and eager to please."

"And she hates Cass and you both." Matilda chuckled.

"And that makes it even more satisfying. Binta is truly a broken creature."

"And the sex?"

"Very good, I must say," Ronnis said, taking another large drink. "I can take my aggressions out on her since Cassandra is off limits, assuming we find her. Unless we can incorporate rape into our tortures?" he asked, hopefully.

"Absolutely not! There are no exceptions. She must be a virgin for my sacrificial ceremony to succeed."

"A pity."

"And I assure you, dear Ronnis, we will find her," Matilda added.

Ronnis shrugged as if he didn't care, but Matilda knew he wanted her. If he couldn't rape her, he could at least assist with Cass's torture of the unfortunate wretch.

"I feel Binta is a distraction. Perhaps I will kill her," Matilda said.

She watched Ronnis's reaction to gauge his true feelings. He only shrugged again, and she could tell he honestly didn't care if Binta died. She shifted her gaze to the girl and realized she was sobbing softly, curled in a fetal position. Her anger flared at how much time they wasted waiting for Cassandra. Matilda thought of Cerus, petrified and in the desert a few miles away. She needed to go to him and find a way to remove his curse, but she was trapped here, waiting for Cassandra to appear. The more time she spent waiting, the more anxious she became.

She focused on the medallion once more and received the same vague message—Cassandra was very close, so close that Matilda should be able to see her from where she sat. However, Cassandra remained hidden somehow, and Matilda knew that if she went outside, she wouldn't find her, although the medallion indicated otherwise. The frustration grew, and Matilda took a deep breath to control the anxiousness inside her. Something had to happen soon; Matilda needed to rescue Cerus quickly, and she contemplated reaching out to the great wizard Malikai. His stronghold was in the desert, not far from their current location. His magic was powerful enough to tear Cassandra out of her hiding spot and restore Cerus. The price would be high, and he would sexually dominate Matilda as compensation over and over again. She chewed her bottom lip as she thought of the possibilities. Malikai was an excellent lover, after all.

Cass returned, shaking off the chill from the cold night air and breaking Matilda from her thoughts. She stopped and looked at Binta, who was still curled in a fetal position but had gathered herself, and only the occasional sniffle indicated she was conscious. An evil look spread across Cass's face as she looked upon the helpless girl. Cass was far too reckless to leave alone and in charge of Cassandra's capture, assuming the little witch would eventually come out of hiding. The thought troubled Matilda, and she felt trapped, having no confidence in Cass or Ronnis to ambush Cassandra properly in her absence. However, Matilda couldn't keep sitting and doing nothing; the frustration was overwhelming. As important as finding Malikai was to her, she simply couldn't leave her two allies in charge of finding Cassandra.

Ronnis and Cass whispered, each pointing or nodding toward Binta, who appeared asleep then. They chuckled and whispered some more, enjoying her misery. Something in that act made Matilda's blood boil: she had lost her husband, perhaps forever, Cassandra was well hidden, and the remaining Gorl warriors would be restless without their leader. Matilda was in a difficult spot, and Cass and Ronnis were playing games, seemingly without a care. She would have to make some tough decisions soon.

MUCH LATER THAT NIGHT, MATILDA AWOKE WITH A START. THE MOON was full, and that was always a time when she felt close to her demon lord. She couldn't see the moon within the confines of the magical cottage, but she knew it was there, a holiday for Marnelphion. She rose and quietly donned her priestly robes as Cass snoozed on the second small couch and Ronnis slept on the floor near the fire. Binta slept curled up in the corner of the room, still naked, her clothes nowhere to be found. Matilda assumed Cass had them hidden away someplace safe. The girl wore her collar, but the leash wasn't attached—Cass must have that stashed away as well.

She made her way to Binta, careful to move silently and not awaken anyone. She looked at the pathetic wretch, her anger at the situation boiling over. She gritted her teeth, grabbed Binta by the hair with one hand, and covered her mouth with the other. Binta jumped at Matilda's touch, and her eyes widened. She yelped, but Matilda's firm hand muffled her cry.

Matilda didn't speak but motioned to the door with her head. Binta nodded understanding, and Matilda removed her hand from the girl's mouth. She helped her stand, never releasing her fistful of hair. She pulled Binta to the door, opened it, and moved outside. As Matilda expected, strong moonlight bathed the area.

Once the door to the cottage was closed, Matilda released her and said, "We have not had a chance to talk."

Binta said nothing and only stood there with her hands crossing her naked breasts. The cool desert wind made the girl uncomfortable, as did her nakedness. Matilda didn't care; her patience had worn out.

"Where is Cassandra?" Matilda asked, moving close.

"Can I at least get some clothes?" Binta asked, ignoring the question.

A knife flashed into Matilda's hand from the folds of her robe. She took a step toward Binta, who backed away nervously.

"I am not playing, little girl. I want to know where Cassandra is. You came to help her, and her trail led you here to us. How did you find her?"

Binta held her hands up in surrender and said, "I've told you already. The Mystic sent me here."

"I am supposed to believe your story that you had a god-like wizard send you to this spot because you beat him in a duel of wits? And at the same time, you give yourself to Cass as if you were a wanton whore?" Matilda asked, moving so that she was between Binta and the cottage.

"Yes," Binta whispered.

"I don't believe you, but I do think you know where Cassandra is," Matilda said, taking a step closer.

Binta took another step back, moving toward the cliff face. "Matilda, I don't know where she is. I came here just like you, trying to find her."

"And you still expect to find her before me and steal her away?" Matilda's anger was growing.

Binta said nothing and lowered her hands to her sides.

"Here is what I think: you know where she is, and you are biding your time until you can take her from me," Matilda said, brandishing the small but vicious-looking knife and moving closer. "In the meantime, you act powerless before Cass and Ronnis so they keep their guard down. Am I close?"

Binta continued to back away while Matilda followed menacingly.

"No, that is not how it is," Binta explained.

She moved as far to the drop as she could and stopped, teetering on the edge. Behind her loomed a massive fall from the cliff face. The wind was stronger here, and her footing seemed unsure. Matilda continued to advance, determined to have her answers.

"Tell me the truth, or I'll run you through now. What is your plan?"

The look in Binta's eyes told Matilda there was more to the story than a girl searching for her friend. Something there gave Matilda pause; something warned her that Binta was dangerous. Matilda was about five feet from her but stopped. A warning screamed in her mind. It was apparent that her earlier suspicion was correct: the girl was a distraction and was better off dead.

"You wouldn't believe my true story. I am here to find and protect Cassandra from you or anyone else who would harm her. I truly don't know where she is, but I plan to find her before you do. And rest assured, Matilda, I will kill you if you don't give up your quest to find her."

The sudden change in Binta's demeanor surprised Matilda enough that she lowered the knife and stared in amazement at the young girl.

"If you are truly as powerful as you suggest, why the farce with Cass? Why not just kill her? Why not kill all three of us? You obviously hate us all and know what we will do to Cassandra when we find her."

Binta only smiled, and Matilda matched it.

"It's complicated," Binta said.

"Let me simplify it for you," Matilda said, grabbing her holy symbol.

Matilda began casting a spell that would leave Binta immobile and vulnerable. Before she entirely spoke the first word, a rock the size of an apple hit her hard in the temple.

"No, vile woman. Today, you will force me to destroy you to protect the one person I love," Binta said.

The spell fizzled, and Matilda crumpled unconscious to the stone floor of the small mountaintop.

BINTA LOOKED AROUND THE AREA, SEARCHING FOR A LARGE ROCK. The powers bestowed upon her by X'lor, the fallen god, had given her godlike mental abilities. Usually, she could read a person's mind or even control their actions, but her powers had failed her against Matilda, Ronnis, and Cass. She learned that mind control didn't work on strong-willed individuals and was especially difficult against non-humans. For whatever reason, she couldn't read or control the minds of her captors, especially Cass. She felt powerless in that one's presence, hopelessly defeated by the demon milk she had consumed twice now.

The area they stood in was nothing but smooth stone, and she had been lucky enough to find a good-sized rock to incapacitate Matilda before she had completed her spell. She intended to complete the task quickly. Matilda was dangerous and could not be left alive. The evil woman had inadvertently taken Binta far enough away from Cass that her mind cleared in the night air. She could access her unique powers of the mind once more. A trail ran down the mountainside on one end of the clearing, which Binta knew eventually led to the foot of the mountain. Closer and behind her, the cliff face dropped hundreds of feet into a boulder cluster. On the other two sides, rock walls jutted into the air, which left little debris for her telekinetic powers to manipulate into a weapon.

She reached out with her mind to the rock she had just hit Matilda with. It rose into the air and hovered above the prone woman. Matilda moaned slightly, unconscious but still very much alive. Binta tried not to look at her; after all, she was about to commit murder. Binta concentrated on the rock and tried futilely to pretend she wasn't about to snuff out a life. She told herself that she had to do this for Cassandra. If not, this evil woman lying wounded before her was going to kill her true love. She had no choice. The rock was above Matilda, floating ten feet in the air, right above her head. Binta was going to bring it down and smash her skull, but she couldn't bring herself to use her hands. Perhaps if she didn't touch the rock, she would be removed from the act and somehow not guilty of murder. Her concentration waned, and the rock quivered as she battled with her moral conscience.

Binta made the mistake of looking upon Matilda and seeing the trail of blood trickling from her temple. She thought back to her adventure beside Cassandra and recalled the moment she killed the goblin with her magic to save her friend. She had felt overwhelming grief for a moment afterward. However, it had saved Cassandra from being attacked by a creature intent on hurting her, and the guilt had quickly faded.

Before she could bring the rock to bear, she saw a flash from the corner of her eye, and the rock exploded into many pieces. Binta turned away to avoid the flying debris as small pebbles rained down on her and Matilda.

When she turned back, Cass was standing over Matilda, Ronnis behind her with his black sword in one hand and a lantern in the other.

"You've been a bad girl, Binta," Cass said.

Binta was familiar with the spell that Cass had used to disintegrate the rock. It was the same magical dart of energy Binta had used to kill the goblin, and now it had stripped her of her only weapon. She lost all her bravado in Cass's presence, and her submissive nature resurfaced. She fought the old feeling the best she could, trying to maintain the brief freedom that Matilda had inadvertently given her by bringing her outside and away from Cass. Her mind was disciplined enough, but her inner desires betrayed her.

Cass's attire, see-through silk top and tiny underwear, drew Binta's attention. Ronnis was shirtless and wore thin pajama pants. He knelt to examine Matilda, setting the lantern down to do so. He rose soon after examining Matilda and wore a concerned expression. He was maskless, and the lantern light made the scar on his cheek seem more horrific than usual. Binta couldn't help but compare his physique to Malikai's perfect form. The old wizard had sexually used her like Ronnis did, but the comparisons ended there. While Malikai was a thorough lover with an ideal body, Ronnis was inadequate and he repulsed her, but at that moment she wanted him again. She needed him to take her.

"No, this stops now, Cass," she said with as much conviction as she could summon, ignoring those thoughts.

"Nothing stops," Cass said, revealing a tiny vial of white liquid.

Binta's heart raced, knowing what evil lurked within the small container. It was nepalin milk. Cass had fed the milk to Binta back in Pelesea, and she had gladly consumed it out of her desire to be dominated by the cruel girl. Her lust had overridden her better judgment, and she had consumed the concoction without knowing its origin. She had regretted that decision ever since. The vile substance had become her bane. Then Illa, the demoness, had fed her more, and now she was powerless against it. Her newfound mental disciplines made her powerful, and she could do miraculous things with them, but she felt helpless in the presence of Cass and the threat of the milk. Her powers faded and her thoughts focused solely on sex when Cass was around.

Binta took in her surroundings. There was no escape other than jumping off the cliff. She looked over her shoulder and wondered if she could levitate to the bottom of the drop. She wasn't sure she could handle that much weight. She didn't want to abandon Cassandra, but it would be no good to her friend if she died. Still, she was trapped, and the cliff seemed the only option to escape Cass's clutches. She knew Matilda wouldn't be lenient with her if she survived the rock attack, and it wouldn't be wise to be around when she recovered.

She calculated her options too long, and before she could move toward the drop, Cass was upon her, grabbing a fistful of hair and jerking her back. Cass's scent overwhelmed Binta and had a soothing yet electrifying effect.

"Where do you think you're going?" Cass whispered in her ear.

She held the vial under Binta's nose, and her legs nearly buckled. Binta leaned heavily on Cass and would have fallen if her tormentor hadn't been there to hold her up.

"Take her back inside, Ronnis, and tie her up. Give her this if she causes you any grief," Cass said, handing him the vial.

The fumes from the uncorked vial affected Ronnis when he took it. His expression changed, and he fell to one knee, overwhelmed. Cass was there to quickly apply the stopper and end the effects of the powerful milk. It took him a moment to recover, and he shook his head vigorously, trying to shake the wild, lustful thoughts that Binta knew raced through his mind.

"She ingested that?" he asked, nodding toward Binta.

"Yes," Cass answered with a wicked smile. "Now take her inside and make sure she's secure. She is more dangerous than we give her credit for," Cass added, glancing at Matilda's prone form.

Ronnis nodded and led Binta inside the cottage. He threw her limp form onto a couch and dug in his supplies for rope. When he finally found it, Binta gave him a sexy look, although he repulsed her. The milk was having its way with her, and she needed him. She could tell the lustful thoughts hinted at by the milk fumes he'd inadvertently inhaled resurfaced. He tied her hands tightly in front of her, all the while staring lustfully at her. She let him and locked gazes with the repulsive man, licking her lips slowly and seductively. She subconsciously pushed all thoughts of escape to the recesses of her mind.

After ensuring her hands were secure, Ronnis quickly undressed. Binta couldn't move her hands, which excited her, the rope burns driving her wild with lust. She waited while he tore free of his clothes, her breathing heavy with anticipation. He eventually fell over her and had his way with her. She didn't resist, and though they had just performed this same lewd act hours earlier, both quickly fell into their lustful and passionate dance. Two lovers lost in the act, their animal urges getting the best of them. Binta bit her lip and tried not to scream as Ronnis worked her over mercilessly. She loved it and lost track of time as he made her orgasm many times in rapid succession. At some point, Cass reentered the cottage, Matilda leaning heavily on her. Binta did not notice when.

Ronnis finished his task eventually and pushed Binta onto the floor, where she writhed, her lust torturing her. He quickly dressed and stood beside Cass, who helped Matilda lie on the second couch. Her head still bled, and her eyes fluttered open occasionally, but she was seriously injured. Binta tried to watch the events unfolding in front of her, but her sexual desires were too much, so she closed her eyes and played.

"What can we do for her?" Ronnis asked, concerned for Matilda.

"I'm not a healer, so we'll clean and bandage her wound and hope for the best," Cass said, giving Binta a hateful stare. "I have a feeling my slave just made a grievous error, one that will have her life forfeit."

Ronnis watched Binta as she continued to squirm on the floor, lost in the throughs of lust. She licked her lips and beckoned him. He shook his head, and Cass joined him to stand over her, watching her unbridled act of masturbation. They mocked her, but she didn't care. It was evident they weren't going to help her reach orgasm, so she did it herself. Thoughts of Cassandra were lost in a fog of lust.

NEARBY, AS CASS AND RONNIS ATTENDED TO MATILDA'S WOUNDS, Cassandra sat against the dead end of the long hall she had traversed in the magical pocket of space Kane had created. The hall was about one hundred yards from the stairs she'd descended when she first entered. She had dozed for a bit, that she was sure of, but she had no idea how long she'd been sitting there. The place had overwhelmed her senses and seemed to draw her essence into the walls. She stood and stretched her stiff legs, trying to come to terms with her next action. Unlike the first cave she'd entered with her traveling companions, this one contained no monsters or traps—not yet, anyway. Lines of blue energy coursed through the walls like forks of lightning, giving the place an eerie blue glow. She glanced up the hallway, and although she couldn't see them, she knew the stairs were a short trek away.

She recalled that at the top of the stairs was the secret entrance. She'd been lucky to find it so quickly, being pursued by people who wanted her dead. Luck had been with her when she saw the door in a reflection from a nearby stone wall. She'd been quick enough to discern the password: Notel X. She had discovered the password months earlier at the end of the first disastrous adventure she'd taken into one of her father's caves. At the end of that quest, instead of finding Zolmex, her birthright, she had discovered an old, dried-up scroll with the words "Notel X" scrawled upon it. That ill-conceived adventure had nearly cost her her life, but this time was different. Zolmex was here; she could feel it.

"Ronnis and Cass," she whispered, recalling a clear image of both appearing near the secret door after she had entered.

She had narrowly avoided being captured by them, using a powerful spell that Baxter had used to save her from a nest of giant spiders in the first cave. It was an advanced and complicated spell that Baxter hadn't taught her, and she'd practiced it for a long time alone in her jail cell in Pelesea. She remembered its components, and luckily, it worked at just the right time to avoid the ambush Cass and Ronnis had set for her. It was a spell that created a rift in space, a door that let the caster step through and travel a short distance. Cassandra had used it during her trek up the mountain, jumping short distances to avoid capture.

There was also a second woman, a powerful adversary with giant spider-like legs. She had easily held Cassandra with a spell just as Cassandra had backed into the secret cave. She'd then been held immobile at the precipice of the entrance as the woman searched all around, looking for her. Luckily, she hadn't been able to see the cave or Cassandra, but there were many tense moments as the crazed woman tried every trick to uncover her hiding spot. When the spell finally released its hold on her, Cassandra had turned and walked down the stairs, away from her pursuers. The stairs led to this single hallway and subsequent dead end. There was nowhere else for her to go. She stomped her foot in frustration and ran her hands through her hair.

"What am I missing?" When no response was forthcoming from the cave, she added, "And who is that woman with Ronnis and Cass?"

She laughed at the absurdity of it all. She had escaped a trio of people, and barely so, only to find refuge in a cave with no answers. She knew that whoever that third adversary was waiting outside for her, she was powerful. Cassandra couldn't leave without Zolmex if she hoped to survive. She watched the blue energy arch through the walls, speeding down the hallway and back. Blue flames danced on torches at twenty-foot intervals. She recalled summoning a minor light spell before she descended the stairs, and that light had been surprisingly blue instead of the typical orange. A rune in the wall at the top of the stairs had absorbed her spell and created blue lightning in the walls and the torchlight.

"It's from me," she whispered.

Then it dawned on her—she was part of the place. She could bend the energy to her will! No monsters or golems that would tear her limbs from their sockets were lurking in the dark this time. There were no traps or riddles to solve; there was only the blue energy to use as she saw fit. She sat and stared at the smooth wall at the dead end. She watched the energy flow through it and saw abundant arcane symbols dancing around her. All she had to do now was manipulate it into what she needed.

"But how do I do it?" she asked, lightly touching the wall.

The energy answered her touch as the blue streaks of lightning moved to her fingertips. She could feel its power within the wall. She closed her eyes and concentrated. The arcane symbols were there, behind her eyelids, dancing and awaiting her orders. They answered her call but danced independently, creating a synergistic bond between witch and cave. Suddenly, Cassandra could smell food. She opened her eyes and pulled her hand away from the smooth wall, breaking the trance. The wonderful scent of roasted turkey, cooked apples, and mashed potatoes lingered briefly in the hall. She realized then that she was starving, and the magic of the place had sensed it.

"So, we work together, then?"

She took a deep breath and closed her eyes, then reached back to the wall. The energy responded in kind and swirled about her hand. She could vaguely feel it gathering, and she focused her control over it. One of the torches extinguished, its blue flame absorbed into the wall and propelled to Cassandra's connection with the place. A second and then a third torch followed. The energy coursed through her, and she squinted her eyes tight, the blue light blinding her even when they were closed. She eventually screamed as it felt like the energy would tear her apart. Then her world went dark as she lost connection with the wall and slumped to the floor.

A LONG WHILE LATER, SHE OPENED HER EYES AND FOUND HERSELF lying on the hallway floor. She smelled the aroma of cooked meat once more and slowly sat up. She grimaced and brought a hand to her temple as pain stabbed at her. She was dizzy and closed her eyes for a moment to steady herself. When the fit passed, she slowly opened her eyes and found a doorway before her at the end of the hall, where before there had only been a smooth wall.

"Amazing," she whispered.

She could see a quaint little study beyond, and the smell of food overcame her. She stood slowly, realizing that whatever she'd done to create the doorway had taken a lot out of her. The dizziness returned, and there was nausea with it this time. She steadied herself against the wall until it passed. Then she made her way into the cozy study. Inside, she found a fireplace. The flames burning the logs were blue, just like the energy that pulsed through the walls and floor of the place. A comfortable chair awaited her and a table of foodstuffs: a roasted turkey, cooked apples, mashed potatoes, and hot bread. They were all her favorite things to eat. Her mouth watered at the sight. Flasks of ales, wines, and pure water sat on a smaller side table.

Draped across the large chair was a blue robe. Cassandra approached it and noticed the initials "C.R." on the breast, stitched in a deeper blue.

"The color of the stone in Zolmex," she whispered.

She felt the soft material, pinching it between two fingers. It reminded her of a similar robe she'd had when she was small, one that Unis, her first surrogate mother, had made for her. Had she subconsciously created it, or had the cave read her memories and added it to her experience? Cassandra looked down at her travel attire, dirty from the desert sand, and the scimitars hanging from her hips now seemed so bulky. The weapons were gifts from her friend Sitra, the very sleeth that had turned Matilda's husband, Cerus, to stone. They didn't seem to belong in the study, nor did her filthy clothes.

"This place is perfect," she whispered, looking around the room. "I cannot soil it."

A log popped in the fireplace, and she realized all the comforts she desired were in the room. And she knew it was all her father's doing, but was any of it real? It felt and smelled real to her. She took a small bite of the bread, and it was delicious. She determined that everything she witnessed was real and created by magic. It was a joint effort by her and the cave, a collaboration that resulted in the perfect room for her. She had dreamed of such a place to call her own, even as a child at the orphanage in Oldorburg. All that was missing were her friends and family.

With a sigh, she undid the belt holding her scimitars, letting them fall to the floor. She shimmied off her pants and shirt, piling them outside the room in the hallway. Once she was naked, she grabbed the robe and made her way out of the other side of the room. Somehow, she knew exactly where that small hallway led. She traversed it and, at the end, took a left and entered a bathhouse. Heated rocks warmed the pool, and bars of soap lined the edge. Cassandra stepped into the shallow pool after laying the immaculate robe far from the water. She eased herself in; the water temperature was perfect. The silent blue strokes of energy lighting the ceiling and walls only added to the ambiance.

She bathed, using the nearby bar of soap made from cedar grass, her favorite scent. She was hungry and eager to return to the study where the food awaited her, but she also knew it would be piping hot and ready to devour no matter how long it took her to get back to it. She even caught herself humming a song, something she hadn't done since childhood. She finished her bath and leaned against the pool's edge. She closed her eyes and smiled.

"Is this paradise?" she whispered, and drifted slowly to sleep in the warm water.

She awakened much later and realized that her hands had pruned. The water temperature was still perfect, but the thought of sleeping for a long time bothered her. She had to remain focused, or she could get lost in the place. Time was of the essence, so why was she lingering? Kessi needed her, and Sitra, her husband Mateon, and Cassandra's little fairy friend, Gophia, were in a cruel world filled with evildoers. Why was Cassandra being selfish and enjoying the magical cave? She panicked then and stood. Again, she felt weak and nearly fell back into the water.

"I just need food."

She quickly dried herself and donned the comfortable robe, which felt magnificent. She closed her eyes and hugged her arms to her chest, lavishing the feel of the material, lost in bliss. Suddenly, her eyes flew open, and the smile faded.

"I'm doing it again!" she said, realizing how easily she could fall within the comforts of the place.

She quickly made her way back to the study. She cursed herself for leaving her weapons there. To her relief, her clothing and scimitars were where she'd left them. She entertained the idea of putting them back on, but the soft feel of the robe convinced her not to.

She sat at the table, poured herself an excellent wine, and began making a plate of food. She loved how the robe felt; it took her back to when she was young and didn't have a care in the world. She smiled at the thought and recalled images of Kessi and herself, young and full of life. They had shared a good existence at the orphanage with Unis. But that hadn't lasted long. The smile slowly faded. How had things gone from that perfect, innocent life to a life on the run where people kidnapped and tortured her and murdered her family? What had she done to deserve the life she was living? And why did she have to be mixed up in some evil prophecy?

She thought of Kessi and her dead mothers. Did Kessi even know Sera was dead? Where was Kessi? She felt the urge to find Zolmex and take vengeance on the three fools who waited for her outside the hidden cave. She knew she could destroy them all, and once they were out of the way, she would use Zolmex to find Kessi. A terrible thought occurred to her then: what if Kessi was dead as well? She had considered that a possibility, but deep down, she wanted to believe her sister was still alive. She needed to find her and hoped Zolmex could do just that.

She sat back in the chair with a resounding sigh. She would enjoy her meal, eat slowly, and experience this cave, a gift from her father. The place would hopefully supply the answers to her many questions soon enough. She would realize her quest to find Zolmex, and when she did, she would be more powerful than any wizard alive! Cedric had predicted it, and she believed it. With renewed vigor, she sat up and ate heartily.

She tried to savor the perfectly delicious food and enjoy the refreshing drink, but it was hard not to think of Zolmex or the incredible knowledge she somehow knew the cave possessed. She ate her fill and re-dressed. She felt recharged after bathing and eating, and the weapons felt comfortable on her hips. She folded the perfect robe and laid it back where she'd found it, rubbing the stitching longingly with her fingers. She wished Kessi could witness the room, but that would have to wait. It was time to find her answers and become legendary, as Cedric had once told her.

She returned to the torch-lined hallway where fewer torches burned, used up by her effort to create the study. Now it was time to find Zolmex, and she would need to make the next room in the wondrous place. She put her hand on the left side of the hallway, and the energy answered her call again, gathering at her hand and surging through her arm. She now knew the routine and how to manipulate the magic, but she swooned as the effort made her dizzy once more. This time she remained conscious, and when she opened her eyes, she saw that a second door was before her.

It was dark inside initially, but as the energy finished creating the room, several lanterns on a large table flared with blue fire, illuminating the small area. Cassandra was disappointed that she hadn't found the room in her dreams that housed Zolmex. She'd expected it to be there, as she had focused on just that as she'd created the doorway. She knew then that she only had so much control of the magic found in the place, and she would have to play her father's games, no matter how trivial.

She glanced at the study to her left at the end of the hall and stepped into the new room. Aside from the table and the two lanterns glowing from atop it, there was a rolled-up scroll in the center of the table. Beside the scroll was a tiny vial of blue liquid, which seemed to glow like the energy. Large bookcases lined all four walls. Void of any books or scrolls, they stretched to the ceiling.

"What is this place?" she asked, knowing this wasn't something she'd created subconsciously, as the study had been.

She sighed and approached the table. She didn't have time for games; she needed to find Zolmex. This room, this setup of scroll and potion, reminded her too much of the first cave she had traversed with Binta, Greyson, and Cass months earlier. The room had to be a test, and she was in no mood to entertain it.

She sat on the lone chair before the scroll and looked over the magnificent table. It was made of marble or something similar, as was the surprisingly comfortable chair. The scroll had a wax seal with a "K" marking it.

"Kane," she breathed.

She studied the scroll momentarily and thought of the one she'd found in Leo's tomb, deep in the first cave. That scroll had been such a disappointment to her, and her heart raced at the conjured memories—she could not fail in the quest to obtain Zolmex again. Finding the scroll felt too similar, although the one she now held wasn't as old and brittle as the first one, and the wax didn't crumble at the touch.

"Fine," she whispered and raked off the seal.

She unrolled it and spread it across the table, placing a lantern on each top corner to hold it in place. She leaned over it and read the words scribed upon it:

Dear Daughter:

If you have made it this far, you are indeed worthy of your birthright. However, I will not easily hand over something so precious without you truly earning it. Part of your test will be physical, most of it mental, but I will supply you with answers before you take that final exam.

You have been left in the dark most of your life, and now I offer you the chance to learn the answers to your many questions that I am sure still exist. Quaff the entirety of the potion, and everything will be revealed. Who are your parents? Does your birthright exist? How is the prophecy going to work? How can you stop it? Many questions that I am sure remain unanswered will finally be discovered. Do this, and you will be armed fully with the knowledge of who you are and your true purpose. Only then will you be worthy of the final test.

There was no signature, although she knew it was from her father. She released the ends of the scroll, letting it roll back to the lanterns of its own volition. She sat back in the chair and studied the tiny vial. She remembered how excited she was the night she met with Cedric in the bowels of the temple in Pelesea. He had been Kane's agent, the one person who could provide her with answers. He had sought her out and had provided a few of those answers. Now, she had the opportunity to discover the rest of it. She could finally rest easy, knowing her identity. She needed this as much as her father wanted her to have it.

She took up the vial and eyed the glowing liquid. Her heart thumped in her chest, and she could hear it in her ears. She suddenly wanted to return to her room in Oldorburg with Kessi, penning a spellbook and learning magic just as she did when she was twelve. That seemed like a lifetime ago, and it dawned on her that it was almost her and Kessi's birthday. It would be another one spent alone. Tears formed in her eyes.

After many moments, she uncorked the vial. She had to do it, not just for herself but for Kessi. She hoped one day she would be able to tell her sister all her discoveries and the adventures she'd undertaken to find them.

"Very well, Father, show me your secrets," she said and threw her head back, draining the tiny glass container.

She tried to put it back on the table, but her world spun before she could complete the motion. The table was no longer before her, and she vaguely heard the vial shattering on the floor. She couldn't focus as the room seemed a mix of lights and colors, the blue energy from the lanterns streaking it all. Her eyelids were heavy, and she felt compelled to sleep. She felt herself slip from the chair and fall to the floor, but she never experienced the sensation of hitting it. She was floating, weightless as if she were in water. The colors slowly faded to darkness, and she finally closed her heavy eyes. She was at peace and unaware of her surroundings. She was comfortable and safe, so she succumbed to the darkness.

Then, the dreams began.

Less than one hundred miles north of Witch's Rise and deep within the Yaddaton Desert, Jak, the last free member of the Serpent Tribe of barbarians, was pushed face down into the sand by his captors. He spat out the grainy substance and began to rise when one of the men kicked him in the back, knocking him down again.

"Stay down, you Serpent Tribe dog," one of his captors said.

Jak swallowed his pride and obeyed; after all, he was the one who had turned himself over to the Culiem Tribe barbarians. He was desperate and needed their assistance. Unfortunately, his king, Maltor, the lord of the

Serpent Tribe, had just killed Boskel, the Culiem Tribe's king, in an act of vengeance for the death of Cassandra Rho. Maltor blamed Boskel for Cassandra's death because the fairy gifted to Maltor by Boskel had escaped its cage and bit her. Cassandra was to be his queen, and he blamed jealousy for Boskel's murderous plot. Quick to anger, Maltor had challenged Boskel to a fight to the death. He had won, making the Culiem Tribe an enemy.

In hindsight, Jak understood the truth of Cassandra's fate. She wasn't dead, far from it, as she had healed Jak, saving him from certain death months after Maltor had buried her. She was alive and living at the edge of the Yaddaton Desert with a strange sleeth woman and her blind husband. He was happy she lived and felt compelled to tell Maltor the fantastic news if he saw his king again. Jak wondered as he lay face first in the sand if Maltor even lived. The last he saw him, his king was hanging limply from a tall pole near the royal tent at the Serpent Tribe grounds.

He had snuck close enough to his home to witness the spectacle without being noticed. The interlopers had captured what remained of the tribe. They tracked Cassandra Rho into the desert using their dark magic and knew she was once Maltor's captive. Jak had witnessed the raw power of the invaders as they had raised their own dead against them in a bloody battle near their burial grounds. Their magic was unnatural and unholy. Now, they had Maltor, along with a few who were weak and infirm. Jak had spied no other warriors. They were simply gone.

With Maltor near death, Jak had been forced to turn to the Culiem Tribe, the one that Maltor had recently declared war against. The Culiem Tribe was their closest neighbor, so he'd come to plead his case and hoped for mercy. He dared not move other than to raise his face from the sand to see who was before him. His captors had thrown him before a large man seated on a wooden throne, surrounded by shamans and other advisors. Jak assumed the young warrior was the new king of the Culiem Tribe, but he didn't recognize him.

He slowly raised his head and took in the sight. The man on the throne was young and muscular, not over three decades old. His lack of scars indicated to Jak that he'd seen few battles, if any. Jak would not consider any barbarian soft, but this young one looked like he'd spent his life playing in the sand and not sparring with the other youths. He was nice-looking, kept his blond hair shorter than most men of the Culiem Tribe, and trimmed his beard to match. The shamans whispered in his ears, one on each side, while the other surrounding warriors looked at Jak with frowns and revenge burning in their eyes. Not the new king, though; he surprisingly remained stone-faced as Jak lay before him. The man finally rose and walked to Jak, while his guards followed vigilantly.

He said, "Why have you returned to our land, warrior of the serpent?"

His words were not venomous but spoken with genuine curiosity. Jak dared to crane his neck to look the king in the face. "I have returned to request help for my tribe."

"You kill our beloved king, then have the gall to return days later to ask for help? What could trouble the Serpent Tribe enough for you to want to die?"

"We have a common enemy that has invaded Yaddaton."

The king wrinkled his brow and thought for a moment. One of the shamans whispered something in his ear, which he waved off.

"What is your name, warrior of the snake?" the king asked.

"I am Jak, son of Cring, high warrior, and friend of King Maltor."

The warriors surrounding him bristled, but again, the king remained emotionless. Jak waited what seemed like an eternity, straining his neck to see the king's reaction. Eventually, he offered a hand to Jak, who tentatively took it. The young king helped him to his feet, and Jak was surprised at his strength.

"I am Gress, son of Plor, killer of sleeth, and King of the Culiem Tribe."

The two stood face to face, the young king nearly as tall as Jak's large frame. The king respected Jak, and Jak's perception of the man grew. He no longer thought Gress was a soft barbarian, and his opinion changed dramatically over the exchange.

"Tell me of your trouble, Jak, son of Cring."

"Devil-magic-wielding outsiders have handed the Serpent Tribe a deadly blow."

"Interlopers have invaded Yaddaton?" Gress asked curiously.

"Yes, and I ask you as a fellow barbarian to come to Maltor's aid," Jak said.

"Maltor is a dog!" one of the nearby warriors screamed, and many of the others shared the sentiment with angry nods or grunts, and some even spat at the mention of the king's name.

The king held a hand up, and the commotion eventually died. "We owe nothing to Maltor, and I do not care what happens to him," Gress said calmly.

Jak didn't know how to respond, so he said nothing but gritted his teeth and braced himself for a fight. He would not let the men of the Culiem Tribe bad-mouth his king. He had not come to them for that and would not tolerate it.

"However, I have no love for outsiders, especially those who wield devil magic. They are weakling wizards, then?"

"They are shamans of an evil god, I believe, one that can raise the dead to fight at their side. I witnessed them desecrate our graves in just such a way. If they come here next, they will do the same to you, uprooting your properly buried dead."

The warriors looked at each other, understanding now the seriousness of Jak's visit. Even the talkative shaman was silent as Gress pondered Jak's words.

After some time, he nodded and said, "The Culiem Tribe will answer the call of the Serpent Tribe."

Jak nodded and relaxed as the gathered warriors looked at one another, understanding this was the first test for the young king. It was the barbarian way to evaluate a new leader and look for flaws. Weakness or unpopular decisions would result in replacement by means of the challenge circle. Jak could sense the doubt forming among the men, see them watching intently, judging each move. They had just lost their king to the tribe that Gress offered to assist. However, Gress's following words wiped away those doubts and permanently entrenched him as the new king.

"On one condition," Gress added. "From this day forward, the Serpent Tribe no longer exists. The Culiem Tribe will absorb all members of the Serpent Tribe. I will have the four brides of Boskel returned to my possession, unharmed, and I will take the Rho girl as a fifth bride."

There was an immediate uproar from the surrounding warriors as they stabbed their weapons into the air, shouted, and made guttural noises that had even the stone-faced king crack a smile. Jak didn't know what to do other than accept the offer. Otherwise, they would kill him, and that would mean the death of his tribe anyway. He decided not to tell the young king that Cassandra no longer lived within the tribe. He wouldn't mention that or the fact she had escaped Yaddaton by faking her death. He nodded, and when Gress reached out his hand to shake on the deal, he took it. The barbarians cheered all the louder.

Ill-Fated Voyage

MANY OF THE POPULATION OF PELESEA GATHERED AT THE northern harbor, where the great ship *Hope* was anchored. Kringus and the New Order had christened it nearly ten years ago to serve as the official vessel for passage over the seas if the New Order ever ventured forth. They'd never had reason to use it until now. It was a spectacular boat, armed with six ballistae, three on the port and three on the starboard side. It had two decks, the main and the captain's, with the latter about ten feet higher than the main deck. *Hope* had three masts and a crew of two hundred. The figurehead adorning the bow was that of an angel, her wings spread wide and sword pointing straight ahead.

Harold, the dockmaster, and the captain of *Hope*, Ruby Declin, had hand-selected the ship's crew. Years ago, Pelesea saved Ruby's mother and father from a slaver, and they were granted citizenship in the great city to begin life anew. Ruby had been born shortly after and quickly grew fond of the water, volunteering her time on the docks as a kid to learn all there was to know about boats. She became a sailor at sixteen and made hundreds of voyages over the next six years before being promoted to first mate on a merchant vessel named *Sea Belle.* By the time she was twenty-five years of age, she was captain of that boat. At twenty-six, Kringus and Penelope had selected her to captain their ship. The king and queen had known Ruby all her life, and it was an easy selection that they were both very comfortable with.

Ruby was honored to accept the position and brought her first mate from *Sea Belle*, Wendle Esslor. He was only a few years older than Ruby, and although they were considered by many to be too young to lead a ship, their vast knowledge and skill level fit perfectly with what Kringus was looking for. The royal couple approached Ruby in the early weeks of summer, and she and Wendle worked diligently with the dockmaster to find the perfect crew of two hundred men and women.

King Kringus stood at the docks with his queen, Penelope, and watched the hand-selected crew load the cargo hold with food, water, and supplies. He had given a speech to the city a few days earlier, announcing the New Order's plans to travel to Varish and fight the budding prophecy that threatened the world. The people of his great city had responded positively for the most part. Although the mission held uncertainty for them all, the fate of the world rested on the shoulders of the New Order. The people of Pelesea understood that the king and queen had to venture forth. They had been happy with the selection and introduction of Jamison Oland as the city steward in the royal couple's absence.

Kringus looked around at the mass of people and the many city and castle guards assembled to maintain order. Thousands of citizens gathered, hoping to catch a glimpse of their king and queen before they boarded the magnificent ship. Those who couldn't get close on the street found perches on nearby rooftops or on balconies of those buildings. Others were on boats, gathered close to the docks to witness the spectacle. As was tradition in Pelesea, many people had thrown flowers at the feet of Kringus and Penelope as they passed, littering the street with many colorful petals. Kringus looked back and waved as citizens screamed for his attention. Some waved back, while others cried. It was a mix of emotions, and he knew his people were trying to be brave but were scared. His eyes drifted to the carpet of colorful flowers decorating the cobblestone street, making him think of death. He didn't understand why such a bright display made him have such awful thoughts, and he considered it a bad omen for the voyage. So, he kept those thoughts to himself; he had to be strong in front of his people.

Beside the royal couple was Jamison Oland. He was a wealthy and honest Pelesea citizen and had already rescued Binta from Cass. He and Binta were unofficially engaged and had resided in his mansion in Pelesea before his move to the castle a few weeks earlier. Now, Binta was missing, and Jamison fretted over her as much as he did the thought of running Pelesea in Kringus and Penelope's absence. Baxter had taken Binta on a unique quest to find Cassandra at Binta's urging, so Baxter had said. But they hadn't heard from her since that journey to the east over a week ago, and Jamison worried that his love was lost to him. Kringus didn't know the details of Binta's quest, but he could tell her disappearance didn't sit well with Jamison. The steward wore a smile as he walked with the royal couple, but Kringus knew where the man's thoughts lingered. He hoped it wouldn't hamper his ability as steward.

Beside Jamison were his advisors appointed to provide input for the tough decisions he was sure to encounter. Franklin Ruben was the most prominent because everyone knew him in Pelesea. He owned a merchant fleet of ships and was one of the city's wealthiest citizens. He also happened to be the father of Cass Ruben, Cassandra's and Binta's nemesis. The other two advisors, Sam Velt and Raul Franz, were honorable but not nearly as prominent as Jamison and Franklin. However, Kringus knew them both and believed in their strong political views and willingness to say what was on their minds. The king and queen trusted each of the four powerful men to run things in their absence.

On Kringus and Penelope's other side stood the messenger of the prophecy, the one who had first warned them of the events unfolding in the world. Inuentas, the half-demon, had been sent to the New Order to warn them of the Great Summoning that the agents of Marnelphion had planned. His master, another demon lord quite jealous of Marnelphion's plans, had sent Inuentas to call the New Order to action and hopefully ruin his rival's return to the human world. Inuentas carried a massive sword called Slebel on his hip. It was designed to kill demons, and more specifically, Marnelphion. The half-demon was a true warrior and was confident he could destroy Marnelphion with one stroke of Slebel. His mission in the human world was to kill Marnelphion if the New Order failed to stop the summoning.

Victoria and Penelope had researched his word and believed it was true. His message was short and straightforward—the New Order, consisting of precisely twelve members, would venture forth to stop the summoning. They were only to venture forth as twelve, a powerful representation of the goodly races. Kringus and the New Order had hand-selected powerful allies to bring their membership from eight to the desired twelve. As they prepared to set sail, Kringus's silent objective was to destroy Matilda or Cassandra, whichever option saved the most lives. He hadn't let his beloved wife be privy to his plans because she would disapprove. But the world relied on their quest to succeed, and he would take no chances at failing.

In truth, Kringus didn't trust and cared little for the half-demon, starting with the fact that he came from the bowels of hell with his message. Inuentas had reddish skin; dark, beady eyes; horns; and a long, sharp tail that always danced behind him, seemingly ready to impale someone. Kringus knew there was more to the creature than he was letting on; his arrogance and boots, made from human skin, were just glimpses of the evil that Kringus suspected dwelled within their strange visitor. And to make matters worse, Inuentas seemed too familiar with Penelope, as if they were old lovers. She hadn't elaborated on how they might have met in the past, and he hadn't asked her. His wife was half-elven and had lived centuries before Kringus was born, yet looked young and beautiful, as elves were known to live close to ten centuries before old age took them. She would outlive Kringus; they knew that going into their relationship. However, Inuentas's interest in the queen did not sit well with the king.

The rest of the New Order had already boarded the ship: the elven brothers and Penelope's cousins, Von and Lenore, both excellent archers; Arrin, the captain of Kringus's army; Lady Victoria, the grand wizard; Daro the ranger, Keeper of the Woods; Sasha De'Formen, ice carofex and master sword-wielder who was born with goddess-like beauty; Max Smithston, former sheriff of Oldorburg where Cassandra was born; Baxter Von Glord, the high-ranking wizard in Victoria's School of Magic; and two knights of Pelesea, Erik and Marcus. The last two were temporary members until they could find their two missing members, Alleah Mansuell and Greyson Kavince.

Inuentas insisted that if the New Order were to stop the return of Marnelphion successfully, they had to venture forth with only twelve members. According to the prophecy, taking an army or even a thirteenth ally would spell disaster for the group, and they would fail. Kringus, not trusting

Inuentas's word, thought the notion foolish, but he had to rely on Victoria and Penelope to decipher the half-demon's prophetic message. Regardless of how ridiculous that sounded, they had determined he was correct, so Kringus was forced to believe that the small band could accomplish the impossible.

Hope's first mate, Wendle, quickly approached the royal couple, having disembarked the ship and spotted them. Kringus could see the top of Captain Ruby's fanciful hat bob to and fro on the captain's deck of the great ship. He knew it was time to leave. He turned his focus back to Wendle, the heavy-set man's red cheeks puffing with the exertion of his brisk pace. His outfit was as fancy and colorful as Ruby's, and Kringus couldn't suppress his smile. The two took their jobs seriously, and he knew his friends and fellow heroes were in good hands.

Wendle finally arrived and bowed respectfully. "My king and queen, the ship's stores are full. We may launch when you are ready."

When he rose, his eyes briefly met Kringus's, but the king watched the man take in the gathered mass of people surrounding the docks. It was relatively quiet for such a large gathering, the mood tame, and perhaps the big man hadn't noticed at first what a vital mission this was to Pelesea and the world.

He swallowed hard and added, "Whenever you are ready, no rush."

"Thank you, First Mate. We understand your readiness and will be along shortly," Penelope said, punctuating her response with her beautiful smile.

Wendle nodded and bowed deeply once more, removing his plumed hat as he did. When he rose, he smiled, turned, and walked briskly back to the ship.

"A peculiar one," Inuentas said with a smirk.

Kringus began to turn toward the half-demon to give him a piece of his mind, but a gentle hand on his arm gave him pause. He knew whose hand it was before he saw Penelope's genuine smile. She was always there to keep his temper in check, and he relaxed as her touch melted his anger away.

"And so, we venture forth," Kringus said to no one in particular, but kept his loving gaze on his queen.

"The people are restless, and I feel their tensions growing, my king. Perhaps a happy stroll to the ship would be just the right thing for them," Jamison said.

Kringus looked back to the crowd and tried to ignore the dying flowers that littered the street. He saw worry on most of the faces, mixed with fear. The quicker they left, the sooner Jamison could take over and the people could adjust. Pelesea was safe, and even if the New Order failed to stop the summoning, Kringus was confident he could return to Pelesea to protect his people from whatever evil was unleashed upon the world. He nodded and stuck out his arm for the queen. She placed her hand in the crook of his elbow, and the group started for the ship.

"The people already love you, Jamison; you will do splendidly in our absence," Penelope said.

"I wish I shared your positive outlook, my lady. I cannot fill either of your shoes, but we will try to make the people of Pelesea comfortable and happy," Jamison said, holding a hand toward his advisors, who nodded eagerly.

"Yes, we will have them calmly disbursed and going about their lives before your ship is fully out of sight," Franklin added.

"We have the highest amount of faith in all of you," Kringus said, trying to tune out the faint cries of desperation he heard through the crowd.

They were calling for him to stay, not to leave them. The people of Pelesea were not excited for the king and queen to venture across the ocean; they feared the unknown. Kringus couldn't blame them. Still, he had to be strong to show the people this journey mattered and would have a cheerful ending, although he wasn't convinced that was the case. Something gnawed at his conscience; it felt wrong. He glanced to Inuentas, who smiled back, seemingly not a care in the world. That upset Kringus more than anything else. He waved to the people, and Penelope followed suit. It was a long walk along the docks until they reached the boarding plank. Once there, they turned to Jamison and his fellow advisors.

"Jamison, thank you for doing this," Penelope said.

"It is an honor to do my duty, dear lady," Jamison said, gently kissing the back of her hand.

"We will not be long," Kringus added, and he shook the hands of the steward and his three advisors.

He approached Inuentas and stood menacingly before the half-demon. "And so, we are off on the wild chase you have convinced us we must take."

"A wise decision, I assure you," Inuentas said with a slight bow.

"This is a fool's errand, and I do not believe in your long tales, half-demon."

Inuentas only smiled more and glanced over Kringus's shoulder to view the queen. Kringus's neck muscles tightened, and he struggled to remain calm in front of the citizens he knew were watching his every move.

"But you believe in your queen," Inuentas said.

Kringus took a step closer and stood within inches of the half-demon. To his credit, Inuentas's smile grew, and he didn't back down. His tail wagged behind him as a cat's might when agitated.

"Yes, and my friends. All of us will be back with the mission completed. And if I find you have lied to or betrayed us in any way, you will answer me."

The smile faded from Inuentas's face, and he studied Kringus, understanding the threat for what it was. Instead of backing down, he stepped closer and whispered, "You have my word, dear king; whatever I have told you is truth. Do not presume you will survive, but I hope at least some of you make it back."

Kringus knew he was referring to his wife, and that had him at boiling point. He was about to lash out, when Penelope was suddenly there, putting a hand on his shoulder.

"Is everything all right here?" she asked.

"Everything is perfect, dear queen," Inuentas said. "The king and I were discussing how I will assist you if the quest fails. I am on your side, and I hope you can take care of this threat so I don't have to get my hands dirty."

Kringus didn't know if the half-demon was being cryptic with his words. Did he mean he hoped the New Order took care of the threat so Inuentas didn't have to draw his weapon against Marnelphion, or did he refer to Penelope keeping Kringus under control so Inuentas did not need to draw his sword against him? Either way, Kringus was tired of the creature's antics.

"If you are so honorable and brave, why don't you come with us?" Kringus asked.

"You know why, dear king. The prophecy states that the only chance any of you have is with a team of twelve brave souls. No more, no less. You did not invite me to join your group."

"Right, I keep forgetting that part of this suicidal mission," Kringus said, then offered his arm to Penelope once again.

Penelope locked stares with Inuentas, who smiled suggestively and again got under Kringus's skin. "I do hope to see you soon, Inuentas, and with the good news that we succeeded," she said.

"I look forward to that day, and in the meantime, I will take advantage of your hospitality and enjoy the fruits of Pelesea while I await your return."

Kringus's jaw clenched as he watched the half-demon kiss Penelope's hand, lingering with it and looking up to Kringus, his lips pressed against her skin. Something about that seemed perverted to the king, and it took all his control not to lash out. Eventually, the mercenary from hell ended the kiss and smiled at the royal couple.

Kringus and Penelope boarded the ship and waved to the gathered masses. The people cheered, mostly, but a good number cried. Once aboard, they quickly made their way to the captain's deck, standing at the railing along the stern and waving some more. Soon, the anchor raised, the sails unfurled, and the first adventure of the New Order officially began.

DORIN MCVALE WATCHED THE SHIP SAIL OUT OF PELESEA'S HARBOR and into the vast Nepress Sea. It appeared no more than a tiny dot on the horizon before he could pull himself away from the image. He and his fellow dockhands had the honor of loading the king's galleon with foodstuffs and other supplies, and he was overwhelmed to be hand-selected by the good dockmaster. He and his friends had come to Pelesea over five years ago in preparation for this day, and it went perfectly as planned. They had earned Harold the dockmaster's respect and trust, so much so that seven of his ten friends had been part of the group hand-selected to load the ship.

Harold approached the gathered men as the crowd began to disburse and said, "You've done a fine job, men. You have played your part in assisting the New Order and seeing to it that the world is a safer place."

"It was an honor to help," Dorin said in his usual humble demeanor.

The other dockhands, fifteen in all, nodded in agreement and welled with pride as the dockmaster shook their hands and patted them on the shoulders. Dorin and his friends did their part, smiling and taking the praise in stride, as they had for the last five years.

Dorin glanced back to the sea and could barely see the giant ship on the horizon. The New Order was on its way, and he and his friends were partly responsible, if only in some minor way. A new life in Pelesea was beginning under the watchful eye of Jamison Oland. It was a strange feeling for them all, but Dorin and the others slowly returned to their posts and lost themselves in their work until the sun colored the sky a bright red. As they had done since their earliest days in Pelesea, they left the docks and returned to their homes that evening. However, unlike all those previous times, Dorin and his ten friends quickly packed their things and made their way to the city's south side.

Once there, very late into the night, they secretly boarded a large cargo ship heading to Mecca-Loraine. The eleven dockworkers left the city under darkness just as quietly as they had first entered Pelesea. They gave no notice to Harold or any of their coworkers, several of which Dorin had befriended and truly cared for. However, this was business, and they had to stick to the plan. Harold and the other dockhands would be sorely understaffed the following day.

Early the next morning, just before the sun crested the horizon and when the ship was miles away from Pelesea, Dorin and his friends met for an early breakfast deep in the hold of the merchant ship. They found a corner far away from any other paying passengers or crew members, surrounded by wooden crates full of clothing, leather goods, and other non-perishable items. The corner was dark, and Dorin lit a single hooded lantern, which made shadows dance on the large crates. The smell of sawdust and tanned leather was thick.

They rummaged through their packs and pulled out the travel rations they had brought: hard bread and dried meat for the most part. They ate silently, not speaking but making plenty of eye contact as they chewed. It was as if there was excitement among the friends, and they were all waiting for Dorin to speak. They were very disciplined, having waited five years to get to this point, and so they ate silently because a few more moments didn't seem like much time. Once he was confident no one was about, and the sound of light snoring of the late-rising passengers reverberated through the hold, Dorin lowered the hood on the lantern, extinguishing most of the light in their little corner of the hold.

His dark eyes and neatly trimmed beard looked more sinister than usual in the weak lighting, the shadows distorting his handsome features. He was young, barely thirty years old, and had been tapped as the leader of the group long ago, although he was younger than half of the men gathered around him. They trusted him and followed him without question. He looked around the circle of men, making eye contact with each and taking his time before he spoke. Only when he had everyone's attention did he do so.

"And so, it is done," he whispered and finally allowed himself to crack a slight smile.

He rolled his sleeve to reveal a skull tattoo on his left forearm. The other ten did the same, each showing an identical tattoo.

"So, tell us again, Bryce, how the great ship will sink," he instructed the man to his left.

"You know how, Dorin, we have been over this a hundred times."

"I know, I just want to hear it again," Dorin said as the others smiled and nodded eagerly.

Bryce displayed a large grin and said, "Very well. As you know, the metal tube we hid at the bottom of the food stores in *Hope*'s cargo hold is filled with corrosive acid. It will take nearly two weeks to eat through the thick metal container. Once it does, it will dissolve the wooden crate we hid it in, and moments after that, it will eat a hole in the bottom of the ship. The ship will sink, I assure you, and by the time it does, they will be deep in the Nepress Sea."

"And the smaller lifeboats?" Dorin pressed.

"As you know, four are usually used to carry up to thirty passengers to and from the ship to a dock or beach. We added a healthy amount of acid into each, so it will eat the bottoms away by the time they are needed."

Dorin nodded, and the rest of the men silently rejoiced, smiles plastered on their faces as they chewed their tasteless food. Disciplined as always, they didn't make a sound.

After their quick meal, Dorin looked to make sure no one was around or eavesdropping, and once satisfied they were alone, he said, "And now we go to the second stage of the plan. We travel to Mecca-Loraine and from there to Oldorburg. As the New Order drowns, we will quietly take up residence in the town Cassandra Rho grew up in. And thirteen months from now, when they sacrifice the girl and our lord, Marnelphion, returns, Oldorburg will become the base of operations for our people.

"We will be close enough to assist Marnelphion as he establishes his kingdom in Novafontera. Legions of our brothers and sisters patiently wait for the end of next summer and will march to us once it arrives. Then we will have Oldorburg. With their royal couple dead, Pelesea will not dare move to assist the minor forces standing in our way, especially knowing that the summoning will transpire and that the New Order failed miserably."

"Any word from Annabella?" a man named Lars asked.

"Not for five years. As you know, we couldn't take the chance to communicate. We will trust in Marnelphion that she has firmly established the trust of the local officials in Oldorburg."

The men nodded eagerly, hoping that she had done just that. Annabella was Dorin's wife and had been tasked with establishing roots in Oldorburg while Dorin and his men infiltrated Pelesea. The men soon found corners of the hold to unroll their bedrolls and sleep for a few hours. The excitement was still palpable, and few found sleep, especially Dorin, who longed to see Annabella again.

"WHAT TROUBLES YOU? YOU HAVE BEEN SULLEN THE ENTIRE TRIP THUS far," Penelope asked Kringus.

They had been at sea for nearly a week. As the summer faded into fall, Ruby, the captain, had warned that they could encounter choppy weather along the way. So far, the Nepress Sea had been primarily calm, and Ruby thought they could reach Port Racip in less than a month if the weather continued to hold. The king and queen lounged on the captain's deck on a comfortable bench that Kringus had installed before the trip, which butted against the rail that wrapped around the stern. The ship's wheel was in the middle of the deck, and Captain Ruby operated it as the royal couple spoke in hushed tones. The vessel's crew hastily went about their business, rushing up and down the steps leading to the main deck. The sails were full, and the ship cut efficiently through the mighty sea. The first mate, Wendle, rushed up the steps, nodded briefly to the king and queen, and then began speaking with the captain.

"This trip seems irresponsible to me, as I've said before," Kringus replied.

"The prophecy?" Penelope asked.

"Yes; twelve against this evil, if it exists as Inuentas describes, is suicidal."

"Perhaps, but the prophecy is specific. We cannot venture forth with an army, or we guarantee our failure."

"What if I don't believe in the prophecy?"

"But you do," Penelope said with a smile, understanding her husband's doubts. "Why else would you have assembled the New Order and gone on this doomed mission unless you believed at least a little?"

"No, my love, I believe in you. We are only here because you and Victoria backed Inuentas's tale and supported the idea that the New Order could pull this off. But I still don't understand how we were unaware of the prophecy before Inuentas brought it to our attention."

"Victoria and I did our research after the half-demon came to us. The prophecy hid in tomes usually only read by evil men. We were unaware of its existence because it originated from hell, and unless you research such writings deeply, they are challenging to discover. But after researching it, I do believe Inuentas is correct."

They sat silently, listening to Ruby bark orders and the sea break against the ship's hull. The rocking of the boat and the smell of saltwater mesmerized Kringus, and he let Penelope's words sink in. As always, he found her words soothing, and he decided to remove the doubt from his thoughts and focus on completing the task. He was their leader, and his actions spoke volumes; it was time to stop doubting.

"I am sorry, my queen. I should not doubt you or Victoria."

Penelope smiled and said, "That is the burden of being a leader. You worry about the safety of your friends. The fact that it shows makes you human. Do not apologize for fretting over friends; it just shows the size of your heart."

"And my insecurity?"

"Perhaps, but something more. Very few times have I seen you jealous, and your jealousy over Inuentas is abundantly clear."

Penelope's words had Kringus off balance. She was right, of course; his jealousy tarnished his view of the annoying half-demon. He had tried to discover the source of his uneasiness concerning the creature, but in doing so, his queen had quickly picked up on his struggle.

"You are amazing," he whispered.

She moved closer so their foreheads rested against each other and said, "*We* are amazing, my love. And to keep us as such, we must keep our communication open and honest."

"I agree. So, tell me, is my jealousy well warranted?"

"Of course not, but Inuentas and I have a history I should have told you about upfront. It is minor, so I elected to keep it from you, which is my weakness. I should have told you immediately."

Kringus smiled and kissed her lightly on the lips. "I love you."

"And I love you," she answered, kissing him back more fully.

Kringus immediately felt the tension washing away, now understanding that there was nothing for him to worry about. He couldn't believe his mood had been so foul because of it. Still, a sixth sense told him the trip was cursed, something that didn't involve petty jealousy. He thought of the flowers on the cobblestone street back in Pelesea and how he thought of death at the sight of them. Something intangible did not sit well with him, but he couldn't focus on that. It was time to overcome the negative feelings and focus on the mission.

"Tell me the story of Inuentas," Kringus said, pulling away and looking into her beautiful green eyes.

"A little late in the day for a sparring match, I would say," Arrin said.

The two looked over and noticed for the first time that their friend was standing nearby. Neither had seen him, as engrossed as they were in their conversation.

"Never too late for that," Kringus said with a mischievous smile.

Penelope leaned in close and whispered, "You beat me at our next sparring, and you shall receive the information you desire."

Kringus's thoughts ran away with him. Sparring was a ritual they performed almost daily, and the two skilled sword-wielders were evenly matched. Penelope was slender and lithe and was quick and effective with her small blade, while Kringus was large and strong, and his powerful strokes were accurate and deadly. Against each other, there was rarely a consistent winner, despite the difference in their technique. But those sparring matches always ended the same way, and Arrin knew this—with passionate lovemaking. It fueled the fire of their love, and Kringus always looked forward to their matches.

They both turned to Arrin and smiled. He rolled his eyes and said, "The New Order is ready."

He motioned with one hand toward the steps leading to the main deck and the door to the sleeping quarters and conference room below the captain's deck.

"Deal," Kringus said and stood, offering a hand for his lovely wife.

Although she didn't need his assistance to stand, she played the part, placing her tiny hand in his larger one and letting him pull her up. They shared one last knowing smile and followed Arrin, who could only laugh at the spectacle as he descended the steps.

The ornate oaken door that led to the sleeping quarters had the words "New Order" carved into it, and above that was the flag of Pelesea, which had white angel wings on a red background. The three allies walked through the magnificent door, and Arrin led the way below the deck. The design was simple but effective: a long hallway ran the length of the captain's deck, with ten rooms, five on each side. The captain's quarters were immediately to the right, and it was the finest room of the ten, sporting many luxuries the other rooms didn't have, such as a fully supplied bar, a large wooden tub for bathing, and a grand mirror. Across the hall from that was the first mate's room. The final eight rooms were quarters for the New Order.

Since the New Order designed the ship when they had eight members, there were only eight rooms, which Kringus later admitted was a mistake, to which the queen had said, "I told you so." The sleeping arrangements for the voyage had been modified so that Kringus and Penelope shared a room, as did the brothers Von and Lenore. Also sharing quarters were Victoria and Baxter, who were as comfortable as siblings doing so, and the knights Marcus and Erik. Those lucky enough to have quarters to themselves were Daro, Sasha, Max, and Arrin.

The trio passed all the rooms until they reached the end of the hallway, where another large, ornate door stood. This one also had the words "New Order" engraved on it, with the ship's name "*Hope*" inscribed above it. Arrin opened the door leading to a plush meeting room with a large oak table and a dozen oversized chairs lining it. This room also contained a fully stocked bar and an extensive library, with books and scrolls adorning the east wall on large bookcases. A globe on a marble stand stood in one corner. Many lanterns burned brightly in various spots, showing clearly the many paintings that Kringus and Penelope had commissioned for the room: wilderness scenes with colorful flowers in bloom; angels gathering around a mountain top, blessing an injured warrior; a rendition of the original twelve members of the New Order; a painting of the castle of Pelesea; and the largest one, reflecting *Hope* sailing along the seas, her sails full of wind, splitting the ocean waves.

The other members of the New Order were already there, along with a thirteenth person, Parson Minks, the city's official cartographer. He stood when the royal couple entered, while the rest of the group remained casual, although the chatting subsided and the ones standing found their seats. They were one chair short, and Kringus offered his seat to Parson.

"I couldn't possibly, my king," Parson said, hesitant to sit in the offered chair.

"Parson, forget the fact I am your king. In this room, we are all equally important. I'm offering you my chair as a friend, and I will be offended if you don't take it."

Parson looked to the queen for support, and she only raised her eyebrows as if waiting for him to take the seat. She did so with a warm smile.

He reluctantly sat and said, "Thank you, my …"

He never finished his thought, trying to follow Kringus's instructions on equality within the walls of the place. There was a moment where Parson struggled to find his words, and everyone watched him as he squirmed in his seat. Kringus finally let him off the hook, patted his shoulder several times, and chuckled. Parson smiled, but his face remained red for a long while. Kringus made his way to the bar, pouring a sweet ale, one of Penelope's favorites, and a harder one for himself. He walked over and offered his wife her drink, which she took with a smile.

He looked around the table for many moments, measuring the expressions and reading the mood of his friends, both old and new. He couldn't help but let his gaze linger on Sasha longer than it should have. The woman was the most stunning creature he had ever seen, and he didn't want to make her uncomfortable by staring at her. She was already self-conscious of it, and the ship's crew had ogled her every time she came to the top deck over the last week. For reasons unknown to Kringus, the inhabitants of Iciale, the castle where she lived in the ice world of Glacies, found her hideous. Her life, living as a prisoner in the dungeons of the castle, had been filled with ridicule concerning her ugliness. But whatever they saw was a mystery to everyone who met the beautiful woman. She was breathtaking.

Her face was unblemished and perfect, with crystal blue eyes and full pouting lips. Her blond hair was long and wavy and just as gorgeous as her face. The size and shape of her nose was a work of art, and her ears were perfectly symmetrical. Kringus realized that he'd been staring at the young woman for too long, lost in his thoughts because her expression spoke volumes. He quickly shifted his gaze to Daro, the ranger, who was sweet on Sasha. Kringus wasn't confident they were a couple, but he could tell from Daro's behavior that the ranger desired more than friendship. He gave Kringus a look of disdain, so the king moved his gaze to Penelope, who crossed her arms knowingly and gave him a look that indicated he was caught. Her beautiful smile was the only thing that kept him from delving into a complete panic.

"All right, let's get things underway, shall we?" Kringus asked, trying to break the uncomfortableness.

"It's not your fault, Kringus; everyone does it," Daro said, calling him out on the misstep.

Sasha turned her head sharply toward the ranger, who sat near her. Kringus watched his eyes widen as he took in her beauty. She then sighed and reached into a pocket to produce a silk scarf.

"What are you doing?" Daro said, the sight of the scarf breaking him from his trance.

"This," she said, wrapping the fabric around her face, covering everything but her eyes and tying it at the back.

"There, does that help either of you take me seriously? Can you please stop? I must hide from the bumbling idiots who work the ship because they stare at me. I want to sit amongst my friends without feeling the same way."

Kringus had a hard time remaining focused on her words. The covering accentuated her magnificent eyes and made her look more desirable. He just gawked at her for a moment, then looked to Penelope, who cocked her head slightly.

"Ughh!" Sasha finally growled, and she crossed her arms in frustration.

That seemed to snap Daro out of his trance, and the ranger cleared his throat and looked away. However, Kringus could tell the ranger agreed with his assessment of the scarf, and looking at the other people in the room, it was evident that Sasha couldn't escape her beauty. Even the ordinarily tame elven brothers, Von and Lenore, seemed to take great interest in her at that moment. She tried to ignore it, and Kringus vowed not to stare at her again. As the leader, he had to set a better example. He kissed Penelope on the cheek for strength, and she gladly offered it to him and uncrossed her arms, obviously happy with his response.

"We have been at sea for one week now, and according to Captain Ruby, we could make Port Racip within another two or three weeks. We should probably meet here at least once weekly as we journey across the Nepress.

"The queen just pointed out that my morale has been low thus far on our quest, and for selfish reasons. That stops now. The prophecy has tasked us with the most important mission humanity has known since the original New Order banished Marnelphion 665 years ago. I am up to the task and will answer the call. I hope the rest of you will join me."

"That is why we're here," Arrin said.

Daro stood then and lifted his flagon. "A toast to our tireless leader, whom we'll follow to the ends of the world and back. There is no issue here, Kringus; we are with you."

"To Kringus," Victoria added, holding her drink toward the king.

"Hear, hear," Arrin said.

They drank, toasting their king and washing away Kringus's doubts about being a suitable leader. He took a long draw of his ale and then looked to Penelope. He found his courage there.

"So, it is settled. We continue forth, and we conquer anyone who stands in our way! We are the chosen twelve, and we will venture forth undeterred," Kringus said, raising his glass and draining it.

A rousing cheer supported his words, and all drank their fill as Kringus passed the floor to Parson, who brought forth a wooden scroll case and opened it, pulling a new map out and unrolling it. The map was eventually fully displayed with the help of strategically placed bottles on the corners. In an exercise they had already participated in many times, the cartographer went over the major cities of Varish and the location of Nesin in relation to Port Racip.

"Nesin is close to Racip, only twenty miles west of the city. I understand the starting point of your journey is Racip because that is where the search for Lady Alleah and Greyson begins. But remember, just to the west, you will find the target of your mission, the mountain fortress known as Nesin.

"Also, please note the location of Tara, Greyson's hometown. As we have discussed, that could be a location Alleah's group traveled to."

"So, if they aren't in Racip, we must decide to go to Nesin or Tara," Kringus said.

"Yes, and as the map suggests, Tara is roughly two hundred miles north of Nesin."

"So, we dock at Port Racip and hopefully find Alleah and Greyson and all the sisters of Sinnis there. That is the perfect scenario. However, as we've discussed, they are probably not there, and we'll need to pick up their trail, which will likely lead to Tara," Kringus said.

"As we've discussed before, it would be wise to find the designated members of the New Order before moving on to Nesin," Marcus suggested. "Erik and I are glad to fill in until you find Alleah and Greyson, and we're glad to provide the eleventh and twelfth members of the group so the New Order may follow the prophecy's instructions. But we will both gladly step down and return to the ship once the New Order finds them."

"I appreciate the loyalty of both of you. Your actions are honorable and selfless, and we are in your debt," Kringus said.

Many nods and agreements around the table followed that proclamation, ending with Arrin patting Marcus on the shoulder.

"Besides," Kringus added, "we know all too well what can happen when we venture forth without priests for healing."

He directed the comment toward the two knights, who nodded solemnly, remembering their disastrous trip to Oldorburg nearly a year prior. Arrin almost died on that quest because Alleah hadn't journeyed with them. Erik and Marcus had suffered a great deal from their injuries due to the lack of healing.

"Therefore, I prefer to find Alleah and Greyson before tackling Nesin. If anyone disagrees with that course of action, please speak now," Kringus said.

He paused and looked around the table. When no one suggested a different course, he said, "Very well, to Racip and then Tara if we don't find our friends conveniently waiting for us at the port city."

Kringus turned to Parson, adding, "Thank you for the wonderful map."

Parson beamed and rolled the map, stuffing it back in the case and capping the end. "Although I will not venture forth with you, I give you this map for reference on your journey. I hope it serves you well."

He handed the case to Kringus, and they clasped hands. The cartographer then left the room, leaving the New Order alone. Kringus asked for their attention as conversations had flared up around the table.

"My friends, we will meet again in another week. During that time, as we have nothing else to do on this voyage, please consider any weaknesses in our plans so we may discuss and analyze them when we meet. You may call an emergency meeting if urgent business arises before then."

Kringus adjourned the meeting, but Penelope stood and added, "Please enjoy your sailing experience. This ship was built for one purpose: to sail the New Order worldwide when needed. Kringus and I have spared no expense creating this marvel, so please relax as much as possible. Once we reach Racip, I'm afraid our opportunities for downtime will be few and far between."

There was another toast to the queen's words, and the meeting became a social gathering, as it usually was at the end of the New Order's business.

AS THE GROUP ATE GOOD FOOD AND DRINK, KNOWING THEIR TIME TO enjoy each other's company was short, the acid finally eroded the metal casing that housed it deep in the hull. It quickly began to dissolve the thick wooden crate which stored it. Dorin and his men had placed that crate underneath several others so it would be difficult to reach once the crew discovered their sabotage. The intent was to have the stack of goods and supplies crash through the hole once the acid ate through the hull. The New Order faced a pending doom far worse than Port Racip, and no one suspected a thing.

LATER THAT NIGHT, AS SASHA UNDRESSED FOR BED, THERE WAS A SOFT knock on her door. She put on her robe and made her way to it. She hesitated and felt compelled to grab her mighty sword, Iustia, the artifact sword from her native world. But then she remembered where she was, and instead, Sasha found her silk scarf and covered her face as she had done earlier.

She listened at the door for a moment. There was no detectable sound, so she called, "Who's there?"

"It's me, Daro," came the muffled reply.

"Daro? Why have you come?"

"Can you please open the door?"

Sasha did, and a giant bouquet greeted her. Daro peeked from behind it with a smile. "Special delivery, my lady."

She hesitantly took the flowers and looked at them like she'd never seen a bouquet before. "What is this?" she asked.

"It is a bouquet for you."

"I don't understand. You gathered a bunch of flowers on a ship far out at sea?"

"Well, Lady Victoria had to assist me," the ranger admitted.

"And what do I do with them?"

"You've never received flowers before?"

"Of course not."

"That makes sense," Daro said with his hands on his hips. "It is a tradition in this world. When a guy likes a girl, he'll give her flowers. They're supposed to make her feel special."

Sasha turned them over in her hand, brought them to her nose, and breathed in the fresh scent. "They are nice," she finally said.

"They are also a means for men who do stupid things to apologize. So, I want you to have them to say I'm sorry for making you feel uncomfortable at the meeting."

Sasha just stared at him and took another whiff of the flowers. She seemed unimpressed, though, and still didn't invite him in.

"I also brought you these," Daro said, rummaging in a large sack on his side.

He produced two red apples and held them up for her. Daro knew they were her favorite food, so she knew he was genuinely sorry. Her eyes widened, and she tossed the flowers on the floor. She pulled Daro into the room by the front of his shirt, lowered the scarf, and kissed him deeply. Daro kicked the door shut behind him, never breaking the kiss.

When Sasha finally pulled away, she quickly untied her scarf and tossed it aside. She grabbed the apples, sat on her bed, and devoured the fruit as Daro watched—he always seemed to enjoy watching her eat them. She smiled at him between bites but couldn't help but devour the delicious fruit. She became lost in joy, letting the juices run down her chin.

⚜

It was during those moments that Daro wished he were an apple. He watched the beautiful woman eat like a rabid animal, and he couldn't help but smile. She was perfect, regardless of her lack of etiquette.

"So, do you forgive me?" he asked.

Sasha stopped chewing, her mouth full of fruit, and thought about it momentarily before saying, "No."

Then she went back to her eating frenzy. Daro shook his head and picked up the flowers. He set them in a basin, then sat on the bed beside her and waited, enjoying her pleasure. It didn't take long for her to finish them off, and she snapped out of her feeding frenzy, seeming to understand she was making a spectacle. She licked her lips, wiped the juice from her chin, and then looked at Daro. She smiled and kissed him again, devouring his mouth like she had the apple.

She fell over him and kissed him harder, straddling him on the bed. Daro grabbed a handful of her hair and kissed her deeply, his passion for the woman taking over his instincts. His hands wandered as they kissed, from her hair down to her backside, pushing her against him as they ground against each other.

A sudden thump caused them to break the kiss, and both stared at the wall separating Sasha's room from the royal couple. A few moments later, there was another thump, and this one was louder.

Sasha jumped off the bed and quickly unsheathed Iustia. The powerful blade resembled a giant icicle and held great magic, which Sasha had spent the summer mastering. Daro was also up, and the two hurried out into the hall. There, they met Arrin, his sword drawn, and Von and Lenore, shirtless and looking like they'd just awakened. Each held their bow at the ready, arrows notched, and quivers strapped to their backs, holding more deadly arrows.

Arrin quickly tested the door as another thump sounded in the room, followed by a small yelp and a crash. He found the door unlocked, so Arrin rushed in, followed by the elves. Daro and Sasha approached the entrance and stopped at the sight that greeted them. The room was a mess, with furniture tossed here and there, the bed covers strewn about, and several bowls and dishes lying on the floor, broken. Kringus had Penelope pinned in the corner of the room, the king shirtless and the queen only in a thin shirt and underwear. They were both panting and sweating profusely. Kringus turned to regard the intruders, not breaking his hold. A fresh cut on his cheek showed the seriousness of the altercation.

"What is it, Arrin?" Kringus asked, struggling to hold the queen still.

He turned back to her and said, "I have you, now yield!"

"Never," Penelope whispered.

"We thought there was trouble," Arrin said.

"What? Oh, no, nothing like that, just sparring," Kringus said.

The distraction cost him as Penelope headbutted him in the temple. Typically, that tactic wouldn't work against Kringus, but the angle gave the queen the perfect opportunity, and she took it. The king lost his grip on her. She slipped away, and everyone quickly discovered how little she wore. Her sweat-covered clothing hid little of her perfect form.

"All right, everyone out," Arrin said as he turned and tried to herd the elven brothers away.

Arrin usually oversaw the sparring matches when the couple had them in the castle garden in Pelesea. The couple tasked him with observing the contests to ensure no one got hurt, and then when things progressed to where they were, he gave the order for the guards to leave and give the couple their privacy. He was used to the seriousness of the bouts, but Von and Lenore were not, and they were hesitant to leave. As Penelope's cousins, they were very concerned.

"Penelope, are you safe?" Lenore asked.

"What? Are you serious, Lenore?" Kringus asked.

Again, the distraction cost him as Penelope kicked him in the ribs, knocking him off balance and stumbling into the wall with another loud thump.

"Never better, Lenore!" Penelope shouted, not relenting in her attack.

She soon had Kringus on the bed, her legs wrapped around his injured ribs in a powerful scissor hold.

"Give!" she shouted as Kringus grimaced and tried to break the hold.

"Never!" Kringus answered, then looked to the spectators. "Will the lot of you get out of here? You're costing me the match. She owes me information, and I intend to get it!"

Soon, the five of them were standing outside the room, and Arrin quickly shut the door. Ruby Declin exited her room, wearing her pajamas with her saber in hand.

"What commotion abounds in the room? It is enough to sink my ship!"

"Nothing, Captain," Arrin said. "It's the king and queen sparring."

"At this late hour? How is anyone supposed to sleep?" Ruby asked.

Kringus's scream of anguish interrupted Arrin before he could explain, followed by Penelope's muffled cry, "Give!"

Kringus's painful response followed Penelope's command: "Never!"

More muffled dialogue and thumps followed, and it sounded like they were destroying the room, which Daro considered likely. Ruby looked at Arrin, then to the door as a wide smile spread across her face. She eventually laughed, but Arrin had a hard time hiding a smile.

Wendle poked his head out of his room, his hair a mess. "Everything all right, Captain?"

Ruby still laughed and waved Wendle back into his room. "We'll find out tomorrow, my friend. Everyone is safe. Go back to sleep."

The captain returned to her room, still chuckling, and shut the door. Wendle, confused by the exchange, shrugged and nodded to Arrin, then ducked back into his room, closing his door. The elves seemed a little confused by what they'd witnessed.

"Don't be alarmed, my friends; this is normal for the royal couple," Arrin explained.

"Normal?" Von asked suspiciously.

"Yes, they do this all the time, and to be honest with you, if you're concerned for Penelope, don't be. Kringus usually takes the worst of the beating."

That seemed to convince the elves, who looked at each other and shrugged, then nodded to Daro and Sasha and headed back to their room. Soon, only Arrin, Sasha, and Daro remained in the small hallway, with only the occasional thud and subsequent groan from the royal couple's room breaking the awkwardness. Daro realized that he and Sasha still had their weapons drawn.

"Well, goodnight then," Arrin said.

He returned to his room, leaving Daro alone once more with Sasha. He immediately thought of returning to their kissing, which he hoped would lead to more. He was ready to be intimate with her and suspected she felt the same. More thumps and the sound of Kringus groaning filtered out into the hall, snapping him from his contemplations and making them both uncomfortable.

"Shall we return to your room and finish what we started?" Daro asked hopefully.

Sasha thought about it briefly, then kissed his cheek and said, "No, let's go top deck; this noise is distracting."

"Top deck?"

"Yes, I've been down here all day, and the crew will be mostly asleep now. We can sit under the stars and chat."

"Chat? Yes, great," Daro said, disappointed.

Sasha didn't pick up on his sarcasm and gave him another quick peck on the cheek. "Let me dress, and I'll meet you up there."

"Great," Daro said with a fake smile as Sasha ran to her room.

"Release me, woman!" Daro heard Kringus roar.

Penelope's curt response followed: "Never! Give!"

"Thanks a lot, Kringus. I hope your missing information is worth it. Kick his ass, Penelope," Daro whispered, then made his way to the deck.

He found Baxter at the ship's bow, watching the stars and lost in thought. Daro approached him, turning to see who was handling the wheel at the late hour. He saw a young female crew member on the captain's deck. She saw Daro and saluted him with a smile. Daro nodded, then turned back to the bow. The few crew members he passed along the way acknowledged him, most with a nod or a smile or even both. It appeared that only a handful of the crew were working the night shift, and Daro felt comfortable with what he saw from them. They seemed proficient and trustworthy, making him feel safe this far out at sea. He knew little about sailing but felt the New Order was in good hands.

Baxter didn't hear him approaching—Daro was a master at moving silently, so he was close to his friend before clearing his throat to announce his presence. Baxter turned toward him, surprised at first, but a genuine smile found his face soon after, and Daro joined him at the railing.

He'd become good friends with Baxter over the last year, first meeting him while searching for Cassandra and her friends during their disastrous mission into the cursed mountain near Pelesea. They'd bonded during that search and had joined forces once more to rescue Sasha from her uncle. During their time together, Daro had learned how much the powerful wizard was in love with Cassandra. Daro had never met Cassandra but had seen her from afar several times. He was not impressed—the young woman seemed to cause trouble wherever she went, or perhaps it followed her. Either way,

Daro thought Baxter should leave her be. However, he wouldn't tell his friend that because he knew how much Baxter loved her.

"Beautiful night," Baxter said.

"Yep, as long as you're not trying to find peace below."

"What happened? Did Sasha forgive us for acting foolishly at the meeting?"

"Sasha isn't the problem; it's Kringus and Penelope."

"What? Are they all right?" Baxter asked, suddenly alarmed.

"Yes, just sparring, but maybe a little too wildly for the inside of a ship!"

Both laughed, and Baxter said, "Yes, Arrin has told me the tales of those two going at it. I'm sure it's a sight to behold."

"Definitely. Also, to answer your question—no, I don't think Sasha forgives any of us for being idiots."

"I don't blame her. I'm sure this world is quite an adjustment for her. The constant stares would have to get old, right?"

Both fell silent, and Daro's thoughts lingered on Sasha. Who was he to believe he could win her heart? He was a simple man who lived with wolves, deer, and other wildlife. She was too sophisticated for him yet childlike in many ways. He sighed louder than he intended and scratched his neatly trimmed beard. He felt the fool trying to win her over; she could have any man she wanted, so why settle for an average-looking forester who had no riches to offer her?

"Don't worry, Daro, even if she doesn't become your woman, you have kissed her, and I think most men would die for that opportunity," Baxter said, as if reading his thoughts.

Daro glanced at Baxter and saw the genuine smile there. The man was humble, electing to dress simply and not in the flashy wizardly robes most wore. He didn't carry magical staffs or wear pointy hats like the typical magic-users Daro had run across in the past. Baxter's dress was very similar to Daro's—a loose shirt and pants, but instead of swords, he wore a single wand on his side and many small bags filled with various components. He didn't look the part of a wizard at all, and Daro imagined he would fit perfectly out in the wilderness if a wizard's life didn't work out for him. He felt Baxter was the brother he never had.

"She does like to kiss a lot," Daro finally said with a smile.

"You're fortunate," Baxter said, looking up at the stars.

"You're thinking of Cassandra, aren't you?"

"Always, my friend."

They both stared at the stars briefly, letting the silence speak volumes. Eventually, Baxter said, "Do you remember when we camped on our way to search for Cassandra? You know, that first night when I desperately wanted to keep moving, you were set on making camp?"

Daro smiled and said, "I remember it took a lot of convincing before you finally caved and set up camp."

Baxter turned his gaze from the stars to focus on Daro, and the ranger could see the sadness behind his eyes. "I feel that anxiety all the time with Cassandra. I feel like I'm chasing the wind and can never catch her. I kissed her once, and it was the most amazing experience I've ever had. It was the best moment of my life to be that close to her, smell her, taste her."

"I remember that kiss. That was quite impressive."

They shared a laugh, recalling when Baxter had kissed her just before she made a move to strike at Kringus. If he hadn't done so, she would be dead, Daro knew. It was true; the young woman was reckless. As hard as it was to love Sasha, he couldn't imagine trying to love someone like Cassandra Rho.

"I just wish I could capture that moment and make it last. I think of things we could do or a life we could share. I want her to be my wife and a mother to my children. But I can't even have her beside me to begin courting. Her life seems so chaotic and filled with one tragedy after the next. I worry about her. I love her and want a simple life for us. You're lucky with Sasha; at least she's accessible.

"The truth is, Daro, I don't even know how she feels about me. The last time I spoke with her was right after the kiss, and then Kringus's men whisked her off to the jail. I don't know if she liked the kiss or even likes me. Perhaps to her, I will be nothing more than her instructor at Victoria's school."

Daro hadn't considered it in those terms and felt pity for his friend. Perhaps Baxter was right; Daro at least had a chance to win Sasha's heart because he was often beside her. Why couldn't he ask the impossible and win the hand of the most beautiful woman who ever lived?

The sound of a dropped bucket had both men turning to see a ship hand trying to right a pail of water he was using to swab the deck. He wasn't even looking at it and was struggling with it, still awkwardly holding his mop. Another nearby man slipped on the spilled water and fell to one knee, banging it hard on the deck. He grimaced and rubbed the wounded knee, but both men seemed preoccupied by the vision that was Sasha De'Formen. She had walked by them and now looked over her shoulder at the spectacle.

Daro's heart raced at the sight. She wore the scarf over her nose and mouth, which did little to hide her beauty, but her outfit was the cause of the chaos she left in her wake. She wore thin pajama bottoms, nearly see-through, which hugged every curve of her hips, and the matching top left little to the imagination. She was seldom cold because she came from the world of ice and was quite comfortable in freezing temperatures. Therefore, she rarely wore much clothing—another bonus he enjoyed courting the beautiful woman.

"You're doing it again!" she shouted as she made her way over, crossing her arms over her breasts to hide them.

Daro shifted his gaze quickly to Baxter, who mirrored the action. Both men then turned to face the sea and shared a slight chuckle.

"Good luck, my friend," Baxter said. And as Sasha arrived, he turned to leave. "Sasha, how nice to see you. I was just leaving, so I'll let you two enjoy this wonderful starry night."

"Hi, Baxter. You don't have to leave because of me."

"Don't be silly. I'm just tired and need rest. I have a lot on my mind."

"You're thinking of Cassandra? And maybe Binta?" the insightful carofex asked.

Baxter looked as if he'd been slapped, and Daro realized that Binta was also part of the man's pain. He had taken her on his magical carpet to a place far to the east just a few days before the New Order had left Pelesea. She had coaxed him into doing so, and her purpose was to find Cassandra and bring her home. Baxter had left her in a dangerous situation but wouldn't say much about it. The grief held him, and Daro wished he'd noticed it before. He made a note to speak to Baxter about Binta later.

"You are as observant as you are beautiful, Sasha. Please don't change," Baxter said. He smiled, then gave Daro a nod and went below deck.

Sasha took his place at the railing, and the two stood silently. Then, her perfume attacked Daro's senses, and he took her in, feasting on her with his eyes. She looked at him puzzled and slowly untied her scarf. As soon as it dropped from her face, Daro kissed her hard, and she returned it.

She broke the kiss just as quickly and said, "I know what you desire, Daro. I don't know if I'm ready."

"I understand, Sasha," Daro said.

He turned to the stars and watched intently, hoping to hide his disappointment. It wouldn't be fair for him to be angry or push Sasha on the idea of sex. He'd never allowed himself to fall in love, which was frightening.

"Can we just stay out here for a bit?" Sasha asked.

"Of course," he answered and summoned a smile.

There were a few moments of silence before Sasha added, "Also, I like kissing you, you know that, right?"

That made Daro feel a little better and he drank in her beauty again. She moved close to him, and he melted in her presence.

"I like it more than apples," she breathed in his ear.

The two potential lovers embraced and kissed passionately. Daro's hands eventually roamed her perfect body, and she accepted his forwardness. The crew watched intently.

As Baxter walked past Kringus and Penelope's room, he heard muffled voices followed by laughing. He paused at their door to listen. He knew he shouldn't, but he found hope in their playfulness. He longed for Cassandra and him to reach that point, to be a perfect couple like his king and queen. More muffled speaking, then a loud smack from within the room, followed by Penelope's magical laugh, broke his trance. He smiled at the giddiness of the royal couple. They seemed not to have a care in the world, but he knew better. He suddenly felt guilty for lingering, so he left them to their play and turned in.

Kringus and Penelope were unaware of Baxter's brief presence and had tuned out their surroundings. Currently, they were the only two occupants in their world. Penelope's long, toned legs still scissored Kringus, and his ribs were close to snapping.

"Your stubbornness is going to cost you," she warned.

"I was about to say the… same… thing," Kringus replied, trying hard to break the hold and not his ribs.

"How will it look with you saving the world with broken ribs, my love?" Penelope teased.

Suddenly, Kringus stopped trying to pry her legs apart and instead grabbed her foot.

"No, Kringus, don't you dare!" Penelope screamed, releasing her hold and trying to back away.

It was too late, however, as Kringus had her foot, pinning it tight to his side with the crook of his arm. With his other hand, he began to tickle his extremely ticklish wife. Penelope screamed and laughed and eventually cried as her husband mercilessly tickled her foot. She squirmed and desperately pulled at Kringus's arm, but he had her. He looked on as she struggled to breathe, tears flowing freely down her reddened cheeks. He felt terrible for her but continued the barrage—he would have his answers concerning Inuentas.

"Yield!" he demanded.

Penelope continued to laugh and cry and squirm. He continued his assault, and she eventually conceded, nodding her defeat. Kringus released her, and she propped herself against the wall to catch her breath. They were sitting on the bed, or what remained of it, most of it strewn around the room. Penelope's face was flush, and tears and sweat glistened on her face and neck, which Kringus found arousing. Her ordinarily perfect, fiery red hair was disheveled, which excited him even more. She panted, making her small breasts heave in her tight shirt, which was too much for the king.

"And now I'll collect my prize," he said, crawling toward her like a predator about to pounce.

"You cheated."

"I always cheat," he replied with a shrug, then fell over her.

Their embrace was sexually charged from the hour-long match that had led to that point. Kringus greedily kissed her, and they tore each other's clothes off. They made passionate love for the next hour, making almost as much noise for their neighbors as they did during the sparring match. Once finished, Kringus lay back with his arms crossed behind his head while Penelope laid her head on his chest. She absently played with his chest hair, a contented smile on her beautiful face. Kringus wore a look of satisfaction and breathed deeply.

"So, tell me of Inuentas," he said.

She turned to look him in the eye, her chin resting on his chest.

"This is why you almost made me break your ribs? You wanted to know about him that badly?"

Kringus thought about it briefly and eventually said, "Yes."

"Very well, but I'm afraid there is not much to tell."

"I'm listening," Kringus said and closed his eyes, promising himself he wouldn't become jealous or angry. Penelope deserved that from him.

"We met nearly sixty years ago."

"Before I was born."

"Yes, and before I was queen of Pelesea, but that's a different story." She smiled, turning her head to lay it back on his chest.

She began playing with his curly chest hair again and continued, "I was in a brothel."

"What?" Kringus said, immediately breaking his silent oath.

Penelope sat up and propped herself on one elbow. "I wasn't working there; I was trying to save someone."

"Of course," Kringus scoffed, hopefully playing it off.

"Anyway, he was a customer that night and had just paid to be with the woman I was there to rescue. He agreed to let her go if I stayed with him and answered ten questions honestly."

"And you agreed?"

"I was young and dumb and felt it was a small price to pay given the amount of gold he had paid for a night with the woman."

"What were the questions?"

Penelope looked at him, eyebrows raised, and said, "Mostly very personal and mostly sexual in nature."

Kringus tried to swallow his jealousy, but he must have done a poor job because Penelope caught on to it immediately.

"Remember, we just talked; there was no physical touching."

Kringus ground his teeth. His breathing was ragged as he tried to control his temper. He knew something had transpired between his wife and the half-demon, but that was many years ago, even before he was born.

"Continue," he finally said.

"Well, I answered his questions, and he became increasingly interested with each answer. I could feel his eyes roaming my body, and it felt like he was staring into my soul. His final question surprised me—he asked what race I was."

Kringus opened his eyes and asked, "You didn't tell him, did you?"

She sat up, looked into his eyes, and gave him that look, telling him everything was all right. He loved it when she did that and chalked it up to her age and wisdom. She could always extinguish his anger and, in this case, jealousy.

"I had to. I swore I would answer honestly."

"But I thought only Victoria and I knew your secret," Kringus said dejectedly.

"Inuentas is the only other being to know."

"But how could you trust him?"

"I'm coming to that, and you will not like that part, my husband."

The cryptic comment had Kringus sitting up straight in the bed and staring at Penelope, waiting for her words with bated breath.

"And so I told him honestly that my mother was an elf, and my father—"

"Was an angel," Kringus finished for her.

"Yes, and so this stranger, this half-demon, knew my secret."

"And Penelope, you don't like people knowing your secret. So, what deal did you make to ensure his silence?" Kringus asked, trying to control his jealousy.

"He said he would keep my secret if I did one thing, and he offered me another bag of gold to do it."

"Gold?"

"Yes, remember, this was before my queenship, and a bag of gold was handy, then."

"So, what was the act?" Kringus asked, his nostrils flaring.

"Please, my husband, know that this was long ago and meant nothing to me," she said, touching his cheek.

Kringus closed his eyes and gently took her hand, kissing it and calming immediately. "I know, my love."

"He asked to see my wings."

"Your wings?"

"Yes."

"And you showed him?"

"I removed my shirt and showed him, stretching them out wide."

"So, he saw your breasts?" Kringus asked, again struggling to control the anger that boiled within him.

"Yes, but he didn't touch me. He sat there looking me up and down, and as I stood there, he became aroused. Finally, he began to masturbate."

"What did you do?"

"I hid my wings, put on my shirt, and hurriedly left."

"And what did Inuentas do?"

"He continued to pleasure himself, and just before I opened the door to leave, he thanked me for a good time and told me he would never forget me."

"And he recognized you immediately that day Daro brought him to us," Kringus said, "Did you remember him?"

"Of course."

"And you elected not to tell me?"

"Yes, and perhaps that was wrong. However, I knew you would be jealous, and I didn't want it to interfere with the mission."

Kringus relaxed, and Penelope laid her head on his chest again. "So, are you mad?" she asked.

"Of course not," he lied.

"Good. I love you," she whispered.

"I love you as well."

Her breathing soon became shallow, and he knew she'd fallen asleep on him. Kringus's mind whirled with the information, and he struggled to keep calm. He wasn't usually a jealous man. Still, he knew Penelope was very selective when it came to choosing lovers, and the fact that Inuentas had seen her partially naked and against her will infuriated him. He vowed to stay calm for Penelope's sake but did not trust Inuentas. Unlike his wife, sleep eluded him most of the night.

$YLOR WOODS

He woods seemed ominous to Kessi. She wasn't sure why, but she'd been uncomfortable since they entered them. There was something intangible here that she couldn't place, and she would be glad to clear the forest. They were nearly twenty miles northwest of Nesin, deep in Sylor Woods, a strange and mysterious forest stuck between Nesin and their destination of Attins. Kessi was second-guessing the wisdom of not taking the road to the west that would eventually circle the forest and take them right to Attins's doorstep. However, the group of women she traveled with, women Kessi felt so close to she considered them sisters, had all agreed not to take the road in the hopes of remaining hidden from their former captor, Matilda, the priestess of the demon lord, Marnelphion.

Kessi looked around at the women, and her heart filled with love. She had spent so much time in the jails of Nesin, Matilda's mountain fortress, that she couldn't imagine life without them, especially Sabrina, her best friend. They all walked silently, hot in the midday sun. Even with fall so close, the woods were unseasonably warm. The journey wasn't just hot but slow, as they often had to cut their path with the swords they'd stolen from Nesin's guards.

Kessi still couldn't believe they were free. They had all been thrown into Matilda's jails months ago so Matilda could eventually sacrifice them to her demon lord, Marnelphion. She thought of the special jar she carried in her pack. It wasn't heavy or a burden. Kessi was overjoyed to hold it because it contained something special to her and her friends: the gaseous form of Emiline, the vampire. Without her assistance, they never would have escaped Matilda's vile clutches. Kessi, using the powers granted to her by her god, Adlesk, had helped coax Emiline into the gaseous form and maintain it during the day as they traveled. Emiline couldn't enter the sun for fear of perishing, so Kessi kept her nice and safe in her dark pack.

In addition to Sabrina and Emiline, Kessi traveled with twenty-one other women, all virgins collected by Matilda and her evil husband, Cerus, except one. They had jailed Patricka in a different part of the jail system in Nesin, one to house prisoners forced to serve in various capacities. Patricka was a beautiful woman with a perfect figure and, therefore, was used nefariously by Matilda and Cerus in their bedroom. She was the only one among them, other than Emiline, who wasn't a virgin. However, they all knew she would have been sacrificed, along with the virgins and any other captives Matilda had in her possession on that fateful night.

Shortly after their miraculous escape, Sabrina concocted the idea to travel back to Attins, the small town Matilda had kidnapped her from a year earlier when the priestess first started her quest to find Cassandra. After some discussion, the group agreed. The theory shared by all was that they had nowhere else to go, and nearly half the group was from the small farming community. They reasoned Matilda wouldn't look for them there because of the depleted population. It wouldn't be worth her and Cerus's time to revisit the town. In truth, Kessi knew that the evil couple were preoccupied with finding Kessi's sister, Cassandra, who was the centerpiece of the ritual. For whatever reason, the summoning wouldn't work without Cassandra. Kessi planned to foil the attempt to capture Cassandra. She would not be staying long in Attins.

Once night arrived and the evening grew cold, the women set up camp. They elected not to start a fire because they didn't want to draw attention. They had stolen food, water, and supplies from Nesin but didn't have enough blankets to protect them from the cold. So, as with the previous nights, they would sleep close together and share body heat and blankets as much as possible. Kessi opened her pack after the sun had fully set and released Emiline. The vampire quickly exited the jar and re-formed into her true self—that of a beautiful and perpetually young elf maiden. At first glance, one would not suspect her of undeath, but all had seen her feed, and she was indeed a vampire.

She looked around, gaining her bearings, the group watching her intently. Only Kessi felt comfortable around her because she'd spent time with Heinsvick, Emiline's master and greater vampire, back in Novafontera. Heinsvick had bitten Kessi twice, and she could still feel the shame of it pulse through her veins. She was lucky, and he hadn't fed on her long enough to turn her as well. He would have if he hadn't needed Kessi to fool Matilda—a failed scheme. During her time with the great vampire lord, Kessi had discovered a softer side to the creature, and she indeed saw that in Emiline, only to a much greater extent.

"Where are we?" Emiline asked meekly.

"Still in Sylor Woods," Kessi said with a comforting smile.

The vampire looked around suspiciously. Her actions validated Kessi's doubts, but she didn't find comfort in them. Some of Kessi's friends backed away, including Patricka, who was the least familiar with the vampire. They could all sense Emiline's nervousness.

"What is it, Emiline?" Sabrina dared to ask, moving to stand beside Kessi.

"It?" Emiline asked, focusing her gaze on Sabrina and tilting her head slightly to the side, a habit she had developed when she didn't quite understand a question.

"Yes, whatever it is you sense," Sabrina answered nervously.

Emiline's gaze drifted back to the woods behind them. It was dark, and the only sounds were those of insects buzzing, the few hearty enough to survive the first few weeks of fall, as well as the rustling of the leaves in the cool breeze. The women huddled close together, staring in the same direction. Kessi sensed the evil there, just like Emiline, and now she believed the others could feel it too.

"I am hungry. I will hunt quickly and return," Emiline said.

"Of course. Be safe, my sister," Kessi said.

Emiline smiled, a rare feat for the undead creature, and touched Kessi's arm gently where the healed-over puncture marks from Heinsvick remained.

"Sister," the vampire whispered.

Before Kessi could reply, the vampire moved into the darkness with blinding speed.

The group stayed huddled together, with blankets around the ones on the perimeter of the tight circle, shielding them all from the wind. Kessi whispered a simple spell, and her holy symbol, a piece of copper shaped like a teardrop that she wore around her neck, flared to life with a magical light. She kept it low to the ground so the wall of blanketed women would hopefully dim it from predators or anything else nearby.

They took a quick inventory of the food and, to many groans of protest, rationed what they had. Kessi didn't like doing that, but they would be in trouble this deep in Sylor if they ran out of food. Sabrina and the others from Attins all had experience of farming, but that wouldn't sustain them now with the cold weather coming and no crops to tend.

After eating a quick meal and nervously looking around the dark woods, they began to turn in. Sabrina, Kessi, Natasha, one of the more vocal members of their group, and Patricka remained awake, sitting at the edge of the camp. The nights were getting cooler as summer slowly gave way to fall and much spookier the deeper they went. Kessi knew that soon they would require a fire. She hoped to be far from Nesin before then but wasn't sure how long they could go without a light source to penetrate the thick, unsettling darkness. Kessi's light still lit the immediate area as she couldn't bring herself to dismiss it. None complained.

"How long will it take to trek these woods, Sabrina?" Natasha asked, breaking the silence.

"Well, I don't know for sure, but I believe I overheard Cerus tell Matilda after my capture that Nesin was roughly two hundred miles from Attins. So, if it is truly two hundred miles from here and we can travel five to ten miles daily by foot, we should get there before the weather turns too cold. Perhaps within six weeks."

They sat silently for a bit before Patricka asked, "What is the place called Tara that I've heard you mention sometimes when you talk about Attins?"

A shadow came over Sabrina's face as she recalled the events of that fateful evening when Cerus's men destroyed the two peaceful communities. She seemed to stare off into the distance as if she were somewhere else or, most likely, reliving a nightmare.

Eventually, she replied, "Tara was a community of priests found on the side of a mountain, only a mile or two from Attins, located at the mountain's base. I was there, living in Attins after my parents died. I was beginning a new life, one full of uncertainties."

Sabrina stopped, her eyes watered, and she seemed to stare off into space once more. Kessi instinctively put an arm around Sabrina's shoulders to comfort her.

"Your parents didn't die during Matilda's raid?" Kessi asked.

Her friend wiped her eyes and found the strength to continue. "No, they died years earlier when I was but a toddler, killed by a band of raiding ogres. Fortunately, I escaped death that night, and a merchant caravan found me wandering not far from our quiet home in the prairie fields.

"They took me in and cared for me. As I grew, they learned to love me in their way. I feel they loved my usefulness to help with the caravan as I grew more than they loved me. One night, when I was sixteen, one particular merchant decided to introduce me to sex. Luckily, his wife caught him, and he never had the chance to touch me. But that night, that woman, who held a lot of sway over the group, decided I should be discarded from the caravan at their next stop so I wouldn't seduce her husband again."

"So, they left you at Attins?" Kessi guessed.

"Yes; I had only been there about a week, feeling sad and alone. I missed my parents, and I wanted a family again. I was there on the night of the Harvest Festival, a holiday celebrated by the people of Attins, or it used to be before the invasion. It was a night of blessings, and some of the younger women gathered to meet the priests from Tara."

"Why?" Kessi asked.

Sabrina blushed and said, "Well, believe it or not, it was for the sole purpose of conceiving a child."

"Out of wedlock?" Natasha asked.

"Yes, well, you must understand, it is considered a blessing by the god of creation, a goddess named Phena, to conceive on that night. Also, the blessing doubled if the father was a priest of Tara."

The young women looked at each other in disbelief, and Sabrina smiled, found her courage, and said, "I was one of the virgins prepared for courting that night."

"What?" Kessi asked, wide-eyed.

"It's true," Sabrina said, shrugging in defeat. "Please understand that I was alone and needed the blessing. I had no family, and I thought that if I conceived on that night with one of the priests, the townsfolk of Attins would welcome me as one of their members."

"They don't sound like very nice people," Patricka said, and the others nodded their agreement.

"Oh no, the people of Attins were very nice and accepted me. They had taken me in without question once the merchants dropped me off and had always made me feel welcome. But I was alone, always alone. I missed my mother and father, and I thought maybe if I had a child, I would have a family again."

"But you were just a child yourself," Kessi added. She wasn't judging; she knew Sabrina understood that as they locked gazes and smiled.

"Yes, true enough, but I was ready to give myself. I needed something to live for; a child would have been it."

"But Matilda had other plans?" Natasha added, and they all shared a brief, uneasy laugh.

"Yes, she did, and it was a pity, too. There was supposed to be a handsome priest visiting that night, a prodigy of Tara."

"A prodigy?" Kessi asked.

"Yes, their god, Plath, was rumored to have a young prodigy living in Tara. Rumors circulated that he was quite good-looking and an effective lover."

Sabrina caught herself and blushed as the other women stared at her in disbelief. Kessi smiled to alleviate the tension, and Sabrina returned the smile and continued, "Anyway, he was supposed to be tall, handsome, and kind and would have made an incredible father for my child. A true blessing that never came to fruition.

"I also had this fantasy that perhaps he would make love to me, gently and caring, then in the process, fall in love. He would give up his god and become my husband and father to our child. We would farm the fields and live in Attins, raising a loving family with many kids."

"So, he's dead?" Patricka asked sadly.

Sabrina looked at her hands, fidgeting in her lap, and nodded, nearing tears again. "Yes, as far as I know, Cerus's men murdered everyone in Tara. They took most of the people in Attins as hostages, except the old and the sick, who they murdered. I overheard Cerus tell Matilda such, but I was lucky enough not to witness it."

Sabrina stood, brushed off her pants, and said, "Well, that's it. You asked what Tara was, Patricka, and that is the long answer."

Kessi stood with her friend and hugged her. "Thank you for sharing."

Sabrina hugged her back, and Kessi whispered, "And to think, you were almost a mother!"

They laughed and cried and hugged tighter. The tale was just one of many tragedies the young women had gone through, and it was just another thing that brought them closer together, especially Kessi and Sabrina. They had shared so much in the bowels of Nesin, each day filled with doubt and fear. During their time there, they had always felt at death's door. There was no future for them in Nesin, only death. Those nights huddled together and afraid had made them close. They somehow grew closer that night in Sylor Woods after Sabrina shared so much personal and painful information.

Kessi dismissed her light spell, and the four bedded down shortly after. They huddled together and shared one of the ten blankets the nearly two dozen women had taken from Nesin. It was cold, and Kessi was having a hard time falling asleep. There had been no further sign of Emiline, which was not uncommon, but the night was mysteriously quiet. She noticed as she lay there that the few bugs in the area had grown silent. Only the wind and the soft snores of a few of her friends kept her company.

A snapping twig close to camp had her turn and stare into the darkness. Her heart pounded in her chest, and she lay there frozen with fear. She thought she spied two yellow eyes not far from her, but they disappeared quickly. It might have been her imagination, but her gut told her something was out there watching them, something evil. She slept little that night.

THE FOLLOWING DAY, KESSI AWOKE TO A BEAUTIFUL SUNRISE. THE fast-rising sun burned away the slight chill of the late-summer night. She sat and stretched away the aches of sleeping on the ground. She was the first to be awakened by the snores of a few of her friends sleeping nearby. Then, to her horror, she realized this was the first morning since they'd escaped Nesin that Emiline hadn't awakened her before dawn.

She panicked and quickly rose, finding her pack and, shortly after, locating the glass jar that had served as Emiline's quarters during the day. Kessi's heart raced as she discovered what she already knew—the jar was empty. Emiline hadn't returned to the camp that morning, and now the sun shone brightly in the early-morning sky. The trees were thick where they had made camp and still held their leaves, although some were starting to turn vibrant colors as fall drew near. However, it was not enough to protect Emiline. If she was anywhere nearby, Kessi feared she had already expired. There was nowhere for Emiline to hide from the sun.

"Sabrina!" Kessi called, kneeling and waking her sleeping friend. Others stirred as Kessi's panicked voice disrupted the peaceful morning.

"What's wrong?" Sabrina asked, sitting up and rubbing her eyes.

Kessi held the empty jar before her friend and said, "Emiline is missing!"

That snapped her friend from the sleep from which she stirred. Fear quickly engulfed Sabrina's face. "Oh, no," she whispered.

Sabrina rose, and she and Kessi quickly awakened anyone still slumbering, although most were stirring by then. They took a quick count, and luckily, no one else was missing, but sadly, no one had seen Emiline since the previous night. They quickly formed a search party and scoured the area. The trees were thick, and the land was primarily flat, with many tangles of thick, viny weeds growing abundantly nearby. No ravines or water were in the area to pose a hazard, and they found no blood or signs of a struggle. It took several hours to search the immediate area, and when they found no signs of Emiline, they returned to their camp, tired and worried.

Kessi sat and took a small sip of water from her canteen. Sabrina and Natasha joined her, and Kessi passed her water around. They were tired and sad, and the sun was high in the midday sky. Others of the party sat somberly in small groups, and some began to eat.

"Please ration your food until we get to Attins. We will pack up camp and leave after a small rest," Kessi announced.

Some nodded in response, while others seemed too shocked even to acknowledge Kessi had spoken.

"What do you mean?" Natasha asked. "Are we leaving Emiline?"

"I don't know what else to do," Kessi said with tears forming.

"There must be something we can do, Kessi," Sabrina said.

"Even if we found her, the sun will have destroyed her by now," Kessi answered.

"We don't know that," Sabrina argued.

"Tell me what we can do. I'll stay and wait for Emiline if you think it prudent. We have limited supplies and probably shouldn't linger this close to Nesin. Tell me, my friends, what should we do?" Kessi pleaded.

The three sat for a moment in contemplation, none providing an answer to Kessi's question. Eventually, Natasha spoke. "Something bad must have happened. She wouldn't just wander off."

"I agree," Kessi said, nodding.

"Do you have a spell? Something like the power you displayed against the creatures in Nesin?" Sabrina suggested.

Kessi shook her head sadly. "I don't think I have anything to detect her or give us a clue to her whereabouts. Let me pray while the rest of you eat and see if Adlesk offers me anything."

Kessi wandered off to the side of the camp, whispering a prayer. She noticed Sabrina and Natasha share a knowing look as she departed. They understood the severity of the situation, and Kessi feared she would never see Emiline again. The group ate while Kessi prayed.

DEEP IN A CAVE, ABOUT FIVE MILES SOUTH OF KESSI AND HER FRIENDS, a battered Emiline was tossed to the stone floor at the foot of a large wooden throne. The two men who had captured her in the woods were large and muscular, with unkempt hair and beards. They wore clothing typical of farmers—pants and shirts made of cheap materials, dirty and tattered. But Emiline sensed these were not just ordinary farmers, especially those living deep in a cave. Also, they secreted a strange scent that wasn't human, and although their language was understandable, grunts and growls peppered it. The most telling thing about them was their stench, especially their breath, which reeked of rotted meat and spoiled blood.

The men had crudely wrapped Emiline with a rope, wet with a strange liquid that burned her and made her weak. They'd caught her at night and had easily overpowered her. They were strong, even for the likes of the stout vampire. They had quickly tied the rope around her, not only keeping her arms immobile but also sapping her strength. She now lay on her back, moaning as the ropes burned her arms. One of her captors pulled her by the hair until she was on her knees, facing the throne. She hadn't noticed before, but now she saw a large, naked woman sitting on it, one leg hanging over the arm.

The woman looked more significant than the men, and her dark hair was equally unkempt. She even had pieces of foliage and dirt matted within the large tangle. A smaller throne sat beside but slightly behind the woman's. A man sat casually on that one, looking at Emiline with disgust. The woman kicked her leg quickly back over the arm and sat straight on her throne, towering over Emiline's more petite frame.

"So, Vlord thinks he can invade our territory and not suffer consequences?"

Emiline stared at her, puzzled at her words. She cocked her head to the side, trying to digest the words the strange woman spoke. Who was Vlord? The woman became enraged by her lack of response and backhanded her, sending her tumbling to the stone floor. Emiline lay still, moaning as the hit was more brutal than anything she'd experienced before. The two men retrieved her, dragging her by her arms and scuffing her knees on the stone floor. Soon, she was kneeling before the large woman once more.

"Explain yourself," the woman said, following that with a low growl.

"These two men wrapped a rope around me, which leaked burning water, hurting me. They then dragged me here. If not for the rope, I would have torn their throats out."

One of the men kicked her in the ribs, knocking her over, and the woman laughed at the brutal display. Once more, Emiline was pulled to her knees by her hair. These people were vicious, and Emiline knew her doom well before determining who they were.

"You're a feisty one! That is unlike Vlord to keep unruly females about," the woman said.

"I don't know Vlord," Emiline said.

The woman's visage grew severe, and she stood then, towering over Emiline. It looked like she struggled to control her anger. She seemed to want to throttle Emiline, and the vampire knew she could do nothing about it if she decided to follow through with it.

"Eat her heart, Kir," the lanky, much smaller man on the second throne said.

"Shut up, Densor, we do not eat spoiled meat!" the woman said, glaring at him.

The man seemed to wilt under her gaze, and soon, Kir's attention was back on Emiline. She bent low so they were face to face, and Emiline could smell the stench of her breath as she had with her two captors.

"I don't like liars any more than I do trespassers," she said with an evil smile.

Emiline cocked her head in confusion, and that made Kir somehow angrier. "Fine, tie her to the table with fresh ropes and bring the holy water. We will get her talking in no time," she said.

The two men roughly pulled her to her feet, taking her deeper into the cave. Kir and Densor followed closely behind, the giant woman with a stern and eager look on her face and her smaller mate rubbing his hands together anxiously.

It was an all-too-familiar feeling for Emiline, held against her will, deep in a cave. She had just escaped that exact situation. However, in Nesin, the priests could control her actions, whereas these people could overpower her. And the ropes burned her skin and sapped her energy. Being a prisoner to the rough and unruly people was somehow worse than being Matilda's captive.

They threw her on a slab that was more like an irregularly shaped, polished rock than a table. Several other men joined the task, bringing new ropes that dripped with burning water. Emiline whimpered and tried to break free, but she had little strength, and the large men easily held her. They tied her arms and legs to the stone slab with the fresh ropes, the nasty water burning her so much that she screamed. Her cries echoed down the massive cave tunnel, bringing more evil men and women to watch the spectacle.

Soon, Emiline was sobbing quietly as the ropes were wrapped around her torso after her limbs were secured. She felt as if her skin were on fire. Soon, the half dozen men who had secured her to the table backed away, giving Kir plenty of space to approach her. Emiline had never felt so helpless. She struggled with the ropes, but she couldn't break the binds. She thought of turning into a gaseous cloud and escaping, but it had to be daylight outside by now, and the sun would burn and destroy her. Besides, without Kessi's help, she couldn't possibly shape-change.

Kir was suddenly there, a wicked smile on her face. She held an empty chalice in her large hand and waved it at Emiline. "We will find out why you are in our territory and who the humans you travel with are."

Emiline could only moan in response. As the woman spoke, Emiline discovered a light wafting of smoke coming from the ropes. As her eyes focused on the drifts of smoke, she realized, to her horror, that it was not the ropes burning but her skin! She was afraid, and she didn't understand the strange phenomenon.

Several large, wild men struggled to carry a full and heavy barrel next to the table. They sat it down next to Emiline's head. Kir held out the chalice for Densor to take and opened the lid. Many more of her strange captors packed into the room to watch. All shared common traits—they were large, some barely clothed or completely naked, with wild hair and an almost animal-like demeanor. They seemed vicious and eager for what would come next for their captive. Emiline was in deep trouble and wished Kessi were there to help her.

Kir, the group's apparent leader, retrieved the chalice from Densor and dipped it into the barrel. Emiline was uncertain what could be in the large container and was relieved to see that the liquid which spilled over the cup and splattered on the floor appeared to be ordinary water. Her relief was short-lived.

"Do you know what this is, vampire?" Kir said, holding the dripping chalice toward Emiline.

Emiline didn't answer; she was too afraid of what would come, and the pain from the burning ropes was overwhelming. She didn't understand what the woman wanted. With a wicked smile, Kir brought the dripping goblet over Emiline's face, and when a few drops fell on her face, they burned as boiling water might. The water hissed, and the smoke from her burned skin filled her nostrils. She screamed in agony and shook her head, trying to dislodge the hateful, biting liquid. Kir grabbed her by the hair and held her still, bringing the chalice close to her face.

"This is holy water, you corpse, and it will burn your perversion away and reveal your true, dead self. It is what soaks your binds, which burn your undead, filthy body and sap your strength. Shall I pour it in your eyes and blind you?"

Emiline screamed again and closed her eyes tight, afraid the unpredictable and cruel woman would do just that.

"Or how about I pour it down your throat and burn you from the inside out?"

Emiline closed her mouth tight and reopened her eyes to find Kir handing the chalice back to Densor, carelessly spilling some of the contents as she did. Emiline flinched as a good bit of the water splattered on the floor. Densor took the water, sniffed it, and shrugged as if he didn't understand how the water could hurt Emiline. A fight broke out nearby as a few attendees jockeyed for position to witness the torture.

Kir seemed not to notice and turned Emiline's head toward her, using her tight grip on her hair as a handle. Emiline wasn't used to being handled so easily.

"Tell me your name," Kir said.

"My name?" Emiline repeated, not understanding the question, the pain in her arms making it difficult to focus.

"Perhaps this one is broken or daft, and Vlord kicked her out," Densor said from over Kir's shoulder.

"Shut up, Densor!" Kir growled. "Vlord would not do that to one of his own. He sent this one to guide the humans, that much is clear."

Kir had mentioned the name "Vlord" again, but Emiline couldn't hope to understand who that might be. She could only think of Heinsvick, whom she suspected was dead, and her new friends, who were in danger, out in the woods alone. She had failed Kessi and the others, and for that, she was sad.

"Emiline," she said quietly.

Kir turned from Densor and refocused on Emiline, a broad, wicked smile engulfing her face.

"You see, she understands what we say, Densor. She isn't daft, are you?" Kir said, bending even closer to Emiline's face. "Now tell me what you're doing with the humans in our woods."

Emiline's delay in responding seemed to enrage the volatile woman. "Tell me, or I'll burn you alive, vampire!" Kir screamed.

"We're passing through the woods. We mean no harm," Emiline spat out, panicking.

"Why did Vlord send you here? He knows our rules, and you and your undead brethren are not allowed on this side of Sylor."

"Sylor?" Emiline asked in confusion.

"Don't play dumb with me, you rotting corpse," Kir said, reaching for the chalice, nearly knocking it from Densor's grasp.

The wild woman poured a few drops on Emiline's immobile right hand.

It burned and ate at her skin, and the pain was exquisite. Kir quickly wiped it away just as the skin began to bubble.

"There, you see, Emiline? I can burn you alive, or you can talk. Do you want to talk to me now?" Kir asked.

Emiline nodded, balling her burned hand to alleviate the pain. The skin was blistered but not badly. None of the burns that wracked her body were severe yet. But she now understood what it meant to come in contact with that hateful water. She couldn't survive that. She would tell them whatever they wanted to know.

⁕

Later that night, Densor sat in a chair next to the bed that Kir and he shared. She was his wife, but his status in the hierarchy of men within their community was much lower. Kir used him as a scapegoat for most of the problems she encountered or the failures that they endured. He accepted that status because he was safe from attacks within the group. He was Kir's chosen, and she would kill anyone who threatened him. Still, it came with a large share of degrading experiences for the small-statured man, one of which he endured as he sat next to his marital bed.

Kir was atop her lover, grinding and growling like an animal, with an occasional moan. The man was one of many of Kir's lovers and was much larger than Densor. The man's name was Brustin, and he stood nearly seven feet tall. He was muscular and had the stamina to be one of Kir's favorite lovers. Densor tried not to let the copulation bother him, but the occurrence was becoming more and more frequent.

"So, she is lying then?" he asked his wife, who seemed to be enjoying herself at that particular moment.

He sighed and waited patiently for her moans to subside, staring at the ceiling and trying not to peek at the spectacle. Kir insisted he watch because she knew it insulted him. That gave her great pleasure and, according to her, made sex all the better. She bit her lover on the shoulder hard enough to draw blood, which made them increase the intensity of their lovemaking.

Once satisfied, she rolled off Brustin, panting and enjoying the effects of their lovemaking. Brustin got up, gave Densor a derisive snort, and left the room. The king and queen of the community then had a brief opportunity to talk before Kir's next lover arrived.

"She isn't lying. She was afraid for her miserable life. I could see it in her eyes. She isn't part of Vlord's clan," Kir said.

"And you believe she is traveling with this group of humans?"

"Yes," Kir said, propping herself up on one elbow. "I also think they're just randomly traversing Sylor Woods."

"Only fools would do so. Everyone knows that Sylor Woods is most unwelcoming to humans."

"Yes, so perhaps they aren't from around here. Brustin reported that he glimpsed the gathering, and they seemed to be novice travelers who don't belong in the woods."

Densor shifted uncomfortably in his seat at the mention of her favorite lover and one of her most potent and dangerous hunters. "Then why didn't he capture them?" Densor dared to ask, his annoyance with the large hunter evident in his tone.

"Because, my stupid husband, he was cautious for the community. If they'd been ravenkin, it could have been disastrous."

"Ravenkin? Aren't they extinct?"

"Of course not. Don't be foolish, Densor. Besides, now we know they're harmless and they'll be brought here for our hunting pleasure."

Densor couldn't help but smile at the thought. "They were mostly women, according to Brustin, correct?"

Kir sat up on the edge of the bed and, with a smirk, said, "Yes, they are young and female. Even you'll be able to join the hunt."

Densor took the insult without complaint. Kir was right; the last time they'd hunted men, he'd found himself in a precarious situation and needed help. That wasn't befitting Kir's mate, so Kir forbade him to hunt unless the prey was female.

"The full moon is in three nights; we should capture them now before they find their vampire friend missing," Densor said.

"Brustin is already working on it. They'll be ours tonight."

"And what of the vampire?"

A wicked smile spread across Kir's face, and she said, "On the night of the full moon, we will nail her to the cave wall so she can watch the hunt. Then, as the sun rises, we'll enjoy the roasting she'll endure as the sun burns her flesh away."

"A perfect ending to a most wonderful night."

"Yes, a perfect ending," Kir purred as she noticed her next lover entering their room.

Maxis was the most prominent man in the community, which was two hundred strong. He had dark hair and darker eyes and was far crueler than any other hunter in the community. He entered the room naked and ready to please the queen. He was muscular without an ounce of fat on his perfect body. He kept his eyes on Densor as he approached, and even as he mounted the bed and Kir nibbled on his chest and neck, he kept a stern visage on Densor. The king squirmed in his chair, wilting under the man's gaze like everyone who witnessed it. Finally, when he started making love to Kir, he turned his attention to her. Of all of Kir's lovers, Densor hated Maxis the most.

GREYSON KAVINCE, ALLEAH MANSUELL, AND CHLOE FRALAND HAD fled Port Racip about the same time Kessi and her friends had escaped Nesin. The three companions now found themselves in the thickest part of Sylor Woods. They were a mere fifty miles east of where Kessi and her friends searched for Emiline, oblivious to the proximity. Lud, the goblin scout gifted to them by Glime, one of the leaders of Racip, had led them deeper and deeper into the most dangerous part of the woods. Besides the occasional rest so that the strange little goblin could refer to his map, their guide rarely stopped, pushing the party further away from Racip and the dangers lurking there.

Alleah and Chloe were priestesses of the goddess Sinnis, and they had sailed from Pelesea with Greyson to find out who was behind the raid that had destroyed Greyson's home community of Tara. He had narrowly escaped death during that awful day, having witnessed his best friend's murder and the dead bodies of his mentors and friends. Greyson had escaped with a powerful scroll that had teleported him to Pelesea and into the lap of Alleah Mansuell. The two had grown close since that day, and when Alleah invited Greyson to join her and her sisters on the journey to Tara, he gladly accepted.

However, the captain of the ship that had sailed from Pelesea's ports and across the Nepress Sea to Port Racip had betrayed them, resulting in the deaths of all the sisters of Sinnis except Alleah and Chloe. They discovered the betrayal at Racip's docks, and during the surprise attack, Greyson and Alleah escaped into Swamp Ikma. Cerus and his men, the same ones responsible for murdering the sisters of Sinnis as well as the people of Tara, had followed them in, taking Chloe hostage to coerce Alleah into surrendering. Luckily, the swamp's denizens had saved them, including a mighty dragon named Malebak and a strange druid named Breeston. Together, they chased off Cerus and his men and saved Chloe from certain death.

After burying the sisters of Sinnis and summoning beautiful wildflowers to adorn the gravesites, the three, along with Lud, had left Port Racip. To escape the dangerous port city, they had to trick the self-appointed local lawman, Sebastian, and his gang of bullies. Now, outside of Racip and away from the protective realm of their influential acquaintance, Glime, the party was vulnerable and would be in grave danger if Sebastian and his men followed them. So, no one complained as Lud continued to push them deeper into the thick and unforgiving vegetation of Sylor Woods.

But when they finally stumbled across a small river, they convinced the guide to stop and set up camp early so they could bathe and wash their clothing. Lud scouted the area quickly before agreeing and, after a few moments, returned with a nod of approval, a black substance smeared across his lips and chin.

"Lud thinks ugly… I mean, humans will be happy here tonight. No monsters," Lud said, then cursed himself for nearly insulting his travel companions, a nasty habit he had difficulty controlling.

The little goblin considered all humans extremely ugly and wasn't shy about sharing his opinion. Glime punished him when he did, usually making Lud smack or hit himself if he slipped up. Also, Lud's propensity to consume any dung he found during their trek had disgusted them all, but now used to it, no one said a thing about the substance on his face, knowing exactly what it was. Lud sat on a rock and studied his map as the rest set their sleeping rolls and positioned themselves close so they could sleep in protective proximity.

Greyson studied the setting sun and understood that to find Tara, they needed to keep it setting to their left and rising to their right. Lud was a little strange but was proficient at his job because they'd achieved that alignment thus far. Greyson was soon distracted by Alleah assisting Chloe with removing her armor. The leather armor with metal studs had been custom-made by Glime's armorer back in Racip, so it fit them well. But a full day of walking in the tangled mess that was Sylor Woods wore on them, whether the armor fit comfortably or not.

He watched intently from the corner of his eye, pretending not to notice. Chloe was a little younger than Alleah and Greyson, perhaps eighteen, with strawberry-blond locks and dark eyes. She was a pretty woman, and Greyson enjoyed the view of Alleah stripping her down to the cotton dress she wore underneath. Chloe was attractive, and Greyson didn't mind sneaking a peek. However, Alleah was a natural beauty with long blond hair, bright blue eyes, and one of the prettiest faces he'd ever seen. She was one of the most beautiful women he'd ever met.

He was in a relationship with Binta Mulay back in Pelesea, a true beauty in her own right with a passive nature. He loved Binta and longed to return to Pelesea to get reacquainted with her, and hopefully with Cassandra Rho if the king ever let her out of jail. But Binta wasn't beside him, and Greyson's needs had him longing for Alleah. She was a true friend, but sex was usually something he thought about often when he was around her. Unfortunately, Sinnis required her followers to remain chaste, so neither Chloe nor Alleah could fulfill his current needs.

Oddly enough, back in Ikma, while staying with the druid, Breeston, Greyson had been introduced to his wife and encouraged to sleep with her. Her name was Zeva, and she was a sleeth, a race of people with snake-like attributes. Sleeth were always born with a curse and a blessing. Zeva's curse had been her ugliness, and the sight of her repulsed Greyson. However, she had the power to read his thoughts and shape-change into something he desired. She had taken the shape of Alleah, and he'd gladly had sex with her. He thought about those times often and wondered how accurately Zeva had portrayed Alleah's perfect body and her nakedness. Had her actions reflected how Alleah would look and act, caught in the joys of lust? He wished he could find out. He absently licked his lips as he spied on his two friends.

He sighed and looked at his magnificent staff that leaned against a tree near his sleeping roll. The gnarled wood from which it was made came from Swamp Ikma, and the large green gem came from Zeva's loins. Just as Breeston had predicted, the woman had given birth to a gem conceived on one of the many occasions Greyson had slept with her. Zeva's blessing was the ability to birth the powerful gems every so often. The gem, a product of Greyson, now acted as a conduit with his god, Plath. It also amplified his powers, making him quite formidable. He entertained the idea of charming both women into sleeping with him. He would have already done so if Alleah wasn't such a good friend.

Unfortunately, his conscience wouldn't allow it. He couldn't bear the thought of being the one who lured Alleah away from her goddess. He picked up the staff, stared into the bright green gem, and wondered why he shouldn't try. After all, he should do it before another man did. And if she did give in to his advances, as Glime hinted that she might, he could convert her to be a follower of Plath. His eyes widened as he thought of it—he'd already converted Binta. If Alleah followed, he could start a harem of beautiful women, all followers of his most influential and extraordinary god.

"Greyson?" Alleah's voice came from behind him.

He jumped and nearly dropped his staff. He turned to see Alleah standing near him with a quizzical look on her beautiful face.

"Sorry, did I startle you?" she asked.

"Uh, no, of course not. I was praying," he stammered.

"Sorry to interrupt. I thought Plath preferred a morning prayer?"

"Yes, he does, but I was trying to summon a protective spell before we camped," he lied.

"I see. Well, Chloe is off to the river to wash up, and Lud seems engrossed in his map," Alleah said, nodding to the curious goblin who was now eating fistfuls of dirt as he studied the parchment.

Greyson chuckled and said, "Yes, he is, and he's currently only eating dirt, which is an improvement."

Lud quickly said, "Lud hears you. Goblins hear everything," without looking up from his map.

"Sorry, Lud," Greyson said as he and Alleah grabbed their soap and left the camp.

They hurried out of the campsite, holding in their laughter until out of Lud's earshot. They soon found a secluded place for each to bathe privately in the river and wash their clothes. Luckily, Glime had supplied them with extra clothing so they could let their fresh wash dry on the branches of nearby trees. Later, as the sun set, painting the sky bright red, Greyson and Alleah sat on their bedrolls, eating a small meal. The three had set their camp to form a triangle as they slept, one friend's head near the other's feet, creating a protective area where Lud, as usual, would sleep, perfectly centered in the human triangle. Chloe had already turned in and was resting comfortably. Lud lay in the middle of the group with no bedroll or blanket, completely comfortable lying on the ground with no cover.

"She feels safe because of you," Alleah said, nodding toward Chloe.

"What?"

"You gave her hope, Greyson. You gave us both a chance to survive this. Without you, I would have surrendered to that monster, Cerus, and Chloe and I would both be dead. You saved our lives."

"Then we are even."

There was a long silence as they slowly chewed their dried meats and fruits. The only sounds were the numerous crickets, the occasional hooting of an owl, and the rigid snoring from their goblin guide. They had no fire for fear of attracting predators, but it was late summer, and the nights grew cold, so the fire would soon be necessary.

"Thank you for coming to Tara with me," Greyson said, breaking the silence.

"Of course, that was the main objective of our journey here."

"Yes, but we already discovered the source of the murders, and we need to relay that information to Kringus and Penelope. The world may be in grave danger."

"That is very true, Greyson. However, you need to understand that you gave us closure. We buried our sisters, as hard as it was, and we blessed their journey to the afterlife. It would be best if you had closure as well. You need to bury your friends and bless their bodies properly. We're close to Tara, so we'll go so you can find peace, and then we'll find passage back to Pelesea."

A moment passed between them and they fell into each other's eyes before Alleah smiled and squeezed his hand. He returned the gesture, and shortly after, Alleah turned in. Greyson offered to keep the first watch over camp for a few more hours, so he sat on a nearby rock while the other three slept. He kept his staff with him, and his thoughts lingered on Alleah. She was a good friend, and the dangers and tragedies they'd endured since arriving at Varish had made them closer.

Their trip through the thick woods of Sylor had been uneventful, and he was confident that no one from Racip was following them. It had been nearly a week, and there had been no sign of Sebastian or his goons. Still, Greyson couldn't help but consider the predicament they would be in if

Sebastian and his men were tracking them. He realized then that he'd never seen Alleah in action, either with her mace or spell powers. Greyson knew that the priestesses of Sinnis had a reputation for being very dangerous with both. He hoped he would never have to see her use either; he didn't want her in a situation where she would need to use her skills. He felt the same about Chloe, but his main concern was Alleah, who, as much as he hated to admit it, took up most of his thoughts recently.

Just then, Alleah stirred in her sleep, kicking a leg out of her bedroll and revealing a generous portion of her thigh. Greyson knew how warm the sleeping rolls could be, and his friend needed the cool air at that moment. He was glad of it as he took in her perfect leg. He wished they'd lit a fire so he could have a better look. His thoughts traveled back to Swamp Ikma, where he had bedded Zeva multiple times, each visit giving him a glimpse of Alleah's nakedness as the sleeth shape-changed into his friend. He'd wondered how accurate the sleeth had been in her ability to duplicate perfection. Glimpsing just Alleah's leg made Greyson think that she hadn't done Alleah justice.

He swallowed hard as lustful thoughts filled his head. Glime's words echoed in his mind, hinting that Alleah could be his if he pushed the issue. Glime was a telepath and had read something in Alleah's thoughts. Greyson looked at his staff and the green gem adorning it. He'd not done so yet, but he understood that any spell he summoned through it to charm a woman like he had Cassandra would be nearly impossible to deny or break. He could have Alleah if he chose to. He shook the thought away as quickly as it had come. Alleah was a friend, and he couldn't betray and break her connection with her god—could he?

He struggled with his desires as he examined the perfect leg Alleah unwittingly presented him. She eventually grew cold and tucked it back in her bag. He turned in shortly after, waking Chloe to take the next watch. It took him quite a while to find sleep as he lay there, his thoughts on bedding Alleah festering. He eventually drifted off into a restless slumber, and soon enough, it was daybreak. Everyone rose, ate briefly, and then broke camp before the sun was high in the eastern sky. It looked to be a beautiful day, and after Lud had studied his map again, he declared they would reach Tara within two or three weeks. Greyson felt a tingling in his soul at the proclamation. He would finally be back in Tara to lay old ghosts to rest.

LONG AFTER GREYSON AND HIS FRIENDS BROKE CAMP THAT DAY, KESSI and her party of Nesin escapees were still at their camp, and their mood was dour. They'd spent the entirety of that morning combing the area, hoping to find a clue to Emiline's fate. They had found nothing. Kessi had prayed for answers, but none were forthcoming. As the sun rose to its zenith, the women had to decide—did they proceed without their friend or search some more? Kessi and Sabrina sat together, quietly discussing their options.

"We can't leave her," Kessi said, fighting back tears.

"I agree," Sabrina said, placing a gentle hand on Kessi's.

"I knew you would, Sabrina, but what of the others? We can't ask them to stay if they don't want to. After all, Emiline attacked Kimmie and nearly killed her."

"Yes, Emiline was forced to do the bidding of that evil priest, Merrik, remember?"

"Still, she did it, and I'm sure it was awful for poor Kimmie. And although Kimmie split from us and traveled to Ikma, everyone else remembers the attack, I assume."

"Yes, you would know," Sabrina said, turning Kessi's arm to reveal the bite marks on her forearm.

"That's different," Kessi said, pulling back her arm. "I let Heinsvick bite me; Emiline forcefully bit Kimmie."

"Well, I'll stay with you if you decide to stay. The others can decide what they want."

"We can't blame them if they carry on to Attins."

"I know, Kessi. They're our sisters, and we won't hold their decision against them," Sabrina said with a smile. "But I'm confident they won't leave her."

Natasha was the first to break up the private meeting, coming over with a tired smile and saying, "The others are curious about our plans."

Kessi looked beyond Natasha and noticed Patricka had her gear on and was ready to proceed, several others joining her.

"It seems some have already decided," Sabrina said.

"Yeah, they're just afraid that whatever took Emiline will return. Also, if someone comes looking, we aren't that far from Nesin," Natasha added.

"We can't leave without Emiline! She helped us escape, and we owe her our life," Sabrina said, standing and letting her voice carry more than she intended.

Her outburst gained the group's attention, and they all looked on, waiting for the answer. Kessi stood and put a gentle hand on Sabrina's shoulder. When she turned to her, Kessi smiled, which relieved most of the tension on Sabrina's face. Kessi moved to stand before the small band of women.

"I have a solution," she began, and they gathered closer.

"We can't linger, that's true, and we all did our part looking for our sister, the one we owe everything to. I don't blame any of you for wanting to make haste to Attins. At a good pace, we'll arrive in less than a month, according to Sabrina."

Kessi turned toward her friend, who gave a weak smile in response. Kessi continued, "However, we know nothing of these woods and their dangers. Emiline is our first casualty, and it breaks my heart to leave her behind. I hope that if I were the one missing, you wouldn't so easily give up on me."

Kessi paused there, and Patricka looked at her feet, unable to make eye contact. She absently kicked at a small rock, the guilt weighing heavily on her.

"If you want to go, there will be no judging. We were all locked up in that evil hole in the mountain, and none of us want to go back. We all want a chance to live a life of freedom again, and I hope we can find that in Attins. I only ask one favor of all of you. I hope we can stay together for the safety of the group. I say we go and begin our quest for Attins anew."

"What?" Sabrina asked with a gasp.

There was murmuring and whispers from the gathered women, some nods, and more than one look of astonishment. Kessi only smiled and clarified, "I propose we walk straight toward Attins, side by side, twenty feet apart, and search for clues as we head toward our new home. That way, we give our lost friend a final chance of being found as we travel. We can cover a lot of ground with all of us lined up like that. If we find nothing, then at least we have tried and not given up so quickly on Emiline. If we find something, perhaps there is hope we can find her. What do you say, my sisters?"

They immediately agreed, and no one decided to leave the group. It warmed Kessi's heart to know they all shared such a strong bond and indebtedness to one another. They were a family, so they wouldn't give up their search for Emiline, though things looked bleak for their friend. Kessi turned back to Sabrina to find her smiling, and the two unofficial leaders of the group shared a nod. The group broke camp quickly and were soon on their way, hoping they would somehow find something to lead them to their friend, but they were also happy to be moving once more.

They positioned themselves just as Kessi described so they could stay close but cover much ground. Kessi and Sabrina remained near the center as Patricka and Natasha, armed with swords they'd taken from Nesin, took up the most dangerous spots at the end of the line. Lila carried a third sword, while Sabrina and Kessi carried the remaining two weapons, but none of the five sword-wielders knew anything about using them.

That was the best formation they could muster to offer the most protection, given their limited supply of weapons. They all knew what would happen if they encountered anything hostile. Kessi hoped they would travel without such an event, but most of all, she hoped they'd find some clue about Emiline's whereabouts. It broke her heart to think of leaving her.

The afternoon quickly became humid, and the bugs bit at them as they methodically made their way through the thick vegetation of Sylor Woods. They still found no sign of their friend, and Kessi understood that Emiline was probably lost to them. The vessel she carried in her pack felt empty yet heavy on her back. As they walked that afternoon, it dawned on her that fall was almost upon them. The warm days would become a rarity in the next few weeks.

That also meant her birthday approached. She thought of Cassandra, then, and how much danger her sister was in. After they found Attins and Sabrina and the others claimed it once more as their home, hopefully with full cupboards, Kessi would leave. She had to find Cassandra and warn her about Matilda and Cerus. They planned to kill her, and Kessi had to stop them. Her thoughts were heavy, as was her mood as they trudged onward. That was why she barely heard the alert coming down the line from the west, Natasha's end of the line.

"Sabrina! Kessi!" Lila, one of the younger survivors of Nesin, no more than sixteen years of age with red hair and freckles, called as she ran toward them from up the line.

She was one of the awkward sword-wielders, the weapon unbalancing her as she ran. By the time she reached them, she was breathing heavily, and her usually pale cheeks were flushed. She stopped in front of them but had to bend and catch her breath before she could speak. Sabrina drew her sword and looked to the west. The line had stopped, and the ones nearest her shrugged, obviously at a loss for what was happening.

"Easy, Lila, catch your breath and tell me what's going on," Kessi said, gently touching her shoulder.

"Natasha has found something," the girl said between pants.

"Emiline?" Kessi asked hopefully.

Lila shook her head and said, "No, a place, a large rock and wagon tracks."

Sabrina and Kessi shared a concerned look before Kessi said, "Good, Lila. Please continue relaying your message until you reach Patricka and give her the news. Then bring everyone on that side of our formation up to the place you speak of."

Lila nodded, then ran on. Kessi, Sabrina, and everyone else who'd heard the news quickly moved west to find Natasha. Many were already gathered around the area when they arrived. It was nothing unusual, just a large, flat rock and a trail leading away to the north, precisely where they were heading, that looked partially overgrown.

"I almost missed it," Natasha said. "It was about thirty feet to my left, but I glimpsed the strange rock before we passed it, then sent Lila to retrieve you."

Soon, the group stood around the rock, looking for clues. It had scratches from what looked to be claws, but they were more extensive and more profound than something a normal animal could inflict. The grass around the rock was matted and showed signs of recent use. The trail leading away from the strange rock led north toward Attins, and although slightly overgrown, its use was evident in the thick understory.

"So, what do you think?" Sabrina asked Kessi.

"It's strange, and at first glance, I thought it might be for sacrificing, but I see no blood stains."

"Yeah, it hits home after our experiences in Nesin, but I agree there's no blood anywhere. So, what is it used for?" Sabrina asked.

"I don't know, but we should follow the trail. It's the first sign of a possible settlement in these woods," Kessi said.

After some discussion, the group followed Kessi's advice and traveled along the trail, two abreast with Sabrina and Kessi leading the way and

Natasha and Patricka bringing up the rear. It wasn't long before they spotted a lone wagon moving toward them, pulled by two donkeys and driven by two men, one much older and with a white beard. Both men were dressed modestly in what appeared to be farmers' clothing.

"Should we hide?" Sabrina asked.

"No," Kessi said, shaking her head. "We need to make contact. Hopefully, they can provide information concerning Emiline. If not, we outnumber them and hopefully aren't in danger if they're hostile."

They waited, and when the older man saw them, he slowed the wagon and eventually stopped it about fifty feet away. Kessi could see that his companion wasn't a man but a boy closer to her age. The two whispered to each other and eyed the women suspiciously.

Finally, the older man spoke. "Who are you?"

"And what do you want?" the younger man added.

"We're looking for a friend," Kessi answered, walking toward the wagon. The others followed her lead.

The older man grabbed a long staff from the back of the wagon, which was hauling several large barrels. The staff was wooden and wrapped in a leafy vine with large, purple flowers sprouting all along its length. He stepped down from the wagon, moaning with the effort. The young man jumped down to join the older one, and that was when Kessi's life forever changed.

The young man had curly brown hair, a slender build, a chiseled chin, and a perfect face. He was beautiful, and Kessi immediately found breathing hard as she watched him approach. They locked eyes, and she suddenly felt they were the only two in the woods. She didn't even notice the similarly awkward look that washed over his face. Kessi realized she wasn't breathing; her body was no longer able to function properly. Even her heart fluttered in her chest. She felt hot and light-headed and couldn't turn away from his mesmerizing gaze. She swallowed hard and managed to start breathing again before she fainted. He was before her, and she couldn't speak. The two looked into each other's eyes, lost in the moment.

"I …" the handsome young man said, but that was the extent of their conversation.

Kessi noticed peripherally that Sabrina tried unsuccessfully to hide a giddy smile as she watched her. Kessi felt her face flush, but she couldn't pull her gaze from the beautiful young man before her.

"I am Grandpa, and this is my Kody," the young man finally blurted out, motioning with one hand toward the man with the white beard.

Sabrina and several nearby girls giggled at the error, but the younger man had no idea he'd said anything wrong and stared at Kessi wide-eyed. She was equally unaware of the mistake and still speechless.

"Damn it, Kody, get away from her; she could be dangerous!" the old man said, pushing Kody back, stepping between the two, and brandishing his marvelous staff.

He held the staff before him to ward off Kessi and her friends and said, "Back, or taste the poison of my staff, creatures of darkness!"

No one moved for a long while as Kessi and Kody seemed lost in each other. No one expected the interaction and didn't know what to make of it. Eventually, Kessi snapped out of her trance, sharing an astonished glance with Sabrina, whose giddiness was suddenly lost.

"Grandpa, put that down. I don't think these women are werefolk," Kody said, placing his hand on the staff and gently lowering it.

The older man didn't resist, and soon, the tip of the flowered staff was touching the ground before him. Sighing, he said, "I guess you're right, Kody. Apologies, ladies, one can never be too careful in Sylor Woods."

"No offense taken, but did you say werefolk?" Kessi asked the curly-headed dream, whose name may or may not have been Grandpa.

He approached her and nodded slightly. "Yes—creatures of the night, killers, all of them."

"Oh," Kessi managed to whisper, but she soon lost her voice.

She was melting under his gaze again, and she considered if it could be a spell or a trance she was under. She knew the truth of it, though. She had never had a great interest in boys, and even at nineteen, she had never had a boyfriend. But there was no mistaking this: Kody had her attention.

The older man interrupted the again-forming trance by placing a hand on Kody's shoulder and gently pulling him back as he stepped between Kessi and Kody. "What my grandson is trying to say is that this part of Sylor Woods is crawling with werewolves."

That broke the spell quickly for both Kessi and Kody. Kessi turned to Sabrina, whose face reflected the fear they all felt.

"We have a friend missing, and we're looking for her," Kessi told the older man.

"Here, in Sylor Woods?" Kody asked.

Kessi nodded.

"Then your friend is already dead," Kody's grandpa answered. "Kody, come and help me get the barrels in place," he continued, returning to the wagon.

"Wait!" Kessi and Sabrina said together.

"We can't just leave her out there," Kessi said.

"Grandpa, we should help," Kody said, moving up to the man and whispering.

Kessi waited as the two discussed things in hushed tones, the older man occasionally looking over Kody's shoulder to take in Kessi and her friends. Kody became more animated and began to flail his arms as he spoke. Kessi knew he was pleading their case, this incredible young man whose soul was just as pure as his physical perfection. His grandpa stubbornly shook his head, then climbed back into the seat with a huff.

A dejected Kody approached Kessi and Sabrina. This time, his mind focused as he looked disappointed and helpless. "I'm sorry, but my grandpa—"

"Said no," Kessi finished for him.

Kody lowered his head and nodded.

"Kody, let's go. The sun will be down in a few hours," his grandpa said from the seat of the small wagon.

Kody sighed and said, "I must complete this chore. Follow the trail the way we came, and it will take you to our home. It's just a small community of hardworking people. They may not let you in; tell them Samuel and Kody invited all of you. We'll return shortly."

Kessi still had trouble focusing, becoming lost in Kody's brown eyes again. Luckily, Sabrina still had control of her senses and asked, "What is the chore?"

Kody was already backpedaling toward the wagon and said, "We have to deliver these barrels to the offering rock."

"What's in them, and what are they for?" Kessi managed to ask.

"I'll tell you when we return," Kody said as he sat beside his grandpa, Samuel. "Go, now, before the sun sets. If they have your friend, they know of you and will be hunting when the sun sets."

Samuel whipped the donkeys lightly to get them moving with an exaggerated, "Ya!"

The donkeys started up, and the members of Kessi's party parted to let them through. Kody and Kessi shared a long look as he passed. A slight nod and smile from the young man made her blush, especially when Sabrina grabbed her arm and squeezed it. Kessi turned to her and saw the smile engulfing her friend's face.

"What?" Kessi said, but she couldn't contain her smile either as the two touched foreheads and giggled, barely containing their laughter.

"What was that all about?" Patricka asked as the group huddled around Kessi and Sabrina.

"Nothing," Kessi said, fighting the butterflies in her stomach.

"Nothing?" Lila repeated. "You two were gushing over each other!"

"Yeah, as if you two were lost lovers seeing each other for the first time in years," Patricka said with a smile.

"Don't be ridiculous! Let's get back in order and travel the path as Kody instructed. Perhaps the people of his community can help us—at the very least, give us some knowledge of who or what may have Emiline," Kessi said, starting to walk.

The others whispered about the strange encounter, and Kessi heard her name several times. They weren't vindictive conversations meant to hurt her; they'd simply witnessed one of the greatest moments of her short life. Danger and evil surrounded them, lurking in every corner of the strange woods, but Kessi couldn't have been happier. She made sure no one saw, but she allowed a smile to crease her pretty face as she picked up the pace, hopefully leading her friends to safety and another chance to see Kody.

As Kessi and her friends traveled down the weed-infested trail to the unknown community from which Samuel and Kody had come, Greyson and his friends traveled through a more rugged part of the woods. The ground was broken and littered with rocks, competing with the abundance of trees and vine tangles.

"Uh oh," Lud suddenly said and stopped.

"What is it, Lud?" Greyson asked.

"It is time," the goblin guide replied.

Greyson's grip tightened on his staff. He called forth its power, which seemed to vibrate in his hands. The weapon opened his mind to Plath, and he was ready. He was prepared for whatever danger might be before them. However, nothing prepared him for what happened next. Lud hastily unrolled the map and then dropped his pants and squatted. It was simply time for their guide to relieve himself.

"No, Lud!" Chloe screamed, but it was too late.

She turned and fled into a thick group of bushes. Greyson and Alleah followed, all three laughing when they reached the center of the tangle. It took a few moments for them to gain control of themselves, and by then, they were each nearing tears.

"He is quite charming," Greyson added after they regained control of their senses.

That started them up again, and it took a few minutes before they quieted down. The day had been very humid, the worst day for traveling thus far during their trek through the woods, and the setting sun was dropping the temperature to a more reasonable level. They each found a seat, Chloe and Alleah sitting on an old log and Greyson propping himself against a tree. He took out his waterskin and drank, watching Alleah and Chloe share small talk and giggle, probably at Lud's expense.

Occasionally, Alleah would look over at him, and his heart would race each time she did. Sitting against the tree also reminded him of Swamp Ikma, where he and Alleah had run for their lives and stopped to rest against the old trees of the swamp, like they were doing now. He loved the way she looked at him.

Chloe suddenly stood as something caught her attention near to where they sat. Greyson vaguely heard her say, "What is that?" as she walked out of the thick bushes.

He barely noticed Chloe leave as Alleah held his attention. They shared a look that spoke volumes about what potentially awaited them in the coming days. Alleah smiled, and Greyson decided he'd never seen her more beautiful. The moment enveloped him, and he fell into the trance of Alleah Mansuell.

"Alleah, come look! It's a field of butterflies," he vaguely heard Chloe say from beyond the brush wall.

He went over and sat beside Alleah, and she smiled that beautiful smile. She was stunning, making his heart flutter in his chest.

"They are so friendly! Three are on my hand, colored blue, red, and orange. It's an amazing sight, guys. Come out here and see for yourself," Chloe's voice echoed in the background.

Greyson looked hard into those beautiful blue eyes, and the smile melted from her face. She looked nervous, and he understood why. She was faithful to her goddess and always had been. Now, her faith wavered, and he knew he was to blame. Yet, he had to have this woman. The sample offered by Zeva was not adequate; he needed the true Alleah beneath him, writhing in ecstasy.

He inched closer, and Alleah looked like she wanted to say something but lost her courage to speak. She turned her face toward his and watched intently as his lips moved closer to hers. He heard the bushes rustling but didn't care. His moment with Alleah was upon him!

Chloe interrupted the connection as she forced her way back through the thick brush to stand beside them again, ending the spell they found themselves under.

"Alleah!" she said, focused on the blue-winged butterfly on her hand.

She didn't notice that they were in the middle of something special; her gaze locked on the large butterfly that slowly raised its wings and crawled on the back of her hand. Greyson wanted to inform her that she was intruding and that maybe she should take her insect pet for a walk. Before he could, Alleah ended the connection. He knew she would be stronger around Chloe and, at that moment, started thinking of ways to get Alleah alone as they traveled.

Alleah stood and said, "What?"

"I've been calling you. Didn't you hear me?"

Alleah shared a glance with Greyson as he stood, too. The enormous butterfly had moved to the tips of her fingers. It was nearly half a foot long, according to Greyson's estimate.

"There's a field full of these. Come look," Chloe said excitedly.

"What? Show me," Alleah said.

Chloe moved through the thick brush again, and Alleah and Greyson struggled to pass as the plants tugged at them. However, the sight on the other side of the clump of wild growth took their breath away. An open field stretched out in front of them. Thousands of butterflies littered the ground, their colorful wings slowly opening and closing as they all seemed to silently applaud the friends' arrival.

"Dear Sinnis, I've never seen anything like this," Alleah breathed.

Greyson was at a loss for words. The sight was the most beautiful scene he had ever discovered while trekking in nature. The butterflies had brightly colored blue, orange, red, yellow, green, and purple wings. And the setting sun seemed to reflect off the beautiful carpet of winged insects. All three stood there in silence, taking in the incredible sight. He heard Lud whistling as he approached from behind them, and Greyson made his way back through the clinging vegetation. Their scout stood there with his tiny map rolled and tucked under his arm. It looked as if he were about to speak, but he stopped as Alleah and Chloe moved through the thicket to stand beside Greyson.

Lud stood there with his eyes as large as saucers, pointing to the butterfly on Chloe's finger. His mouth moved up and down slowly as if he were trying to speak, yet he made no sound. He appeared to be terrified of the little friend Chloe had found.

"What is it, Lud?" Greyson asked, stepping closer. Alleah and Chloe followed, and Lud recoiled from Chloe, his lower lip quivering in fear.

"It's just a butterfly," Greyson said, now very concerned with the goblin's behavior.

"No, they're fligs," Lud whispered.

"What's a flig?" Alleah asked, now standing beside Greyson.

"This thing has a face!" Chloe screamed suddenly, and she shook the butterfly from her finger. It flew out into the clearing with its brethren.

"A face?" Greyson asked as Chloe wiped her finger on the grass as if she'd just touched something icky.

Greyson turned back to Lud to ask for clarification only to find a snevol clutching Lud from behind, a knife pressed against the little goblin's throat. The snevol were a race of beings related to the sleeth. The snevol looked like humans at first glance, but their pupils were much more prominent, their skin a light green, and they had six fingers adorning each hand. They also moved quickly, and Greyson had encountered several in Glime's court back in Racip. He knew then what it wanted.

It smiled at Greyson as it called out, "Sebastian, I have them! Over here!"

Greyson could hear Sebastian, the ruffian from Racip, approaching and talking excitedly, which meant there were others with him. Greyson had charmed Sebastian and a group of his friends, tricking them into helping bury the bodies of Alleah's and Chloe's sisters in the faith, who had been ambushed and murdered by Cerus the Grey back in Port Racip. Greyson had promised a fun-filled night with Alleah for their help, then had escaped the foul city before they could collect their fee. He remembered Cassandra's adverse reaction to learning of the charm spell he once used on her. She'd smacked him hard several times and was furious with him. Cassandra was a friend, so he could only imagine what Sebastian and his cronies would do if they discovered his charm.

They'd tracked them, using the snevol, and now they were in serious trouble. Greyson studied the creature that had Lud and recognized him as the one that had hit Alleah in Glime's court. His anger got the best of him, and he lost his connection with Plath through the staff.

"Aren't you one of Glime's men? The coward who hits women and picks fights with frightened goblins?"

"I work for whoever pays the most, and Sebastian paid me a lot to track you down," the creature said with a wicked smile.

"Fligs," Lud whispered, nearing tears.

"Shut up," the snevol hissed, and he shook the little fellow so hard his teeth chattered.

"Leave him alone," Alleah said.

The snevol regarded Alleah and recognized her, a smile widening on his face.

"Kavin Lightbringer," a voice came from behind the snevol, who dragged Lud out of the way so Sebastian could make his grand entrance.

The man wasn't wearing armor but had his sword on his side. His shirt was soaked, and his hair was wet with sweat, lines of it making little rivers down his dirty cheeks. Greyson understood that Sebastian and his men had forgone their armor to travel fast and keep up with their snevol tracker. It had taken over a week, but they'd finally tracked them down. Ten others came spilling in behind their leader, all of them a part of the group Greyson had charmed at Port Racip, and they all looked eager for revenge.

"You owe me, Lightbringer, and I intend to collect my fee," Sebastian said between gasps as he tried to catch his breath.

He produced a waterskin and took a long draw, wiping his mouth with the back of his hand. Greyson moved to stand between the evil men and his friends. The fool still referred to him as Kavin Lightbringer, the moniker Greyson had used to conceal his identity when he first entered the city.

"Over my dead body," Greyson said.

Sebastian looked to the other men in his group, and they all laughed at Greyson's expense. "As you wish," Sebastian said, drawing his sword. The others followed, and Alleah and Chloe drew their tiny maces.

Sebastian and his men advanced. Greyson focused on his staff and called to his god. Then things really got out of hand.

MORTEMUS KANE

ASSANDRA WAS DREAMING. SHE KNEW THAT, BUT THE DREAM was vivid and quickly becoming a nightmare. She knew her physical form was left sleeping in the magical cave and wanted to return to it and awaken before the dream could start fully. She felt a chill and sensed an underlying evil that spoke of death and power. In the dream, a black fog surrounded her. She couldn't see it, but she could *feel* a presence. Her breath caught in her throat as the mist began to swirl away. She could suddenly smell many pleasant scents, ranging from cinnamon to honey. She wondered if she was in a bakery at first, and when her vision cleared, she knew that wasn't the case.

Once the fog was gone, she stood in what appeared to be a small but cozy log cabin. A fire blazed in the hearth, and a large black cauldron hung over the flames, steam rising from it. The cabin had only one room, which included a dining table and two chairs, a bed, and, in the corner, several smaller tables with books, scrolls, and various trinkets and components littering them. Cassandra knew it was a wizard's play area, for she'd had one in Oldorburg a few years earlier, albeit less interesting. She was relieved to find such a pleasant little place, and the sense that this might be a nightmare slowly faded.

There was a scream so sudden and loud that Cassandra jumped and covered her ears. She turned to the source and realized someone was lying in the bed. It was a woman, but not human. She seemed long, and Cassandra imagined she had to be seven or eight feet tall, although it was hard to determine with her lying down. Her hair was black with streaks of grey coursing through it. Her face was hideous, with a large crooked nose, pointy chin, and several warts dotting it. Her skin was a sickly greenish color, and she was skinny. Looking at the creature, Cassandra knew this dream wouldn't be pleasant.

"Wake up," she whispered to no avail.

The creature thrashed and screamed, kicking the thin blanket off her. The strange woman was naked, and although her form was lithe, her stomach pouched slightly. She was sweating and obviously in a lot of pain. Cassandra, unable to control her feet, unwillingly moved to between the creature's legs and discovered she was in the throes of childbirth. The woman was dangerous, Cassandra knew without a doubt, but she also pitied her for being in this much pain and alone with the task of birthing a child. Cassandra noticed that with each scream and each painful push, many arcane symbols came into vivid focus around the creature.

Cassandra unfocused her vision and searched for the symbols. Suddenly, they were everywhere! The room was thick with them, so dense that when she looked for them, it was hard not to stay focused on them and stare in awe. There were many that she'd never seen before, and they piqued her curiosity. She started examining them, reading them, and quickly understanding the purpose of each. She was so enthralled with them that she soon tuned out the screaming and thrashing woman on the bed. The many pieces to the magic puzzle known as spellcasting were before her. Cassandra reached out to them, mentally calling them, and they collected around her. She was mesmerized and had no idea how long she studied the magical air in the small room. The sound of a crying baby finally broke her from the trance.

She looked at the woman, losing track of the symbols, which slowly faded to nothingness. She was just in time to see the woman sever the umbilical cord with a serrated knife. Once freed from the placenta, the woman cradled her newborn to her naked breast, where it latched on, instinctively suckling. Cassandra felt compelled to approach the bed, the fear rising within her as she did, still unable to control her movements. It was a baby boy, and although birth membranes covered him, he looked like a normal human baby despite his mother's appearance.

"That's my boy," the new mother cooed, stroking his head, covered with dark hair.

She hummed to him as he fed and lovingly wiped him as he ate. "Eat, my son. Soon, you will enjoy the blood of the innocent and not just the milk from my bosom."

The statement confused Cassandra, and what seemed a lovely moment, regardless of how horrific the strange creature looked, now seemed a thing of nightmares. Would she feed her newborn blood of the innocent? What was this awful creature, and who was the child? Why was she dreaming of this and unable to awaken when she knew perfectly well this was just a dream?

Then she understood it wasn't just a dream or a nightmare but a little of both, most likely. More importantly, it was a vision, one from her father. She couldn't wake up until she experienced it and understood what he wanted to share. She tried to be brave but feared what she'd learn. It felt to Cassandra as if she were watching a historic event unfold. It had to be important to her father and, therefore, necessary to understand him and perhaps the prophecy.

"Magic conceived you, and the pureness of the blood will make you the most powerful warlock ever to exist," the creature purred, and her humming grew louder.

Cassandra noticed that the air was thick once more with the arcane symbols, most concentrated around the babe. She focused on them again. They overran the place just as before. Did the creature say that magic conceived the baby? It made sense to Cassandra and explained why so many arcane symbols gathered around the child. It also stood to reason that there would be no father as she couldn't imagine a mate for the hideous beast before her.

The strange creature danced around the room, naked with her newborn, happy and content. The vision grew foggy as the slim, hideous woman approached where Cassandra stood. The image frightened Cassandra, but she was rooted to the spot, again unable to control her movements. The image disappeared in a thick black fog just when the creature neared.

THE DARKNESS CLEARED ALMOST IMMEDIATELY, AND NOW CASSANDRA was on the other side of the room, near the table where a bowl of mush sat before a cranky baby, who squirmed and fussed in a high chair. Cassandra assumed it was the same child, maybe six months old now. He was a cute baby, and his black hair was wild on his head, just like his mother's. A scream from below the floor stole Cassandra's breath, and the child stopped crying and seemed to listen intently. The scream was short-lived, and Cassandra stared at the baby, whose dark eyes seemed to understand the desperation of that scream. Cassandra knew without a doubt that it was a child's scream, and she listened carefully to make out any other noises from below the floor planks.

"A cellar," Cassandra whispered.

The only sound was the occasional sighing of the baby as it bravely recovered from crying, shuddering with each breath. After several moments of silence, footsteps approached from below, and a shiver coursed down Cassandra's spine. A trapdoor near the bed opened, and the woman, the mother of the miracle baby, appeared, wearing a plain brown dress. She looked healthier now and taller, her crazy tangle of hair nearly touching the eight-foot ceiling. Whatever the creature was, it was imposing, and Cassandra felt unsafe around it. She looked at the baby, kicking his legs excitedly at the sight of his mother. A large smile, showing several tiny teeth, made the cute baby even more adorable.

"Well, my angel, I have some more special formula for you," the mother whispered.

The creature carried a large glass of reddish liquid. It looked like blood, and given the circumstances, Cassandra assumed it was. The mother sat at the table, poured a generous portion of the glass into the bowl of mush, and stirred it with a wooden spoon.

Once the white, mushy food was dark pink, she said, "Now, let's feed my big boy. Soon, you'll be able to use the powers of the arcane and will become a most proficient warlock."

To Cassandra's horror, the woman spooned a giant mound of the mush into the baby's mouth. He ate hungrily, and the mother smiled, quickly feeding him several more helpings before adding more red liquid. The baby fussed when the food stopped.

"Patience, little one, the blood is thick and pure. You must consume it slowly or else—"

The door suddenly splintered inward, flying across the room with large pieces landing on the bed and over the trapdoor. What appeared to be a wizard stood at the door, a smoking wand in his hand. The mother, baby, and Cassandra were startled, and Cassandra yelped in surprise. The mother growled and stood tall. Cassandra could see the symbols gathered around her, answering her silent call.

"She knows magic?" Cassandra whispered to herself.

"The witch is to the right of the room, a baby near her. Careful, she will be tricky," the wizard calmly said before several heavily armored men rushed through him.

He seemed to disappear, and Cassandra realized he'd used magic to survey the room and wasn't standing near the entrance. Four armed men entered the room wearing chain-mail armor and brandishing swords. The witch immediately collected and organized the symbols floating all about. Cassandra had never seen anyone use them so proficiently and quickly. She knew that no one in the room could see them except her and the witch because the men rushed into them before realizing there was a problem.

The witch made a few hand gestures, and the symbols swarmed the first man. He couldn't see them, but according to his reaction, he could feel them. Cassandra didn't recognize what spell the witch was casting, but the man stopped and shook violently, blood leaking from his eyes and ears. His sword clanged to the floor, and his lifeless body followed soon after.

The second assailant came on with a roar, undeterred, until the creature funneled hundreds of the mystical symbols into his mouth. His face scrunched up in confusion just before his head exploded, raining gore around the room and at Cassandra's feet. The baby cackled as his mother waved her long arms about, directing the next attack, a hateful sneer on her face. Cassandra had never witnessed anyone able to manipulate the magic so quickly and with such deadly precision.

Two more men rushed toward her as a third appeared in the doorway brandishing a longbow. He strategically fired two arrows in rapid succession between his two attacking friends. In the middle of casting, the witch had to redirect the arcane symbols into a protective shield. She barely had the spell in place when the arrows struck. Both were held in midair just before her face, then fell harmlessly to the floor. The baby laughed some more and clapped his hands awkwardly.

Now, the witch was hard pressed as two men came at her, swords swinging and maneuvering her away from her baby. She had to dodge the attacks and retreat toward the bed. Cassandra could tell she was concerned for the baby, but the little one seemed to think the spectacle was hilarious. The nervous mother didn't believe so; Cassandra knew she was overmatched and her child was at risk. That made her even more dangerous.

A sword slashed from her right as the second one aimed for her skull with a powerful overhead chop. She sidestepped the chop and instinctively caught the first blade with her gnarled hand. It cut deeply into her palm, but she held it tight. Judging by the surprised look on the sword-wielder's face, she was strong and soon pulled the weapon from his grasp. Simultaneously, she summoned a globe of energy using her free hand, throwing it at the second attacker, striking him in the face with it and taking most of his head. The man's body fell to the ground, smoke pouring from his badly burned head.

"Your days of spreading your evil magic in these woods are over, Agatha!" the unarmed man said as the witch slashed at him with a clawed hand while throwing his sword out of reach.

The man barely dodged the attack and backed against the table, where a bowl of bloody mush hovered high in the air and fell onto his head. Agatha and Cassandra looked to the child, who giggled and clapped gleefully, thinking the whole thing was a game. He had levitated the bowl and used magic at only six months old.

A smile spread across Agatha's face as she beamed with pride. She struck with a claw that tore the man's throat open, and he staggered away, holding his wound and wearing a bowl as a hat. Blood squirted from between his fingers, and his torn neck would most definitely prove fatal. His body finally gave in and fell, adding a fourth corpse to the small room.

"My son, the warlock," Agatha said proudly.

The beautiful moment shared between the mother and her young child was one of the few they had, and their time together was too short. The delay cost the witch everything as two arrows struck her chest. She fell back against the wall from the short-ranged impact of the mighty bow and stared wide-eyed at the attacker, who was still at the doorway and reloading his weapon. The baby stopped laughing and stared at his wounded mother, suddenly on the verge of tears.

The man took a new bead on the witch, and she screamed in denial, quickly working her magic to make the door slam on him. The arrow fired and landed with a dull thud on the floor near the table. The man screamed in agony as the door crushed his arm, snapping bones and tearing skin.

The witch held a shaking hand toward the portal, using all her effort to keep it shut. She looked over proudly to her baby, whose eyes welled with tears. Cassandra couldn't believe the intelligence she saw within the infant's eyes. He somehow understood the intruders were trying to kill his mother and she was hurt.

A bolt of lightning smashed through the window and struck Agatha, knocking her to the floor. The child cried and held his arms toward his mother. She sat against the wall, her upper body, neck, and part of her face burned severely from the lightning strike, her wild hair dancing crazily on her head. Her arms lay limply by her side, breaking the spell she'd used to hold the door shut. The archer with the now nearly severed arm fell back as three more men rushed in with their swords. The wizard followed and stood at the doorway, the wand smoking from the lightning discharge. The witch was doomed.

She tilted her head to her son and smiled. "I love you. Avenge me," she said.

Just before the three new assailants were upon her, she turned her head toward the sword she had tossed earlier. It lay in the corner near Cassandra. With a flick of her arm, the sword flew toward the wizard, who yelled out in surprise. He was powerful and had enacted several spells of protection that should have defeated her attack. However, he didn't realize how many arcane symbols covered the projectile and how they easily penetrated his magical shields. The sword impaled him in the stomach, all the way to the hilt.

He fell dead, the last of Agatha's victims. The three men hacked her apart right in front of her delirious child. The men were frightened and cut her to pieces out of sheer terror.

Only a strong voice from the doorway stopped them. "Halt! The witch is dead, gentlemen!"

They stopped their panicked strikes as if they'd awakened from a trance and then realized the horrific scene before them. All three studied the area, themselves, and each other—blood covered their swords, armor, and even their faces. Once they realized she was dead, they turned to regard the voice. A man in holy vestments stood at the doorway and silently said a blessing before he crossed the threshold. Cassandra guessed he was older, perhaps in his fifth decade. He was handsome and wore a sword on his side. He had scars on the left side of his face and neck, which appeared to be battle wounds, possibly from a sword. It added character to the man, Cassandra thought.

"There, there, little one," he said, reaching the baby and lifting him gently. "We will get you back to your parents soon enough."

The baby cried and pointed to the bloody corpse of his mother. "Yes, the bad witch is dead. You are safe now," the holy man said.

"We have saved this one from an awful fate and must find the other children. Check for a cellar, and be careful," he ordered the three men.

They nodded and began looking around. They quickly found the trapdoor that Agatha had used, and as they descended the steps, Cassandra watched the exceptional child interact with the man. The man's intentions were good, but Cassandra understood he had no idea how aware the baby was. The man took the infant outside. She could hear him gently singing to the child. Soon, the crying stopped, and Cassandra was left with the massacre. She took in the tragedy, her heart aching for Agatha and her baby.

The men, although thinking they'd done an honorable thing, had just murdered a new mother, leaving her baby orphaned. Sure, the witch was hideous and fed her baby blood from who knows what, but did she deserve to die so horribly? Cassandra wasn't convinced justice had been served. That was until the three men returned from the cellar with two dozen emaciated children, all under the age of ten. Cassandra felt suddenly ill as the image fogged and faded away.

WHEN THE IMAGE CLEARED AGAIN, CASSANDRA WAS RELIEVED TO FIND herself in another small but normal-looking home. She was no longer in the blood-soaked room of murder where the witch had been slain. This house had two rooms, and she stood in the living area near the front door.

A woman in a simple blue dress and wire-rimmed glasses, with brown hair and streaks of silver accentuating her locks, sat in a rocking chair near Cassandra, knitting what looked to be a blanket. She was pretty, but more importantly, Cassandra felt comfortable being near her. The woman had a good soul, unlike the witch Cassandra had just witnessed.

"Mari, have you seen my mustache tonic?" A man's voice came from the other room, which appeared to be a bedroom from Cassandra's vantage point.

"No, Jed, I've never had use for the stuff," Mari replied.

A man popped his head around the corner of the room with a curious look. The woman had her back to him and kept to her work, a large smile spread across her face. It was contagious, and soon Cassandra joined her. The man was very handsome and looked tall and strong. His mustache was dark and full, and his hair peppered with grey. Cassandra found him distinguished.

"Well, then, that is good because I would not like to be married to a bearded woman, regardless of how pretty she may be," Jed said.

Mari couldn't contain her laugh then, so she dropped the knitting to her lap and turned to Jed, obviously her husband or partner. She was even more beautiful when she laughed, the crow's feet at the corners of her eyes not detracting from her good looks. The man smiled and came to her, kissing her gently. His pants and shirt weren't extravagant, and he wore suspenders dangling by his legs. The couple's attire told Cassandra they weren't wealthy, and Jed's calloused hands indicated he was no stranger to manual labor. His large, rough hands gently grasped Mari's cheeks as he kissed her. The two seemed in love.

A sudden knock on the door interrupted their moment, and Cassandra broke out in a cold sweat. After what she'd just witnessed, she could only assume something terrible was about to happen. Jed stood tall and pulled his suspenders up and over his shoulders. He then licked his fingers and tried to straighten his untamed mustache. Jed gave Mari a knowing look as he did, and she stuck her tongue out to tease him. He stifled a laugh and opened the door.

The man from the witch's cabin stood at the threshold, holding the baby. Cassandra's nervousness doubled as she recalled the horrible events of that battle. The infant wore nice clothes and appeared content but perhaps not happy. Cassandra studied his face as the two men greeted each other.

"Jed. Mari." The man nodded, looking past the big man to Mari, who had sidled up to her husband.

"Hi Vincent," Jed said.

Mari repeated the greeting with a smile. When she saw the little boy, she lit up. The baby smiled and shyly tucked his head into Vincent's neck.

Vincent laughed and said, "He's taking a liking to Mari already."

"Oh, but he is a handsome one and a flirt," Mari said, playfully pinching his leg. The infant squealed and cackled.

"So, what brings you by at this late hour?" Jed asked. "And with a baby to boot? I know this isn't your child."

"No, it's not!" Vincent said, and they all laughed. "But that's why I'm here, Jed and Mari. May we come in?"

"Of course," Jed said, stepping aside.

"You may come in if I get a chance to hold the youngster," Mari teased, holding her arms to the baby.

He still lay his head on Vincent's shoulder but had a giant smile on his cherub face.

"Well I'm the only one he'll let hold him, Mari. I don't mind, but—"

The baby lurched forward suddenly, arms held out to Mari. "Oh my," she said, gently taking him into her arms.

She carried him back to her rocking chair, forgetting the two men, who looked on in astonishment. She whispered baby talk to the small boy and tickled him. He cooed and laughed in response. They bonded, and it looked to Cassandra as if they were meant to be together.

Vincent entered, and Jed shut the door behind them. They watched the interaction, both sharing a smile at the spectacle.

After a moment, Jed said, "May I get you a drink, Vincent?"

"No, thank you. I won't be staying."

"Well, please sit, then," Jed offered, motioning toward a large, plush chair.

Vincent nodded and took a seat. Jed pulled up a chair and sat next to Mari since Vincent was now sitting in his comfortable smoking chair. She was rocking and humming, and the baby was tired, closing his eyes and resting comfortably on her bosom.

"Where did you find such an angel?" Mari whispered.

"Well, that's why I'm here, Mari," Vincent said, then turned to Jed and continued, "We found him with the Witch of Weston."

Jed's and Mari's eyes widened, and Jed said, "Old Agatha? He's lucky to be alive if that old hag had him."

"Yes, you're correct, but we killed her, Jed. She's dead."

"What?" Jed asked, sharing a look of astonishment with his wife.

"It's true. By the grace of the gods, we killed her, but it wasn't without a cost, including Stu," Vincent said.

Mari gasped and held a hand to her mouth. The baby stirred, and she began humming again. However, the sadness did not leave her face.

"Stu? Dead?" Jed asked.

"Yes, and four others in the attempt."

"When?" Jed asked.

"Three days ago. We freed two dozen tortured children, this one included."

Mari looked at the baby and struggled to hold back her tears. Jed put a hand on her shoulder and smiled. She tried to return the gesture, but it was a poor attempt.

"Two of the children died from their injuries, but the others were all returned to their parents."

"And why do you still have this one?" Mari asked.

Vincent sat up and cleared his throat. His look was stern, and he, too, looked on the verge of an outburst. "We don't know who he belongs to."

"What?" Mari and Jed asked in unison.

"It's true. He belongs to no one in town, and all of our riders but one have returned from the neighboring lands. No one has claimed him."

"So, how can we help?" Jed asked.

"Well, I know how the two of you were never able to have children of your own," Vincent started, then smiled at Mari.

Her eyes widened, and she whispered, "You can't be serious?"

"The elders of the church have voted on it, and we want you to have him, assuming the last rider doesn't find his true parents."

Mari stood and hugged Vincent, then her husband. She cried on his shoulder, and the baby stirred. She was too excited to sit, so she walked and hummed, though her voice cracked. Jed and Vincent shook hands, and it looked as if the big man would weep like his wife.

"What do we need to do?" Jed asked.

"Well, if you need to talk about it first, I understand. I mean, this is a life-changing event, and you may want to think it over," Vincent said.

"Look at her, Vincent. That's all the answer you need. We've wanted a child for a long time now and have considered adopting. The way Mari bonded with that baby makes me think he is a gift from the gods."

They watched Mari walk around the house, humming happily and crying simultaneously. Whenever one of her tears fell on the baby, she whipped it away. It was the most beautiful thing Cassandra had ever seen, especially being an orphan.

"Well, I have the things for the babe: diapers, milk, and other things. They're in my coach. I'll fetch them," Vincent said.

Jed grabbed his arm and held him. Vincent turned to the man, and Jed said, "She has grown attached to the child. How long realistically do we have before we can call him our own?"

Vincent thought about it, and Jed released his grasp. After a few moments, he said, "Jed, if I had it my way, he would be yours from tonight forward. However, if the true parents come knocking in the next few months, we must turn him over. And that assumes the last rider won't return with news of the child's parents."

Jed nodded, and Vincent returned to his carriage to retrieve the baby's things. Soon, he was on his way, and the new parents watched their baby sleep peacefully in the crib Vincent had left. They held each other, and Mari still occasionally wiped a tear away.

"He is perfect, Jed."

"Yes, he is that."

"What will we name him? Vincent said they didn't know his name."

"Well, we already agreed that if we had a boy, we would name him Mortemus. Is that still what you want?"

"Yes, of course," Mari said. "Mortemus Kane, what a wonderful name."

The image began to fog over again, preparing to take Cassandra to the next scene of the disturbing history. However, she no longer focused on what was before her, her thoughts inward as she contemplated what she'd seen thus far. She had suspected the baby might be her father, but now she knew for sure. Mortemus Kane had to equate to Kane, the lich-god. He was born to a mother unnatural and evil. And according to her, he was conceived by magic. How could that be possible? Cassandra had witnessed him using magic well before he should have been able to. She took a deep breath and focused as the image cleared again.

Mortemus looked ten to twelve years old, a handsome kid with dark eyes and hair matching her dreams of him. He seemed content, sitting at the lone table in the tiny home, putting pen and quill to paper. His mother rocked and knitted just a few feet away. Mari's face was older and showed a few more creases, and her hair was primarily grey now. But she was happy, and it showed as she hummed a song. Although not biological, mother and son had bonded over the years, and the love in the room was evident.

His father sat in another chair, puffing on a pipe, and Cassandra could smell the sweet tobacco smoke that filled the room, even though she knew it was just a dream. The family was happy and content, and the focus of the vision settled on young Mortemus. Everything else in Cassandra's field of vision became smoky and unclear. She watched her father age a few more years in the blink of an eye, and when the peripheral smoke cleared, he was a young man near her age, now with a beard. He was handsome, and his eyes were kind. He sat in the very spot at the same table, still writing away with his quill and ink.

Cassandra looked around and noticed the house was empty. Mortemus was so engrossed with his work that he didn't hear the wagon arrive. Cassandra could hear it but tuned it out, intent on looking upon her father if that was who sat before her. She couldn't see any resemblance of herself in his features, but she was mesmerized by how engrossed he was in his work. Was he penning a spellbook? Probably not if he was a warlock. Was it schoolwork or a journal of some kind? Then she saw it—he stuck out his tongue ever so slightly as he concentrated, which was one of Cassandra's habits. She smiled when she saw it—this was her father, she had no doubt.

A soft knock on the door startled both.

"Mom? Dad?" Mortemus said with a smile, gently putting his quill down and rushing to the door.

He was tall and lithe, and his smile engulfed his face, reflecting his true feelings for his adoptive parents. Cassandra knew something was wrong before he reached the door. There was something in the air, a pending doom, and Mortemus felt it, too, as he put a hand on the doorknob. He stopped, the smile slipping away as he thought of the situation. After all, why would his parents knock? He shrugged, and the smile returned as he opened the door.

Vincent stood at the threshold. He appeared very old to Cassandra, a far cry from the man who had led the group to slay Agatha and rescue the children she'd imprisoned. His hair was grey, as was his beard. His vestments were stark white, except for the telltale splotches of blood that covered most of the front and some of the arms. It looked like a strong breeze would knock him down. Several other priests were with him, but Cassandra didn't recognize them. Their robes were similarly stained.

"Vincent, are you all right?" Mortemus asked.

"No, Mortemus, everything is not all right."

"What? Why are you covered in blood? Are you hurt?"

"No, Mortemus."

"Well, Mom and Dad will be home soon if you need help," Mortemus said, panic edging his voice.

The young man was breathing heavily, and the smile was long gone. He was in denial but had to know why Vincent was there. Still, he played along, ignoring the obvious. "They went to pick up vegetables from the market and perhaps a side of bacon. You know how my dad loves bacon," Mortemus continued.

"Mortemus," Vincent said, taking the boy by the shoulders.

Mortemus pulled away, delaying the inevitable and trying to come to grips with his suddenly bleak future. "Yes, sir, they will be home soon. If you want to leave a message, I'll be sure they get it."

Vincent grabbed him again, this time more firmly. "Mortemus, my son, your parents are gone. Bandits ambushed them on their way back home. They were murdered and robbed. We found them, but it was too late."

The young man's eyes filled with tears, and he shook his head. "No, they'll be back, you'll see."

"I'm sorry, Mortemus," Vincent said.

The young man finally broke down and hugged Vincent. He sobbed hysterically as the old priest gently patted his back, and the other two looked at their feet. Mortemus Kane cried for a very long time, heartbroken and now orphaned for the second time in his life.

Cassandra shed a tear as the image faded away.

CASSANDRA WAS HEARTBROKEN BY THE LOSS HER YOUNG FATHER SUF-
fered. It was sad, and she knew what he was going through, having also lost
two mothers by the same age. The similarity was uncanny, and she wondered
how much control her father had over her life. Had he meddled with her
life since her birth? Could he do such a thing being a self-made god? How
much control did the gods have over human lives? The prophecy made her
think it was a lot.

As the image returned, she stood at a graveside near Mortemus, whose
expression had changed. He had shed tears, and now his expression spoke
volumes: he had moved on from heartbroken to angry. She knew he still hurt,
but it looked to her as if he swallowed the pain and focused on his reality.

A warm summer rain drizzled over the service, and Vincent intentionally kept it short because of it. Cassandra wasn't close enough to hear the
words, but she was sure they were heartfelt, given Vincent's history with
Mortemus and his parents. Cassandra approached Mortemus as the crowd
disbursed. She wanted to hug and comfort her father, but her arms wouldn't
work in the dream, as she never felt in control of her actions. Again, it felt
as if her father was manipulating her dream. So, she watched.

"Come, Mortemus, let's go back to the church and have a meal in honor
of your parents," Vincent said.

"I'm not hungry."

"Well, come with me and get out of this rain."

Ignoring him, Mortemus said, "Is it true that the gods bless us by raining
on our funerals?"

Vincent smiled the best he could and nodded, clapping the young man
on the shoulder. "Yes, Mortemus, I believe it is so, and I doubly believe it
for your parents. They were good people and will be well maintained in
the afterlife."

Only Mortemus, Vincent, and Cassandra remained as the funeral party
quickly disbursed. Two gravediggers sat nearby, respectfully waiting for
everyone to depart. Vincent whispered something to Mortemus, which
Cassandra couldn't hear. Afterward, they hugged, and Mortemus thanked

the old priest for the excellent service. Vincent nodded to the gravediggers and walked away, leaving Mortemus alone.

The two men walked over with their shovels, and one began to fill Jed Kane's grave with dirt. The hollow sound of it landing atop the coffin gave Cassandra chills. The second man, young, probably Cassandra's age, approached Mortemus, shovel in hand.

"I assume you knew them," the man said, nodding to the gravesites.

Mortemus nodded.

"Losing someone you love is tough. I know all too well," the young man said, leaning on his shovel and staring into space. After a few moments, he snapped out of his daydream and continued, "My name is James."

He extended his hand, and Mortemus shook it. They stared at each other momentarily, both seeming to search for the right words. In the end, James smiled and started toward Mari's grave.

"Wait," Mortemus said after he had taken a couple of steps.

James turned back, and Mortemus approached, taking the shovel from the gravedigger and rolling up his sleeves.

"What are you doing?" James asked.

"Paying my respects. I owe these two everything."

Mortemus started refilling the grave. He stopped after a couple of shovelfuls of mud and called to the man filling his father's grave, "You, stop that. I'll do it."

"What?" the man said, looking puzzled at Mortemus, who began working again.

James and the other man shrugged at the strange request. The man stabbed the shovel into the dirt and said, "As you wish. Come on, James, let's get some food."

The man walked away, and James watched for a bit. He then turned to Mortemus, who was in his own world and focused solely on his chores. "This is a lot of work. Are you sure you want to do this yourself?"

"I do," Mortemus said without stopping or making eye contact.

It looked to Cassandra as if James wanted to say something. He started away but returned after a couple of steps and said, "I can help."

Mortemus didn't slow, saying, "I said I'll do it."

"I'm not talking about the work."

The heartbroken young man stopped then and looked at James with more than a bit of curiosity. James looked around to ensure no one was watching, leaned over, and whispered, "Necromancy."

"What?"

"Necromancy. It's an art and a way for you to speak to the dead," James explained.

"You're referring to magic?"

"Yes, but not just any powerful magic. It can have you saying farewell to your friends here or perhaps even bring them back."

Mortemus's eyes widened, and his breath caught in his chest. "Did you say bring them back?"

"Yes, in some instances, if you're powerful enough in the art of necromancy."

"James, let's go, I'm starving!" the second man yelled.

The man was nearly fifty feet away, waiting impatiently. James waved him off, then continued his conversation. "I know someone powerful enough. I can't explain it now. Meet me at the cemetery on the north end of town tomorrow night as the sun sets."

James hurried away, but Mortemus called after him, "Blackland Cemetery?"

James turned but didn't slow, saying, "The one and the same," before turning back around and catching up with his fellow gravedigger.

Mortemus watched until they were out of sight. The rain seemed to die down a little. He stared into the grave at his mother's coffin for many moments, lost in contemplation. He eventually began his work again. He worked without tiring and didn't stop until he'd filled both graves. By then, he was sweaty and dirty, and the sun was low in the sky. Satisfied that he'd successfully buried his parents, he took a quick look around. Confident no one was looking, he finally broke down and cried well into the night. Cassandra wanted to reach out and comfort him, but she couldn't. She was stuck in the vision and helpless to move of her own accord.

THE FOLLOWING NIGHT, SHE WAS THERE WITH MORTEMUS WHEN HE arrived at Blackland Cemetery. At the front gate, true to his word, stood James. The sun was very low, nearing dusk, and the shadows were thick, but it was unmistakably James. He seemed overly excited to see Mortemus and approached him with a giant smile that almost glowed in the twilight.

"I knew you would come," James said.

Mortemus shook hands with the young man, and James led him deeper into the cemetery, an arm draped over his shoulder.

"You will not be disappointed with Basith," James said.

"Who?"

"Basith Sinclourgh, the necromancer."

Mortemus seemed uneasy, and Cassandra felt uncomfortable. The idea that a powerful necromancer was awaiting his arrival in a cemetery at sundown made the setting mysterious and dangerous. Her feeling of doubt was amplified once James brought Mortemus before a large mausoleum and then looked around to check there were no witnesses.

"What are we doing?" Mortemus asked. He still seemed to be reeling from the death of his parents, and even though he seemed a little suspicious of the situation, he didn't catch on to James's strange behavior. Cassandra wanted to interfere because something was happening that made the hairs on the back of her neck stand on end.

James used a rock to knock on the door. The loud thud echoed through the massive tomb, which startled Mortemus back into reality. He looked around, confused and more than a little anxious.

"Don't worry, my friend, it's a secret club, and you're invited," James said, patting Mortemus on the back.

"Why do I feel we're doing something wrong? Isn't someone buried in there?" Mortemus asked.

"No, they moved the body to a larger mausoleum a few years ago, and now we meet here."

"Larger? I find that hard to believe," Mortemus said, his eyes taking in the massive structure.

It was made of marble, and at least one side of the structure was overrun with vines, although Cassandra couldn't tell for sure in the darkness. There were angels or gargoyles lined along the roof, but the dark made it hard to tell which it was.

"Perhaps we should leave," Mortemus said, now having second thoughts.

"Mortemus, don't be nervous; you'll want to do this. I know it's a strange setting, but Basith likes his privacy because some people frown on the idea of a necromancer in the town. But listen, a few months ago, he allowed me to say goodbye to my grandfather."

"Really?"

"Don't be naïve," Cassandra whispered, but neither could hear her because she wasn't there.

"Of course. Basith is very good at this, and since the people you lost—"

"My parents," Mortemus said flatly.

"Yes, your parents. Since their deaths occurred recently, their spirits are still linked to our world. Therefore, he can use his magic to speak with them."

Mortemus seemed to lose his nervousness then and said, "Really? Will I be able to speak to my parents?"

"Maybe. If it *is* possible, Basith can make it happen."

A small peephole opened in the large structure, and a muffled voice from within said, "Password?"

"Sin of death," James whispered.

The peephole closed immediately, then there were sounds of the door unlocking from within. It creaked open just enough for James and Mortemus to squeeze in, and Cassandra followed before the door shut behind her. She could hear James whispering with the door opener. There was total darkness initially, but eventually sparks flew as the doorkeeper struck flint and steel to light a torch, revealing a small hallway lined with several sarcophagi resting in cubbies on either side. Soon, the torch was ablaze. The man holding it looked creepy to Cassandra. He was tall and very thin, almost too thin. He looked unhealthy, and the flickering torchlight didn't flatter his hollowed face.

"Mortemus, this is Riggs, our doorman," James said.

Mortemus looked nervous but shook the strange man's hand. "Hello," he whispered.

"Nice to meet you, fresh meat," Riggs said with a toothy grin.

The look on Mortemus's face spoke volumes. He was repulsed and uncomfortable. Cassandra felt the same and wished there was a way she didn't have to witness what lay in the bowels of the great tomb. If Riggs were any indication of what was ahead, the rest of the tour would not be pleasant.

"This way, Mortemus," James said with an outstretched hand.

Mortemus walked beside James, who seemed too eager and maybe a little nervous, with Riggs behind them, bearing the torch. At the end of the small hallway was a trapdoor. It was open and looked to Cassandra to be a newer addition to the old stonework floor of the mausoleum. Plenty of light was coming from below, and Riggs quickly doused the torch.

"Enjoy your first session, fresh meat," he said with a wheezy laugh.

"Leave him alone, Riggs. He's going to say his goodbyes to his parents, who just passed," James said, putting an arm around Mortemus's shoulder.

The smile melted from Riggs's face, and he nodded. It was dark, but Cassandra could see his teeth almost glowing in the dim light as James and Mortemus descended the ladder nestled at the lip of the trapdoor. Riggs was smiling as if he knew something the other two didn't. That didn't sit well with Cassandra. She followed the other two down the ladder as Riggs shut the trapdoor behind her.

The ladder led to a large room carved into the earth shaped like a five-pointed star. Each point was a hallway, narrowing to an end, where a door stood. Chairs with hooded men sitting motionless lined the five hallways. The room was about ten feet tall and had many wooden support beams built along the dirt walls to hold the stone ceiling above them. Several large stone columns stood near the center of the room to reinforce the structure. Carvings of skulls and strange symbols decorated the columns. A raised, circular stone stage adorned the middle of the room.

The men sitting in the chairs spooked Cassandra; she could tell Mortemus was also uncomfortable. She estimated at least one hundred chairs lined the five hallways, all filled with creepy, hooded men, save for two chairs at the base of one of those star-point hallways. The men all wore black robes with white skulls emblazoned on them, and each robe had a large hood that they wore. Cassandra assumed they were men, but she couldn't be sure, for the hooded robes hid their features. Two large braziers burned on either side of the stage, casting dancing shadows on the walls. Neither emitted smoke, and when Cassandra focused on them, she could sense that magic created them. James led Mortemus to one of the two empty chairs closest to the stage, which were on either side of the widest part of one of the star points.

"That chair is mine," James said, pointing to one of the two. "I must change into my robe. I'll be right back."

"Wait. You're leaving me in here?" Mortemus asked in a panic.

"Don't worry. These are all necromancers, and they welcome new students. I'm also new, so all the 'fresh meat,' as Riggs calls us, sit closest to the stage, at the base of each point. The older students sit near the smaller ends of the points. Relax, I'll be right back."

James walked to the point of one of the stars and disappeared into the doorway found at its end. Cassandra disapproved; something was wrong with this place. From her father's expression, she knew he felt the same. Every seat was filled with lifeless necromancers, assuming that was what they were, and each sat perfectly still. She believed they would have greeted and welcomed her father if it had been a legitimate school. None did, and the silence was thick in the room. It was very creepy and made Riggs look like the life of the party. Cassandra knew Mortemus was in trouble and didn't believe James was returning.

Cassandra's nervousness grew as the moments passed. Looking closer, she realized, to her horror, that the star-shaped room was a pentagram! She wanted to take Mortemus and flee the place, but as was the case during each previous vision, she couldn't move of her own accord and was helpless to do anything but watch the events unfold. She understood these were past events, and she couldn't change the outcome, but they felt natural, as if she were there experiencing the horror her young father was now feeling.

Just as it looked like Mortemus might rise from his chair and flee, James returned wearing one of the black robes with skulls adorning it. He sat near Mortemus and winked at him before draping the large hood over his head, hiding most of his face. Soon, he was sitting still, facing forward and silent like the others.

Mortemus looked around nervously, eyeing the ladder, the one means of escape the strange place offered. Cassandra imagined that he now wondered how he'd found himself in such a dangerous situation. In unison, all congregation members began reciting a mantra in a tongue that Cassandra didn't understand. It was apparent to her that Mortemus didn't either. Even James joined in, evident by his moving chin, which was the only thing visible from the large hood.

Then, a tall man with a shaved head appeared at the southern pentagram point. He wore a similar black robe, but the skull pattern found there was painted red instead of white. He looked in his early forties, with bright blue eyes and a large nose. His bushy eyebrows were the only trace of hair on his head, and his skin was a sickly grey. All the congregation rose. Cassandra didn't understand how they saw him or knew to rise. Surely they couldn't see through the obstructive hoods. James didn't look over but raised his arm toward Mortemus, indicating he should rise. He slowly did so.

The cadence of the mantra increased as the man, obviously the necromancer, made his way to the stage where Cassandra currently stood. When he reached it, he held his hands out to his sides, and she could hear him whispering something under his breath. She suspected it was a spell, so she focused on the arcane symbols to see if she could find any in the strange tomb. Sure enough, they answered his call, and the intensity of the braziers decreased because of it. In unison, the congregation sat. It took Mortemus a moment to understand he should sit. He glanced around and quickly found his seat.

As Cassandra stood on the stage beside the man, she was overwhelmed by a sense of repulsion. Not only was the man unattractive and his soul corrupt, but he stunk of death as if he were a rotting corpse. She knew it to be a dream, yet she could smell the stench as if she were there. She turned to Mortemus. His face shone in the diminished light, and she knew he was sweating. He was afraid, and she understood his discomfort.

The man spoke. "For our lone visitor today, I welcome you."

He looked right at Mortemus and smiled. His teeth were black and rotted, and his breath smelled of decaying carcasses. Cassandra wanted to run, just as much as it appeared Mortemus did. Instead, her father was glued to his seat with fright and didn't budge.

"My name is Basith Sinclourgh—"

All in attendance interrupted him with a shout of "Basith!"

He smiled and continued, "I am a necromancer and leader of this group of fine men and women."

He extended his hands and twirled slowly to encompass the entire pentagram-shaped room.

"Tell me, young Mortemus, have you ever heard of the god Marnelphion?"

A unified shout of "Marnelphion!" from the congregation followed.

Mortemus looked around the gathering nervously and shook his head. "No, I have not. But I am also not a religious person, Mr. Sinclourgh."

"Please, call me Basith."

Another shout of the necromancer's name followed, and it appeared to Cassandra as if the deranged man just enjoyed that automatic response as much as being the center of attention for the group. A chill ran down

Cassandra's spine at the mention of Marnelphion, as this was obviously the first time her father came to discover the beast's existence.

"Marnelphion is a demon lord, young man, and favors the human race," Basith continued.

"Demon?" Mortemus whispered, and his eyes widened as he took in his surroundings with renewed interest.

"Yes, but he does not wish humankind ill will. He is the lord of the undead and is an important bridge between life and death. He is the one who conceived the undead and blessed our world with the knowledge of how to create and command them. So, think of him not as a demon but a god."

Basith stepped down from the stage and walked to Mortemus. He smiled and put a calm hand on the young man's shoulder. "He will give me the power to communicate with your parents so that you may tell them goodbye."

Mortemus nodded, still seeming unsure of himself. Basith patted his shoulder and returned to his place on the stage. There, he led the congregation in prayer, walking around the circled platform, facing each point of the pentagram, and addressing the followers. The sermon was short, and Cassandra's concern for Mortemus's safety grew with each passing moment. The man glorified a cruel demon lord with his speech, and the worshippers absorbed his words and responded with cheers and hails to the necromancer. Cassandra watched Mortemus as the meeting grew old. He fidgeted in his seat and frequently looked around at the gathering, seemingly unsure of himself.

"Run, Father," Cassandra whispered.

"And now, the climax of our gathering! Our guest wishes to say goodbye to his parents, who were senselessly murdered only a few days ago. Disciple James enlightened him about our organization and our purpose. And now he is here," Basith said, motioning toward Mortemus.

In unison, the congregation said, "Praise Marnelphion!"

Basith moved toward Mortemus as the gathering rose. With a smile, he said, "Are you ready to experience something that few have the opportunity for?"

He put an arm around Mortemus's shoulders and motioned with his other arm toward the door at the end of the hallway where Mortemus sat. Her father turned in that direction and saw the doorway, dark and uninviting. Mortemus made no move and looked toward the ladder and the exit of the strange place.

Basith followed his gaze, and his smile melted away. "You may go if you wish, of course. However, the opportunity to say farewell to your parents slips away with every passing moment."

Cassandra approached, wishing once again that she could interfere. Mortemus made no move and seemed to struggle with the options.

"Disciple James, please come here," Basith said, turning to Mortemus's newest friend.

James stood and pulled back his cloak. He approached Basith and bowed respectfully. "Yes, my lord?"

Basith turned back toward Mortemus and said, "Shall I have James prepare the sanctuary for the communication, or do you still contemplate leaving?"

Mortemus made no move, and Basith moved closer. "With all due respect, young man, time is of the essence."

James looked on hopefully, and when Mortemus glanced his way, he smiled slightly. Eventually, Mortemus caved. "Yes, let's go."

"Excellent! Disciple James, please prepare the sanctuary for communication," Basith said. James bowed once more and hurried off through the doorway.

Basith gently led Mortemus behind him, a friendly arm around his shoulder. Cassandra followed, an uneasy feeling growing in her stomach. As they passed the members of the congregation, each turned to face the necromancer. Soon, they entered the doorway, and once they disappeared into the darkness, the gathering said in unison, "Praise Marnelphion!"

"I will guide you through the darkness, Mortemus. Just relax," Cassandra heard Basith whisper in the pitch black ahead of her.

It was so dark that she couldn't see her hand before her face, but she knew the dream would guide her, so she let it. She felt the ground slope further downward, and the smell of sulfur and earth grew thick. Finally, a flame lit a small room ahead of them, and shortly after, James appeared in the doorway with torch in hand. Basith led Mortemus to the room, and James stepped to the side so they could enter.

Inside was a small stone altar, the top flat and smooth like a table, large enough for a human to lie on. Cassandra was suspicious of it immediately.

There were shelves of ointments, oils, and potions on the wall to the right, and a mural depicting a large fire with a demon's face in the center adorned the wall to the left. A small wooden door remained tightly shut on the far wall. Implements lay on a table next to the stone altar. Cassandra recognized the similarities between the evil place and the cacti prison, where the barbarians had performed a brutal ritual known as the Warrior's Heart on her. She shivered at the memories of it.

James put the torch in a sconce near the mural; the flames on the wall magically began to move, and the demon's face seemed to float freely about the inferno. Mortemus took a step away as he studied the strange art. James only smiled and waved his hand at it with a nod to relieve any anxiety Mortemus felt, as if the mural were an ordinary piece of art you'd find anywhere. Cassandra unfocused her eyes to pick up the arcane symbols floating around the mural. They were thick and ancient. Most she did not recognize; whether due to their age or their complexity, she did not know.

"To speak with the deceased, you need to open your mind," Basith said, walking to the shelf, rummaging through the many vials, and breaking the spell the strange mural had over Mortemus.

"Is this place safe?" Mortemus asked James, perhaps as a last and desperate effort to reassure himself he wasn't making a horrible mistake.

"Of course. Lord Basith is looking for the catalyst to allow you to speak with your parents. I've seen it before, and it's quite spectacular."

"Will you be staying through this?"

"I will, Mortemus, and you will be amazed and thankful once we complete the experience."

Basith returned holding a vial with a purplish-colored liquid. It was small and made from decorative glass. The necromancer handed it to James and smiled again, showing his blackened teeth. Cassandra did not trust that smile.

"And now, I will meditate to reach out to your parents. You need to drink the contents of this vial, which will open your mind and prepare you for communication. I shall return shortly."

He then turned and exited through the small door in the back of the room. Although the door only opened briefly, Cassandra smelled the unmistakable stench of death wafting from it. It shut quickly, and the strange leader of the group was gone. She wanted Mortemus to flee while he had the chance. She didn't trust anyone in the place, not even James. She thought of how young and naïve Mortemus was. From the vision she'd seen, he'd led a normal and happy life thus far, and although he'd witnessed his biological mother's death, he seemed far too innocent to be among the necromancers. He didn't see the potential danger, but with her vast experience thus far in her young life, Cassandra knew he was in trouble. Still, she could only watch.

"James, this feels wrong. He's strange, and I'm not too fond of how he looks or acts. I feel that his intentions are not pure. How well do you know him?" Mortemus asked as soon as the door had shut.

"Do not fear, my new friend, Basith is strange but harmless. Have you ever met a necromancer before?"

"No, of course not."

"Well, this is pretty much how they all look and act," James chuckled.

"I don't want to be here. Also, how did he know the deceased are my parents? I didn't mention that, but he knew."

"I told him about your parents when I left to change into my robe. Also, I understand your hesitance, Mortemus. The guy worships a demon, right?"

"Don't you?"

"Yes, technically. I'm here to learn the skill, not to become a priest of a demon. I hope you will join me after you go through this amazing ritual. We will learn what we can from Basith and then leave together to provide this service ourselves."

"But you hardly know me. You expect us to go into business together?"

"Yes, I would do it for the coin, and you would do it to help people. We would be perfect partners," James said with a laugh.

Cassandra watched as Mortemus thought it over. He studied James's face, which was pleasant, and the story seemed genuine enough. Her father was probably considering what his new future entailed at that moment, now that he had no parents. How would he feed himself, finish school, learn a skill, and, most importantly, live in an empty house once so full of love and life? He would be lonely and sad. James was giving him an alternative existence that could help people in his situation and provide them with closure if he learned the skill.

Cassandra watched in horror as Mortemus took the tiny cap off the vial and sniffed the contents. He didn't react, indicating to her that it was odorless. He looked at James once more to gain reassurance he was safe.

The strange young man only smiled and nodded. With a slight nod of his own, Mortemus downed the liquid and waited for an aftertaste or perhaps something worse. When nothing seemed to happen, he returned the empty vial to his new friend.

"You won't regret this," James said, patting him on the shoulder, then returned the empty vial to the shelf.

Before James had even reached the shelving, Mortemus appeared disoriented. He leaned heavily on the stone altar and shook his head as if trying to remove cobwebs.

"Oh, and don't worry if you feel dizzy; that just means the elixir is working. It opens your sensory receptors for communication," James said over his shoulder.

James returned and seemed unaffected by Mortemus's disorientation. He put a hand on his shoulder and asked, "Not feeling so well?"

Mortemus tried to speak, but his mouth moved only slightly with no words forthcoming. The smile on James's face turned into a smirk as he watched the young man struggle. Mortemus grasped the altar tighter, and James just watched it unfold.

"Well, it seems that our special serum may have some side effects," James said with a chuckle.

Basith reentered the room, leaving the door open behind him. The stench of decay followed him, and the light projected from the dancing flames from the mural couldn't cut into the darkness beyond that door. Cassandra understood there could only be evil in the room, but she was more concerned with Basith's appearance. He was naked, having lost his robe somewhere in the impenetrable darkness. Unfortunately for Cassandra, the rest of his body was as hideous as his face. He was too thin, with his ribs visible through his tight, grey skin. His body was as hairless as his head. The most disturbing thing was that he was erect and fondling himself.

Mortemus didn't even notice, now losing his balance and leaning heavily on James. Basith came to the other side of them and helped James to keep him from crumpling to the floor.

"He is ready," Basith said. "Help me get him onto the altar."

Mortemus couldn't interfere as James and Basith worked together to get him face up on the smooth stone altar. His eyes were wide with fear, and his mouth moved occasionally in an attempt to protest, but his quivering lips produced no words. Basith leaned over him and looked into his eyes. When he noticed the dilated pupils, he smiled evilly.

"Excellent! James, bring me the components," Basith said, and he began his self-stimulation again.

James went to the shelf and rummaged momentarily, eventually returning with a few vials and a small stuffed bag. He took up a position on Mortemus's right side, opposite where Basith stood.

"Dear Mortemus, I have good news and bad news for you. The good news is, you will meet your parents tonight, as we promised," Basith said excitedly, waving a hand toward the dark room he'd just exited.

Mortemus couldn't hope to move enough to turn his head; from what Cassandra could tell, he was barely even breathing. Soon, two figures moved out of the room, walking with a strange, slow gait. Cassandra gasped when she recognized the animated corpses of Jed and Mari Kane. They slowly approached their new master, still dressed in fine burial clothes. Mari had a large gash on her throat, now sewn shut.

"You see, I am a man of my word. Now, the bad news is that you will be joining them soon. The serum you have consumed will not heighten your senses to speak with the undead. Instead, it will prepare you for undeath. Now, sit back and relax; soon, you'll be one more zombie in my collection. After all, the more undead that populate our world, the closer we become to Marnelphion," the necromancer said while rummaging through the small bag.

"You will make a great zombie," James added with a wicked smile.

Cassandra noticed Mortemus's eyes move slightly toward James, but she could tell even that was a struggle. As her young father endured the burdensome transition, Basith produced a handful of ashes and sprinkled the contents of one of the vials atop them. The ash began to smoke on contact.

"Can I tell him my secret before you kill him?" James asked hopefully.

"Yes, my disciple, now is the time if you wish to tell him," Basith said, smearing the moistened ash on Mortemus's forehead and cheeks.

James leaned down as Basith did his work and whispered, "I killed your parents. I stabbed your father forty-seven times because I always stab my victims forty-seven times. Your mother cried while I did, and I felt bad for her. Therefore, I slit her throat and got it over with. I made an exception for her concerning my stab-count rule. It took your father a while to die, but your mother went quickly."

"And you got in our way when my disciples tried to collect the bodies," Basith said as he smeared ash on Mortemus's arms and hands.

As Basith finished the task, the zombie versions of Mortemus's parents finally reached the table, taking up positions on either side of the necromancer. Neither had decayed much, but the early onset of rigor mortis had begun. Despite the nasty scar across her throat, Cassandra found Mari still beautiful. Both looked lifeless, and Cassandra understood that that was precisely the case as the abominations were not Mortemus's parents.

"Can I take his eyes?" James asked.

Cassandra didn't know what the deranged man meant, and she wished she could sever the vision because she didn't want to find out. Unfortunately, she had no choice but to watch the events unfold.

"You take his eyes while I take his mother," Basith said.

James's smile grew even wider, and he smacked his hands together excitedly. He moved quickly back to the shelves and grabbed a metal flask with a glass stopper. As he did, Basith commanded Mari to lean over the table so her face was close to her son's. Basith lifted her dress and began rubbing his genitals once more. Cassandra looked on with horror, and her heart broke for her young father. She could see his eyes water, but he couldn't do anything but watch the events unfold.

"Let me start your process into undeath as James gives you a final, painful gift. You and your father can watch your mother give herself fully to me," Basith said, smiling and showing his black teeth again.

Basith waved his hand that wasn't in use over Mortemus's body, closing his eyes and whispering a few arcane words. Cassandra could hear Mortemus suck in a deep breath, and it might have been his last as a spell washed over him. As it took effect, Basith moved behind Mari and slowly entered her, repulsing Cassandra as he found yet another way to desecrate her corpse. What little movement remained in Mortemus's body slowed, and his skin slowly began to tighten and grey as his mother rocked back and forth from Basith's thrusting. Her face was expressionless, regardless of the ecstasy plastered across Basith's face.

"Want to know a secret?" James asked, leaning in beside Mari. "You weren't supposed to be here, but since you wouldn't leave the gravesite so we could take your parents' bodies and prepare them, I took the opportunity to recruit you. Basith approved of having the whole family, so here you are!" James continued, then laughed hysterically.

Basith moaned and exclaimed, "The old woman has some mileage on her, like an old pack mule, but she's still a nice ride, right Jed?"

James nearly dropped the flask, laughing so hard. Jed's animated corpse stood nearby, watching his dead wife being abused by the evil man, showing no reaction to his words. The scene repulsed Cassandra, but she saw that the mural of flames on the nearby wall shifted strangely, which neither James nor Basith noticed. It was almost like a glitch in the magic that gave the fire life, and it didn't seem to be instigated by the necromancer. Cassandra reasoned that there had been a hiccup in the magic that maintained the burning wall.

She unfocused her eyes and searched for the arcane symbols. She sucked in a breath as she saw them flowing from the wall and swirling around the altar. Cassandra didn't know if it was part of the spell Basith had just enacted on Mortemus. Still, she had a feeling that her young father was gaining his footing as a warlock, trying to stop the events with an effort of magic manipulation. The arcane symbols were wild and uncontrolled, but he was finding his footing again, not having done it since he was just a few months old.

When James finally gained control of his chuckling, he removed the stopper from the metal flask, leaned in close, and said, "I am going to take your eyes; you won't need them anyway. No need to do it, but I thought it would be fun to watch."

Mortemus's skin looked like death, and it was taut across his face, arms, and hands. She imagined the spell's effects caused the change and that the rest of his body looked the same. His eyes were still open, and he didn't seem to be breathing. She knew he was still alive as a tear ran down his pale cheek, and the gathering arcane symbols continued to mass around him.

"And now, some acid for your eyes," James said, bringing the flask toward Mortemus's face.

At that exact moment, Basith groaned and closed his eyes tight, close to an orgasm as Mari's body rocked violently over her son's. It was too much for Mortemus, who lashed out at both men using what control he could muster over the symbols. Cassandra's jaw dropped at the glimpse of unbridled power that her father possessed. He formed two copies of an advanced telekinesis spell, one that Cassandra couldn't hope to cast or understand. The results of the spell told her precisely what he'd done.

The flask turned and spilled on the hand that held it. James screamed in agony as his hand and wrist smoked. He backed away a few steps and grabbed the flask with his uninjured hand just before he dropped the container. The incident broke Basith's bliss, and he disengaged with Mari and looked on in shock at James's plight. Before he could speak, he was lifted off his feet and thrown violently into the shelving as if a tornado had tossed him. The corresponding smash of the shelving, along with the many vials and bottles, was satisfying to Cassandra as the necromancer crashed to the floor amid the rubble.

James stood, staring dumbfoundedly as his master moaned and lay still. He was vigorously wiping his burned hand on his robe, leaving a trail of smoke as the acid disintegrated the cloth. Cassandra knew the young disciple had no idea what had happened, but James looked at Mortemus as if silently accusing him. Clenching his teeth and ignoring the immense pain in his wounded hand, he advanced on his shriveling victim, who now looked more dead than alive.

"You will not deny me this," he hissed, shoving Mari out of the way so he could more easily reach Mortemus's dying eyes.

The symbols began to retreat, and Cassandra knew Mortemus's battle was over. As short-lived as it was, she was impressed. However, once James poured the acid into his eyes, a new level of disgust rose in the back of her throat. His eyes popped and burned and James jumped excitedly at the display, tucking his bad hand under his good arm as he did. Mortemus didn't move as the acid ate away his eyeballs, black smoke wafting from the sockets and blood pouring from them and pooling in his leathery ears. A faint wail gurgled up from somewhere deep within Mortemus and leaked between the remains of his curled lips. It was barely audible, and the only thing that hinted he was clinging to life. He was alive and felt the anguish of the attack.

"Take that!" James cried victoriously.

The young disciple then moved to Basith, who was slowly recovering his wits. He helped his master stand. Several cuts adorned the necromancer's body in various places. None were severe, but Cassandra was happy about her father's small victory.

"What happened?" Basith asked, looking around.

"I think he did it," James said, pointing to Mortemus's still form.

"Impossible," Basith said through gritted teeth.

The two approached the altar where Mortemus's eye sockets were still smoking heavily. Basith pulled Mari out of the way and smacked her head, making her dirty but still beautiful hair fly with the strike. It didn't seem to hurt the undead creature, and Cassandra was sure she didn't feel it.

"Get back, you fools!" Basith yelled, pointing to the far wall.

Both zombies stumbled away to where he indicated. The evil men studied Mortemus, who lay on their altar, and Cassandra's eyes watered as she bore witness to the death of her father. It occurred to her that he was indeed dead and that this scene had probably occurred many centuries before she was even born. Still, she was heartbroken by it.

As she pondered the possibilities, Basith said, "What is that?" as he leaned over Mortemus's face.

James leaned in as well, and the last of the smoke cleared the hollow eye sockets. He gasped and moved away a few steps, but Basith remained, studying the strange sight. He even pulled down the skin of Mortemus's tight cheeks the best he could to get a better look. Cassandra noticed then that two red dots glowed from those sockets. She also saw the arcane symbols increasing in activity, not chaotically as before, but smoothly and controlled. They floated around the room as if on a river's current, awaiting guidance to form a spell.

"This is impossible. I performed the ritual to create a zombie, yet he has the eyes of a powerful undead, like that of a lich," Basith said.

He looked inquisitively to James, who stood a few feet away, mouth agape. "I cannot create a lich. Or anything more powerful than a simple zombie."

James returned to stand beside his master, waving the remaining smoke away with his uninjured hand.

"Marnelphion will bless me as the congregation grows strong, I assure you, Disciple James, but to create anything other than a zombie is currently beyond me."

"Then how?" James asked.

Before the necromancer could answer, a withered but strong hand shot up from the table and grabbed Basith by the throat with a vice-like grip. James screeched with surprise and stumbled backward. Basith's eyes grew as wide as saucers as Mortemus sat up, holding the kicking necromancer off the floor by his neck. Cassandra watched in amazement as he casually tossed the evil man toward the mural of flames. Tendrils of smoke suddenly escaped the painting and grabbed the flailing man. The smoke wrapped tightly around his throat and torso and then secured his arms and legs, holding him taut against the wall.

Even though Mortemus was untrained in using magic, Cassandra knew he was born with the ability. She realized then that no one else knew of the hidden talent he possessed, not his parents, Vincent, or even Mortemus himself. The transition to undeath had heightened his abilities, and he quickly mastered spells far more significant than anything Cassandra could hope to cast. He was naturally powerful, and the words of his mother, Agatha, rang in Cassandra's head: *Magic conceived you.*

James backed toward the pentagram, ready to flee the place. Sensing his desire, Mortemus pointed a dried and wrinkled finger toward the exit where the remaining disciples of Marnelphion sat and awaited Mortemus's procedure. A small dart of fire shot forth from his hand, and James had to step aside to let it pass into the main gathering chamber. Shortly after, there was a blast, and for a few horrible moments, all the air was sucked out of the room to feed the inferno. Even Cassandra couldn't breathe temporarily, even though she understood she wasn't truly there witnessing the event as it happened.

Flames billowed from the main gathering area, licking James's robe, but died away just short of consuming him. Then, screams began to echo throughout the small room as the fire consumed the congregation. All the necromancer's followers, save James, were dead or dying within moments. Mortemus levitated off the floor, his feet a few inches from the ground.

"Stay away from me, freak!" James cried, brandishing a knife with his good hand.

Mortemus ignored him and began summoning the energy for a powerful spell. There was nowhere for James to run, and his exit was now a raging wall of fire. Mortemus pointed toward Basith, and Cassandra could see the many arcane symbols quickly answering his call. She was astonished to see the burning flames of the mural suddenly become real and begin burning the flesh of the necromancer. He screamed and thrashed and burned along with his congregation. James watched it unfold, eyes wide and on the brink of crying.

"I'll cut you, Mortemus!" he yelled over the roaring fire and dying screams of his master.

Mortemus responded by summoning a crackling ball of energy and shooting it forth to strike James's hand that held the knife. The attack took most of the flesh from that hand. Skeletal fingers dropped the weapon, and it rattled to the floor. James fell to his knees, holding his newly injured hand to his face, screaming at the immense pain. The tears began then as Mortemus reached his hand toward the dropped weapon, and it flew to his waiting grasp. He easily lifted James with a telekinetic spell with his other hand and pulled him through the air to the altar. There, he slammed the young disciple onto the stone surface. He hit his head hard and nearly lost consciousness. James had now taken Mortemus's place, lying face up on the altar.

"My name is no longer Mortemus," the powerful warlock said, holding up an arm and turning it over, examining the greying, tight skin that covered it. "Call me Kane."

Cassandra didn't know what to expect from the once peaceful, young Mortemus, who now seemed powerful and vengeful. Contrary to what Cedric had told her, her father hadn't lived a long life in search of immortality; he'd had it thrust upon him at a young age. The place was quickly filling with smoke, and although it didn't affect her breathing, it was making it hard to see. She saw Mortemus's parents standing quietly in the corner of the room. Basith was still, his body engulfed in flames, melting the flesh from his bones. It dropped to the floor in gobs with sickening splats.

What happened next repulsed her, but she understood that Mortemus, or the lich named Kane as he was now known, was exacting a punishment suitable to the crimes that James had committed against his family. He held James still with magic with little effort but ignored the frightened young man's pleas for mercy. Cassandra tried to look away, but the vision held her once more, making her watch the dastardly deed. Kane meticulously carved out James's eyeballs and tossed them on the floor. James wailed and begged for mercy. The act was brutal, but Kane never wavered. His actions were determined and precise. Next, he slit the young man's throat in a fashion similar to the wound on his mother's corpse. As James gurgled and died from the vicious wounds, Kane stabbed him precisely forty-seven times, just as James had done to Kane's father. Kane left the knife in James's chest with the last strike.

"Your victims, including my parents, are now avenged. Go forth to the afterlife and the hell that awaits you," Kane said calmly.

James lay still on the table, and little remained of Basith other than a blackened skeletal figure. The cries of the immolated disciples had faded away as the evil congregation met their tragic fate. The entire group of fanatics was gone, and the small room where Kane stood slowly filled with smoke. The red dots that now served as his eyes focused on the undead creatures that used to be his parents. He kept his gaze on them, silently studying them. Cassandra assumed he was looking for a trace of his parents in their lifeless forms. They only stood perfectly still and showed no signs of the parents he had come to love so dearly.

He pointed to a nearby space with his right hand, his skin so thin that his hand seemed little more than skeletal with a tight wrapping of dead skin. A doorway appeared at the spot, one that Cassandra recognized. It was the same spell that Baxter had used to save her once before, and it was one she had difficulty learning. It was complex, and Kane had mastered it without training. She was mesmerized. She knew it was a doorway to lead out of the place. It wouldn't take Kane far, but it would be enough for him to escape the inferno.

He approached his father and said, "I love you, Father, and I'm sorry for what these men did to you. I have avenged your death the only way I know how."

He then went to his mother, and Cassandra could sense the terrible pain he felt. The earlier visions had indicated just how much he loved his mother. They were close. "I love you, Mother, and I will always remember the love you showed me. I will never forget you," he said, stroking her cheek.

Cassandra openly cried, then, remembering the loss of her surrogate mother, Sera, not so long ago. Her heart broke all over again as she watched Kane say goodbye to what remained of his parents.

He finally stepped back and said, "I know what I see before me is a perversion, not my parents. However, I hope you heard my words and that you may safely travel to the afterlife now. I cannot put you back in your graves, so I will destroy the abominations that you have unwillingly become. I will cremate your bodies in the hope that you may find peace in the afterlife. Goodbye."

Nothing happened for many moments as Kane wallowed in his sorrow. The smoke filled the room. If any living creatures had occupied it, they would have succumbed to it. Yet, Kane stood still, silently saying his goodbyes, the magical door waiting to take him away. After many moments, he waved his hand, and flames from the burning wall that had consumed Basith rolled through the air to the zombies of his parents. They didn't move or cry as the flames quickly consumed them. Kane didn't move until their corpses fell in a heap upon each other, appearing to hug one final time.

Cassandra barely saw his dark form move through the doorway. She could see nothing but the shining door, so she walked to it and stepped through. She exited at the top level of the mausoleum and saw Riggs leaning over the trapdoor that led to the lower levels. It looked like he'd just shut the trapdoor and was waving his hand as if the door had burned it. Smoke was starting to fill the tomb. Riggs stood and backed away, unaware that Kane and Cassandra were behind him. The magical door that had brought them from the bowels of the place vanished.

Riggs turned to flee, only to run into Kane. He shrieked and bounced off the immovable creature Mortemus had become, falling to the floor, his eyes wide with fear. Riggs had no torch lit this time, but the light from the fire below seeped through the trapdoor edges and gave enough for him to witness his doom.

"Who… who are y-you?"

Kane bent and said with a hiss, "Fresh meat, remember?"

Riggs only shook his head and tried to back away toward the trapdoor, deciding that burning alive was a better ending than what was before him. Kane grabbed him by the leg and pulled him back. Riggs screamed and yelled for help, but there would be none for the last known survivor of the evil guild. Kane lifted him by his hair, and he brought his hands up to try to pry the grip loose, kicking his feet and screaming. Having heard enough, Kane plunged a bony hand through the man's chest, easily breaking his sternum and ripping out his heart.

He went limp and hung there, the light fading from his eyes as he stared at his heart, now presented before him. Kane tightened his grip on the bloody organ, squashing it and spraying Riggs's face with blood. The corpse formerly known as Riggs didn't notice.

Kane released the dead man and turned toward the door of the mausoleum as flames lapped through the edges of the trapdoor. Smoke was quickly filling the small space. Kane made a powerful wave toward the tomb's door, and it flew off its hinges, landing far away with a loud crash. He floated out of the mausoleum, his feet barely a foot above the ground, and when he cleared the threshold, he floated straight up into the night sky. Cassandra rushed out of the tomb to see where her now powerful father had gone, but he was nowhere in sight.

The vision faded once more.

BALE ARRIVES

A MERE FIFTY YARDS AWAY FROM WHERE CASSANDRA'S SLEEPING form tossed and turned in a troubled sleep on the cave floor, Matilda dragged a battered and bruised Binta out of the magical cottage they'd lived in the last few weeks. Cass and Ronnis followed closely behind, concerned about what she would do next. Matilda had finally awakened from Binta's near-fatal attack that had left her unconscious for days. She had awakened under the care of Cass and Ronnis, who attended to her the best they could. The pain was overwhelming when she first opened her eyes, and it took her some time to adjust to the dim light in the room offered by the fireplace.

She had to administer a healing spell to alleviate most of the pain in her head. Cass recounted the story for Matilda of how Binta had used a telekinetic power to attack Matilda with a rock and probably would have killed her if not for Cass interfering. Binta was powerful and only controllable by Cass, which meant she had to go. Matilda couldn't keep her around any longer, despite the fun Cass and Ronnis had with her. She stood at the edge of the summit of Witch's Rise, near where she believed Cassandra to be hiding. She threw Binta down in front of her, and the girl landed hard on her hands and knees, crying out with the pain as her skin tore from the impact. Matilda grabbed Binta's hair and pulled her to a kneeling position, holding a knife to her throat.

"Cassandra Rho! Come out, or I'll kill your girlfriend!" Matilda demanded.

"Matilda, no," Cass pleaded nearby.

"Do not come any closer, Cass, or I will slit her throat."

Cass and Ronnis stopped, and Cass put her hands in front of her as if to indicate she wouldn't interfere. Still, Matilda knew how much Cass enjoyed tormenting the young woman and didn't discount the idea that she'd try something foolish.

"Matilda, please, this won't work," Cass said.

"I'm tired of waiting. I'm done with the games. Cassandra comes out now, or her little whore girlfriend dies. It's a win-win situation for me. I either capture Cassandra and complete this exhausting search or kill this annoying distraction. Binta is far too dangerous to keep alive."

Ronnis crossed his arms over his chest and wore a smirk. It was one of the few times in recent days that he wasn't wearing his mask. He carried it, and Matilda noticed he didn't have the powerful Black Adder. She deciphered two things from that: one, he valued the mask more because he was so embarrassed by his disfigurement; and two, he had no plans to try to stop her if she did kill the little whore. She only needed to focus on Cass, and the pain in her temple told her that Binta must die.

Binta was scared and showed no signs of fighting back. Matilda didn't know if that was because she was powerless due to Cass's proximity or if she was faking. Binta was powerful, and Matilda believed she was hiding her abilities, making her even more dangerous. Matilda couldn't take any chances that the girl would interfere or even prevent Cassandra's capture.

"Last chance, Cassandra! Surrender to me, and I'll release her," Matilda said.

She waited for a response, but the only reply was the slight whistle of the air blowing through the rock walls. Matilda's anger boiled, and her patience thinned. She took Binta's left arm and sliced it from her wrist to her elbow. The cut was deep and would be fatal. Binta screamed and brought her right arm around to grab Matilda's hand. With the power of Marnelphion pumping through Matilda's veins, the girl had no chance of stopping her.

Blood gushed from the wound as Matilda released the pathetic wretch. She turned to Cass, whose shoulders visibly slumped, but she didn't interfere. Ronnis stood passively by with an amused look on his face.

"Let's make a trade, Cassandra. You for her," Matilda said, pointing her knife at Binta, who cradled her arm and rocked back and forth to ease the pain.

Matilda waited with a smirk. She knew this would coax Cassandra from her hole. Her girlfriend would die without healing. Her wicked smile faded as the moments passed. Matilda knew her prey was nearby and had to be witnessing the torture her friend was enduring, yet she still did nothing to stop it. Of course, Matilda had no intent of releasing Binta; the girl would die on the mountain range in short order. However, she was giving Cassandra no choice but to surrender or watch her friend's murder. With no answer forthcoming, Matilda angrily pulled back on Binta's hair once more and put the knife to her throat. Binta's eyes streamed rivers of silent tears, and her arm gushed blood, despite the girl's efforts to stem the flow.

"Your silence speaks volumes about your feelings for this one. Binta obviously means nothing to you. Now she dies unless you crawl out of your filthy hole."

Matilda waited for an answer, her fingers grasping the knife so tight that her hand shook. The sharp edge cut slightly into Binta's delicate neck, which spurred a pathetic whimper from the tortured girl. Still, Cassandra did not answer. Matilda prepared to end the standoff and applied pressure with the knife. She'd hoped to trick Cassandra into surrendering, but the ruse had failed. Nevertheless, Matilda had to kill the dangerous girl. She would have to find another way to capture Cassandra.

She pressed the blade into Binta's soft flesh, starting another stream of blood. Binta tried to squirm free but to no avail; she was growing weak from the loss of blood. Before the knife could cut too deep, she heard footsteps approaching behind her, and a voice called out, "I hope that's not Cassandra Rho."

It was male, but it wasn't Ronnis's voice. Matilda withdrew the knife and dropped Binta, who crumpled to the ground. She knew the voice, and her eyes grew wide. She couldn't turn around and stood over Binta, only a few feet from the cliff face. There was no sound other than the desert wind buffeting her. Then the footsteps continued their approach, sounding like an army. Still, Matilda couldn't turn and face the new arrivals. She swallowed hard and turned the bloodied knife over in her hands nervously.

The newcomers finally stopped once they were very near. It was Bale, she knew, without turning. Bale was a man she despised despite being a devout worshipper of Marnelphion. His appearance could only mean one thing—Marnelphion was replacing her! Her mind swam, and her breathing became labored. How could this be? She had the blood of her god coursing through her veins; she was the chosen for this task, hand-selected by Marnelphion. She should see it through!

Matilda's surprise slowly faded and was replaced by anger once more. She glanced down at Binta, and the girl tried moving away from her, still trying to stop her lifeblood from spilling out. Her eyes fluttered, and she was near unconsciousness. She was no longer a threat, but Matilda still considered running the dagger through her chest. Instead, she steeled her resolve and slowly turned around. Sure enough, ten feet away was Bale, the arrogant, unpredictable man Matilda hadn't seen in over ten years. He was there to replace her, she did not doubt that. She watched as his men spread out behind him, blocking the trail that led down the mountain. Ronnis and Cass stood to the side, helpless and confused by their presence. They said nothing, recognizing the robes of Marnelphion that the new arrivals wore.

A few held torches, giving Bale an ominous look, something he didn't need assistance with. He was naturally intimidating with his metal teeth, which now reflected the flickering torchlight as he smiled. He was tall, and she knew he was equally strong. He was a thorn in her side and had returned to her at the worst possible time. Matilda couldn't let him take over the sacrifice when she was this close.

"Well?" he asked, sporting that evil smile she remembered.

"Well, what?" she asked, subconsciously brandishing the bloodied knife toward him.

"Is that the Rho girl?" he asked, nodding toward Binta.

Matilda took a slight glance behind her and quickly dismissed the notion. "Of course not; that would ruin the sacrifice."

"Yes, it would."

"Why are you here, Bale? The sacrifice is mine! Marnelphion brought me back from the gates of hell to complete this, and I intend to do it."

"Relax, Matilda, I'm not here to take over. I'm here to get you back on track."

"What are you talking about? I have Cassandra Rho nearly in my grasp. I don't need you."

"Actually, you do. You have grown sloppy, and I'm here to clean up your mess. The sacrifice is still yours if you are deemed worthy."

"You speak with a forked tongue, Bale! As usual, you spit lies. Nothing about what I do is sloppy. I am in control and do *not* need your assistance," Matilda answered, now considering running the knife through her old adversary's chest.

"That is not how Marnelphion sees it," Bale said, his smile growing wider and his teeth more prominent.

A figure flew out of the shadows to land on his shoulder. Matilda's heart dropped into her stomach—it was an imp. That meant that Marnelphion was with Bale. The knife nearly fell from her grasp as her eyes were transfixed on the mighty creature. Matilda knew what she had to do. If she failed the test, she would die. She had felt confident that she was Marnelphion's hero, but now, with the imp choosing Bale, she was suddenly doubtful.

She dropped her knife but didn't hear it clang to the mountain floor. She was focused on the imp as it smiled mischievously, its tail wagging over its head. Matilda knew the ritual of a Marnelphion imp, so she slowly stuck out her hand, palm up, and waited. She couldn't control her trembling. Was all her work for nothing? Did Marnelphion still trust her? Thoughts flittered through her mind like butterflies.

Then, the imp took flight from Bale's shoulder. It flew toward her upraised hand, and time slowed for Matilda. She could see the flap of the imp's wings as it made the short distance in just a few pumps. The tail shot forward, and Matilda knew what venom it contained. It never landed on her but flew past her hand and struck it with the barbed tail. Matilda didn't move or follow the path of the imp. Instead, she focused on the immense pain coursing through her hand and waited for death to call her. If Marnelphion still had faith in her, she would live; if not, her heart would stop when the venom entered her system. It took only a few moments for her to find her answer.

The pain was horrific, but the venom didn't affect her. With a smile, she turned to find the imp had landed on Binta's unconscious form and was sucking the blood from her gashed forearm. Its tail gently rubbed on her naked belly as if the creature were trying to soothe her while it sucked out her life's blood.

"I am still the chosen!" she said to Bale, presenting her bleeding palm.

He nodded and smiled. "As I told you, I am only here to get you reorganized."

"I don't need your help, Bale."

"Marnelphion disagrees. Why else would he send an imp from Nesin to me instead of you?"

She half turned to regard the imp, who was now licking the spilled blood from Binta's breasts. "What do you know?" she asked Bale.

"I know that you have lost control of Nesin, for Neclesious was one of the imps assigned to guard your fortress. He fled and may be the only imp to survive the uprising of the prisoners you held there."

"What uprising?"

"While you chased the Rho girl, the prisoners escaped, and Nesin is vacant."

"How? I had it guarded well, and the prisoners had no way of escape," Matilda argued, trying to absorb the stunning news.

"According to our new friend, Neclesious, the virgins led the uprising, along with your pet vampire," Bale said with a wicked smile.

Matilda let the words sink in, shocked that Nesin was lost. How long had it been since she and Cerus left the fortress to hunt down Cassandra? It had been a few months. Perhaps her focus on tracking Cassandra *had* made her sloppy. Maybe she needed Bale and his men. She looked over Bale's shoulder to the many men watching, all priests of Marnelphion. A feeling of relief washed over her, and her heart opened to the possibility that Bale and his men were there to help, not stop her.

"Where are Cerus and his men?" Bale asked, looking around.

Matilda's thoughts refocused on her husband at the mention of his name. She turned to her left to where the Yaddaton Desert loomed at the base of the small mountain. It was dark, and she couldn't hope to see anything. Even if the sun was at its zenith, she knew she couldn't see Cerus from the vantage point. But he was there, somewhere far below, petrified and waiting for her to free him.

She turned back to Bale and whispered, "We should talk."

Bale nodded and commanded his men to set up camp. They had a covered wagon drawn by two horses and loaded with supplies. They were efficient and organized and began unloading the wagon and building a fire while others set a perimeter watch. As they worked, Matilda stole another glance at Binta, who had to be near death by then. Binta was still unconscious and bleeding, and now the imp was shaking her wounded arm over her face and breasts, coating them in fresh blood, then dropping her arm long enough to lick up the mess.

"I agree. However, we must start purging these non-believers," Bale said, waving a hand toward Cass and Ronnis.

"They are friends and allies to the cause."

"Regardless, I will make this decision so you can focus on the task. That's why I'm here," Bale said, holding up his right palm so she could see the healing wound of the imp's sting.

Matilda understood that he was right. If he deemed Cass and Ronnis a distraction, he would kill them. He was there at Marnelphion's will, and she wouldn't stop him. Perhaps Cass and Ronnis had served their purpose. He approached Cass first as three priests surrounded Ronnis, who now wore his mask but was still weaponless. Both seemed to understand the danger that Bale presented.

"And why should we suffer your presence, beautiful one?" Bale asked Cass.

"I hate Cassandra, and I want her dead. Matilda has also promised I am her torturer, and I plan to see it through," Cass said, her voice growing louder, obviously panicking at the thought of losing that opportunity.

"You? What do you have to do with anything, my dear? You are a non-believer and have no rights within this company," Bale said, motioning with his hands to the surrounding priests.

Cass looked to Matilda for help, but Matilda could only shrug. She couldn't help Cass; she would have to plead her case. "I have helped corner Cassandra here, and without me, Matilda wouldn't have been close. That is the deal—I help catch her, and I get to torture her," Cass argued, the desperation rising with each passing word.

"I see no need to keep you now unless you have some worth I haven't thought of," Bale threatened, his smile melting away and a few priests moving closer to Cass.

"She is my slave!" Cass said, pointing to Binta, where the imp was still playing.

"I'm afraid your slave is dead."

"Not if you heal her and get that thing off her."

The imp perked its head up before smiling and sticking its tongue deep into Binta's wound. She moaned, indicating she was indeed still alive.

"See! She lives. Please heal her. She's valuable to us!"

"No, Bale, she's too powerful. Let her die," Matilda intervened.

"That pathetic creature is powerful?" Bale asked doubtfully.

"She is," Cass said. "But I can control her. I can force her to do things sexually, and she's quite proficient at them. Perhaps that is enough reason to keep her alive for you and your men?"

"Interesting. How can you do this if the whore is powerful enough to worry Matilda?"

"With this," Cass said, showing him the small flask of demon milk.

"Perhaps I will take that and control her myself."

"You could try. But I don't think Marnelphion would be happy with that decision."

Bale chuckled, as did the nearby priests, who all sensed a kill was imminent. "Then enlighten me, young lady, what purpose do you truly serve?"

"I'm closer to your god than you might think, and I will be one of his chosen ones once he arrives," Cass said, the whites and pupils of her eyes suddenly turning black.

The change gave Bale and the priests pause as they watched Cass's metamorphosis. After her eyes turned pupilless and dark, two tiny horns sprouted from her forehead, and lastly, she unfolded her large bat-like wings. Bale's eyes widened as he witnessed the transformation, and he appeared amazed yet pleased with what he saw.

"Magnificent," he said, sighing, and the surrounding priests looked upon Cass's enhanced form with a newfound appreciation.

"Forgive my doubting nature, Cass. I'm here to protect Matilda and ensure she completes her mission. Now I see that you are truly an ally of our cause, obviously sent by Marnelphion," Bale said, stepping close and gently running the back of his hand across her cheek.

"I hope that you and I can grow close as we continue our unholy quest to bring our lord back to the playground of the human world," he added with a smile.

"Not a chance," Cass said, "unless you save her."

She pointed to Binta's still form, where her new appearance seemed to hold Neclesious's attention. The imp still sat upon Binta's chest but no longer played with the dying woman. Instead, the imp wore a suspicious look and didn't seem pleased with Cass. It flew to hover near Bale, its nostrils flaring as it took in Cass's scent.

"Half-blood," the imp screeched, pointing a clawed finger at her.

"This half-blood will wring your neck, imp," Cass said, not backing down from the insult.

"She's not nepalin. She is a tainted half-breed," the imp complained, landing on Bale's shoulder, his tail wagging menacingly.

"She is perfect, Neclesious, and a strong ally if I allow it," Bale said, still staring longingly at Cass.

The imp spat but said no more, possibly seeing the wisdom in Bale's reasoning. Matilda thought about taking that opportunity to stab Binta and end the threat before Bale made the erroneous decision to save her. She looked for her knife that she'd dropped, only to find that one of the priests held it and wagged a finger at her with a shake of his head. None of her priests would have defied her as this one did; Matilda knew she had to follow Bale's wishes, even if she was still in charge of the Great Summoning.

She realized then how careless she had indeed been. Her priests were all dead, having sacrificed themselves to become powerful undead guardians she left behind at the barbarian tribe. They watched over prisoners that may or may not still be there. She had lost Cerus and Nesin. There were still followers of Gorl with her undead minions, but they might have left without Cerus to lead them. If that was the case, her undead guardians would probably be destroyed, and her barbarian prisoners would have escaped. Things were falling apart around her, and she hadn't realized because of her desperation to catch Cassandra. She decided she would pose no threat to the priest who held her knife. She bowed and stepped away, suddenly overwhelmed with how much she had lost in the last few months.

Bale went to Binta, but it took him a long time to pull his gaze from Cass, who remained in her half-demon form. She looked exquisite, Matilda could not deny. The girl barely wore anything and showed most of her perfect figure to Bale. Her allure was probably the only thing that prodded Bale into action. After all, Matilda knew the man was not in the habit of saving people. He knelt and picked up Binta's injured arm, checking for a pulse.

"She is cold," he whispered.

"We feast on her organs, then," Neclesious hissed, still perched on Bale's shoulder.

"No," Bale said with a slight shake of his head. "She lives. There is a slight pulse."

Cass rushed up to Bale, and several priests followed in case she threatened their leader. Ronnis tried to move, but priests brandishing wicked serrated daggers quickly surrounded him. He held his ground, raising his hands slightly to indicate he would cause no trouble. Cass knelt beside Binta, a concerned look on her pretty face. Matilda didn't know if she was trying to maintain Bale's attention to manipulate him or if she were genuinely concerned she would lose her sex slave and the stay atop the mountain would become much more drab for her and Ronnis. The one thing Matilda knew was that Cass cared nothing for Binta.

Bale nodded to Cass and whispered, "Dear Marnelphion, I don't ask for healing much because neither you nor I believe in it. However, I ask that you give me the strength to heal this wretch, not to save and protect her, but to further your will by torturing and abusing her. Please heal her arm, but not in a good way. I ask that you leave a nasty scar and that it will pain her until the day she dies."

A spell unfolded in answer to his request, making his hands glow brightly. He held Binta's injured arm in them, and the energy slowly seeped into the wounded girl. As the brightness in his hands diminished, the nasty gash in her arm closed. Binta moaned slightly and turned her head back and forth as if the process pained her. She never regained consciousness through the procedure and appeared as if in a deep sleep. At its conclusion, her arm was whole again. An angry red line of scar tissue ran the length of her petite arm, and Bale smiled at his master's work.

Bale made eye contact with Cass, who wore a big smile. "Thank you, that was impressive," she said.

Bale stood, and Cass followed, no longer concerned with Binta.

"She is a threat to us and our cause as long as she lives. I task you with keeping her under control. She will never leave your side, and I always want her arms bound. If you do not abide by these rules, I will kill her myself. Do you understand, Cass?"

"Yes, of course."

The imp spat at her again and growled, showing his teeth. Cass only stared hatefully at the creature.

"Relax, Neclesious, there will be others you may torture," Bale said, trying to defuse the imp's displeasure in Binta being saved.

Bale motioned to one of the priests, who brought rope and carelessly flipped Binta over. She didn't awaken and moved very little, only showing discomfort when the priest roughly tied her freshly healed arm. Matilda was impressed with the priest's knot-tying proficiency. When he finished, he dragged Binta to the newly lit fire and laid her beside it. He produced a blanket from the wagon and tossed it to Cass, then melded back into line with the other followers of Marnelphion.

It was cold on Witch's Rise as fall set in, and the higher elevation made it very uncomfortable. Binta wore only her underwear, and Matilda knew she had to be cold. Cass seemed to consider giving her the blanket but thought better of it, showing the newly arrived priests her cruel side by keeping it. Binta's proximity to the fire would keep her from freezing to death as Cass folded her wings and wrapped the blanket around her shoulders.

Bale smiled with approval, catching Cass's eye once more. She seemed to welcome the attention, whether to keep herself alive or attempt to seduce the hideous man, Matilda couldn't tell. Bale strolled over to Ronnis next, who was surrounded by the priests. He stood tall and proud before Bale, but Matilda knew he had to be nervous. He had no weapon, and she knew he would be much more confident with the Black Adder strapped to his side.

"And who might you be, masked one?" Bale asked.

"Ronnis D'Breeth."

Bale was taking charge of eradicating things that might not interest Marnelphion, and Matilda had to respect that. She wanted to vouch for Ronnis's character since they would have lost Cassandra's trail in Mecca-Loraine without him. She knew her opinion wouldn't influence Bale, so she remained quiet.

"And why should we suffer your presence? You aren't a worshipper of Marnelphion."

"Because I hate Cassandra Rho. She has taken everything from me and ruined my life. I want to see her dead, and I support your cause if the result is just that."

"Why the mask?"

"Cassandra attacked me a few years ago, one of many injustices I have endured at her hands."

The imp still sat atop Bale's shoulder, and Matilda was sure if Bale wasn't enough of an imposing figure, the imp added to Ronnis's nervousness. Cass glanced Matilda's way, silently asking if she could somehow support their ally. Matilda shook her head slightly and broke eye contact. Cass looked on, intrigued, but seemed to understand Ronnis's fate was his own, and they couldn't help him.

"Remove it," Bale said, taking a step closer.

Ronnis stood momentarily petrified as the imp grinned and waved his venomous tail. Ronnis slowly found the courage to ease the mask off his face. Bale's smile widened when he witnessed the terrible wound.

"That must have hurt, and your anger with her is well founded. However, I see fools such as you every day, and I bet you're thinking that you want to kill her yourself, maybe even have your way with her. Is that what's going through your mind, Ronnis D'Breeth?"

"Of course. But I have tried twice and have failed twice. I'm no longer interested in exacting my revenge personally. I'll gladly let Matilda handle that as long as I witness her death."

"And why should I trust or even believe you?" Bale said, motioning with a hand to one of the priests.

A wiry little man stepped forward with an evil smile that reminded Matilda of the imp. He produced one of the serrated daggers she'd witnessed several carrying. She knew that Marnelphion preferred the weapon because it was easy to gut victims with. Cerus had used one to slaughter the inhabitants of Tara a few years ago, and the Sinnis priestesses more recently. She knew what damage the weapon could cause.

"I want Cassandra captured, tortured, and ultimately killed, just like you," Ronnis said, sweat forming on his brow.

"We have plenty of allies here to do just that. Why do we need you? What is keeping us from gutting you now?"

Ronnis looked around nervously as the five priests immediately surrounding him withdrew weapons similar to the dagger Bale waved in front of his face. The imp clapped his hands together and issued an evil little cackle. Bale nodded, and the priests began to move in.

"Because I would do anything to see it through! I would carve a hole in my other cheek to witness her demise!" Ronnis said, his voice cracking with desperation.

Bale stopped, and his smile became even more substantial and somehow more evil. He motioned with his hand for the priests to halt their advance. They complied in unison, backing away to give him some space. Once Bale determined they'd distanced themselves properly, he tossed his dagger at Ronnis's feet, and it rattled on the mountain's stony floor. Ronnis looked at the weapon stupidly, trying to comprehend what Bale intended.

"Do it," Bale finally said.

"Do what?" Ronnis asked in confusion.

"Cut a hole in your other cheek."

Ronnis's eyes widened. Neclesious clapped hysterically and jumped up and down on Bale's strong shoulder.

"Do it, and I'll know that I can trust your word," Bale said, patting a hand in the air to calm the imp.

Ronnis didn't move for a long time, and Matilda could see his breathing become slightly labored as if he considered undertaking the cruel deed. Matilda thought about interfering. If Ronnis did it, would he blame Matilda for his newest disfigurement? Before she could react, he grabbed the dagger and held it up, displaying it to Bale. The imp clapped some more.

"Go ahead, Ronnis, it's the only way I know for you to prove I can trust you," Bale prodded.

Ronnis brought the large dagger to his face with a slightly trembling hand. The only sounds were the howl of the wind and the continued clapping from Neclesious. He took a moment to make eye contact with Cass and then Matilda. His breathing became more ragged. Matilda could only shake her head, and he immediately looked away, probably understanding that no one would help him.

He instead focused on Bale and the hysterical imp. He opened his mouth as his labored breathing reached an animal-like level. Matilda knew he was trying to mentally prepare for the task. A growl issued from somewhere deep inside him, and he took the blade and stabbed it into his cheek with one quick motion. He screamed as blood gushed from his mouth and down his chin. Neclesious laughed and pointed at the pitiful man.

Ronnis started sawing his cheek, screaming all the while. Matilda assumed the louder he cried, the less he felt, as his mind focused on something other than the pain. He cut a circular piece of flesh the best he could as more and more blood ran down his face and dripped on his clothes and the rocky floor of the mountain. When Ronnis completed the macabre act, he threw the bloodied knife on the ground and, with a trembling hand, put the flesh that was once his left cheek into the palm of his hand. He presented it to Bale, who approached. Matilda found a new level of respect for the man at that moment.

"An incredible display, Ronnis D'Breeth!" Bale said cheerfully, seeming genuinely impressed.

Ronnis was breathing hard and grimacing. Tears began to flow down his cheeks as the pain got the best of him. Once Bale was before him, examining the self-inflicted mutilation, Neclesious snapped a hand to grab the severed flesh and stuff it quickly in his mouth, clapping and humming as he enjoyed the bloody snack. It looked like Ronnis would say something but he thought better of it. Instead, he dropped his hand to his side.

"I have a newfound respect for you, Ronnis. I didn't think you had it in you, but you've earned the right to travel alongside us," Bale said. He turned toward Cass and added, "Both of you have."

Ronnis couldn't speak and seemed to struggle with the pain. His breathing was still sporadic, and he occasionally blew a bloody bubble from either his nose or mouth, to the imp's delight.

"Do not heal him," Bale said, looking over the gathered priests. "I want the wound to heal on its own."

He then looked to Ronnis and grabbed him firmly by the shoulder. "Embrace the pain, and understand that it is your key to gaining what you want—Cassandra Rho. We will have her soon, do not doubt, and you will be there when we capture, torture, and kill her.

"It is also a symbol of our trust for one another. When you look in the mirror and see the wound Cassandra gave you, turn the cheek and see the other wound you had to endure because of her. Use that hate to assist us, not to hamper us in any way. I will not tolerate it. Do we understand each other?"

Ronnis looked at the dagger lying nearby, then back to Bale. He slowly nodded, and Bale clapped him on the back.

"Then we have an understanding. Men, these two are to be left unharassed. They are here because I will it. Cass, you and Ronnis are to watch over your slave there. If I catch her about without at least one of you beside her, I will kill her and remove you both from our group. Understand?"

Ronnis nodded, and Cass, still standing beside Binta, said, "Of course, that's what we've done for weeks now."

"Good. Matilda and I have much to discuss. Disciples of Marnelphion, set a perimeter. I want at least six of you to watch for Cassandra during two-hour shifts. Matilda believes she is here, on this mountaintop, but is hiding with the help of her weakling father. She cannot stay hidden for long."

"Hail Marnelphion!" the priests said in unison.

Bale motioned to the magical cottage, and as she walked toward it, Matilda glanced back and saw the efficiency of the new priests. They were some of the most devout known to exist. They were disciplined, just like her priests, but were more focused. She felt good about the idea of them being around. She knew she could relax in the cottage, and they would actively watch for Cassandra. She didn't have that confidence in Cass and Ronnis, fearing they would murder the girl upon sight. She took a glance at Binta, still unconscious and lying by the fire, the priests stepping over her as if she didn't exist. She seemed to be breathing normally, and Matilda wondered if sparing the powerful telepath was a good call on Bale's part.

She looked at Cass and Ronnis, who stood side by side near Binta, watching over her. Cass had reverted to her human form and remained wrapped in the blanket intended for Binta. Ronnis now held a cloth to his wounded face, probably obtained from one of the priests who would now respect them both as members of the group. She gave them a slight nod, and they nodded in return. For the first time in a long while, Matilda's heart began to fill with hope. Perhaps Bale and his men were the final cog in a machine that promised such sweet results. She entered the cottage, eager to speak with Bale and happy the imp followed. The door shut behind them, concealing them from sight.

JAK LAY ON HIS STOMACH, PEERING OVER THE GIANT DUNE THAT GAVE him a perfect view of his home, or what remained of it. The sun was high in the Yaddaton sky, and the last remaining members of his tribe were herded together and exposed to the beating sun. Many tents that belonged to the Serpent Tribe lay in shambles, and some were burned to the ground. The interlopers remained and continued to abuse the prisoners, people Jak knew and cared for, some even good friends.

That was upsetting enough for Jak to want to destroy all the invaders, slaughter them, and free his people, but that wasn't the worst part of the atrocity that lay before him. As the last few days had passed, he'd been forced to wait patiently as Gress, the new king of the Culiem Tribe, strategized the best method of attack. In those days of waiting, Jak witnessed the interlopers erect a ten-foot-tall pole and hang Maltor from it by the wrists. His king appeared dead to Jak, but he wasn't sure. Blood matted his head, back, and chest, and he'd hung from that pole for over two cycles of the sun. If he were alive, it would be barely so.

They had hung him there in front of the prisoners, and Jak reasoned it was to diminish morale or remind them that they were indeed at the mercy of their captors. Jak even thought that perhaps the invaders were trying to instigate a fight, to slaughter the old, weak, and infirm so they would not endure the burden of keeping watch over them. They seemed restless without their leaders, the small woman and the large man with the mighty spear. They had even become so bold as to drag Maltor's brides from the procreation tent and rape them at the foot of Maltor's pole. They seemed to grow more unruly and more brutal as the days passed.

The only thing that seemed to give the vicious outsiders pause was when the sun set and the moon took over the Yaddaton sky. At that time, they retreated to their tents, and six creatures of death, worse than the abomination he once knew as Vixa, roamed the desert settlement. They seemed comprised of the devil magic Cassandra possessed, making Jak think these invaders were tricksters, even more so than Cassandra had been. They floated unnaturally, and their skulls burned with a purple flame that never seemed to consume them. They only came out at night, and during the day, they disappeared into one of the larger tents Maltor used for entertaining guests from other tribes. The undead creatures were powerful and kept a watchful eye on the prisoners, so Jak was preparing an attack in the middle of the day when the creatures would be weak.

Finally, Gress was ready, so Jak surveyed the area again, looking for any deviation in routine from the previous two days. He found little, the only change being the increased viciousness of the interlopers. He gave the signal to Gress and the other members of the neighboring tribe who waited at the bottom of the dune. Everything was in place, and the unruly men holding his brethren captive were ripe for an attack. It was time to liberate what remained of his home. Gress nodded in confirmation, and Jak smiled. He had his eye on one of the invaders who appeared to be in charge without the real leaders.

That particular fool liked to taunt Maltor, having prisoners kneel before the pole from which Maltor hung and beat them until they cried for mercy. Maltor hadn't budged, and Jak had a feeling he was dead. But that mattered little to him now. The evil man was subjecting the remaining members of the tribe to whatever tortures he felt necessary. He was a coward and a weakling and was about to discover what happened when you declared war on the Serpent Tribe. The acting leader would be the first to die.

Jak stood and calmly reached to his back, where his quiver was strapped, and retrieved an arrow. He had obtained a few dozen of the well-made weapons at the site of the massacre his people had faced near the burial grounds. Now, he would use them to avenge all of those who had died during that attack. Jak was the finest archer the Serpent Tribe had, making him deadly with a bow, even at a range of nearly one hundred yards, his current distance from his target.

He stood tall atop the dune, took aim, and fired. Before the arrow reached its mark, some of the gathered interlopers noticed him and began to stir. Their leader was also alerted to his presence, and he stopped his beating of an elderly barbarian to turn toward Jak. As he did, the arrow found its mark, impaling him in the throat. Jak could imagine the surprised look on his face as he stumbled around holding his neck. Jak watched stone-faced, but on the inside, he was delighted with the shot. Soon, their wounded leader was face first in the sand, the fall impaling the arrow further through the back of his neck.

"That was for you, Maltor, my king and friend," Jak whispered as he notched another arrow.

He then looked to the sky and saw two swarms of fairies flanking the invaders, who were gathering their weapons and forming an attack stance.

They were too focused on Jak to notice the two small clouds of dangerous creatures several hundred feet above them. Jak fired another arrow, but it was only a distraction to keep their attention on him. They easily dodged the attack at that distance, but the fairies grew close. He smiled and grabbed another arrow as a small contingent of about two dozen vile men rushed up the dune. He fired twice more as they charged, killing another and wounding a third before turning and walking back toward Gress's men.

When the men of Gorl crested the dune, ready to unleash their pent-up anger on Jak, he stood casually with his giant sword at the ready and three hundred of Gress's men beside him. The first wave of Gorl warriors stopped and stared in surprise, and the ones behind them pushed them forward, not understanding the delay. It took a moment for the situation to register and for each interloper to understand their doom. However, they were warriors of Gorl, hearty and fearless. They made a circle, back to back, and waved on the barbarians. Jak recalled the battle at the burial site when they first met these warriors and how the witch had called for their dead to fight against them. There was no magic to help the fools this time. Now, they were outnumbered, and Jak would avenge his brethren who died fighting the zombies. Jak smiled and advanced along with Gress's men.

Just before he reached the Gorl warrior, he heard the commotion on the other side of the dune—the fairies had made their presence known. His vengeance and confidence in knowing they would slaughter these invaders of Yaddaton nearly cost him as his foe surprised him by throwing his spear. The Gorl warrior's aim was true, and Jak barely deflected enough of the spear to keep from being skewered. He clipped the weapon with his sword, and it drew a crease of blood on his upper thigh as it passed dangerously close.

The surprising Gorl warrior sprinted behind the spear, a serrated dagger now in his hand to finish him off. The warrior understood his doom, seeing that the spear had failed to hit its mark. Still, he didn't relent in his attack and ran straight for Jak, the dagger leading the way. Jak ran forward, up the dune, equally ready to defeat his foe. The Gorl warrior let out a crazed scream and threw the dagger just before they clashed. Jak turned slightly, and it embedded in his shoulder. He barely felt the bite of the wicked blade, concentrating only on his opponent.

Despite the fact he'd thrown all his weapons, the man launched himself at Jak, fearless and confident. Jak stabbed straight toward the warrior's gut, and his sword sank in deeply, the momentum of his attacker assisting with the ghastly wound. Soon, the two men stood eye to eye, Jak's sword buried in the man to the hilt. Time seemed to stop, and Jak looked the dying man in the eye. The interloper's look of surprise and pain spread a smile across Jak's face. He immensely enjoyed the feeling of his sword cutting through his flesh.

The sounds of battle swarmed them, but Jak was only interested in watching the light leave his victim's eyes. The man eventually fell, sliding off Jak's sword and lying dead at his feet. Jak spat on the man and said something he did not expect: "That was for Cassandra."

He moved away, leaving the dagger in his shoulder and helping Gress's men complete the onslaught. They made quick work of the overwhelmed warriors, then quickly climbed to stand atop the dune. The fairies had done their job as many Gorl warriors lay strewn about the sand at the base of the pole holding Maltor. The prisoners had also entered the fray, taking the spears of the dead interlopers and attacking alongside the fairies any Gorl warrior that remained. The barbarian prisoners were elderly and not as fast or skilled, but they were fighting for their lives and homes.

It made Jak proud as he took in the spectacle, but it broke his heart. They would win the day, thanks to the Culiem Tribe, but this was also the end of the Serpent Tribe. Gress's men charged down the dune, ready to continue the onslaught. Jak finally pulled the dagger from his shoulder and watched them go. He followed the wave of hearty barbarians, but the battle waned when he arrived. The interlopers were primarily dead, either from the fairies' venomous bites or barbarian blades.

Jak met one of the armed prisoners, an old barrel-chested blacksmith named Vral, son of Kem. He was nearly eighty, and his long grey hair lay matted to his neck and shoulders. Vral had forged Jak's sword, and when the two found each other in the chaos, Jak held his bloodstained blade up and nodded to the old barbarian. Vral grimly returned the nod, then looked up to Maltor's lifeless form hanging from the pole. Jak turned to regard his king as the fighting around them died.

"Give me a lift?" Jak asked.

Vral nodded, and they made their way to the pole. Maltor's bare feet hung at face level with Jak, and blood dripped from his toes, forming a red stain in the sand. The sight gave Jak hope as he understood Maltor had to be alive if he was still bleeding! Vral knelt so Jak could stand on his back. Once he had his balance, he was face to face with his king. The fighting stopped then; the barbarians must have noticed Jak's actions. They gathered around quickly, wanting to know if their king still lived. The men of the Culiem Tribe also looked on, curious.

Jak stopped and looked around briefly before turning back to Maltor. Dry blood caked the right side of his head, and he was missing an ear. His eyes were closed and his face bruised from the beatings the interlopers had administered. There was no doubt in Jak's mind that Maltor had lost his battle with the outsiders only because they cheated or used devil magic to weaken him. He had never seen Maltor lose a challenge or a fight. The sight broke his heart.

"My king?" Jak finally managed to say.

There was no answer, so Jak took his sword and sawed the ropes holding Maltor to the pole. Many of the remaining members of the Serpent Tribe gathered close to catch their king when he fell. They grabbed his legs, and as the ropes began to give and Maltor inched downward, they reached up and grabbed his waist.

Before Jak could complete the task, he heard Maltor whisper, "She's alive."

Jak nearly fell, caught off guard by Maltor's sudden spark of life. He smiled wide and there was a cheer from those gathered around, as their king was indeed alive.

Jak said, "Who, my king?"

"Cassandra, my queen."

Maltor returned the smile and nodded at his hands to indicate Jak should continue. Jak did, making quick work of the ropes that held Maltor to the pole. He fell gently into the waiting arms of the barbarians who supported and believed in him. They laid him in the sand, and one of them turned him on his side to examine the vicious wound in his back. The look of those witnessing the injury spoke volumes. Jak knew Maltor would need healing quickly if he were to survive. Jak turned to Gress, who was nearby, and made his way to stand before the young king. Jak knelt and bowed his head.

"Rise, proud warrior," Gress said.

Jak did and looked the king in the eye. "We are indebted to you, and we will honor the agreement you offered us, but I ask that you heal him."

Gress looked over to Maltor's still form and the many wide-eyed barbarians awaiting his response. After many uncomfortable moments, Gress sighed and motioned for the shamans to assist Maltor. They quickly went to the injured king and began healing, summoning every ounce of curing magic Strenna offered. Soon, Maltor was awake and aware of his surroundings. He lay in the sand for a few moments as the remaining members of his tribe pawed at him, overjoyed at his consciousness. A few women wept, and even some of the old, proud warriors became teary-eyed at the spectacle.

Maltor slowly sat as the shamans backed away. His people assisted him or began to before he waved them off. The proud king then stood on shaking legs to the gasps and murmurs from those witnessing his resolve. He looked close to death, with the side of his head still matted with blood and the garish wound in his back from Cerus's spear still bleeding, even after the extensive healing. Jak backed away as Maltor started to walk toward Gress, who crossed his arms over his chest as his guards gathered close.

It took Maltor a long while to make the small trek to stand before the much younger king. Jak couldn't believe Maltor was still alive, much less capable of standing and walking on his own. He had hung from the stake for several days without food or water, slowly bleeding out. He had baked in the intense Yaddaton sun, and anyone other than a proud native of the harsh, sandy world would never have survived the ordeal. But Maltor was no ordinary barbarian. He was prouder and more stubborn than anyone Jak had ever known. He was the same height as the new king and looked around the area, taking in the strangers from the Culiem Tribe before finally settling his eyes back on Gress.

"Gress, son of Plor," Maltor whispered, his throat dry and raspy.

Gress nodded and replied, "Maltor, son of Gron, former king of the former tribe of the serpent."

"Former?" Maltor asked, and Jak noticed the nearby guards bristling.

Gress stood his ground fearlessly and said, "Yes, I have made a deal with this one," pointing toward Jak.

Maltor's eyes followed the pointing finger to eventually fall on Jak, who wilted under Maltor's stern gaze. "What deal?" Maltor finally asked.

"Your fearless warrior, the lone one left in your once proud army, asked the Culiem Tribe for help to save you. I agreed, but only if the Serpent Tribe disbands and the Culiem Tribe absorbs the remaining folk," Gress explained.

There was an immediate uproar from the few remaining members of the Serpent Tribe. They shouted in denial and lifted the weapons they'd used to battle the interlopers: rocks, sticks, whatever they could find. They rallied behind Maltor, growling in defiance at the strange proclamation.

"Furthermore," Gress interrupted, "Maltor is banned from Yaddaton from this day forward."

There were further grumblings and increased shouting from the small group of tribe members. Maltor smiled at his tribe rallying behind him, and Jak saw Gress frown in response. Jak knew that if Maltor made a stand, all was lost. The remaining members of the Serpent Tribe were much older, and the Culiem Tribe was better armed and called the vicious fairies allies. To stand against the Culiems was suicide. Luckily, Maltor understood this, and he turned to face his people.

"My loyal members of the Serpent Tribe, I am proud of your determination, and it does my heart good to see you rally behind me once more against impossible odds," Maltor said.

"Draw a challenge circle, Maltor!" Blesk, the old tent-maker, yelled.

The others around him cheered and nodded their agreement. Although grey and feeble now, the man would have made a good king, Jak thought. He was charismatic and strong, and Jak momentarily worried that the older man would change Maltor's mind. However, Maltor raised his hands to his people and nodded.

"No, there has been enough bloodshed. It ends now. You are all safe with Gress; I have known him since he was a small child. He is honorable and just, and he will make you a great leader," Maltor said and looked back to Gress, who nodded in agreement.

"Where will you go, my king?" an old, haggard woman asked after many moments of silence.

"Do not concern yourselves with my well-being. I will leave the Yaddaton Desert as proud as ever, with my head held high. I have a destiny that will take me from the desert, never to return."

Maltor's words calmed the small crowd and subdued the fighting mood of Blesk and the other aging warriors of the group. They would follow his commands, regardless of how awful they felt about them. The proud tribe would be no more; it was hard for the people under Maltor's rule to grasp that reality. It brought a tear to Jak's eye as he witnessed their final realization that their tribe was no more than a memory.

There was silence among the barbarians of the now-lost Serpent Tribe, but Maltor stood firm before them, battered, bruised, and bleeding. He would be true to his word, Jak knew. He would honor the agreement for the safety of the few that remained. He cared and was honorable enough to see it through.

He turned to Gress and said, "There is one thing I must do before I leave the desert."

Gress frowned and said, "What is your last request, former king?"

If the barb stung Maltor, he didn't show it, and his focus settled on a nearby tent, which Jak knew contained the mighty creatures of undeath. Jak had watched them the last few nights, patrolling the area, toying with the prisoners, and displaying tremendous power. As they didn't venture out in the day, Jak believed they would be weaker now as the Yaddaton sun hung high in the sky.

"I will destroy the filth that haunts my home," Maltor said, nodding to the tent that housed the unnatural creatures.

Gress and his men turned to regard the large tent, the front flap blowing in the slight breeze, giving a glimpse of the interior. It was dark inside, but with each peek inside, they could make out the creatures roaming the darkness, agitated yet helpless in the midday sun. The purple devil magic burning their skulls licked the air, giving faint glimpses of the creatures. Their presence was unnerving, even for the hearty barbarians. Still, Maltor didn't flinch.

He turned to Gress with an outstretched hand and said, "Lend me a weapon, and I'll rid my… your land of these vermin."

The two kings stared intensely at each other as the rest waited for a response. After what seemed like an eternity to Jak, Gress nodded to his closest guard. The man returned the nod and presented his sword to Maltor, hilt first. Maltor took the weapon and nodded one last time to Gress.

Then he turned to Jak and said, "You have arrows?"

Jak smiled and reached over his shoulder to his quiver, bringing forth one of the arrows. He removed his bow from his back and notched the arrow, ready to serve however Maltor needed him.

"Burn it down," Maltor said, then walked to the tent, sword at the ready.

One of Gress's men assisted Jak in wrapping the arrowhead in cloth and setting it ablaze. Once burning, Jak notched the arrow and aimed. There was a moment before he let it fly when he saw his king standing at the front of the tent, waiting for the strike. He was ready to take on the evil that lurked inside. Maltor was a hero to Jak and any barbarian who called the Serpent Tribe their home. Killing the abominations would be his final task as king, even if it killed him. Jak let the arrow fly, which struck true, quickly igniting the camel-skinned structure.

Maltor stood unflinching as the tent became engulfed in flames. Thick black smoke billowed into the bright Yaddaton sky. Jak drew his sword and took a step toward his king. Gress was there suddenly, stopping him.

"No, proud warrior, this is Maltor's task. He asked for this one honor, and I have granted it. However, he will do it alone," Gress said.

Jak stood silently before replying, "Then his victory will be even more legendary."

Gress smiled at Jak and turned to watch the battle play out. Jak sheathed his weapon and stood beside the culiem king. His heart raced as the flames quickly diminished, revealing the perverted creatures of undeath that awaited Maltor. There were six wraiths of Marnelphion, and they hissed and shielded their eyes from the burning sun. The purple flames engulfing their heads seemed diminished in the daylight. They were disoriented as well, the sun seemingly disrupting their thought process. Jak noticed that they still wore the robes of what he assumed were the interlopers' shamans. They were black with human skulls depicted on them in white paint.

Maltor strode into the smoldering remains, picking up speed as he went. The Culiem Tribe and the remnants of the Serpent Tribe gathered around and took in the strange sight of a defeated and exiled king fighting for the freedom of people who were no longer his subjects. Jak wanted to rush in but understood this was Gress's call. The king allowed this and might stop it if Jak interfered.

One of the creatures finally noticed Maltor and rushed toward him, floating several feet above the desert sand. The flames on its head intensified as it centered its focus on Maltor. Its hands were suddenly engulfed with the magical flames, bringing them to bear against Maltor, and ready to claw the proud barbarian to pieces. The other five noticed this and soon joined their brethren, closing in on Maltor.

Maltor didn't flinch and looked like he wouldn't even wield his weapon, and Jak wondered for an instant if his king were giving up, preferring death over exile. But then Maltor moved with lightning speed as he brought his sword around in a sudden sweep, lopping off the right hand of the closest creature. The purple flame extinguished once the hand fell to the sand, black and lifeless, from the animated corpse. The beast hissed and swung its other claw at Maltor's face. Although severely injured and dehydrated, the former barbarian king was faster than expected for the undead creature. He ducked, kicked out hard, connecting with the creature's sternum, and knocked it back into two other closing wraiths.

Sensing an attack from behind, Maltor turned and swung mightily with a guttural roar, decapitating the closest one to him. The lifeless body fell to the sand, the skull rolling to the edge of the tent, the purple fire now extinguished. Four of the undead creatures flanked Maltor, with three creatures coming from one direction and one from another. He had no choice but to face the three. Jak winced as the lone creature behind him had an easy target.

Maltor grabbed the priestly robe of the one-handed creature and pulled it forth, onto his extended blade, all the way to the hilt. Then they were face to face, and Maltor only smiled into the creature's lifeless eye sockets. It raked Maltor's forearm with its one good hand, trying to break Maltor's hold. The barbarian ignored it as blood gushed from the new wound, and soon the thing began to tremble, and finally, the magical flames engulfing its head and lone hand faded to nothingness. It fell from Maltor's blade and onto the sand.

Maltor had destroyed two undead perversions, but the creature behind him grabbed his head, and the purple flames traversed from its hands to encompass Maltor's head. Jak knew what would happen once the transfer was complete because he'd seen one of the creatures do that before to a defenseless prisoner. It would spell doom for Maltor.

Jak's king, good friend, and former leader of the Serpent Tribe did not disappoint! He swung his sword at the two attacking undead before him, decapitating both with one mighty swing. Then, at the same time, he screamed that guttural war cry and rammed his head back and into the face of his attacker. Not only did he break the hold and disrupt the devil magic that threatened to burn him alive, but he also dislocated the thing's jaw. He turned to face it as it stood dumbfounded, its jaw hanging at an unnatural angle. Maltor smiled and roared once more as the Serpent Tribe barbarians all cheered, as did a few of the Culiem Tribe. Jak gauged Gress's reaction to that outburst, but the king seemed enthralled by the battle.

Jak smiled, understanding that Maltor would be victorious. He had dominated the creatures, the most potent adversaries the interlopers had to offer, and he had done it injured and without help. He threw his sword like a spear, and it struck a creature in the chest. It fell to the ground, landing on its feet, but then began staggering around, nearly destroyed. Maltor strode confidently in to finish the fight.

The smile melted from Jak's face as he realized Maltor had only fought five of the nasty beasts, and the sixth one emerged from the billowing black smoke at the back of the tent remains. It seemed more substantial than the others and was more cunning, hiding until an opportunity presented itself. Jak wanted to cry out, but his voice caught in his throat as the creature flew up behind Maltor without a sound. Several Serpent Tribe barbarians yelled out to their king, but Maltor either didn't hear the warnings or thought they were screams of support for his fantastic deed.

Just before he reached the staggering and diminishing creature that wore his sword like a badge of defeat, the wraith from behind plunged a flaming claw into the open wound on Maltor's back. The wound was raw, and Maltor indeed felt the attack as he roared in defiance. He stopped, and his body shuddered as the purple energy began to burn his insides. With his free hand, the creature grabbed Maltor by the hair, and the energy flowed from that hand to Maltor's skull. The badly injured king was defeated just as quickly as it looked like he would win.

"My king," Jak whispered, his arms and legs numb and frozen in place by the spectacle.

Suddenly, Maltor found his strength as he grabbed the clawed hand that held his hair in a deathly clutch with both his hands and, with another roar of defiance, began to pull the hand away from his skull. The creature pulled a generous portion of hair from Maltor's scalp as he did. But Maltor was able to free the connection, and the purple fire quickly faded from his head before it could fully form and burn him. However, the creature had several fingers in Maltor's wounded back, and smoke poured forth from that burning touch.

Maltor's eyes were wide as fresh blood from his head trickled down his face. He held the creature's hand tight and bent it at an awkward angle. The wraith hissed and broke his connection with Maltor's wounded back to use that now-free hand to try to pry Maltor's grip from his bent wrist. To Jak's horror, he saw as Maltor turned fully to face the beast that fire poured from Maltor's spear wound. Black smoke rose from his back, and the stench of burning flesh became thick in the air. Maltor didn't seem to notice.

With a sickening snap, the phantom's wrist broke and dangled from its arm. The flame encasing it extinguished, and the creature roared in anger and fear. The barbarian didn't give the beast time to recover—he stepped up and smashed it in the face with a mighty swing of his fist. Teeth flew, and the creature floated haphazardly around Maltor, trying to find its bearings. Maltor grabbed it by the robe and pulled it forward, smashing his forehead into its face. The creature grabbed his hair again, trying to channel the purple energy into his skull.

Maltor somehow ignored the attack and continued to headbutt the thing. His forehead became a bloody mess as he flew into a rage, a roar escaping his parched lips. He repeatedly smashed the creature's face and continued to do so even when it fell limply to the sand. Maltor's firm grasp on the creature kept it from falling entirely. Although it took many long moments, Maltor finally relented his attack.

He was a mess, with so much blood covering his face and matting his hair that only the whites of his broad, wild eyes indicated he was alive. He slowly turned toward the remaining undead filth that was now crawling away in the sand, the entirety of the blade of Maltor's sword sticking up from its back. To Jak's relief, Maltor's back was no longer on fire, and the open wound was now just a mass of blackened flesh. How his friend continued to stand was beyond belief.

Maltor staggered toward the last wraith, which could barely use its clawed hands to drag itself away. He finally reached the thing and smashed its skull with a powerful stomp. There was a loud pop as the bones broke, and Maltor continued his assault, cutting his foot badly on the broken bones. When he was eventually satisfied that the creature was dead, he turned to his people and let loose the loudest, most guttural scream ever heard in the Yaddaton Desert. He then fell face first to the sand.

Jak rushed to him, as did the few remaining members of the Serpent Tribe. They gently turned him over and examined his wounds. Gress made his way over, along with his shamans and many guards, and stood above the mortally wounded king.

Jak looked up to the proud and astonished young king of the Culiem Tribe and said, "He lives."

Jak instantly noticed the shock on Gress's face, but it was short-lived. He quickly motioned to his shamans, who began healing the former king. Jak and the others stepped back to give them room. Jak knew that they faced the impossible. Maltor was far too injured to live through his wounds. But he also knew that if anyone could do it, Maltor could.

SUFFERINGS

KRINGUS STOOD AT THE STERN OF *HOPE*, THE MAGNIFICENT ship that carried the New Order and their crew to Varish in search of Cassandra Rho. Captain Ruby, First Mate Wendle, Von, Lenore, Daro, Sasha, and Max joined him. He looked over the gathered crew on the main deck just a few steps below him. Penelope, Arrin, Erik, and Marcus were walking among them, trying to settle any who were upset. Their mission had quickly proven disastrous, and Kringus appreciated the work of his wife and friends, who were attempting to keep everyone calm.

The crew had furled the sails, and the boat bobbed helplessly in the middle of the deep sea. Contrary to its name, the great ship was sinking quickly, and there was no hope for them to find. The hull had been breached in a troublesome area, underneath crates of foodstuffs and other supplies, making repairing the hole impossible. Three crew members had drowned trying to stem the flow of water into the hull before the king called off the repair attempt. Kringus never took the death of his subjects lightly, and the damage to the ship was intentional. All the lifeboats had been compromised as well, sealing their doom. That was what troubled the king the most: that someone had done this deliberately, with the intent of killing them all.

Still, if they were the chosen group to battle Marnelphion, how could their adventure already be over? He wondered how someone could have bested them so easily. He suspected Inuentas and hoped to have a chance to interrogate the evil creature. But he knew the chances of that were not good.

The sun was high in the noon sky, and the water was calm. He peeked over the rail at the gently lapping waves and noticed the waterline slowly creeping closer to the deck. About six feet of hull was still visible above the water at the captain's deck and less than two at the main deck. Kringus suspected they had less than an hour before the ship sank. He wasn't a sailor but knew enough of the ocean and boats to know that the outlook was bleak. He spotted Penelope in the crowd below him again as she comforted a hysterical sailor. She must have sensed him as she looked up and smiled. He smiled back. What more could he do? His wife was a saint and was always positive despite how bad things were.

His thoughts were interrupted as Ruby told Wendle, "There is no excuse, Wendle. You are in charge of the safety of this ship. How did this happen under our very noses?"

The first mate was at a loss for words and only shook his head dejectedly. Kringus did not blame him for the disaster and did not want the guilt of this tragedy on the young man's shoulders. He was about to say something when Max, one of the newest members of the New Order, beat him to it. Max was the former sheriff of Oldorburg and continued to impress Kringus at every turn.

"With all due respect, Captain, this is no time to point fingers. We should find a solution to the problem and not focus on what has already transpired."

Kringus noticed the look Ruby gave Max and understood that the former sheriff had struck a nerve. The captain was about to reply with a rebuttal but finally calmed and nodded, her face flush. "You're right, Max. Wendle, I apologize. I never thought I would lose a ship, much less my crew and wonderful friends of the New Order. I'm ashamed and didn't mean to take it out on you."

"I deserve your wrath, Captain; I let you and everyone else down," Wendle said, nearing tears.

Kringus was now behind Wendle and clamped a hand on his shoulder, startling him. "It is no one's fault. We blame no one for our predicament," the king said. He then turned to Ruby and added, "All is not lost. Victoria and Baxter have a potential solution, remember?"

Kringus had sent them out on Baxter's flying carpet several hours earlier in a desperate attempt to find land or possibly a vessel to rescue them. Their prolonged absence did not sit well with the king. Before they left, they'd shared a piece of information with him, Penelope, and the captain. They had a magical device that could save them, but its effects were chaotic, and they desired an alternative, so they agreed to take the carpet and survey the area first.

"Aye, my king, but neither is confident in its ability to save us, and it seems only an act of desperation to use it," Ruby replied.

Kringus nodded his agreement and forced a smile. "Let's give them a chance. Perhaps they will find an alternative. If not, we'll soon discover what strange device the fate of this ship might rest on."

Ruby nodded and tried to smile as well. She looked out to the main deck, where several crew members leaned over the railing, peering into the cold, dark waters that might become their tomb. Kringus understood the pain on her face; they held similar roles on this mission, and each felt responsible for the lives on the ship.

He managed to tear his eyes away from the captain, not needing the distraction, and turned to find his beautiful wife walking up the steps. The bottom of her dress was wet, and he realized then that water was trickling over the main deck in several places. They didn't have an hour as he first thought—they were minutes away from sinking. Penelope was a vision from the heavens, her red hair cascading over her shoulders to spill on her green dress. He loved that dress and hated that it might be the one she would die in.

Before she reached him, he turned to Von and Lenore and said, "I know we left our gear and armor below in case the worst happens and we have to tread water. Do you think it's also wise to leave all cumbersome weapons on the deck, such as swords and bows?"

Von answered, "You suggest we take only small weapons, such as daggers and knives?"

Before Kringus could respond, Penelope was beside him and answered for her husband. "Yes, cousin, it will be difficult to swim with large weapons, so we must forsake them. Please relay that information to the captain and the New Order so we may all prepare properly."

Von and Lenore shared a glance, but as always, their faces remained expressionless, and they turned back to Penelope and nodded. Both removed their swords and finely made elven bows, which Kringus knew they would never part with under normal circumstances. They placed them neatly by the railing and moved on to tell the captain.

Kringus felt Penelope's fingers intertwine his. "Our situation is desperate," she said.

"Yes, we all feel it. The captain is guilt-ridden, as is Wendle."

"As are you," Penelope added.

He looked into her beautiful green eyes and saw encouragement, even under the worst circumstances. He turned fully toward his wife and took her tiny hands in his. She was his everything. He needed her more now than ever, and she was there as always. He placed a hand on the side of her face, and she closed her eyes and pressed against his touch.

"When the time comes for us to abandon ship and tread water, our outlook will become dire. It would be best if you promised me that you, Victoria, Baxter, and whoever else can fit on that magical carpet will fly away to safety. Use those beautiful wings to save yourself from this fate."

Penelope opened her eyes, took his hand from her face, and kissed it. "I will not leave you."

"The last two people leaving this shipwreck for safety are Ruby and me. I will not have you die senselessly. You and Victoria can fly and possibly secure several more people between you with the help of Baxter and his carpet," Kringus said sternly.

"I—"

"Will listen to your husband," Kringus interrupted. "You know it's the prudent thing to do. You must carry on the mission without me and whoever else finds a tomb at the bottom of the Nepress. The world is counting on us. Our love can't trump that."

It was one of the few times he'd seen Penelope on the verge of tears. She knew he was right and eventually nodded, gripping him tightly. He hugged her back, threatening to spill his tears. He was glad she buried her face in his chest; he didn't want her to see his vulnerability. Not now, as the mission was at such a critical precipice.

"No, Daro, I can swim just fine with Iustia strapped to my side," he heard Sasha say.

The king and queen looked around. Most had dropped their weapons, but Sasha wouldn't part with her artifact, and Kringus didn't blame her. He sighed, and Penelope smiled, releasing him so he could defuse the situation and most likely save Daro from Sasha's wrath. Before he could step in their direction, Von and Lenore had returned, picking up their bows and strapping them on.

Kringus looked at them inquisitively, and Lenore only pointed to the sky. Kringus turned to see Baxter's carpet returning. At the same time, he heard several delirious crew members announcing the wizards' return, sending the crew into a happy frenzy comprised of relief and nervous cheering.

It quickly quieted to a hushed murmuring among the New Order and crew as others picked up their dropped weapons, following the elves' lead. They were excited by their appearance, but doubts riddled Kringus's thoughts. He knew nothing was near them; Parson, the cartographer, had confirmed that hours earlier when the leak was first detected. Soon after, they had furled the sails as the ship became impossible to sail, bloated with water. They were alone, deep in the Nepress Sea. He sighed, preparing for the news his friends would deliver. A sidelong glance at his queen inspired him to hold on to hope. Perhaps Victoria had found a way.

He was already considering alternative means of escape, though. The wizards had privately told the king and queen about the strange magical device that could save them if they found themselves in this situation. They had asked to bring the volatile item with them because of the slim chance they would need it. Now, he was glad that he'd agreed to allow it. Still, their hesitancy to use it spoke volumes. Just how dangerous was it?

The royal couple was joined by Ruby and Wendle, giving the wizards room to land the carpet. Baxter commanded it to hover about three feet over the captain's deck and hopped off before extending his hand to help Victoria. Once they stood on the deck, Baxter commanded the carpet to lower the rest of the way, where he began to roll it up. As he did, Victoria approached Kringus, a solemn look upon her pretty face.

"There is nothing, Kringus. No land, no ships, just a vast expanse of water," she said.

Kringus nodded, understanding that would be the case, as Penelope added, "Whoever did this knew exactly what they were doing. They knew we would be helpless, far out at sea, and with no one to assist us at this point in our journey."

Baxter joined the small group as the crew and New Order looked on anxiously. All eyes were on the six of them, and any hope or chance to survive the tragedy rested on their decision. Kringus understood this and nodded for Victoria to continue.

"We must use the magical horn," Victoria said. "There is no other choice."

"Wait. What device do you have?" Captain Ruby asked.

"It's called the Horn of Blorgis, a magical device created for sailors in desperate need of saving. From what we can tell, once blown, it will whisk the members of a distressed ship away to safety," Baxter explained excitedly.

"Why haven't you brought this to my attention before now?" Ruby asked.

Baxter's face reddened, and he looked to Kringus for support, obviously not wanting to say something to provoke the young captain's wrath. Kringus knew before she spoke that Ruby didn't like the idea and that it was an act of desperation. Still, he wanted to know more about the device, and the captain seemed to understand something of its lore.

"What does it do, Baxter?" Kringus urgently asked after shouts erupted from the crew that water was flowing over the deck.

"It's only one of three or four known to exist. I purchased it from Franklin Ruben recently."

"Who purchased it?" Victoria cut in.

"Well, the school, but it was my idea."

"Give it to me," Kringus said, his patience growing thin.

Victoria nodded to Baxter, who removed his pack and dug through it briefly before bringing it forth. It looked like a large conch shell.

"You rest our hopes on that?" Penelope asked.

Baxter nodded and said, "It is quite powerful."

"May I?" Kringus asked, reaching for it.

Baxter handed it over, and Kringus studied it, turning it over. It appeared nothing more than an ordinary shell. He handed it to Ruby once he understood he could discern nothing of the item, desiring her expertise. Her brow furrowed as she looked it over carefully.

"Once blown, Kringus, it will take us away from the ship and safely to land. Rumors suggest it holds a powerful teleportation spell, strong enough to save all of us," Victoria explained.

"But there is a risk?" Kringus asked as Ruby sighed and handed the device back to Baxter.

"Yes, it is unpredictable—" Victoria began.

"No, dear wizard, it is cursed," Captain Ruby said.

Everyone turned to look at her, and no one could deny the fear plastered on her and Wendle's faces. They knew the item and were most displeased about the prospect of using it.

"My king, blowing this thing could cause instant death for all of us," Ruby clarified.

"What do you know?" Penelope asked before anyone else could.

"Legend has it that a powerful god created six of them and disbursed them throughout the world to sailors, letting them believe it would save them from drowning in the event of a disaster," the young captain explained.

"And?" Kringus prodded, knowing they had precious little time to debate the reliability of the item.

"There is a legendary tale common amongst sailors of a ship's captain that used one, and the crew was whisked away, never to be heard from again."

There was a moment shared by the six, each looking into the others' eyes, fearing the use of the magical device. Kringus had to make the call—he was their leader and needed to decide quickly, for time was of the essence. So, he took the shell and turned to his captain. She took a step back, her eyes never leaving the item. She was terrified, her eyes wide with fear. It scared her, but it was the only chance they had. He nodded to Ruby, and she swallowed hard, studying his face. She was the captain of the ship, and Kringus respected her. He wanted her onboard with his decision if possible. She studied his face, her eyes darting back and forth, his silent request sinking in. Eventually, she nodded in defeat, but the fear didn't leave her face, nor Wendle's.

He turned to the crew and walked to the top of the steps. They all gathered close as the ship groaned, the weight of the water threatening to snap it in two. Kringus was amazed at how close the water was to spilling over the deck. Now was the time. They would have no chance to study the device or determine its safety.

"Dear crew of our beloved *Hope* and my friends and members of the

New Order, there are no vessels in the area and certainly no land," Kringus began, which started a nervous chatter throughout the crew.

Arrin, Erik, and Marcus climbed the steps to stand with the rest of the New Order. The ship lurched as cracks began to form along the main deck. Water poured forth, and the crew screamed.

Trying to be heard over the chaos, Kringus shouted, "However, we have discovered one chance to avoid sinking with this ship."

He held the horn high so all could see. He saw the looks on their faces. Some recognized the device, lending credibility to Ruby's claim; others were too panicked to acknowledge him. Instead, they hurried away from the water that was now several inches over the main deck.

"It is called the Horn of Blorgis and potentially holds a powerful teleportation spell," he continued futilely.

"Rumors say it's cursed," one of the sailors at the foot of the steps said, and Kringus noticed many of the surrounding crew members nodding in agreement.

They knew of the device, and from what little Kringus knew about sailors' superstitions, he considered it a bad sign. Using the horn could be a disaster, but what choice did he have? He couldn't risk the lives of his wife, friends, and loyal subjects due to a legend that might or might not be accurate.

"I don't know what will happen if we blow the horn, but I do know what will happen if we don't. As your king, I say we take that chance. I say we use the horn."

Kringus tossed the horn to Baxter and said, "Blow it!" as the water flowed over the deck more strongly, nearly washing several crew members overboard.

Baxter took the horn and looked to Victoria for support. Kringus saw her nod her approval with a pleasant smile. He thought of the meeting room back in Pelesea and wished the New Order were there, laughing and sharing a meal. He grabbed Penelope's hand. She squeezed it tight.

"Gather close and draw your weapons! We may find ourselves in immediate danger after I activate the device," Baxter barked.

The crew moved in, the water up to their knees, threatening to take them overboard. The ship groaned again, and more timbers snapped. It felt like the great vessel would break in two at any moment.

"Now, Baxter!" Kringus shouted over the growing chaos as the crew members ascended the steps to the captain's deck.

Everyone with a weapon drew it, including the crew, who all carried a sailor's knife. Kringus drew his massive sword with one hand and still held Penelope's hand with the other. He turned to her, and she had her small sword ready. She offered him a beautiful smile. He nodded and looked around at the other members of the New Order. All were ready for whatever occurred next. The elves were close by, and each held their bow again, arrows notched. Kringus and Lenore shared a nod.

Baxter brought the horn to his lips and blew. The conch made a strange sound, almost like a strained, gurgling note. Kringus saw smoke pour forth from the device. As Baxter finished the long, sad note, the smoke multiplied into a cloud. Baxter was the first to understand something was wrong. Kringus could see it on his face. Baxter's mouth twisted in a silent scream, then turned blue before ice formed. Kringus watched in horror as the smoke spread over the ship, blotting out the sun. It looked like a low-hanging fog at midday, but then the cold hit him, and he couldn't believe the icy death the cloud brought forth. He lost sight of Baxter and anyone who wasn't close. He could only see the lower part of Penelope's tiny arm; the fog enveloped the rest of her.

Kringus felt his hand freeze to his weapon, and then his other one stuck to his wife's small hand. His muscles stopped heeding his call, and he became paralyzed. He wanted to warn his wife, but that was impossible. He froze to the spot. The cloud continued to swirl, and the cold burned his bare skin. He heard the screams of the crew and his fellow members of the New Order. The last thing he felt was a thick layer of ice form on his face and then spread to encase the rest of his body. He briefly experienced the suffocating effects as it cut off his oxygen supply. That soon mattered little to the surprised king as his lungs and other organs quickly shut down from the extreme cold. Soon, he didn't need the oxygen. Soon, he didn't even notice the bite of the cold. His world went dark and silent, and Kringus knew nothing more.

MATILDA STOOD BEFORE THE RUINS OF A STATUE THAT WAS ONCE HER husband, Cerus the Grey. The nasty sleeth creature, Sitra, had petrified him weeks earlier, and Matilda had left him there. She had been on Cassandra's heels and had no choice but to go after the little witch. She had intended to come back soon after and restore Cerus. She had assumed he was safe, a beautiful statue in a garden of sand that no one would bother. However, Cassandra had eluded her, and as the days turned into weeks, she felt unsure of the outcome of the chase. Would she finally catch the spawn of Kane? The knowledge that her husband was only a few miles away and needed rescue compounded her frustration. Alas, she had waited too long, and something had happened to the perfect statue of Cerus. He was the latest casualty in the chase for Cassandra, and Matilda would hold the little witch responsible.

"It's mixed hopelessly with the sand," Bale said, observing the scene but not venturing too close to the crumbled pieces that were once Cerus the Grey.

Matilda fell to her knees, nearing tears. She hadn't felt this level of sadness since she was a little girl when her parents had abandoned her and, indeed, she hadn't cried many times in her life. Yet, here she was, at the site of her husband's demise, the emptiness of his death welling inside of her. Bale put a hand on her shoulder as she surveyed the death scene before her. Bale was right; too much of Cerus's remains had mixed with sand and, in truth, had probably already blown away. There was no way to bring her husband back because there weren't enough pieces to make him whole.

She barely stifled a sob, and even the hateful Bale appeared to sympathize with her situation. His strong hand gently squeezed her shoulder, but he said nothing, giving her a moment. She hardly noticed that his hand had disappeared shortly after. A fragment of the crumbled statue that was once her husband caught her eye. She picked it up as tears blurred her vision. She blinked them away. She held a piece of his face with one eye staring accusingly at her. His perfect face was now reduced to part of a cheek and one eye.

"I'm sorry, my husband, I have failed you. Who did this to you?" she whispered, struggling to get the words out.

As if in answer, Bale said, "Are these the two who owned the structure?"

Matilda put the little piece of Cerus into one of her pouches. She didn't know why; she just wanted to keep a piece to remember him. She rose and walked over to where Bale stood with two other priests. Six of them had ridden from the mountaintop back to the small house Cassandra's friends, including the sleeth that had petrified Cerus, called home at the foot of Witch's Rise. They had taken one of the two wagons, this one more of a prison cell on wheels. Bale had brought it along just in case they did find Cassandra, but their plan now had been to load Cerus in it and take him back to the top of Witch's Rise to keep his statue safe.

Two priests remained with the cell and the two horses that pulled it. She paid them no mind and was so distraught that she didn't even notice the other two who stood with Bale around a burned pyre, two charred human skeletons resting within. Bale kicked his booted foot around the ashes, looking for a clue. Matilda looked them over, expecting one of the skeletons to be smaller in stature if they were the tiny home's owners. They were not; each skeleton was the size of a sturdy warrior.

"Two Gorl warriors," she whispered.

"What?" Bale asked.

"These are two Gorl warriors, used as a distraction to make us think the nasty sleeth and her husband are dead."

"Why do you think this?"

Matilda looked the volatile priest in the face and sternly said, "I instructed the Gorl warriors to keep her alive. I told them to take her eyes. If anything, they would have taken her with them back to the desert, or they would have left her here, blind and alone."

Bale looked toward the home, which appeared deserted from the outside. He nodded to the two priests, and they smiled evilly, each producing a wicked-looking dagger. They slunk off toward the home, and Matilda briefly thought how silly they looked, trying to sneak up to it. She knew if the woman was inside, she had already spotted them.

"I want them alive if you find them," Matilda called out.

They stopped and looked at each other, then back to Bale, who smiled, flashing his metal teeth, and nodded in agreement. Then, the two priests continued on their way. They closed the ground quickly and soon opened the door and disappeared inside. It appeared to Matilda that a great deal of sand had collected against the door before they opened it, almost as if it hadn't been used in quite a while.

She looked back to the skeletons. Perhaps these *were* the two they'd encountered? She remembered one large man and a tiny woman, yet the two skeletal remains in the burned pyre were nearly identical in size. These corpses couldn't be the man and woman whom they'd fought. She was sure of that now, which begged a different question—if these weren't their remains and the house sat dormant, where were they?

Then she remembered the man used a mallet as a weapon, one that could crush a stone statue with but a few strokes! The man who lay dying in a pool of blood had lived? Either that or someone else strong enough to wield the giant weapon had attacked her defenseless husband. There was no other explanation; they were both alive!

She looked back to the house just in time to see the two priests exit and shrug, indicating that no one was inside. They both sheathed their weapons and returned to Matilda and Bale.

"They aren't here, then," Bale said.

"They are hiding," Matilda answered coldly and calmly.

"What do you know?" Bale asked.

"There's no doubt that these are Gorl warriors, and the two responsible for murdering Cerus are the same two we battled, the very ones who befriended and protected Cassandra. They harbored her in that small home and fought us while she ran toward the mountain. Ronnis was lucky enough to see her, but we left before the task was complete. Four strong Gorl warriors remained behind to beat, rape, and maim the woman. She was defenseless, and her fat husband lay there bleeding to death," she said, pointing to a nearby spot in the sand. "They had things well under control. What changed after we left? Perhaps Neclesious can provide an answer," Matilda said.

They looked over to the wagon, which consisted of metal bars on the sides and top, and the imp lay sprawled across the top. The desert sun beat down on the wagon, heating the bars and comfortably warming the creature. He slept soundly, and Bale shook his head.

"No, he'll be cranky, more so than usual, if we wake him up for this. The bottom line is that we came for Cerus but have found him dead. We mustn't deviate from our course. Cerus's murderers don't matter, and we mustn't pursue them. We must return to Witch's Rise at once."

Matilda stared at him as her heart thumped in her chest. Was Bale saying that avenging Cerus's death did not matter? Or was he saying that the idea of Cerus's death didn't matter? Either way, she wasn't happy with his reasoning. She closed her eyes and took several deep, calming breaths

When she finally opened her eyes, she said, "You and I should check the house just to be certain they aren't there."

"And if they aren't?"

"Then we leave for Witch's Rise. I will temporarily put the matter behind me."

Bale studied her face briefly before nodding and ordering the men back to the wagon. She and Bale made their way to the house, and her suspicions were confirmed—no one had been there for a while. Possessions were left exactly as they would have been, complete with clothing and foodstuffs, some now rotting. There was also a grisly scene in the dining room where Matilda assumed the Gorl warriors had tortured the sleeth. The table was bloodstained, as were the nearby wall and floor. It gave Matilda some hope that perhaps Cerus's men had extracted the sleeth's eyes. Maybe she and her husband were already dead.

With a sigh, Matilda said, "Let's go, but mark my word, I will have my revenge if either still draws breath."

She began to walk past Bale and out the door when he grabbed her and turned her toward him. "Yes, make a note of your enemies, my friend. We will be back after the Great Summoning is successful, and we will bring a horde of demons with which these two fools can play. If they are truly alive, they will regret it."

His reasoning made her feel better, and she smiled at the thought. "Agreed! Have your men gather what they can of Cerus and put him on the wagon."

"Matilda, don't hold out hope—"

"I'm not. I just want to give him a proper burial far away from this forsaken desert."

Bale stood unmoving. She was waiting for a rebuttal, just one more thing to make Cerus's death seem insignificant, and she would lose her temper. Matilda clenched her jaw and waited. Eventually, he nodded and ordered his men to do what she asked.

Matilda and Bale discussed their plans over the next hour as the four men gently tried to collect all the pieces of the crumbled statue, and Neclesious snoozed behind them.

Once they'd completed the task, they headed back to Witch's Rise. None noticed the tiny fairy hiding behind an outcropping of rocks, watching the entire display. When they were well out of sight, Gophia, a friend and ally to Cassandra, flew from her hiding spot in the rocks. She beat her tiny butterfly-like wings as fast as she could and quickly covered the five hundred yards to the secret door leading to a hidden cavern.

Sitra and her husband, Mateon, had lived beneath their home for the last few weeks, hiding from the inevitable return of the people searching for Cassandra. They hadn't set foot in their humble abode during that time, fooling Matilda and Bale into thinking it deserted. Their underground cave was a perfect hiding place, offering shelter, water, and plenty of food from their vast subterranean garden. Several rooms comprised the place, with the most significant one housing the garden. They had discovered the cavern decades ago and had built their humble home atop it. The grand secret of their modest home was the paradise caverns beneath it. So, they sealed the door leading from the house to the magnificent hideout, and there they stayed, healing and biding their time.

They had good reason to take such extreme measures. Sitra had been nearly beaten to death by Cerus's men when they first came looking for Cassandra. She had used her curse to gaze into Cerus's eyes just as he was about to abuse her in ways she couldn't imagine. She had turned the evil man to stone where he stood, effectively ending his life. She wasn't proud of the act, but sometimes her curse proved helpful, saving her. The enraged woman leading the hunt for Cassandra, evidently his wife, had ordered her henchmen to beat Sitra and take her eyes, all while Mateon lay dying in the sand, bleeding from a vicious stab wound to his throat.

Sitra gently rubbed her left eye, the skin still black around it, remembering that awful time. She would have lost her eyes, her husband, and probably much more if Binta Mulay, Cassandra's influential friend, had not come along. She had used her powerful mind to dispatch the men and save Sitra and Mateon. Since then, they, along with their little fairy friend, Gophia, had lived under the sandy surface of the Yaddaton, recovering from their wounds in the rocky caverns. Binta had left them as quickly as she'd appeared on her quest to find Cassandra and take her home. They hadn't heard from the young girl since, and so they didn't know if she'd found

Cassandra or if the two were dead. Once healed from their injuries, they would discover the truth of Cassandra and Binta's fate.

Now that Mateon was walking again and could eat soft food and not just drink water and broths, that time was growing near. They had sent Gophia out to discover information about the two missing friends four days earlier. They worried that perhaps the little fairy had met her demise and that those evil men and the fanatical priestess had detected and captured their little spy. It saddened them to think of the possibilities, yet Gophia would give her life to save Cassandra. They were close, having saved each other from the barbarians of Yaddaton.

The two were in one of the smaller chambers, the one that currently served as their bedroom. Mateon was lying on the bed as Sitra dressed his wounded throat with some of Yaddaton's potent bay leaves. Sitra grew them in their garden for times such as these. She was a proficient healer, and her knowledge of the healing powers of various roots and plants had saved her husband.

Sitra, a sleeth with beautiful but deadly green eyes that would petrify anyone looking into them, was slight of build. Her hair, comprised of tiny snakes, was the only indication that she wasn't a human. She leaned over Mateon to apply the leaves with a smile, for his wound was healing. The attack had damaged his vocal cords beyond her capabilities to repair them. So, he now spoke in a whisper and would do so the rest of his days. However, he would live, and that made her happy.

She stared into his sightless, white eyes and felt nothing but love for the man. He was blind, and she could look upon him and not blindfold herself as she was apt to do when others were around. The falinca plants that grew naturally in the cavern clung to the ceiling and walls and generated natural light so she could see her beautiful husband just fine. Their life was once effortless and wonderful. That had changed, and now the future was uncertain. Sitra kissed him lightly on the lips.

He put a hand on her cheek and said in his new whispered tone, "No funny business, doctor, I'm not fully healed."

Sitra chuckled, and they kissed deeply. Mateon sat up, gently slipped her shirt off her shoulder, and said, "On second thought, I'm feeling much better."

"You are a naughty patient!" Sitra teased, the tiny snakes comprising her hair hissing at him in mock annoyance.

Mateon smiled and was about to continue undressing his beautiful wife when there came the sound of a tiny bell from the gardens.

"Gophia!" they said in unison.

Sitra quickly donned her blindfold, and Mateon stood with his wife's help. At first, he was shaky on his legs, but he quickly found his bearings. Soon, they were in the hall, heading toward the garden.

"Gophia, we are here!" Sitra yelled.

They couldn't see it from where they were, but they understood that Gophia had found her way into their hidden paradise using the tiny door that Sitra had created a few weeks prior for their fairy friend. It was next to their secret door, hidden in an outcropping of rocks. Like their door, Sitra had adorned Gophia's with stones and plants to blend in with the natural landscape. They had also built a contraption that the fairy could use when she first entered the cavern, a pulley system with a tiny bell to alert Sitra that she should don her blindfold. The bell was small but was placed in an alcove to maximize its echo when it rang. So, they heard it easily as Gophia tugged on the small cord with all her might.

She stopped once she heard Sitra call out, then spotted the couple on the far side of the garden, near their living quarters. She flew quickly to them and perched on Sitra's shoulder, similarly to how she used to with Cassandra.

"You seem panicked, Gophia. What's wrong?" Sitra asked.

"The bad people returned!" Gophia shouted between large gulps of air, still winded from her quick flight.

"Are they in the house?" Mateon asked, bristling at the possibility.

"Gophia saw them there, but they left."

"So, they came back to check on Cerus?" Sitra asked.

"Yes, and they are displeased."

"Was Cassandra or Binta with them?" Mateon asked.

Sitra and Mateon couldn't see how Gophia reacted. Her silence spoke volumes, though. She and Cassandra were very close, and it obviously hurt the fairy to think Cassandra was in danger or possibly dead. A little sniffle finally broke the silence, and she said, "No, Cassandra is gone."

None spoke for a bit, and Gophia remained sitting on Sitra's shoulder, the closest snakes of Sitra's hair nudging her playfully. The fairy seemed to appreciate the gesture, but she was heartbroken.

"We are almost ready to venture from our hiding spot," Sitra said.

"Gophia, we *will* find our friends. Our enemy's numbers are small, and we can surprise them."

"No," was the only response the fairy gave.

"Why Gophia, we cannot give up on Cassandra or her wonderful friend who saved our lives," Mateon said. "They only have a half dozen in their group, and one of them helped me destroy Cerus, so they aren't as loyal as you might think. If we surprise them, we can win."

"There are many, and one has metal teeth. One is a bat and scares Gophia; it smells of death. It is unsafe to pursue Gophia's friend," Gophia explained, nearing tears as she spoke.

The little fairy covered her face in her hands and sobbed. More of Sitra's snake hair gathered around the little creature, hugging and rubbing against her. Whenever Gophia laughed, which hadn't occurred much since Cassandra's disappearance, it sounded like a tiny bell ringing from her belly. It was strange, yet magical. As she cried, Sitra and Mateon could hear the same bell-like sound but at a much softer and despairing pitch, giving it an eerie twist.

"Well, we can't sit here and do nothing," Mateon said after listening to the fairy's suffering.

Sitra nodded. "When can you be ready to travel?" she asked.

"Within days!" Mateon said proudly.

"When can you wield your magnificent mallet?"

Her words stole Mateon's bluster, and he thought momentarily, gently rubbing his wounded neck. With a sigh, he replied honestly, "Weeks."

BINTA UNDERSTOOD MANY THINGS. SHE KNEW SHE'D DEVELOPED HER mind into something that was nearly god-like. She'd quickly honed her new skills to defend herself against anyone who stood against or abused her. She had come to Witch's Rise to use those same powers to destroy those pursuing Cassandra. She had left Pelesea confident she could deal with any obstacle and vanquish any foe. And she had until her inner desires got the best of her. She couldn't think clearly around Cass Ruben—her enemy, tormentor, and mistress—and couldn't use her newfound skills.

Sure, she understood what she was doing when forced into service by the evil woman, but she was powerless to resist anything Cass demanded.

Binta's strange sexual desires became overwhelming when in her presence, her naughty thoughts overriding her powerful mind. That submissive part of her, which was always most dominant when serving Cass, overrode any good decision she could make. She was a non-thinking fool around Cass, although she could kill people with her powers if she focused on using them.

"That's a good girl," she heard Cass purr.

Binta found herself kneeling before Ronnis, still bound and with his hands intertwined in her locks, using her at will. She hated Cass and Ronnis, but how they used her made her feel alive. It wasn't the first time in recent days that Ronnis had used her orally for satisfaction. Cass was always nearby, shoving the vial of demon milk under her nose any time Binta looked to be regaining her senses. Binta understood why she'd come: to find Cassandra, take her home, and protect her friend from these fools. As she swallowed the filth Ronnis gave her, she thought how ridiculous her situation had become. Her life was forfeit, and her sexual nature was to blame, and perhaps Cass, the demon milk, X'lor, and his assistant, Illa. They had all been part of the process to bring her weakness to the forefront, and now her sexual appetite was all that mattered. She simply couldn't get enough sex and wanted nothing more than to be forced by the very people she despised, the very ones trying to kill Cassandra!

"Go to your corner, slave," Cass cooed.

Binta knew better than to stand, and with her hands bound in front of her, she couldn't crawl. She heard herself say, "Yes, mistress," but it felt like an out-of-body experience, as if she were on the outside looking in.

She tried to crawl the best she could, and she soon felt Ronnis's boot kick her ribs. She fell to her side as he and Cass shared a laugh. It reminded Binta of the confrontation Cass and Cassandra had had at school, where Jabell had kicked Binta repeatedly in the ribs. Ronnis only kicked her once, not wanting to hurt her seriously. He had grown more vicious over the last few weeks since Bale had made him cut a hole in his other cheek, but he still practiced self-control. He and Cass needed Binta uninjured for their perverted sex acts. She couldn't read Ronnis's thoughts, and she knew it was because of the mighty sword that had infected him, but she didn't need to look inside his head to understand how dangerous he was. Ronnis was awful, and she now understood why Cassandra hated him.

She returned to her knees and began crawling again, hoping there would be no second kick to the ribs. None came, and she realized her two tormentors were fixing themselves a drink and whispering, Cass occasionally giggling like a small child. Binta was confident they were already planning their next sexual domination of her. It made her tingle, and when she got to her corner, she curled up in a fetal position and began to play with herself, the fire between her legs far from sated. She wanted to focus on escaping to help Cassandra, but it felt so good to focus instead on her sexual desires. She couldn't wait for Cass to drag her back to Ronnis to pleasure him again.

And as dangerous as Cass and Ronnis were, they paled compared to the evil men that comprised the group of priests following Bale. She picked up their broadcasted thoughts easily, and their motives were clear. The men she found herself in the middle of were the purest evil that humanity had to offer. She had read some of their basic desires and deeds they'd performed in the past to appease their demon lord. Luckily, they weren't focused on her and cared little for her fate. She let out a soft moan as she masturbated, and she heard Cass giggle again at her expense. Binta didn't care, so she continued her self-stimulation.

She was in a terrible predicament, and no one would save her. She had done this to herself. She had been arrogant, thinking she could find Cassandra and bring her home. She was sad that she'd failed her friend and was ashamed to have left Jamison, the one man who seemed to love her, without saying goodbye. He would never know what happened to her. She sobbed as she orgasmed, two opposite emotions derived from her understanding of the personal hell she had made for herself. But then she heard Cass and Ronnis approaching, and her desire to please them overrode those true feelings. She pulled herself together quickly—she needed to please her mistress. Nothing else mattered.

***

Jamison Oland, the new steward of Pelesea, stared at the large painting he'd had commissioned for his beloved Binta. It had cost him plenty of gold, and he'd hired the best artisan in the city to paint his love. She'd done a splendid job, and the price was worth every ounce of gold. It had hung in his manor a few blocks away, but he'd brought it with him after moving into the castle a month earlier. Now, it hung in his royal chambers in the castle. It was still Kringus and Penelope's room, but it was his until they returned.

The New Order would be reaching Varish by now, and their mission to find and bring back Cassandra would begin in earnest once they'd disembarked and begun exploring the wild lands of the untamed continent. Would they find Binta with Cassandra and fill the hole in Jamison's heart? Binta had left him without saying goodbye, but Baxter assured him she cared for him. According to the wizard, she had gone undercover because she knew Jamison would disapprove of her plan, but she intended to return to Jamison's arms once she completed her task.

"What exactly is your plan, my love?" he whispered, running his fingers over her cheek on the portrait.

The painting had no answer for the heartbroken man. Those beautiful brown eyes stared back at him, which had attracted him to her in the first place. Those eyes were a window to her soul and all the goodness found there. She was a sexual person, and that was how he'd met her, prostituting near the southern docks. Jamison had traveled across the city to buy a cursed sword from a shady sailor at those docks. The transaction was intense, and he purchased the item, but not without the assistance of several off-duty city guardsmen he'd hired.

The guards had departed with his treasure, delivering it safely to his manor. He was boarding his carriage that night to head home when he told Tumins, his driver, that he was parched and needed a drink. They were near a rickety old tavern called Poppy's Inn. It didn't look inviting to Jamison, but he had desired a drink badly enough to make an exception. He and Tumins had entered the tavern to deathly silence. All the attention had been on a young, scantily dressed woman walking up the steps to the second floor. Her perfect butt swayed underneath her too-short skirt, and her underwear left little to the imagination. A woman Jamison recognized was leading her up the stairs with a leash.

Cass Ruben, Franklin's daughter, led the beautiful young girl around like a piece of property. So, yes, sex was the first thing that drew his attention to Binta, but when she turned to face the tavern once they'd reached the top of the stairs, his heart had skipped a beat. She was stunningly gorgeous, and those eyes captivated him. Although he and Tumins left shortly after that with a bottle of watered-down ale, he promised to return inconspicuously later. He did, and he met Binta shortly after. The sex had been fantastic—it always was with her. And although he was just one of many paying customers, he immediately fell for her. He returned many times over the next few weeks, his obsession with her multiplying.

Luckily, her soul was as beautiful as her body, and they connected, not just sexually but mentally as well. Luckily for Jamison, he soon became more than just a paying customer. It was shortly after those early conversations that he began to understand Cass forced Binta to work as a prostitute. He didn't want Franklin's daughter to get into trouble, but he had to go to the king with the information; he had to free his beloved Binta from that awful life. And he had, and now they were engaged. Binta had never said yes, but she'd moved in with him and even wore the ring he'd given her. They would wed one day, he was sure of that, but he had to find her first.

A light rap on the door broke him from his contemplations. "Come in," he said but didn't turn from the painting.

The door opened, and he heard the familiar grating of armor as two of his guards moved in to stand on either side of the door. He welcomed the protection, but it wasn't required here in Pelesea.

"He is here," Brack Tompkins, his captain of the castle guard, said in his familiar monotone voice.

Jamison smiled before turning to regard the captain. He liked the man. He was all business, and that was what Jamison wanted in a person in charge of castle security. Brack was standing in the room, just a few feet from the doorway, and as Jamison suspected, two guards stood on either side of the opened door, dressed in their Pelesea plate mail.

Brack was also in his plate armor, and Jamison knew that there was more to that armor than met the naked eye. According to Kringus, the armor contained a powerful enchantment. His large mustache seemed too big for his handsome face and was well maintained, just like his perfect brown hair that never seemed out of place. He was a good man, and Jamison was lucky to have him in the castle. With all he had going on as steward, the castle security was one thing he never had to worry about as long as Brack was on the job.

Beside him stood Sloan L'Shans, the beautiful castle wizard. Once he discovered that Kringus and Penelope didn't have a designated royal wizard, he made an appointment with the instructors of Victoria's school. His demands of the school had been direct—he needed a wizard powerful enough to protect him and wise enough to advise him. The wizard would also need to live within the castle, specifically in the room next to the royal chamber where Jamison slept. The school had taken precisely three days to send Sloan to him, and he couldn't be happier.

He hadn't expected the wizard to be female or attractive, but Sloan was both. She was young, still in her thirties, and unattached. So, instead of an older man with a grey beard and pointy hat like Jamison had envisioned, the castle wizard was beautiful and available. Her dark hair always seemed to curl perfectly around her shoulders, and her blue eyes were magnificent. Her figure was perfect, he could see, even through the usually red or white robes she chose to wear since moving into the castle. Those colors matched the banner of Pelesea: a red background with two white angel wings. She was powerful and loyal. Suffice it to say, Jamison thought a lot of her.

"Where is our guest?" Jamison asked.

"In the study where you requested him," Brack said. "Four of my best men are in the hall guarding it if he tries to exit the room."

"So, you are treating him as a prisoner?" Jamison asked, cocking an eyebrow to emphasize his point.

"Well—" Brack began before Sloan took over the conversation, cutting him off.

"Dear Steward, we cannot be too safe with the likes of Inuentas. His birthplace reeks of betrayal and evildoers. I think it's wise that Brack has him guarded, and I was happy to see that he handed over his great sword at the castle door."

"He's unarmed?" Jamison asked.

"Yes, we wouldn't allow him entrance any other way," Brack said proudly, smiling with the lovely Sloan.

With a sigh, Jamison shook his head and said, "The man is a half-demon, so I understand your caution with him, but remember, the king and queen allowed him to enter this castle to share a meal. He was also allowed to carry his sword. It is the king and queen's wish that he has the same rights as our citizens until he proves he doesn't deserve them."

Brack nodded his concession. "Yes, Steward, you are correct."

Sloan said nothing, and Jamison could tell she wanted to offer a rebuttal. He decided to end the conversation before she had a chance. "Nevertheless, I appreciate both of you doing a tremendous job of keeping me and the rest of the castle safe."

His words brought a smile to Brack's face, and Jamison patted him firmly on the shoulder. "After you, my liege," Brack said, extending his left arm toward the door.

"Excuse me, gentlemen, are you forgetting something?" Sloan said.

Both turned to regard the beautiful wizard, who wore a smirk. She said nothing but approached them and began waving her hand delicately through the air. They both knew she was casting a spell, and Jamison understood her to be a witch who could use spells without a spellbook or the cumbersome components wizards usually relied upon. Ironically, the ability was rare in humans, and the only other known witch Jamison had heard of was Cassandra Rho.

Sloan cast her spell, and Jamison felt it wash over him. He wasn't sure what she'd done, but he knew it was something that would protect them. When Jamison and Brack gawked at each other after the spell was complete, waiting for some sign that the spell had taken effect, Sloan rolled her eyes and chuckled. She walked up to stand between them and poked a finger at each. A light blue veil of energy formed a barrier around each man separately and momentarily became visible when her fingers struck them.

"A protective sphere to deflect most attacks. The duration is short, and it only lasts for about an hour. Only a precise and powerful strike can penetrate it."

Jamison was amazed at how easily she cast the seemingly powerful spell and understood that the act could save his life one day, possibly this very day. Powerful and trustworthy allies surrounded him, and he was thankful to have them. He smiled at his wizard, and he and Brack led the small procession to the study where Inuentas waited.

The four guards remained in the hall as Jamison, Brack, and Sloan entered the large study. The room held six plush chairs, perfect for reading the hundreds of books that lined the bookcases on three walls of the room. On the fourth wall was a fireplace with a smoldering fire. Several small tables were stationed around the room, each with a bowl of fruit, primarily apples from Daro's orchard. Several bottles of Pelesea wine were on the tables, ordered explicitly by Jamison as a treat for his guest. Inuentas stood by the fireplace, one arm leaning casually on the mantel, a glass of wine in the other. His back was to the door, and his tail twitched like an agitated cat's.

"Do you keep all of your prisoners waiting this long, Steward?" the half-demon hissed, not even bothering to turn around.

He seemed mesmerized by the fire as he nursed his drink. Jamison ignored the comment and sat in one of the chairs. Brack and Sloan took up spots on either side of Jamison as the guards pulled the door shut behind them.

Inuentas whipped his head around, and his black eyes were slits as he said, "And you need guards to babysit me?"

He tossed his glass into the fire and turned fully to face Jamison. He was about ten feet away, and Brack put a hand on the hilt of his weapon. A small ball of energy suddenly appeared in Sloan's right palm. Jamison saw the half-demon's point of view but also understood that Brack and Sloan were cautious about the strange creature. After all, Inuentas constantly boasted of his proficiency with the deadly blade he carried, and he worked for a demon lord. Jamison didn't feel safe in the room with Inuentas and was glad of the presence of his captain and wizard. Jamison didn't want to be judgmental with their guest, especially since that would go against what the king and queen believed in, but Inuentas's appearance unnerved him. Besides his pupilless, black eyes, his skin was red, and he had two little black horns on his forehead that matched his black hair. And, of course, the tail continuously flicked and wagged, the barbed end appearing vicious and threatening to Jamison.

Inuentas looked to Brack and growled, "Draw your weapon, and you won't live long enough to regret it."

Brack didn't flinch and, thankfully, didn't draw his weapon. Jamison was relieved but already felt it might have been a mistake to bring the creature to the castle. After all, Inuentas was correct—they weren't treating him fairly.

"And you," the half-demon continued, switching his gaze to Sloan. "You and I can settle our differences in a more secluded and intimate setting. You are quite the specimen."

Sloan bristled and wanted to say something but managed to hold her tongue. Yet, the ball of energy in her palm only grew brighter and began to sizzle with expanding energy. Inuentas watched it and smiled, his sharp canines becoming visible.

"Enough of this," Jamison said, motioning for his allies to stand down.

Both obeyed. Brack removed his hand from his weapon, and Sloan dismissed the energy gathering in her delicate but deadly palm. Inuentas relaxed noticeably, gave one final seductive look to the wizard, and then quickly backpedaled into the nearest seat. He took an apple from a nearby bowl and began chewing, looking Sloan up and down as if his eyes were devouring her as he ate.

"You are not an enemy of the New Order and, therefore, are certainly not an enemy of Pelesea, Inuentas the Indomitable," Jamison said.

The half-demon stopped chewing for just a moment, contemplating Jamison's words. He eventually began chewing again with a quick nod. "Then I'll have my weapon returned, now?"

Jamison saw Sloan and Brack look at him intently, awaiting his answer. He knew he had to use kid gloves with the demon now that he'd been offended. Inuentas had information Jamison needed, and the steward didn't want to insult him further and risk losing it. He eventually shook his head, knowing that giving the creature his weapon would show a sign of weakness and would also undermine Brack and his men.

Inuentas's visage grew stern, but before he could speak out against the decision, Jamison made him an offer. "Although I cannot give you your sword now, rest assured you will get it back as you exit the castle. Also, my two advisors will leave us alone to discuss a matter of great importance."

"What?" Brack and Sloan said in unison.

"He is unarmed, as well as I, so we may speak on even terms. Inuentas is not our enemy; he has come here at my request. Please stay outside the door so that we may discuss things privately and in a civilized manner. Is this a suitable compromise for you, Inuentas?"

The half-demon didn't move or say anything for a long time, his beady eyes examining each of their faces. Jamison knew the protective shield was still in place and that his top advisors would be outside the door. He felt safe enough with that arrangement and hoped his guest would agree to the terms. Eventually, Inuentas nodded.

"But, Steward, this is unsafe," Brack began.

Jamison shook his head and smiled, lifting a hand to stop his captain. "It's fine, Brack. Inuentas and I are not enemies, and he is my guest. I will not have him treated as a prisoner."

Brack and Sloan looked at each other briefly, then at Inuentas before slowly leaving the room. "We'll be right here if you need anything," Brack said before shutting the door.

"There, now we may discuss things privately, and I hope you won't feel like a prisoner."

"Yes, Steward, we may do just that, but understand that I'm never unarmed," Inuentas said with a smirk.

He then grabbed an apple from the bowl beside him and tossed it in the air. As it fell back to the ground, he whipped his tail out and stabbed it with the barbed end. The apple quivered momentarily on the end of his tail and immediately began turning brown, then black, rotting from the tail's venom. Once it was shriveled up and rotten, Inuentas flicked his tail, and the poisoned fruit shot into the fireplace with a sickening splat. The fire hissed, and a cloud of toxic gas puffed into the room.

Jamison didn't flinch, telling himself the demon wouldn't attack him with so many of his allies right outside the door. He had to cover his mouth and nose from the stench of the burned fruit, and it made his eyes water. He understood that Inuentas's tail was as deadly as any blade he could have carried. Brack had erred in his judgment.

"Now tell me, what is so important that you would summon me here, treat me like a second-rate citizen, and offend me by assuming I am defenseless, good steward?"

"Again, my apologies for any inconvenience this has caused you," Jamison said, the foul gas finally dissipating enough so he could uncover his mouth and nose.

He rose, poured his guest a drink, and made one for himself. He walked over to stand before the half-demon, in range of the deadly tail, as an act of trust. He needed Inuentas to calm down, and he needed his answer. To his relief, the creature nodded and took the drink. Jamison retook his seat.

"So, I have researched and found that you were one of the last people to see my Binta the day before she left Pelesea."

"Is that so?" Inuentas said, taking a long draw of his drink.

"My sources tell me that you two had dinner the evening before she left. Is this true?"

"Did your sources tell you we also got a room for a few hours afterward?"

The words hit Jamison like a ton of rock. Had Binta slept with this creature? Was Inuentas lying to him? He understood the nature of demons, and they were expert liars. Was this his way of getting back at Jamison for the harsh treatment he'd endured from Brack and his men? He tried to steady his breathing; he had to focus.

"That's right, Steward," Inuentas said, a smile forming on his hateful lips. "Binta needed information, and I gave it to her. I required a fee, and that fee was steep. She gladly paid it. And I happily took it."

"Binta wouldn't sleep with the likes of you, demon," Jamison growled, feeling his face flush.

"No? Then how would I know that when she is on top of her lover and climaxes, she whips her head back and moans while her little toes curl and dig into your thighs?"

Jamison felt as if he'd pass out, each pump of his heart pounding in his head. How could his beloved cheat on him? Did she not love him? The thoughts of her and Inuentas tangled up in a lovers' embrace raced through his mind, and the half-demon sensed his discomfort.

"Relax, Jamison," Inuentas said, and the lack of title didn't go unnoticed. The creature's smirk disappeared, and he said, "I was only descriptive so you would know that I'm not lying. Men, such as yourself, who are in love are also blind to the truth. Now you know I speak it."

Jamison tried to calm himself. He nodded and sipped his drink. After a few moments of silence, he asked, "Why?"

"Why did she sleep with the likes of me?"

Jamison could only nod. He didn't want to belittle Inuentas because he was part demon, but he had a hard time controlling his prejudice. Binta wouldn't have slept with him unless she was desperate. He needed to know before he lost control and had Inuentas jailed. "Yes, why that? What did you discuss over dinner?"

"She was desperate for information, and I had what she needed. She offered to pay for it with your gold, but I had other ideas." He stopped and took a long sip before continuing. "I mean, Binta is a sexy tart, Jamison. Can you blame me?"

Jamison had had enough. "Listen, half-demon, if you mention one more time how you had sex with my fiancée, I'm liable to do something rash."

Inuentas smiled and said, "Fair enough," raising his hands to calm Jamison. "However, you are not going to like the answer."

Jamison relaxed as his demeanor changed. He knew something terrible had happened to Binta and needed to know what it was.

"Baxter, the wizard, took her far away using his magic carpet. He wouldn't elaborate because he swore secrecy to Binta. Why did she come to you, and where did Baxter take her?" Jamison asked, hoping his desperation wasn't apparent.

"Very well, you have asked, and I shall tell. Your fiancée, as you describe her, has stumbled upon an amazing gift. She is a telepath now, and a mighty one. She was able to—"

"Read my missing book, the one that I saw turn a semi-powerful wizard's mind to mush," Jamison finished for him.

"Excellent, Jamison. She read the book, and it should have killed her. Instead, she became the most powerful human telepath I have ever encountered."

"You speak of her in past tense," Jamison pointed out.

"That's because she's probably dead, and I can't think of a bigger waste," Inuentas said, licking his lips and suddenly staring into space as if recalling his tryst with Binta. He snapped out of it when he noticed Jamison's stare. "I sent her to Vasym to find The Mystic and obtain her answers."

"Vasym? The Mystic? What answers?"

"Yes, Vasym is a desolate forest hundreds of miles from here. It's the home of a creature called The Mystic, a powerful being that was once a god but was cast down from the heavens centuries ago. I told her that he would know where Cassandra Rho was."

"So, she went to find Cassandra?"

"Of course."

"Why didn't you tell the New Order of this Mystic?"

"Because he would have killed them if they'd sought him out. Only Binta's powerful mind had a chance to withstand his mental intrusions."

"And you think she failed?"

"I'm sure she did. No one has ever met The Mystic and left Vasym a free person. He most assuredly melted her brain, and she's one of his many slaves now."

Jamison let the information sink in and had never felt so desperate. He knew the half-demon was being honest with him and that he couldn't focus efforts to attempt a rescue. He had to trust in her judgment and Baxter's as well. Indeed, Baxter wouldn't have sent her to her death. He must have believed she could survive the encounter with The Mystic.

"Unless she brainwashed him into believing that?" Inuentas said, as if he were reading his thoughts.

Jamison nodded and said, "Thank you for being honest. Brack will see you out now."

Inuentas stood as Jamison sharply clapped his hands twice, signaling for Brack to open the door, which he did immediately. He and Sloan slid inside the room as if they'd anticipated trouble. With one last nod shared between half-demon and steward, Brack escorted Inuentas away.

"Did you find the information you required?" Sloan asked once they were alone.

"Yes, I did. Thank you for being here. Your services are invaluable to me. I wish to be alone now if you don't mind leaving and shutting the door behind you."

"Of course, Steward. Are you all right?"

"Fine," Jamison lied.

Sloan stepped out of the room and was about to close the door when Jamison blurted out, "Have you ever heard of The Mystic of Vasym?"

She poked her head back in, and her forehead scrunched as she thought about it. "No, shall I research him?"

Jamison thought about it momentarily, knowing that he shouldn't use the resources at his disposal to find Binta. That was what his mind said, but his heart had other ideas. "Yes, please," he finally said.

She nodded and left, shutting the door behind her. Jamison sat in that study for a long time, drinking his sorrows away. He felt a great emptiness in his soul, and he was sure now that Binta was dead. Eventually, his emotions got the best of him, and he wept for her and the life they could have shared.

Unlikely Hero

The folks of Sylor were very hearty, primarily farmers, with a few other skilled laborers living among them. They were hardworking people, and their small town was self-sufficient. Kessi and her sisters arrived at a closed gate and a tall, sturdy wall surrounding the place. Oddly, the same beautiful flowers that adorned Samuel's staff covered it. Initially, the guards atop the twenty-foot wall denied Kessi's band access. They demanded that each person in Kessi's party touch the flowers climbing the wall. It was a routine similar to what Samuel had put them through, so Kessi and her friends complied. Even so, the gate didn't open. It only briefly opened after Kessi mentioned that Kody and Samuel had permitted them to enter the town.

The guard hastily ushered them in, looking around nervously while the gate was open. They relaxed only when Kessi's party was inside and the gate secured. Kessi immediately noticed that the wildflowers the people seemed to be obsessed with grew abundantly on the buildings. There were fields of them as well, as the townsfolk grew them as crops. As soon as they entered, two men, obviously priests, approached them and touched each visitor's forehead with a silver holy symbol that hung around their necks on silver chains. The symbols were shaped like two hands holding a world in their palms. Kessi knew some of the gods back home, and to her relief, she didn't believe the god they worshipped to be evil. After each passed the silver-touching test, the priests welcomed them and let them be.

Since they had no coins to buy goods or pay for a place to stay, Kessi and her friends were given shelter in one of the town's large barns. As barter for the lodgings, they agreed to work the fields the next day. The barn was large enough for them to unpack their gear and rest. Now that they felt a little safer, exhaustion kicked in. Some of the women immediately decided to catch some sleep. A creek meandered near the barn and eventually emptied into a large pond near the middle of the town. Kessi, Sabrina, and a few others decided to take a bath in a private area of the pond, which was well hidden by thick vegetation. There, they could wash themselves of the filth from Nesin and effectively wash away the remnants of the evil place.

Kessi and Sabrina relaxed in a shallow part of the pond, enjoying the feel of the water, something they hadn't felt for many months. The others had already left, sleep beckoning them after their refreshing bath. The air was cool enough to be slightly uncomfortable, but the place was a little piece of the heavens for the two girls. They lay their heads back on a large stone they shared as a pillow, submerging the rest of their bodies.

"This place seems nice," Sabrina said, her eyes still closed, deep in a relaxed state.

"Yes, too bad we can't enjoy it," Kessi added, her eyes closed as well, basking in the waning sun.

"We'll leave tomorrow night to find Emiline?" Sabrina asked, opening one eye to measure Kessi's reaction.

Kessi had already opened her eyes and was staring at her friend seriously. "We must leave as quickly as possible, for Emiline's sake."

Sabrina sat up but kept her nakedness below the waterline as they were out in the open. "We can't leave at night," Sabrina added.

"No, the next morning. We'll have to work hard enough tomorrow to earn another night's stay in the barn."

"How will we do it? How will we find her or defeat a nest of werewolves?"

"We can't without the townsfolk's help," Kessi said glumly.

"You mean Kody?" Sabrina said with a knowing smile.

Kessi felt her cheeks flush at the mention of the boy. "No! Sabrina, this is serious. We must gain an audience with the leaders of this town and discover information about the werewolves. Where do we find them? How do we kill them? Can they lend weapons or men to help us fight? I'll focus on that, not some boy I may never see again."

Kessi briefly dunked her head under the water and brought it back up, wiping the water from her eyes. She needed to quench the heat building in her cheeks, but Sabrina could see through her façade.

"You should have seen your faces when the two of you met. You were both wide-eyed, like school children with a bad case of puppy love."

"Don't be ridiculous, Sabrina, this is a serious matter. Emiline is in trouble, and we owe it to her to help her. Boys can most definitely wait."

Sabrina sobered at the thought. "We aren't exactly a formidable rescue party, are we?"

"No, especially if some others decide to continue to Attins."

Sabrina lay her head back on the rock and stared silently at the blue fall sky. Kessi could tell she hadn't thought of that, and the truth was sinking in. There was a good chance Patricka and the others wouldn't go back to find their friend. Kessi joined Sabrina, laying her head next to her.

"I won't abandon her," Sabrina whispered.

"I know, and neither will I. However, the two of us can't do this alone. We'll need to ask Sylor's leaders for advice. Without their help, we cannot hope to win."

They lay there a bit longer before Kessi finally said, "We should go. The sun will be setting soon, and we have much to do before we can rest."

"We're going to ask for an audience with the leaders?"

"Yes, and to hopefully catch a glimpse of that beautiful boy," Kessi said with a smile.

She heard Sabrina sit up in the water again, but Kessi held her eyes closed tightly, trying to keep a blank expression. She knew Sabrina was waiting for a reaction, as Kessi remained stone-faced.

"Mayla, you tell me what's going on! You can't say something like that and then feign rest," Sabrina said, using the fake moniker she'd given Kessi when Kessi couldn't recall her name.

Kessi could only imagine Sabrina's shocked expression as she stared at her, open-mouthed. It made Kessi eventually snicker, and soon, the two laughed giddily, something neither had done in months.

"I knew it!" Sabrina said, playfully splashing Kessi.

Kessi sat up and splashed back. At that moment, she was young and free, something she hadn't felt for a long time. She had a best friend, a safe community, even safer than Oldorburg, and a tingling in her soul. She would love to focus on that sensation and get to know Kody better. But Emiline was in trouble, and Kessi could never be at peace if she didn't try to rescue her. Even if they succeeded in that endeavor, there was still the matter of Cassandra. Her sister was also in serious trouble. Boys were not a priority.

The two quickly dried off and dressed, then went to the barn to find their sisters asleep. It was a few hours before sunset, but they were physically and mentally exhausted. Kessi had intended to invite them to speak with the town's leaders. After seeing their friends soundly asleep, she decided not to wake them. She and Sabrina would go alone, letting their friends enjoy their first peaceful sleep in months.

Kessi and Sabrina found their way back to the gate to retrieve information from the guards. However, different guards were now operating the gate than the ones that allowed them to enter. One turned to face them and acknowledged them with a nod. He looked young to Kessi, too young to be a town guardsman. She approached him with a smile.

"Hello, good sir. We are new to Sylor and need your assistance," Kessi said.

He looked back and forth, studying their faces before finally speaking. "Hello, weary travelers. What may I assist you with?"

"You know we are travelers?" Sabrina asked.

"Of course. Sylor is small enough that I know when strangers are amongst us. Also, Kody came in a few hours ago with Samuel. He asked if a group of traveling female adventurers had entered the town and, if so, where they were staying."

Sabrina squeezed Kessi's arm excitedly. Kessi ignored her but felt her cheeks growing warm again. There were too many pleasant distractions in Sylor. She needed to remain focused.

"And you told him of us?" Kessi asked.

"Of course. I had no reason not to. Is that all right with you, ladies?"

Kessi glanced at Sabrina, who looked like she was about to burst with excitement. Kessi knew why: Sabrina was giddy about the prospect of love for Kody and Kessi, which seemed a ridiculous proposition to Kessi since they had only just met. Still, Kessi could barely contain her joy at the prospect. However, she only allowed a slight smile to crease her lips. Emiline needed her, and Kody could wait.

"It's fine. We have urgent business with the elders of Sylor. Can you point us in the right direction?" Kessi asked.

The guard motioned with his hand to the lamplighters, who were setting the street lanterns ablaze as dusk approached. "It's late, and your business should wait. It's our experience that the few travelers we get here rarely have the stamina for farming. I understand you and your friends will barter your lodging by working in the fields tomorrow. It won't be as easy as you think."

"We expect the work to be challenging, but we are up to the task. However, we must speak with the leaders this night," Kessi said.

"Please, won't you help us?" Sabrina asked, hopefully, and with a friendly smile.

He became flustered as she took a step toward him. Kessi realized for the first time how much fun she and Sabrina could have living in a small town like Oldorburg or Sylor. She had never seen her friend mingle in a society before, and the display was refreshing. They no longer had to live with the looming sacrifice or in fear of being beaten. They could think and do things nineteen-year-old girls did; they could be normal, like flirting with young guardsmen.

"If you want to get things done in Sylor, you should see Samuel anyway. We do nothing without his approval," the red-faced young man said.

"Samuel, the man we met on the trail who pointed us toward your town?" Kessi asked.

The guardsman shared a questioning look with a few of his fellow gatekeepers, who nodded in response. "Most likely. Samuel and Kody delivered today, so it would have been those two if you saw anyone outside the gate."

"What did they deliver, exactly?" Sabrina asked.

"Holy water to the werewolves."

"Holy water?" Kessi and Sabrina said in unison, then gave each other a confused look.

"Yes, to protect them and us from the vampires."

"Vampires?" Kessi said as Sabrina blanched at the mention of the undead.

"Yes, to the west. We give the werewolves the water in exchange for protection from the vampires," the young man explained.

"Wait, the werewolves and vampires know of each other? And they don't get along?" Kessi asked.

"Right. You catch on fast," the young guard said with a smile.

"Tell us quickly how to find Samuel," Kessi said, not sharing his joy.

His smile melted away, and he said, "It's easy. Just go through town, and before the fields, you'll see a large white house. It's Samuel's." He pointed down the center of the main street of Sylor.

Kessi and Sabrina did quick work, half running and half walking toward their destination. They found the house and confirmed it was correct by the horseless wagon parked nearby, the same one Samuel had been driving earlier. The fields of corn and other crops were just past the house, but with the sun already set, they couldn't appreciate how vast the rows might be. They made their way quickly to the door and knocked.

"Emiline is in deeper trouble than I thought, Sabrina. I feel selfish relaxing in the pond and sleeping tonight in our safe quarters," Kessi said, the guilt weighing on her shoulders.

"Yes, and working all day in the fields tomorrow will delay us another day."

"We may have to ask them if—" Kessi began, but the door opened, and a pleasant lady with white hair answered with a smile, cutting her off. The smell of fresh food wafted out the door, and both girls realized how hungry they were.

"Well, aren't you two precious," the woman said with a large smile. "We've been expecting you, so come in. You're just in time for dinner."

Kessi and Sabrina shared a confused glance, shrugged, and entered the large farmhouse, where the smell of delicious food overwhelmed them. Kessi detected chicken, apple pie, and other things she suspected, such as corn and potatoes. The house had a large parlor with many finely carved chairs, a large couch, and a loveseat. Kessi couldn't help but notice the intricate carvings on all of them. She ran her hand over one chair arm as she passed, feeling the detailed carving of a bird there.

They followed their host through the parlor and past a large stairway leading to a second floor. The handrail contained more carvings, mostly of flowers, birds, and butterflies. Kessi absently noticed a large vase containing more of the pretty flowers that were abundant in the town. The parlor emptied into a large dining area, where Samuel sat at a table partially filled with hot food. A younger version of Samuel, who had to be his son, and a similarly aged, attractive woman occupied two other seats. Kessi was sure the woman had to be Kody's mother. She had dark curly hair and big brown eyes like her son. She was beautiful, and Kody got his good looks from her.

"They're here, Samuel, just like you said they would be," their guide said without slowing.

She exited the dining area and entered an adjoining kitchen where several younger girls were preparing food. Kessi and Sabrina stopped at the table, not knowing what to do.

"Well, hello, ladies," Samuel said, standing up and smiling.

He wasn't nearly as grumpy as Kessi remembered when they'd first met him on the trail. The younger couple stood as well, and each wore a warm smile. The woman moved around the table to stand before the girls.

"This is my boy, Tomas, and his wife, Ahmee. My wife, Ruth, was the one who showed you in," Samuel continued.

"You are both welcome here. Please join us," Ahmee said, motioning to two large chairs at the table.

"Thank you," Kessi and Sabrina said in unison.

They took their seats as Ahmee poured them some cold water from a pitcher. The two younger girls came out of the kitchen carrying food. Kessi guessed they were both in their early teens.

"These are my girls, Leesa and Lilianne," Ahmee said.

"I am Kessi and this is my friend, Sabrina. We speak for the group."

The girls both smiled as they placed the food on the table. The family looked delighted, and it broke Kessi's heart to know she and Cassandra never had a similar chance. Nonetheless, it reminded her of home, but that time seemed like a lifetime ago. She couldn't wait to share her stories with Cassandra and hug Sera. It had been too long.

Ruth exited the kitchen, removed her apron, and wiped her brow. She went to the stairs as Leesa and Lilianne took their seats, leaving two empty chairs, one next to Samuel and the other next to Kessi. Ahmee took her seat next to Tomas and whispered something in his ear. He eyed Kessi and smiled. He offered her a wink, and Kessi could feel her cheeks flush. She looked away, embarrassed by the attention.

"Kody, get down here. We have guests!" Ruth yelled before taking her seat next to Samuel. "That boy has never been late for dinner. Perhaps he's sick."

"He's fine, Ruth, he—" Ahmee began before Lilianne interrupted.

"Yeah, he's nervous about them!" Lilianne said, pointing to Kessi and Sabrina.

"Lilianne, watch your manners," Ahmee scolded.

"Sorry, Mother," the younger girl said, then looked to her sister, and they shared a quiet giggle.

Kessi didn't like the attention and almost suggested to Sabrina that they leave. Only two things kept her from doing so: her immense hunger and the sight of Kody when he came down the stairs. He was clean, obviously bathed, and his clothes were immaculate. He looked magnificent, and she couldn't look away from him when he entered the dining room. His gaze fixed on Kessi, and when he smiled, she quickly looked away.

He sat next to Kessi and said, "Hello again."

"Hi, Grandpa," Kessi teased with a nervous smile. He smiled back; it was the most handsome thing Kessi had ever seen.

"What stinks?" Lilianne said with another giggle.

"I think it's Kody. He has on Father's smelly lotions," Leesa said, unsuccessfully trying to suppress her laugh.

"Mom," Kody groaned.

"Girls, enough," their mother whispered, and gave them a stern look.

To break the tension, Samuel offered a blessing over the food, giving his thanks to Phena, the Creator. He then took a piece of chicken, plopped it on his plate, and passed the dish. He repeated the process until all the food was flowing. Kessi and Sabrina took a large share. Kessi was somewhat embarrassed by the mound of mashed potatoes that seemed to engulf most of her plate. The look and smell of the food were intoxicating, and even Kody's excess cologne was overwhelmed and nearly eliminated by the aroma.

Samuel got straight to the point as they began to eat. "Obviously, we were expecting you, ladies, tonight, although I thought many more of your friends would come. However, we are glad you joined our dinner table. I told everyone here about you and how we met, so we know where you come from and that you are missing a friend. What we don't know is what you desire from Sylor."

Kessi appreciated the straightforwardness because she felt very uncomfortable with Kody so close and everyone staring at them. "We need people who know how to use a weapon. None of us are proficient," she blurted out.

Samuel and Tomas shared a glance, and from it, Kessi knew their request would fall on deaf ears. It was a knowing look that indicated they would fail any attempt at rescuing Emiline. The weight of the world was suddenly on her shoulders.

"Dear Kessi, Sylor tries its best to appease the were-creatures of Sylor Woods. Going against them to free your friend would cause great trouble for our small town. When we met, Kody and I were on our way to the rock where we leave our holy water for the volatile creatures," Samuel said.

"Holy water?" Sabrina asked, having already heard the tale, but trying to pry more information.

"Yes, we give them the water each week so that they will protect us from the vampires to the west."

"Vampires?" Kessi said. "The guard at the front gate mentioned vampires and werewolves. What kind of place is Sylor Woods?" she continued before catching herself.

"It is our home," Tomas answered.

Kessi could feel her face growing warm, and she said, "I apologize. I didn't mean to offend."

Samuel held up his hand to stop her and shook his head. "No offense taken, young lady. Our home is in Sylor Woods, one of the wildest and most dangerous places on Varish. However, we have been here a long time and have family buried here, so it's worth fighting for."

Kessi smiled weakly and nodded. She decided then would be a good time to enjoy the food, although she suddenly had no appetite.

"How often do the vampires attack Sylor?" Sabrina asked.

"They don't," Tomas answered.

"Because of the werewolves?"

Tomas seemed stumped at the question and turned to Samuel, who smiled. "The bottom line, Kessi and Sabrina, is we cannot offer your group assistance for fear of provoking the werewolves."

Kessi and Sabrina, now with their mouths full, shared a disappointed look and chewed slowly. The food was good, Kessi thought, but did that matter? Emiline was as good as dead without Sylor's assistance, and they were apparently on their own.

"But we will provide wolfsbane, right, Grandpa?" Kody added, sensing their disappointment.

All eyes turned to the young man, and Kessi mumbled, her mouth full, "Wolfsbane?"

"Yes, the flowers that Grandpa grows. The werewolves hate it, and it can protect you, right, Grandpa?"

"Of course. We'll weave it in your clothes in the morning before you leave. We also have silver-bladed weapons that will cut through them like a hot knife through butter," Samuel said. "And, of course, your promise to help in the fields can wait until your friend is safe and sound."

Kessi's relief at the offer of delayed chores they owed their hosts was short-lived. She knew they were in trouble without warriors or at least negotiators. She stabbed at her food with her fork, lost in thought. How could they have gone through the tortures that Nesin had to offer only for Emiline to fall victim to savage werewolves? She had never seen one before, but she was sure they existed. Her thoughts drifted back to when she and Cassandra were little girls and the giant wolves they encountered in the woods near Oldorburg. The intelligence in those eyes indicated they were more than just normal wolves. Were they werewolves? She suspected so.

"Is there something wrong with your potatoes, dear?" Ruth asked.

Kessi refocused on her surroundings and realized she had made a mountain from them. She looked up and saw everyone staring at her. She glanced nervously at Kody, who looked away quickly as if she'd caught him doing something naughty.

Kessi sighed and stood. "No, Ruth, the food is probably the best I've ever had, if I'm being honest. I'm so hungry that I could eat everything at this table and not be full. However, I don't wish to eat because my heart aches over my friend. Without seasoned warriors or someone who knows how to fight the werewolves, we have no hope of succeeding, and our friend is surely dead."

Everyone was silent for a moment, and Sabrina stood slowly. "Perhaps we should go," she whispered, putting an arm around Kessi's waist.

"Thank you for your hospitality, Samuel. We owe Sylor and will work off our debt upon our return," Kessi promised.

Samuel rose and said, "Please return to our home tomorrow at sunrise. We may not have warriors for your trip, but we will have wolfsbane and silver weapons."

"And leftovers," Ruth said, extending a hand to the table with a pleasant smile.

Kessi and Sabrina nodded and turned to leave, but Tomas spoke then. "And tell us, dear girls, what weapons do you prefer? We have plenty of picks, forks, knives, scythes, arrows, and more, all made of silver and deadly against werewolves. Name it, and we'll see that you're well supplied."

Kessi looked at Sabrina, and the sadness displayed on her face spoke volumes. Her friend knew the mission was doomed because none of them could proficiently use a weapon. They couldn't stand against a vicious were-wolf because of it. Kessi decided she would make the best of the situation. She had to set an example, not only for Sabrina but for all of her friends.

"Whatever you recommend, good sir; we cannot effectively use a weapon, so whatever type you supply will be equally awkward for us to handle, yet equally appreciated."

Tomas swallowed hard and looked to be at a loss for words. He eventually nodded and stared at his plate. Kessi turned to leave again but paused to take a sidelong glance at Kody, who was staring at her with those big brown eyes.

"I can teach you," he whispered nervously.

Kessi smiled and bent to whisper in his ear. His cologne was strong but intoxicating. She drank it in and said, "One day, Kody, I hope to take you up on the offer."

His eyes widened even further, and now it was his turn to swallow hard. Kessi and Sabrina left the large farmhouse and silently returned to the barn. They spoke no words along the way because none were needed.

Once they reached the barn and their slumbering friends, Sabrina succumbed to exhaustion and snored within moments of lying down. Despite her tiredness, Kessi couldn't sleep. Did they have much of a chance at saving Emiline? She doubted the odds were good. How many of her sisters would die tomorrow with the effort? Was the sacrifice of ten friends worth saving Emiline? What if they all died trying to save her? To escape such an overwhelming evil in Nesin only to die at the hands of vicious werewolves didn't sit well with her. She did the only thing she could—she grasped her holy symbol and felt its familiar tear shape.

Silent tears ran down her cheeks and pooled in her ears as she prayed, "Dear Adlesk, we need your blessing tomorrow. We face an impossible challenge and cannot hope to succeed without your intervention. Please be with us and protect Emiline until we can find her. I am forever your servant in faith. I love you."

She wiped her eyes and tried to get herself under control. She felt better having prayed to her god. She closed her eyes and began to drift off. She awakened with a start just before sleep took her and added one last thing to her prayer: "Also, be with Cassandra wherever she is. May she have a wonderful birthday, and please make it the last one we have apart."

She drifted off to sleep shortly after, the holy symbol of Adlesk tight in her grasp. Her god blessed her with pleasant dreams that night. She didn't fight the urge to sleep and fell into a deep slumber, the first she'd enjoyed in many months.

MORNING CAME ALL TOO SOON AS PATRICKA SHOOK KESSI AWAKE. It took her a moment to snap out of her dream state. When she did, she was disappointed to find herself in the barn. She looked around, and it was still dark, but the sun was rising. She could see Patricka's fair face in the dim light.

"What is it, Patricka?"

"A woman is here. She has invited us back to Samuel's farmhouse. She said something about sewing flowers."

Kessi rose, and as Patricka woke the others, she went to the open barn door. Kessi found Ahmee there with a smile on her face. "Good morning, Kessi. I hope you were able to rest last night. I know today is a tough day for you and your friends."

"Thank you, Ahmee. Yes, I rested well," Kessi said, yawning and rubbing the sleep from her eyes.

"When your friends are awake and dressed, I'll take you back to Samuel's place, where Ruth has a tremendous meal waiting for you. After you eat your fill, the priests will sew your clothing and hair with the wolfsbane. And, of course, my Tomas has your weapons ready."

"Your town is generous, and we appreciate the help," Kessi said as a yawning Sabrina came to join the conversation.

Ahmee's expression became serious, and she said, "We should do more. We should help."

"Nonsense, Ahmee. I know Sylor is taking a risk just by assisting us. We hope no harm comes upon your fair town due to our actions."

"Do not fret yourself with Sylor; we can handle the furry beasts if they come knocking." They all shared a forced laugh, followed by a moment of silence. Finally, Ahmee added, "Just bring your friend back here safe, and we will have a grand celebration."

"Deal," Sabrina said.

Kessi found her friend's mood contagious and decided it would be a good day. She would put her faith in Adlesk, and he would protect them. After the others had awakened, Kessi gathered them nearby. She wasn't about to force any of them on this impossible mission. She wanted them to have a choice.

Once they were all together, Kessi spoke. "My dear friends, we go now to undertake a dangerous and nearly impossible mission to rescue one of our own. I won't hold ill will toward any of you who wish not to journey forth. Now is the time to speak your mind. None of us are warriors or polished weapon-users, and surely none have experienced these creatures. Deciding to stay is not cowardly and will not be considered such."

There were some nervous looks among the group, but none opted out; they would all make the trek to the werewolf lair. Kessi smiled and went to each group member, sharing a hug or a smile. Joy filled her heart at their bravery and solidarity.

Soon after, they made their way through town toward Samuel and Ruth's large home at the edge of the fields. Some townsfolk gathered at the sides of the street, sitting on the steps of the various buildings or leaning against them. Kessi realized they were quite the spectacle: all twenty-three of them were unprepared and marching to their deaths.

The sight of Samuel's home broke the awful train of thought as Kessi witnessed a strange scene unfolding in his yard, next to the first row of the town's crops. The farmers had assembled several large tables, and a dozen ladies were setting them with bowls of delicious-smelling goodies.

"Wow, that smells amazing!" Natasha said, coming up to join Kessi and Sabrina.

"Yes, it is good. Sabrina and I sampled the food last night," Kessi said.

"Oh, you've been here?" Natasha asked.

"Yes, everyone was asleep except for Kessi and me, or we would have invited you," Sabrina said.

"We came last night to ask for help," Kessi added.

"And what did they say?"

"This is it," Kessi said with a sincere smile.

"They're feeding us? I'm grateful, but aren't they going to help us?" Natasha asked.

"They can't risk it, Natasha. Sylor is at risk of an attack by the vicious werewolves if they assist too much. We should appreciate the shelter they've given us, for I'm sure even doing that runs a risk to Sylor."

"Come, all of you, have a seat, and we will feed you," Ahmee said, disrupting their conversation.

They ate the fantastic food. Kessi didn't hold back or lose her appetite this time. She was famished, and the food hit the spot. She noticed that as they ate, healers gathered nearby with sacks of what appeared to be grains. They spoke in hushed tones, almost as if they knew the journey was suicidal and they didn't want Kessi or her friends to hear them.

Kessi ignored them and noticed Tomas nearby, organizing silver-bladed weapons on another table. Kessi was no expert, but they appeared to be short swords, slightly smaller than the ones they'd found in Nesin.

The morning sun shone brightly that fateful fall day, burning away the light chill in the air. The scene was breathtaking, and Kessi realized in that wonderful moment just how much Sylor was supporting them. She sat back and silently prayed as her friends finished their meal. She felt Adlesk's presence, and it gave her hope.

They were soon herded to the priests as Ruth and the other women packed some leftovers for the journey. The priests said a few prayers, then ordered acolytes to brush a paste-like substance on their clothes. Some girls initially resisted, but Ahmee put them at ease. "Don't fret. This is a special mud for the wolfsbane."

The acolytes continued their work, and Kessi looked around, scanning the area for a certain boy who had gained her attention. Surprisingly, she hadn't seen Kody yet that morning. Her thoughts were so preoccupied with the journey that she hadn't noticed that he was absent.

Ahmee walked up to her with a small sack of whatever the priests had brought. She smiled and said, "We will coat your clothing with the seeds, just as we did for your friends."

She sprinkled a few handfuls of seeds on Kessi's clothing. True to her word, the strange mud absorbed the seeds. A few other women assisted Ahmee, and soon, seeded mud covered all of Kessi's friends. Then, they began to sprinkle a little in each girl's hair. They needed no mud as the seeds stuck naturally.

As Ahmee finished sprinkling Kessi's locks with seeds, she whispered, "He isn't here."

"What?" Kessi asked, startled by her words.

"Kody, he isn't here. You're searching for him, I can see it in your eyes. However, he will not come."

Kessi felt more heartbroken than she cared to admit. She wrinkled her brow in confusion, but before she could speak, Ahmee said, "My boy likes you more than he's willing to say. He left before sunrise to work the fields because he didn't want to say goodbye. He wishes you a safe trip and looks forward to speaking with you again once you return."

Ahmee kissed her cheek and then moved to seed-up the next girl in line. Kessi felt and looked ridiculous, covered in mud and with seeds littering her hair. But she felt a bigger fool at the notion Kody wouldn't see her off. If the situation were reversed, she would be there for him. She could only surmise that the connection she felt wasn't as substantial for him. After all, they had only known each other for less than a day, so what was the big deal? Still, she couldn't help but feel hurt at the slight.

Soon, all her friends had been mudded and saturated with wolfsbane seeds. They all stood in a row as Tomas completed his brief lesson on wielding the swords. Kessi had been distracted by thoughts of Kody and had tuned his instructions out. Sadly, she realized he'd been giving them pointers on fighting the werewolves, and she'd missed most of it.

"You'll want to swing from side to side. Do not thrust your weapon. The werewolves' reach will extend further than your swords and strike you with their vicious claws if you fight them that way. So, again, swing left to right and right to left in a controlled manner to keep them at bay.

"Also, be advised," he continued, lowering the short sword so it pointed to the ground, "their bite is vicious and can infect you with the werewolf's curse. Do *not* let them bite you."

No one spoke when he finished, and they all felt uneasy. Tomas shifted from one foot to the other, the deadly silence uncomfortable to even the hardiest of Sylor's men. He put the sword back on the table, and with a nod, Samuel and the other priests stepped forward to face the twenty-three brave women who were about to undertake a suicide mission to rescue their friend.

"And now we offer you the protection of the wolfsbane," Samuel said as the priests raised their staves in unison and began to chant.

Kessi felt a tingling in her hair as vines grew and blossomed, interweaving with her locks. The mud on her dress sprouted similar growths, and soon, the remarkable vines covered them. They wrapped around the girls, hugging them tight from their bosoms to their waists. It wasn't uncomfortable, and it seemed to Kessi just another layer of protection against their enemies. The vines in Kessi's hair felt like a crown, and she looked on in disbelief at Sabrina and the others as their vines grew. It was a magnificent sight.

She required a few adjustments, as did her friends, and some of the vines pulled their hair or wrapped too tight in some places. Ahmee and the others helped make the adjustments. Once the finishing touches were applied, Tomas walked down the line, handing out the silver swords with a belt and scabbard. Once the belts were in place, Ruth, Ahmee, Lilianne, and Leesa provided them each with a backpack full of supplies, including the leftovers. Tomas then handed Kessi a detailed map of the southern woods so they could find the werewolf lair.

"And now, you are as prepared as we can make you. May Phena bless your journey, and we will watch for your return," Samuel said.

Kessi took one last look around to see if she could spot Kody. When she didn't, she put the boy out of her mind. She owed it to Emiline to focus only on her. She approached Samuel, shook his hand, and said, "Thank you for all Sylor has offered. We are in great debt to your people and will return shortly to pay it back."

Samuel nodded, but before he could say anything, Kessi ended the handshake and started the long trek to the front gate. Sabrina followed suit, shaking Samuel's hand and moving on. The other members of the small troop did the same, and soon they were marching toward Sylor's exit.

As they walked through the town, the townsfolk standing by watching as if it were a silent parade, Sabrina caught up to Kessi and said, "It's as if they know we march to our deaths."

Kessi smiled, and it wasn't a forced reaction. Adlesk was with them, and she thought they would succeed in their quest. Kessi was probably the only one who felt that way, but she knew Adlesk had answered her prayers, and he would work a miracle for them. She only hoped that none of her friends would die with the effort.

Once they were outside Sylor's gate, Kessi and Sabrina turned to face the small town as the gate slowly closed. There were guards posted atop the flower-covered walls, and they somberly waved as if they would never see them again.

With a sigh, Kessi said, "Let's get this done quickly, ladies. We will strike fast and be back here before you know it. Let's go find Emiline!"

There was a small cheer, and the group headed back into the woods the way they had initially come. They followed the trail they knew led to the rock where the members of Sylor offered holy water to the beasts in exchange for protection. Kessi hoped their actions wouldn't doom the small town. They were good people, exposing themselves to an awful danger by assisting Kessi and her friends. They marched silently on that bright, sunny fall morning, growing closer to an unimaginable evil with each step.

At the same time that Kessi and her friends left Sylor that morning, Kir and Densor, the queen and king of the werewolves, were sitting on their thrones, stewing. The long night had provided no results for the hungry werewolves. Brustin had returned empty-handed and had suffered a beating from Kir for it. They had expected to capture the unprotected humans in the woods while the moon was high. However, Brustin had reported that they'd followed the scent to Sylor with no sign of the humans, which didn't sit well with the queen.

They sat on their thrones, alone, to absorb the information. Densor usually remained silent when his wife was in such a foul mood, and this instance proved to be no different. When Kir was in a bad mood, male members of the pack tended to die. He was safe because his status as king usually spared him from her wrath, but that wouldn't stay her hand if she decided he required a good beating. The king of the werewolves waited and let his wife speak first. It took many moments before she did.

"Sylor has given the invaders refuge. They play a dangerous game, my husband."

Densor nodded, not wanting to stoke the flames of Kir's anger. "And the vampire is evidently a rogue and not associated with Vlord in any way. The situation is curious," he bravely added to the conversation.

Kir rose and left their throne room, going to Emiline, still strapped to the rock table deeper in the lair. Densor followed like an obedient dog. When they entered the room, they found the vampire in distress, moaning slightly, with smoke wafting from her rope bindings. They were burning her, and it filled the room with the stench of burned flesh. She was well guarded with two large men just inside the room. One was a good-looking, red-headed man named Gellor, who had recently taken an interest in bedding Kir.

"My queen, you are a sight for my sore eyes," he said, looking over Kir's shoulder to Densor with a smile. The diminutive king didn't react, used to the threats from her potential suitors.

"How is our prisoner?" Kir asked, ignoring his compliment.

He turned to regard Emiline and said, "The miserable creature is helpless before us. Shall we torture her some more?"

"No," Kir said, moving past Gellor to stand over Emiline. "Tonight, when the moon is full, we will have an orgy of delights! Blood will be spilled, and the forest will bow to us! Then, as the sun rises, we will watch this one burn in the morning sun, a grand conclusion to a holy night."

"And perhaps we could couple as we watch her burn?" Gellor said, running a hand over the queen's shoulder.

Kir's strike was quick and powerful, backhanding the man so hard he flew several feet away before crashing to the floor. He looked up at her with a shocked expression, holding a hand on his swollen cheek.

"I am in no mood for your games, Gellor. Tonight is a full moon. Only my husband will bed me on those nights. I will come to you if I'm interested in your services."

She took one last look at Emiline, then left the room. Densor followed, but not before giving Gellor a large, wicked smile.

KESSI AND HER FRIENDS HAD ONLY TRAVELED A MILE FROM SYLOR before encountering a lone person on the path. It was a striking image that made them all uncomfortable. Patricka noticed him first and drew her weapon, but when Kessi realized it was Kody, her heart pounded. He was standing on the path, waiting for them. He hadn't gone to work the fields; he had snuck out of the town. As he walked toward them, Patricka recognized him and sheathed her weapon. They all looked to Kessi, who walked toward the young man unwaveringly. They met on the path, just like they had a day earlier, and Kessi felt the same butterflies in her stomach now as she had then.

"What are you doing out here?" Kessi asked with a dry mouth, her nerves getting the best of her.

"You didn't think I'd let you go on this crazy quest alone, did you?"

"Kody, what we are doing is dangerous, and I can't ask you to come with us."

"Why not? You asked Grandpa last night for help, and I'm helping."

"Your parents will be furious at me."

"No, they will be furious at me, but not so much after we succeed."

They stared nervously into each other's eyes; they needed no words. Kessi just wanted to melt in his arms. She had never felt that way and imagined it would be fantastic. If they survived this, she would like to find out. As it was, she had to focus on her friend.

After a long silence, Kody said, "This looks pretty in your hair," raising his hand to gently touch one of the blooms.

"Thank you, but we all have them in our hair, Kody, remember?" Kessi said, motioning to her friends, who were walking toward the couple.

"Yes, but you make it look nice," he said with a smile that Kessi couldn't help but return.

"Well, Kody, it looks like you have come to rescue us damsels in distress," Sabrina said.

"Hardly, but I do have an idea, unless you've formulated one already."

"We haven't really talked about our plan yet, so I think we should hear him out," Natasha said.

"Agreed," Kessi said. "We know nothing of these creatures, so your wisdom will be invaluable to us."

"Even when I say my idea involves asking the vampires for help?"

"Are you mad?" Lila, the youngest of the group, blurted out.

"No, not at all. The vampires are not our enemies, but they do hate the werewolves."

"How do you know this?" Sabrina asked.

"Since I have been alive, we have never had an encounter with a vampire in Sylor Woods. Yet, the werewolves trade us protection from the undead creatures in exchange for the holy water. Why hoard all the holy water if no threat is there for its use?"

They all looked at each other, trying to find a response. Eventually, Kessi discovered her voice. "We will trust your judgment, Kody, because you know more about the inhabitants of these woods than any of us. Do you think they will assist us?"

Kody shook his head. "That's unclear. All I know is that if we tell them the werewolves are holding a vampire prisoner, that will get their attention. They hold no love for the creatures."

Kessi turned to her friends, the women who had become like sisters to her over the last year. They all looked to her as a leader, but she wasn't. She needed them all to make this decision. "What do you think? Do we allow Kody to prove his theory or keep marching?"

"I guess it depends on how long it will take, and what the chances are that they'll assist us," Patricka said after contemplating.

"That's the bad part of going this route; the vampire castle is to the west and at least a half day's march."

"That will mean Emiline spends another day with the werewolves," Kessi said.

"Even if she's still alive now, this will decrease the chances that she will be when we arrive," Sabrina added.

"It's a tough decision, but there is little hope without their assistance. Either way, I will follow and support you the best I can," Kody said.

They sat and discussed things in detail but didn't delay too long before choosing. The group decided recruiting the vampires was worth the delay. They'd all witnessed firsthand what the creatures could do back in Nesin. Without Emiline, they never would have escaped that awful place.

And so they traveled with as much speed as possible toward the home of the vampires. Kody didn't know much about them, but he told the young women what he knew. The elders of Sylor taught all their children the location and history of the vampire castle. Kody had learned the strengths and weaknesses of them as well. The same was true for the werewolves. Kody had only seen the vampire's castle once when he was ten, and the giant structure appeared as any other castle, complete with a moat and drawbridge. He dared not think what terrible beasts vampires would keep in a moat.

He recited all he knew, including that the vampire living quarters were underground and an enormous catacomb lay under the castle, where the vampire city was. The king of the vampires was named Vlord, and he had a prince named Galish. Kody didn't know any other vampires and, of course, had never met one. They all listened with great interest as Kody imparted his knowledge.

As noon approached, they came to a ridge. Below them was a thick forest as far as the eye could see.

"This is where their territory begins," Kody said. "It's probably best if just you and I continue from this point," he added, nodding to Kessi.

"Why?" Kessi asked, concerned.

"They may not take too kindly to all of us trespassing. The castle is within those woods, and they may be unwilling to help if they discover such a large group of trespassers."

"You aren't helping your case, Kody," Sabrina said with a snort.

"Kody and I will continue from here. The rest of you grab some food and rest. If we're not back by …" Kessi began, then looked to Kody for a time reference.

"By nightfall," the young man said.

Kessi nodded and said, "If we aren't back by then, leave here to carry out the mission. Please don't search for us, and don't wait. Instead, assume there will be no help forthcoming from the vampires."

"We cannot leave you, Kessi," Sabrina said.

"We must assume that Emiline is in greater danger than Kody and me. So, continue without us."

None of them were happy with that idea, but they reluctantly agreed. The girls all gathered around Kessi, embracing her in a tight hug one at a time. Sabrina was the last, and her eyes welled with tears at the thought of parting. "You realize we've been side by side for over a year. I will feel lost without you next to me, little Mayla," she said.

"You are my best friend, Sabrina. Keep your faith. Adlesk is with us, and this will work. We will return unharmed."

Soon, Kessi and Kody were gone, and the remaining women set up a small camp. They ate, rested, and discussed different strategies to go about the rescue, just in case they never saw Kody and Kessi again. Some even practiced their swordplay, using the silver-made weapons as Tomas had instructed, constantly slashing, never thrusting.

KODY AND KESSI WALKED IN SILENCE FOR A LONG WHILE. THE FOREST was thick and unusually quiet. Kody had to stop several times to get his bearings, and after a few hours of hiking, they decided to rest.

"I may not remember the way exactly," he admitted.

"Obviously," Kessi said with a smile.

"But the forest is quiet, which means we're close. I can't find the giant oak that serves as a guidepost. If we find it, the castle will follow."

"Well, let us be on our way. We haven't much time," Kessi said after a few sips from her canteen.

They started again, and Kody broke the silence. "So, your friend is a vampire?"

"Yes."

"And she has never tried to bite you?"

"No, she is surprisingly gentle but is violent when provoked."

"How? I mean, how did a creature like that become your friend?"

Kessi didn't take the comment as an insult; she understood Kody was genuinely curious. She smiled and said, "It's a long story, and when we return to Sylor, I'll tell you all about it."

"Deal! I like the way you think, Kessi Rho."

"Well, I'll let you in on a little secret about me and vampires," she said with a playful smile. The young man swallowed visibly and waited for her to continue. "Emiline is not the only vampire I've met."

"No way!"

"It's true. I met Emiline's master, and he was brutal and dangerous. He bit me several times."

Kody stopped, but it took Kessi a moment to realize he was no longer walking. She turned to find him standing there with his mouth agape. "You've been bitten?"

Kessi nodded and let out a small chuckle as she returned to him. "Yes, twice he bit me."

"And you aren't a creature of undeath?"

"No, I think they have to bite you slowly and at least three times before it takes."

"And you said he bit you twice?"

"Yes, look," she said, showing him her forearm and the old puncture wounds there.

He took her arm and looked at it, wide-eyed and full of awe. His touch was electric and had Kessi freezing in place. She realized this was the first time they'd touched. She could only look on and nod to any questions he had. Her face was a complexion of wonder as she drank in the essence of the wonderful young man before her.

"And here," she managed to say, taking back her arm and lowering the collar of her shirt to show the bite marks on her neck.

"Oh, wow, I can't believe you—" Kody began as he moved in close to look at the old wound.

He caught himself as he did, now apparently understanding the situation for what it was. He looked into Kessi's eyes, and, somehow, her heart beat faster. She became lost in his gaze. It was her turn to swallow hard.

"Kessi," he said huskily.

"Yes," she managed to whisper as he moved a little closer.

"And what have we here, two stray children from Sylor coming into the vampires' terrain to find a hideaway for their lovemaking?" a voice boomed from above.

They both jumped and moved apart on instinct, drawing their weapons. Kody's was a silver-made dagger that he nearly dropped when he unsheathed it. They both looked up to see a pale-skinned man with long blond hair crouched on a limb. He jumped from his twenty-foot perch with ease and landed between them. He was tall, handsome, and somewhere in his twenties. Kessi had some experience with the undead and knew that this man was a vampire. It was how he carried himself with the utmost confidence and the look in his eyes. It reminded her so much of Heinsvick. For a fleeting moment, she wanted him to bite her, even moving her head slightly to the side to give him access. She remembered Heinsvick's charming ways and quickly broke eye contact, recovering her senses.

"No, we're here to seek out the vampires of Denslock, for we need their help," Kody said, and Kessi realized he didn't fully understand what type of creature was in front of him.

"Brandishing weapons and sneaking around our woods?" the man said, and with incredible speed he grabbed Kody's wrist, squeezed, and jerked, making the knife fly into the brush.

Kody fell to his knees in agony, but the man appeared to be exerting little effort in maintaining the powerful hold. Kessi understood that strength, again, remembering her interactions with Heinsvick well. She sheathed her sword and stepped toward the vampire to gain his attention. "Please, he speaks the truth. We are not your enemy."

"And the pretty lass will save her lover from a cruel death, using her feminine wiles to distract me until she delivers the killing blow?"

Kessi shook her head and sighed. "Hardly. I'm a fledgling priestess, and he's a farmer. Neither of us is proficient in weapon use, which should be obvious," she said, nodding to Kody's grimacing visage at the tremendous discomfort the hold was causing him.

"Yeah… and we… are prepared to slay werewolves… not vampires," Kody managed to add between gasps of pain.

The vampire released him and said, "Find your weapon, and I suggest sheathing it when you do."

Kody gained his feet, rubbed his tender wrist, and nodded, backpedaling to where the small blade had disappeared. The creature turned to Kessi, exposing his back to Kody. Kessi hoped her new friend wouldn't try something stupid. She knew it was a test.

"Nice to meet you. My name is Kessi Rho, and this is Kody …" she paused there, not knowing his surname.

"Meece," Kody finished for her, finding his weapon and sheathing it.

Kessi stuck out her hand for a shake, and the creature looked at her strangely, even cocking his head slightly in confusion, precisely as Emiline tended to do. He stared at her hand as Kody walked back to stand beside Kessi. "You realize I'm a vampire, girl?"

"A vampire!" Kody yelled out in surprise, nearly going for his blade again. The vampire gave him a slight glare, and he thought better of it, but he blanched at the realization that he was standing this close to an undead creature. Kessi tried to ignore his behavior because she knew that was no way to win over the man.

"He's cute but not very bright, huh?" the vampire said to Kessi.

"What?" Kody said, and Kessi had to stifle a laugh.

"My question is still without its answer," the man added.

"I know you're a vampire because you act like the ones I've met," Kessi answered.

"What? You know my kind?" the mysterious vampire asked.

"Yes, and one of my best friends is a vampire, and she cocks her head just like you did a moment ago when she finds something confusing."

"Go on," he said, crossing his arms over his chest, refusing to shake her hand.

She wasn't insulted and kept her hand extended for a shake as she explained herself. "Her name is Emiline, and she's in trouble. The werewolves have her and may have already killed her. We came to your people to ask for help against the vicious beasts. I hope that together we can rescue her."

"And she's the one who has bitten you?" he asked, nodding to her neck.

"No, that was a second vampire, her master. He wasn't as nice, but I think he was also not bad. He had a good side."

"So, you play well with vampires? It's nice to meet you, Kessi Rho. I'm Galish, Prince of Castle Denslock, home to the vampires of Sylor."

Kody gasped again as Galish took Kessi's hand but didn't shake it. Instead, he brought it to his mouth, finally showing his fangs. Kessi had no reaction, and after a slight delay, he kissed her knuckle gently and released her.

"If you're a vampire, how are you out in the day?" Kody asked.

"One moment, dear boy," Galish said, raising a finger Kody's way while examining the boughs of the trees above him, appearing to search for something.

Kessi was also curious to know how Galish could move about in the sun. Heinsvick feared it immensely, and she knew Emiline did as well. It made no sense, but she was positive the person before her was a vampire.

"Ah, there's one. Come to me, my servant," the vampire finally said, raising a hand toward one of the larger trees.

Soon, a large bat flew from it and landed on his arm. It looked like a cat to Kessi, and how it clung to his forearm reminded her of a family pet. He stroked it behind the ears and whispered something to it. After instructing the creature, Galish stood tall and held his arm high. The bat turned and flew deeper into the woods.

"There, he will relay the information to my brethren. We may be on our way, but the moon is full tonight. Do you know what that means?"

"Werewolves," Kessi said.

"Yes, and they'll be worked into a fine bloodlust. They will kill anything within five miles of their lair. They will mutilate all wildlife in the area, and their ravenous orgy of killing and sex will last until daybreak. At that point, they will tire out and find shelter within their lair, but your friend, assuming she is alive, will be their final perversion. She will be burned alive by the morning sun."

Kessi's eyes widened at the thought, and she said, "We must be off at once!"

"Lead the way, child," Galish said.

Kessi led the way as they walked, and Kody walked beside Galish, true to his word. He didn't treat the vampires as enemies because he didn't feel that way about them.

"So, the sun doesn't affect you?" Kody asked.

"Now, that could be no further from the truth, young man! You see, my mother was a sun carofex, bitten by my father."

"A caro-what?" Kody asked.

Kessi had heard of carofex. There was a fortress of them in Mecca-Loraine near her home of Oldorburg, or at least, that was what the legends hinted at. She'd never met one that she knew of. She listened intently but kept a brisk pace, for she was truly worried about Emiline. If Galish was correct, she didn't have much longer to live.

"A carofex is a creature similar in appearance to humans, but much more powerful. We can control different elements, depending on what type of carofex blood runs in our veins. I have the blood of a sun carofex, which means the sun is my friend. It gives me powers, and I'm stronger during the day, unlike most of my kind who prefer the night."

"Which is why you were guarding your home during the day while your family sleeps," Kody said.

"Yes, in a way, I can watch after them while they are vulnerable."

"Are you the only one of your kind?" Kessi asked, talking over her shoulder as she continued quickly.

"No, my sister is also a carofex, and she's guarding the western side of the forest today. She doesn't like the humans from Sylor, so be glad you didn't meet her today."

"Why doesn't she like us?" Kody asked.

"Sylor has a pact with the werewolves. You produce holy water for the beasts to hold an advantage over us."

"But Grandpa says that we pay the werewolves to protect us from the vampires, that several murders have been committed over the years by the vampires, and the werewolves protect us so they don't happen again."

"Unfortunately, that's a lie. I'm afraid that the werewolves are vicious creatures, and if I had to guess, they were the ones who murdered your people and then blamed us for it. We have never killed a human from Sylor that I'm aware of."

Kessi stopped and turned to face Galish. "So, if you don't trust the folk from Sylor, why are you so willing to help us?"

Galish smiled and walked up to her. For a moment, she felt the intimidation that Heinsvick used to make her feel. It was the smirk on the man's face; it was arrogant and hinted at a power she didn't want to know. Heinsvick hit her often in the first few days they knew each other, often enough that Kessi had to summon the courage to stand up to him to end that vicious cycle. This one alluded to the same power, but she felt safe around him. Hopefully, Galish was a more amicable member of the undead. Still, she wanted to know why he wanted to help.

"I'm not eager to help Sylor, but I'm always willing to crash a werewolf party, and if there is a promise of saving a vampire in the process, then it's an easy choice. Have I made you feel at ease now?"

Kessi studied him for a moment before nodding quickly. "Yes," she said with a slight smile.

She turned and led the way, and the three walked silently until they finally reached the camp when the sun began to wane. Sabrina and the others were in awe of the sight as a vampire walked along with Kessi and Kody. But it was also a shock to Kessi and Kody as Tomas, Samuel, several dozen men, and a handful of priests from Sylor stood among her friends.

"Pa! Grandpa!" Kody said in surprise.

Galish stopped, far away from the gathering, and intently watched while Kessi's friends greeted her, and Tomas hugged Kody tightly. Samuel and Galish locked stares, and neither gave an inch in that silent stare-down.

"I guess I'm in trouble?" Kody asked.

"Yes! And no," Tomas said. "When we found you were missing, we left immediately, knowing you'd tried to help these young girls. We easily tracked you here and learned from them what your plan was. You are a good boy, Kody, and I can't be mad at you for it."

"And you were right, grandson, these girls do need our help," Samuel said, finally breaking his gaze from the vampire. "We were foolish not to offer more for their brave quest."

"And now, we have two dozen archers with silver-tipped arrows and a half dozen priests," Tomas said.

It made Kessi happy to see that Sylor's people supported them. She felt like they had a chance to succeed now. She silently thanked Adlesk; she knew he would show her the way. Samuel and the priests broke off from the group to approach Galish. She didn't know what would happen but wanted to do something. She began to walk toward them to intercept Samuel and explain that vampires were not necessarily evil. To her surprise, a strong hand grabbed her arm and held her back. She turned to find Kody holding her and shaking his head.

"No, let my people handle it. They'll do the right thing. They need to do this on their own," Kody said.

Samuel walked up to the vampire with the priests beside him, and Galish only wore a threatening glare in response. There was a long, uncomfortable moment of silence. Tomas and the archers wrung their hands on their bows while Kessi's friends watched intently, knowing how explosive an angered vampire could act.

Finally, Samuel spoke. "I've never seen a vampire in the daylight. Are you a true vampire?"

"Truer than you could know, old man."

"Then how?"

"He's a carofex, Grandpa," Kody called out.

"I don't know what my grandson is saying, but I assume that means you're different, and the sun cannot burn you?"

"Exactly," Galish said with a snarl, showing his teeth so the priests knew exactly what he was.

"Then I apologize that my grandson has disturbed you. He didn't have our permission to trespass on your land, which won't happen again. You may return to your home in peace, knowing you and your kind won't be bothered again."

"Well, I see where the boy gets it," Galish said.

The priests looked at each other, momentarily confused, before Samuel said, "Gets what?"

"His ignorance. I'm going to save a vampire. If the people of Sylor want to help, then all I ask is that you stand out of the way when I start gutting your werewolf friends."

"They are most assuredly not our friends, vampire, no more than you are," Samuel said.

"Fine. Just stay out of my way because I plan to rescue that vampire they're torturing over there in that dung heap they call a lair."

Galish started walking before Tomas said, "Are you going now? The moon will be full soon. Shouldn't we wait until morning?"

Galish stopped and turned with an annoying smile. "No, because once the morning sun is upon us, the mission is over, and it will be too late for the vampire captive. We must reach them before dawn. Hopefully, they won't smell us coming."

The vampire continued toward the trail from Sylor to the trading rock like he knew exactly where he was. Kessi nodded to Kody, then the others, and they quickly packed up camp. The priests and archers never said another word, but they all watched the volatile vampire leading the way as dusk settled in.

"We'll follow this creature in the hopes he'll join our cause," Samuel said with little conviction.

"He *is* safe, Samuel. The people of Sylor can trust him," Kessi said.

He looked into her eyes and seemed to find comfort there, so she smiled. He eventually returned the gesture, and the men and women from Sylor joined Kessi and her friends to follow the vampire.

"The moon will be full tonight and bright enough to light our way. Do not light torches or lanterns; our only hope is to catch these beasts by surprise," Galish called over his shoulder.

Soon, they were marching behind Galish, who had never slowed. Kessi's heart raced with the thoughts of meeting the werewolves. She could tolerate vampires because she knew them, but the tales of the werewolves only reminded her of the wolf encounter when she was five. A chill ran down her spine at the thought of it.

They rarely saw Galish that night as he scouted ahead, occasionally returning to lead the party around an area that contained too many signs of werewolves. He looked weak at night, Kessi noticed, which went against everything she understood about vampires. The nighttime was uncomfortable for Galish, just as much as it was for the folk from Sylor, all walking around in the woods without good lighting. She didn't doubt he was still very formidable, but he fared better in the daylight.

They walked for a long time, and wolf howls were eventually a constant sound floating on the night air. They were creepy and sounded close at times, so much so that Tomas would have them stop their march and hide. During those times, the archers would notch their arrows, and the priests would prepare their staves. However, they managed not to encounter any werewolves, and Kessi knew it was due to Galish's guidance.

Eventually, the night waned, and the werewolf activity seemed to diminish. Kessi looked at the brightening sky, and to her horror, she realized they had walked all night in Sylor Woods and dawn was near.

"We may be too late, Sabrina," she whispered sadly, taking her holy symbol and praying hard. She needed one last favor from her god to see this through.

"It's almost morning," Sabrina said.

"Do not fear, ladies, we are at the lair," a nearby Kody interjected.

"Are you sure, Kody?" Kessi asked.

"Very. I've been to the cave several times. It's within a half mile that way," he said, pointing in the direction they were heading.

"And now we formulate a plan," Tomas said, halting the party.

"We'll need you to provide cover with your arrows as we enter the cave," Samuel began, speaking to the archers. "You keep the mongrels occupied while we find the prisoner."

"We'll go in with you," Kessi said, motioning to Sabrina, Patricka, and Natasha. "We're the best sword-wielders amongst us. We also may be able to help find Emiline once inside."

Samuel nodded, and Tomas said, "Leave the other young people in your group under my command, and we will utilize them to the best of their abilities."

Kessi nodded and turned to her friends. "It's time to return the favor. Emiline saved us from Nesin, so we shall save her from these beasts. Sabrina, Patricka, Natasha, and I will enter the caves with the priests. The rest of you will remain out here under the leadership of the archers. Do whatever they ask to the best of your ability."

"Stay alive, and don't do anything foolish," Sabrina added. "We've all been through too much to lose anyone now. We see this through together."

They nodded. But the mood was dour. The forest was becoming lighter as dawn approached. Everything around them was too quiet as the howls that had haunted them all night were gone. Still, Kessi had to put her faith in the hands of her god, so she offered a final prayer before the group split.

"Let us pray," she said, and they all bowed their heads.

Even the priests and the hearty men from Sylor followed Kessi's lead, listening to a prayer to a god they did not know. But that wasn't the point. They were a unit, strong together, and needed a god's blessing to give them the confidence to complete the task.

"Dear Adlesk, it was your will that allowed us freedom from Nesin, and it will be your will if we are to save Emiline. We put our faith in your hands and ask that you help us with this last task. You are good and just, and we will credit you with any success we have here today. Please be with us all. In your name we thrive."

Suddenly, there was a commotion from a nearby bush as a brief snarl was silenced with flesh tearing and a sick, gurgling sound. A giant werewolf, nearly seven feet tall and twice the width of a human, staggered out of the brush holding its torn throat. Galish stalked behind it, wearing a glove that dripped blood from the silver-tipped nails sewn to the end of it.

The archers pointed their bows at the dying beast, but there was no need to fire as it quickly toppled over and gave one last shudder before growing silent. Kessi and the other women stood wide-eyed at the spectacle. The werewolf looked powerful and vicious despite its demise. Kessi looked to Galish, who shrugged.

"They have surrounded you. Whatever plans you've made no longer matter. Form a defense and hold your ground. I've spotted your friend and am going to free her now," Galish said.

"Emiline? She is alive?" Kessi blurted out more anxiously than she intended.

The vampire looked at the brightening sky and said, "For another ten minutes. They plan to sacrifice her to the rising sun."

"We can't let that happen!" Kessi said.

Galish ignored her and said to Tomas, "You, I need archers, follow me."

The vampire then melted back into the brush. Tomas led the archers behind him, trying to keep pace. Samuel started barking orders, and the priests withdrew bags of the wolfsbane seeds. Kessi couldn't focus on them; her attention was on the shaking leaves behind the last of the archers. She couldn't stand around and do nothing, so she moved quickly, drawing her blade and running after Tomas.

"Kessi!" Kody and Sabrina shouted together.

She barely heard them and focused on running to catch Galish. She believed the vampire could pull off the rescue and intended to help. She knew that one of her friends was close behind her, but she couldn't take the time to look. When she heard Emiline's bloodcurdling scream just ahead, she only quickened her pace.

"Kody!" Samuel called, but it was too late.

The boy, not thinking of his own safety due to his feelings for Kessi, ran off after her. The priests managed to keep the other young women gathered in a tight ring, six priests on the outside serving as protectors. They had given their bags of wolfsbane seeds to the young women.

"Throw the seeds all around, deep into the woods, at your feet, all over!" Samuel demanded as the sound of closing werewolves began to unnerve them all.

To their credit, Sabrina and the others controlled their emotions well and completed the task as Samuel instructed. They quickly tossed giant handfuls of seeds all over the area. The priests began chanting as they did and waved their staves. The vines shot up through the soil and engulfed the region, the beautiful blue flowers popping up along the vines at short intervals. Even the seeds they still held took root, and the women holding the bags of seeds had to drop them at their feet. Soon, there was a tangle of vines and flowers around them as the bags ripped open to allow the growing plants room to establish their hold.

The girls were hard pressed to move much, and Patricka dropped her sword during the chaos of growing vegetation and found no way to retrieve it, so thick were the vines. And then the werewolves were there, rushing at them from all angles. They slowed and dug in their clawed feet to stop from falling into the deadly vines. The first row of the large, dangerous creatures fell into the wolfsbane and howled in pain and fear. Some of Kessi's friends were so frightened by the sight that they had to drop their swords and cover their ears to drown out the awful sound.

Any of the werewolves that touched the plants immediately fell to the ground, scratching at their pelts so hard that they drew blood. They retreated quickly but still created a perimeter around the small group. There were dozens of them, large and intimidating, their muzzles covered with fresh blood from a night of killing under a bloated moon. The girls were frightened, and the priests, although having dealt with the beasts for decades, weren't at all comfortable with the turn of events.

"Beware, my neighbors, we are from Sylor, and any attack on us will be viewed as an act of war," Samuel yelled at the surrounding werewolves.

The blood-lusting creatures made no indication if any of them understood him. They tried to reach through the vines to get at the delicious and helpless treats inside. One came close to Samuel, and he batted the claw away with a powerful strike from his staff, which was covered with a high concentration of the bane. The creature howled and backed away, but another took its place, sensing the kill.

Sabrina noticed that Lila's long red hair was tangled helplessly in the vines, which had her standing far too close to the edge, near the snarling werewolves. Sabrina still held her small sword and began the slow, agonizing process of circumventing the vines to try to reach her friend. Two large werewolves, one with fur black as night, were trying to reach her from the other side. Lila screamed and pulled her head away from the monsters, tearing out large clumps of her hair as she did.

The large, black-haired creature was almost to her, ignoring the welts the flowers were leaving on its hairy arms, when Sabrina arrived by her side. She thought nothing of it and attacked in a fashion she was instructed not to, instinctively thrusting the sword into the eyes of the beast. It struck home since the werewolf had little room to dodge the attack. It let out a blood-gurgling howl and fell away. Lila screamed, cried, and held on to Sabrina tightly as she sawed the rest of her hair free from the tangle and moved her away from the perimeter.

Samuel and the priests had a few tricks to keep the beasts at bay, but they were minor inconveniences. They wouldn't hold them for long. Dawn was upon them, which would help, but they needed the archers to have a chance at adequately defending themselves against so many of the volatile beasts. Galish had led the archers away, so they had little chance to fight off the beasts. Another long, sad scream from the hostage vampire echoed through the woods, disheartening the group even more, especially Sabrina and the other young women who called Emiline their friend.

KESSI CAME TO A SMALL CLEARING JUST BEFORE A LARGE, ROCKY HILL. At the base was a cave that was the apparent entrance to the werewolf lair. Outside the cave was a tangle of werewolves, crawling all over each other and writhing in a mass of hairy bodies. The bloody remains of animals, and possibly humans, Kessi wasn't sure, were tossed around as the creatures seemed charged by the blood. To Kessi's horror and disgust, most of the werewolves were engaged in sex, biting each other as they did. The scene was horrific, and Kessi could only watch wide-eyed.

Kody soon joined her, and she was happy to see that it wasn't one of the creatures pursuing her. He was breathing heavily from the run, like she was, each trying to catch their breath and take in the scene. Kessi heard Emiline scream again, and it was such a desperate and pathetic sound. Her friend was frightened, evident in her wail. Kessi followed the sound, looking up the hill's steep slope to find another cave opening about thirty feet above the forest floor. And there, she saw her friend.

Emiline hung from just under that opening, her arms stretched above her and tied with a rope to two metal loops in the stone wall. She was limp and seemed near death. She shook her head, occasionally looking into the morning sky. An opening in the trees gave the vampire a perfect view and allowed the sun to fall directly on her. In a matter of moments, that would become a reality as the sun slowly began its rise. It occurred to Kessi that the werewolves had done that intentionally so their victims could watch the executioner sun devour them. Emiline clearly wasn't the first vampire sacrifice at that cave opening.

Above Emiline were two more of the vile creatures, and like the others, they were having feverish sex. A smaller one, obviously the male, mounted the more prominent female and had her ear in his mouth as he thrust into her. They leaned heavily against the cave opening just a few feet above poor Emiline. Her desperate screams were making their lovemaking more intense. Kessi felt helpless as the first rays of the sun began to show through the trees. Emiline screamed again and thrashed harder as she began to smoke and burn with the morning sun.

"Those are the leaders. Kill them!" Galish said from nearby.

Tomas and his men didn't second-guess the vampire and aimed at the couple above Emiline. Soon, several dozen arrows filled the cave mouth. Several struck the smaller one in the chest, making him disengage. At least five others struck the larger female werewolf, who managed to slink back inside the cave. Several arrows missed, and some came dangerously close to Emiline, who was oblivious to them at that moment and focused solely on the rising sun.

The smaller male stumbled and fell off the cliff face into the crowd of werewolves at the base of the hill. At that exact moment, Kessi saw a giant bat fly from the brush toward Emiline. She'd seen this before with Heinsvick and was confident that Galish was that bat and would save her friend. The thrashing creatures sobered up as their king lay broken on the ground before them. They watched with Kessi and Kody as the giant bat landed softly above Emiline, then changed back to Galish. He reached down with that powerful glove weapon he now wore and slashed the ropes holding her. He then hauled her into the cave and out of the approaching daylight.

GALISH GENTLY DROPPED EMILINE IN A DARK CORNER WHERE SHE would be safe from the creeping daylight. He had no time to spare and knew that the werewolves would slaughter the archers if he didn't assist immediately. Galish ran back to the ledge and began calling on the morning sun. He used his carofexian ability to harness that incredible power. He concentrated it into a weapon, amplifying its effects and dousing the area in pure morning light, with a brightness uncontested.

The effect had the werewolves, Kessi, Kody, the archers, the priests, and all of Kessi's friends shielding their eyes as intense light bathed the area around the lair. Galish quickly defeated the moon's power over the werewolves. The beasts fell to the ground, and their bodies underwent a painful transformation into human form. Bones popped and skin shrank, and they all writhed in the pain the transformation caused.

Satisfied that he'd negated the threat, Galish returned to the cave to fetch Emiline. He found Kir caught between wolf and human form in a strange and unsettling hybrid form. Half a dozen arrows protruded from her chest and side, and blood dripped from her large maw. She held Emiline's head with one massive claw-like appendage and had a glass orb filled with holy water before the petrified vampire's face. Emiline's eyes were wide with fear, but she seemed to understand her surroundings better now that she was far from the sun.

"Kir, you have lost everything today. Your reign in Sylor, your king, your lair, and, most importantly, your life," Galish teased.

"You! I know you, filthy spawn of Vlord!" she hissed back.

"That's right, my father sends his best wishes. Now, I have healers outside that will gladly fix you up if you hand over the girl."

Kir cackled and gasped and nearly fell over from the effort. "She will be my final kill, and you get to watch her die."

AFTER THE BRIGHTNESS HAD WORN OFF, THE ARCHERS FIRED INTO THE crowd of tangled bodies, their silver arrows doing as much damage to the beasts in their human form as they would do in their wolf form. The werewolves began heading into their cave and away from the focused light of the sun. Kessi understood that Galish and Emiline were trapped in there now. She needed to do something to slow the retreating beasts. She prayed and focused on her god, hoping he would offer something to assist.

She blacked out and fell to her knees during her prayer and wasn't aware of her surroundings for a long while. Kody stood beside her, guarding her in case one of the monsters attacked. Energy welled in her tiny tear-shaped holy symbol. Her god helped the meek and the oppressed, and she knew he had something to assist them, so she continued concentrating on her prayer and ignoring the carnage around her. The holy symbol grew warm in her hand, and she felt a powerful spell seep through her fingers and into the air around her. It was almost like a soft, beautiful song carried on the wind. She heard it, and although she didn't know it then, Kody would tell her later that he swore he also heard the song as she prayed.

The wind picked up suddenly, blowing that faint song all through the area. Even Samuel, Sabrina, and the others would eventually hear it, according to Kody. It was peaceful and calmed them all. More importantly, the werewolves heard it and calmed as well. They fell to the ground when they heard Kessi's song, fast asleep in a peaceful slumber. And just like that, Kessi Rho, with the help of Adlesk, negated the threat of a lair of werewolves.

GALISH, EMILINE, AND KIR HEARD THE FAINT SONG AS WELL. GALISH and Emiline, friends to Kessi, felt no ill will from it, but Kir fought to stay awake. She was the leader of the werewolves and the most impressive of the bunch, but she was no match for the song's power and soon fell asleep. Galish moved quickly and used his silver-tipped nails to ensure she never awoke again.

He helped Emiline stand. She watched him curiously as he tore the remnants of the rope from her delicate wrists. He then held them in his hands, turning them over to examine the bright red burn marks.

"Stupid holy water," he whispered.

He looked at Emiline and noticed she was mesmerized by him and that she understood what he was. He gave her a minute and said, "I am Galish, a vampire. I have come with Kessi Rho to rescue you."

Emiline cocked her head to the side as if she didn't fully understand him. She slowly reached out and pulled his top lip, exposing his sharp canine.

"You are like me?" she asked.

He nodded. "Yes, and we need to leave this filthy place. The werewolves will be back soon enough and with more water. Can you turn gaseous?"

Emiline looked out the cave to the bright morning and shook her head sadly. "I am lesser, and can only do so with Kessi's assistance."

"Never say that! You are a vampire, which implies you are so much more. Never lesser. There is only one way for you to leave here unscathed. Do you trust me, Emiline?"

"Trust?" she asked, tilting her head again.

Galish could only smile, then rolled up his sleeve, presenting her with his forearm. "Are you hungry?"

"Famished," she said with a slight smile.

"Then feed. It will heal you and give you protection from the sun."

"The sun?"

"Yes. I'm a sun carofex, and I can lend my powers over the sun to other vampires who drink my blood. It temporarily allows you to travel in the daylight, and we can get you somewhere safe."

Emiline just looked from his forearm to the cave entrance and the brightness of the day as the beams crept closer. "I don't like the sun," she finally whispered.

"I know, but do you trust me?"

Emiline smiled and nodded, and he brought his arm up to her mouth. She gently bit into him, never breaking eye contact. Once she pierced his skin and the blood filled her mouth, she was lost in a state of bliss, closing her eyes and feeding hungrily. Galish smiled as he watched her burn wounds slightly heal as she fed. His blood was making her whole again.

KESSI, STILL LOST IN THE TRANCE OF HER GOD, KNEW THE THREAT HAD been neutralized, but her god still called to her, so she remained faithfully patient. Kody knelt in front of her, waving a hand before her face. She remained unflinching, her eyes wide and her mouth whispering words no one could decipher.

"What's wrong with her, son?" Tomas asked, joining Kody in kneeling before her.

"I don't know. She won't wake up. Kessi did this to the werewolves," Kody said, waving his hand to the sleeping figures littered all about, "but she won't wake up."

Tomas gently shook her, and Kessi was aware they were trying to wake her, but she knew better than to break the trance. The song still played in her heart, but the most potent chord had yet to be released.

Suddenly, her god nudged her in the direction of the cave opening. She refocused on her surroundings, breaking her trance. Kessi immediately saw a relieved Kody before her and a concerned Tomas examining her. She paid them no mind, for she knew her god was directing her elsewhere, and she turned to the cave entrance thirty feet above her. There, Galish and Emiline stood hand in hand in the sun's morning rays. It was the most beautiful thing Kessi had ever seen, and it took her breath away.

Tears welled as she watched her friend fearlessly bask in the sun. Emiline even smiled and brought her arms out to her sides as if calling to the welcoming rays that Kessi knew would usually burn her. Adlesk called to Kessi and beckoned her to release the most potent note of the song. She heard the music clearly and directed it along the breeze to her friend. The faint song danced around Emiline as her hair blew all about in the breeze. The song seeped into her and carried the sun with it. Emiline's eyes widened, and a large smile formed on her elvish face. She no longer appeared as an undead creature but more like a forest sprite. That was her natural form, pure and good, before Heinsvick had taken her. Kessi knew that Adlesk used her as a conduit at that moment, and it felt as if she gave part of her spirit to Emiline during the brief time the vampire heard Kessi's song. The last, powerful note infused Galish's blood with Emiline's, giving her immunity to the sun from that moment forward. The carofexian blood she had ingested became her own.

To those witnessing the sight and hearing the beautiful song, there were no words to describe how amazing the event indeed was. Emiline's unbeating heart was warm for the first time since she'd entered the realm of the undead, the sun's glow grafting to her soul. Tears eventually streaked Kessi's cheeks as she witnessed the beautiful resurrection of her friend. Her god was good, and he had blessed Emiline, who would never have to fear the light of day again. She could be a beautiful elf and frolic in the woods once more, which better matched her wonderful personality. Kessi's friend was now safe. Overwhelmed with happiness and great accomplishment, Kessi collapsed into Kody's strong arms as the weariness took her.

KANE, THE LICH-GOD

CASSANDRA LAY CRUMPLED ON THE FLOOR IN THE MYSTERIOUS cave. Her last vision had been so vivid and disturbing that she had fallen from her chair. She tossed her head from side to side and moaned as the dream unfolded again. She wanted to wake up, to flee the place. It was so realistic. It felt like she was there, experiencing the early days of her father's existence. A sixth sense washed over her as an evil presence permeated the air.

As the fog dissipated, she found herself in a dark wood. Dawn approached as the sky faintly began to lighten. She was alone, and her nerves got the best of her as she glanced around anxiously. The forest was quiet, with not a cricket chirping nor a leaf rustling. However, it was the smell that disturbed her the most. It was unlike anything she'd experienced before, almost as if evil had a scent and was thick in the air.

Cassandra felt uneasy in the place. She knew something approached and sensed someone was with her. She screamed in her dream and made a small gasp as she tossed and turned on the cave floor. It had to be her father standing right next to her, though he was looking toward the sunrise and didn't acknowledge she was there.

It was after the betrayal he'd suffered at the hands of James, the acolyte of Marnelphion. He stood there, tall and unmoving, wearing a large purple robe. Only his head and hands were visible, and they were skeletal. Two little red dots shone in his eye sockets, the only thing that made her sure it was her father. She reasoned that he was telling a tale and showing her things chronologically with the dreams. She was reliving his past in the order that events had occurred. She didn't know how far this vision was from the last one when she'd witnessed his transformation. How he carried himself, emotionless and powerful, made her think a long time had passed.

The forest brightened as the sun crested the horizon. She could sense his discomfort. He didn't like the sun; it seemed to weaken him. She understood that it was the price to pay for being undead. She didn't know why he was standing in the sickly woods, thick with the smell of death, and watching the dawn. Soon, she had her answer as the immediate area brightened so intensely that she and her father had to shield their eyes. She was blinded in that instant and could feel an incredible warmth. The stench diminished significantly, and she felt peace wash over her.

When she could finally open her eyes and blink away the intense sunrise, she found a being standing before her that exuded a sense of power like nothing she'd ever sensed. The large man looked human, muscled with a beautiful face. His golden armor matched his hair, and the giant sword strapped to his hip indicated he was as dangerous as he was physically perfect.

"Phylance," her father said.

Just as the last time she'd seen her father in lich form, Cassandra noticed that his mouth didn't move, and the booming voice seemed to resonate within him. She had little experience with the undead but understood that her father was powerful, and his voice reflected that.

"Kane," the large man said, sniffing the air and taking in his surroundings.

"Must you amplify the light so?" Kane asked.

The man chuckled and said, "The only time an angel makes a proper appearance in the human world is at dawn, and doing so amplifies the first light of day."

Cassandra was standing in the presence of an angel! She was awestruck, and her knees nearly buckled as she finally came to terms with what this man before her was.

"As you've explained before," Kane replied.

"I'm sorry that it discomforts you."

"It doesn't as much as it did when we first met. Now, I relish the opportunity to suffer through the sun and its damning effects."

"So, you're practicing existing synergistically with the sun?" Phylance asked.

"Ever since we made our pact."

Phylance's expression turned serious and he said, "And that is why we meet this fine morning. I have been instructed to check on your progress with your latest artifact."

"It's nearly ready. In two days, it will be fully functional."

"And you call this thing Zormex?"

"Zolmex," Kane corrected.

They were talking about her birthright! How far back in time were they? Was this event occurring before the original New Order? Leo, the great wizard of that famous band of heroes, had used Zolmex, according to what she understood about the artifact.

"You will give it to the New Order?" the angel asked.

"It has already been negotiated."

"So, you have won the trust of Spring Goodwright?"

"Of course; we fight a common enemy."

"One that hunts us even now," Phylance said, drawing his massive sword, arm muscles cording as he did.

"Yes," was all that her father said.

Cassandra's eyes widened as her father produced a silver scepter from the folds of his robe, a large blue topaz adorning the top.

"Zolmex!" she tried to scream, but she couldn't find the words.

Back in the cave, her unconscious form whimpered.

She watched as Kane and Phylance moved back to back and waited. She could sense the evil that closed in all around them, and the smell became nauseating. A shiver ran down her spine, and Cassandra desperately wanted to flee or close her eyes. The dream was in control, though, and she could do neither. Soon, creatures burst through the shrubbery that surrounded their meeting place. They were hideous and obviously responsible for the awful smell. Cassandra retched uncontrollably when they entered the clearing.

Out of the corner of her eye, she watched the beasts close in on her father and the angel. They ran right past her, making her dry heave. Their appearance was just as disgusting as their stench. They wore no clothing, and although shaped chiefly like humans, they weren't human. They ran on all fours and were very quick. They were hairless and had large, pupilless black eyes and toothy maws that swallowed most of their faces. They drooled a reddish-black substance that continuously splashed on the ground, killing any plants it touched. There were six of the beasts, and they all jumped at their prey simultaneously.

Two lunged at the angel while the other four leaped at her father. She managed to recover enough from her fit to watch the spectacle. The creatures sorely outnumbered her father. Phylance recognized this and partially turned toward the lich to assist him. It was too late as all six creatures were in midair as he tried to maneuver to help Kane. Phylance held a hand toward one of the beasts, and it froze in the air. It just dangled there, unable to move or continue its course. The angel impaled the second one with his mighty sword.

That left four on her father, and she wondered how he could defend himself against that many enemies. That was when she saw Zolmex in action for the first time. She had doubted the artifact existed since meeting with Cedric in the temple's cellar in Pelesea. That meeting seemed so long ago now. Although she knew this was a dream, she understood that it was a confirmation from her father that the device was real. Kane held it up toward the evil monsters, and the topaz glowed brightly momentarily. Then, four beams of white light shot forth, striking each creature.

The creatures howled when those powerful beams contacted them. However, their cries of anguish were short-lived as the four exploded. Cassandra expected blood and gore to rain down on the forest understory, but it was just a light sprinkling of dust. Her father had disintegrated them using Zolmex.

"Impressive," Phylance said with an approving nod.

"Yes, and it isn't even as powerful as it will become," Kane said, turning the rod over and marveling at the magnificent creation.

"How so?" Phylance asked, examining the suspended beast that hung before him.

"It absorbs the wielder's energy when it's activated. I feel weak now, especially with that magnified sun you have summoned to bake us."

Phylance laughed but soon became lost in his study of the beast. "The monster knows nothing but hate. Why should these atrocities be allowed to wander the human world?"

"Like I said, I'm working on it. Once I perfect Zolmex, I plan to pass it off to Leo, the grand wizard of the New Order. He, along with his companions, will send Marnelphion and the rest of these demons back to hell where they belong."

The angel nodded his approval, then decapitated the suspended demon with one quick stroke. He released his hold, and it fell to the ground, where its spilled blood made the surrounding vegetation smoke and wilt.

"I have to admit, I am impressed," Phylance said. "However, I must cut our meeting short; these beasts can sense when an angel descends from the heavens. No need to draw more attention."

"Agreed," Kane said.

Phylance waved his hand, and the sunlight grew brighter briefly. It was so intense that Cassandra had to shield her eyes. The heat was nearly unbearable, and she wondered what effect that would have on her father in his state of undeath. When she could see again, there was a rift in the air beside the angel.

"I take my leave, Kane, the Artificer. I will report your progress to the gods interested in your plan."

Kane floated up to the rift and peered inside. Cassandra could see nothing but a bright light within, swirling with clouds that licked the air before her father.

"Easy, lich, the light will not only burn you, but it will destroy you if the day comes that you're allowed to ascend," Phylance warned.

Kane only stared into the tear and said, "I'm also working on that."

"I'm afraid there is no magic to help you with that," Phylance said, and Cassandra could tell he felt bad for her father. "Your body in its current state would never withstand the power that is the heavens. The place is not made for the undead."

"So you have said."

"And yet, you desire to transcend even more now than the day we first met," Phylance said with a warm smile.

"Yes, I want nothing more than to be invited to the heavens and designated a god by those you serve."

"I wish that as well. Your spirit is powerful enough to make the trip, but your body will be hard-pressed. If you visit my home one day, I will show you all the wonders the place offers. I hope your dream of becoming a god someday becomes a reality."

"Marnelphion will be banished, and it will be due to my greatest invention," Kane said, holding Zolmex up to the angel.

Phylance nodded, smiled, and said, "See this through. Banish Marnelphion, and I promise you'll get that invitation."

He sheathed his sword and stepped through the rift. It sealed behind him, and soon, the brightness of the morning light diminished. Cassandra watched her father, who stood perfectly still for a long while. His desire to walk the heavens was abundant; obviously, he had planned to do so for a while.

"Kane, the lich-god," she whispered.

He half turned toward her when she spoke, and her heart raced in her chest. Had he heard her? She stood paralyzed with fear until she heard the baying of more creatures. The demons were coming, and her father heard them as well. He held his arms out to his sides and slowly levitated above the trees. By the time the demons arrived, he was gone, and Cassandra was alone with the stinking beasts. She was not only frightened but deathly sick from the smell as they roamed all around her, smacking the carcasses of their brethren, which were beginning to melt into the ground, and disturbing the dust from Zolmex's victims. She wanted out of those woods badly and was relieved when the vision started to fail. Soon, the demons and pungent air were gone, and a new vision began to form.

THE VISION FOGGED, AND CASSANDRA'S STOMACH SANK AS IF SHE WERE being whisked far away. When the smoke cleared, she realized that wasn't far from the truth. She was in a dark room, and thankfully, the air no longer made her want to vomit. However, it had taken on a stale odor, almost like old vegetables on the verge of spoiling. She could see the outline of a table in the darkness, and it was massive. It was only a few feet before her, surrounded by roughly a dozen high-backed chairs. There were several windows to the room, and the stormy night sky was brighter than the room where she stood. The only sounds were the rain pelting the windows and a strong wind howling just beyond.

A sudden lightning stroke lit the room momentarily, and Cassandra found she wasn't alone. Each of those high-backed, fancy chairs housed a creature similar in appearance to her father. However, she didn't think any of them was Kane. They seemed distant, almost inanimate, as they sat around the table, none of them making a sound or a movement. She watched intently and examined each skeletal being when possible with each flash of lightning. They each wore a robe similar to her father's, but not the rich purple one he wore in the forest when meeting the angel. These creatures wore robes that were dark and sinister. She was pretty sure these were fellow liches. And how she felt in their presence made her think they were evil beings.

From what she had read about liches, they were most definitely evil, but she had a new appreciation for what her father had become. It wasn't his choice—undeath had been forced upon him, contradicting what she knew about the creatures. Was he the only one to ever reach lichdom that way? She thought of the sweet young man he had become who loved his parents, especially his mother. After witnessing that involuntary transformation and now being in the presence of these evil beings, she decided that was precisely the case. Her father was not a bad person, even in undeath.

Suddenly, the liches stirred, little red lights returning to their eye sockets as if they'd been elsewhere. Each looked around as if gaining their bearings. One looked her way, and she held her breath. Although she knew this was a vision, the power of that gaze made her wilt.

"The traitor has returned," one of them hissed.

"To his demise," another responded, waving a hand that Cassandra could barely see in the darkness.

Torches around the room responded and lit in unison. Cassandra took in the enormity of the place as the walls stretched at least thirty feet into the darkness, and she still couldn't see the ceiling. Other than the table and the two large windows, there was a set of massive double doors opposite the windows, which led to the interior of whatever structure this was. She wondered if it was a tower or a castle. It was magnificent and horrific all at once.

Suddenly, there was a loud boom that echoed beyond the doors. Each of the gathered liches looked to the doors and waited. They wore no expressions on their skeletal faces, but Cassandra sensed a fear in them. She assumed only something compelling could elicit such a feeling from a group of a dozen liches. The double doors swung open, slamming against the walls. They were nearly twenty feet tall and looked to be made of solid oak. It would take twenty people to open them and many more to swing them open forcefully. She swallowed hard and waited for the next excruciating moment of the dream which she was forced to bear witness to.

She wasn't so surprised to see a glowing blue light in the dark hallway beyond the doors. The glow of Zolmex relieved her a little—she knew it was the artifact. The light approached, and the creatures stirred in their seats, nearing a panic.

"It's only the traitor. We are twelve, and our powers are combined through the dark magic of Marnelphion. He cannot stand against us, combined as we are," the torch-lighter, obviously the leader of the evil council, explained.

"He knows the traitor is here and has sent the collector. Soon, he will no longer be an issue for us or Marnelphion," another of the creatures agreed.

Her father floated into the room, the glowing blue tip of Zolmex leading the way. He seemed ominous to Cassandra, nearly god-like, and carried himself accordingly. She wondered how much time had passed since the vision with the angel. She also was puzzled by the presence of the liches. Nothing in the history books back in Pelesea indicated that Kane conspired with others of his kind.

Her thoughts were interrupted by the leader of the council. "And so the traitor returns. What has it been now, Kane, ten decades?"

Kane stopped his progress and hovered like a dark angel, a mere thirty yards from the table. "It has been well over a century, Malignes," Kane cooly responded.

Malignes? Cassandra had never heard that name mentioned in any of the books she'd read. She watched as the leader of the group lifted out of his fancy chair and floated to hover above the center of the table. The others remained frozen in their seats, and it seemed to Cassandra as if they were lending the leader their power. He seemed to swell with it, and she could sense the massive energy swirling around the undead creature. However, that was nothing compared to what her father seemed to have at his command. The arcane energy and mystical symbols she'd witnessed her entire life swarmed around him and reached all recesses of the room. If the liches could see what she saw, they wouldn't be as confident.

"You are a fool to come here, Kane! You must know by now that we have joined our essences to become the most powerful undead in all the realms. Marnelphion has granted us this power in exchange for your capture. You have made that part easy for us by coming here, and we are grateful," Malignes said hatefully.

The leader of the strange, undead council lifted his hand toward Kane, and Cassandra was surprised to see Zolmex tear from her father's grasp and fly into the waiting, skeletal hand of Malignes. The lich cackled with glee and pointed a bony finger at Kane, summoning a band of green energy that wrapped tightly around her father, pinning his arms to his sides. The energy band was still tethered to Malignes's finger, holding her father in place.

"Fool! We have you captured and now possess the powerful artifact you planned to use against our lord. The collector approaches, and soon you will bow before Marnelphion and grovel for forgiveness."

The other liches seemed to chuckle at her father's predicament. Then there was another booming sound, and the stale air was temporarily sucked out of the room. A popping sound followed that phenomenon as another presence entered the place. Cassandra deduced that it materialized out of thin air due to teleportation. The beast was hideous and smelled of death, like the demons she saw in the woods with the angel encounter, but this one scared her more. From her studies, she'd learned that the more powerful demons could teleport, so this one had to be especially dangerous.

It stood over a dozen feet tall and was hideous. Its body was a mass of flesh, not well defined, but more of a blob of pink rolls that hung loosely from its neck, arms, legs, and torso. It didn't appear strong, but it was as it carried a human-sized steel cell, similar to a bird cage. Cassandra thought briefly of her fairy friend, Gophia, whom she'd rescued from a similar, much smaller prison. That thought vanished quickly when the beast smiled. Its mouth was full of razor-sharp teeth, and black ichor dripped down its chin and onto its fatty chest. Cassandra was horrified and repulsed and, more than anything, very frightened.

"I have come to collect," it whispered in a low, menacing voice.

"And we have delivered, Great One," Malignes said, holding Kane tightly in the energy coil.

The beast smiled and opened the cage. He lifted a giant hand and curled a meaty finger for the lich to bring his prize. The thing's smile grew even wider, and more black, foul liquid poured from its mouth.

"And now, Traitor Kane, you will suffer at the hands of our lord," Malignes said.

"But you're forgetting one thing, Malignes," Kane said calmly.

Cassandra was frightened for her father and was terrified to witness the awful scene. She knew she wasn't there, and that was the only thing that saved her from fainting. Yet, her father didn't panic, and she noticed the mystical energy he and Zolmex produced filling the air and swirling between the liches and the giant demon.

"Tell me, fool, now that you know your failure, what did we possibly forget?" the lich hissed.

"Notel X."

Cassandra's heart beat rapidly at the mention of the password she had found scrawled on an old scroll. It had been a stepping block in finding Zolmex and was the key to entering the hidden cave where she knew her dreaming body was resting. The strange words obviously meant something more than a cleverly concealed password. Her father had used it long ago, and it was somehow associated with Zolmex. She waited impatiently for the events to unfold. What could "Notel X" possibly mean in the scenario before her?

"Notel X?" Malignes said, obviously not understanding the phrase.

Her father seemed to relax as if all the danger he faced was somehow swept away. Malignes became rigid, as did the other eleven undead. The arcane symbols poured from the topaz resting upon the tip of Zolmex and wrapped around the evil liches. They didn't move, and Cassandra knew it was because they couldn't. Was the silly phrase used to activate Zolmex? That appeared to be the case in this scenario.

The demon's smile faded as it seemed to understand something was amiss. It roared, spilling black ichor on the floor. It was a clumsy-looking creature, so Cassandra was surprised at the speed at which it reacted. With one leap, it covered most of the distance to Kane. However, before the demon could land before the trapped lich, Kane easily snapped the magical binds that held him. Cassandra knew then it had been a ruse all along. Malignes and the combined powers of the other liches had never truly held her father prisoner.

He calmly lifted a hand and held the creature in midair. It grunted, roared, and jerked, trying to escape Kane's hold. Cassandra saw it blink out of existence for a moment, only to appear again in its invisible prison ten feet above the floor. Her father held the powerful demon with little effort and kept it from teleporting. His power was unmatched by anyone in the room. He made the other liches seem insignificant.

As he effortlessly held the thrashing, furious demon, he floated calmly toward the table and soon hovered before Malignes. The topaz atop Zolmex was pulsating with energy, the arcane symbols in the room flowing into the stone. Cassandra also saw the invisible waves of energy that it seemed to be absorbing from the petrified liches. It was drinking their essence, and they were powerless to stop it. Her father had tricked them into activating the artifact by saying the password.

"I'll take that," Kane said calmly, pulling the artifact from Malignes's weakened grasp.

The device still drank from the powerful undead, and the demon roared and complained about its predicament. It spilled more and more of the liquid from its mouth as it threw its fit. The sound of it splashing on the floor was sickening.

"You see, Malignes, you never were the master here. None of you were. Not even combining your strength can you hope to match my power. And now you have added the final touch that will ensure my little toy here will destroy your master and send the filth back to hell."

Malignes shook momentarily as if trying to break free from Zolmex's hold over him, but his attempt was feeble and pointless. The liches were losing their power.

"You see, Zolmex has one flaw—it taxes its wielder. Now, with the essence of twelve powerful liches, it can perform its most important task without affecting the user. The human I have selected to destroy Marnelphion will easily complete the task now. Thanks for volunteering your lives for the betterment of the world."

There was a screeching sound as Malignes finally found the strength to make a rebuttal, but it was too late. Zolmex absorbed the essence that had animated the liches for centuries, and the topaz grew so bright it looked white. Their bodies simultaneously turned to fine dust, their extravagant and colorful robes collapsing onto the chairs, and Malignes's onto the table.

With the task completed and the vile liches easily defeated, Kane turned toward the demon, who had stopped thrashing and hung in the air. Ichor poured freely from its mouth, and the filth covered most of its chest and enormous belly. It stared at Kane hatefully, wanting to tear him to pieces but understanding the lich's power. Kane floated within a few feet of the beast, Zolmex still glowing brightly. Cassandra caught a glimpse of fear on the monster's face, something she didn't think a demon could feel.

"And now a departing present for you," Kane said.

"He knows of you. He will find you. There is nowhere to hide."

"Yes, I've heard this before. Let me give you a taste of what will happen if your master of nothing comes for me."

The demon growled and lunged at Kane but was held firmly. This only enraged the demon, who struggled to break free. He roared and spat his drool everywhere but could not best the power of Kane. Zolmex grew brighter, and the beast stilled. Its eyes grew wide as it watched a sizzling white ball of energy float from the top of the rod and slowly toward its face. It stopped moving again, resigned to the fact it was defeated.

"I look forward to torturing your soul in hell," it said.

"Good luck with that, foolish demon. Why don't you go and wait for my arrival? It could be a while."

The demon growled and was about to respond when the white ball of energy shot forth into its mouth. It jerked to and fro as the energy seemed to eat it from the inside. It wailed and swung its meaty arms at Kane in a final attempt to capture its prey.

"Goodbye, filth," Kane said, then pointed toward the window.

The demon grew even more significant as the energy from Zolmex seemed to expand it. His eyes turned from black, hateful orbs to bright, blinding light as the energy sought a release. Even its skin began to glow. The demon was quickly hurled through the unopened window, following the direction of Kane's pointing finger. The window shattered, and the giant beast took most of the frame with it as it flew through the air under Kane's guidance, growing brighter. Once fifty yards from the tower, Kane turned it effortlessly to face him.

Kane appeared amused as the monster raked its own eyes and tore its skin, trying to release the energy. After a few more moments, it stopped and hung there. It looked toward the window and the being Marnelphion had summoned him to retrieve. Cassandra didn't know if the beast could see anymore as white beams shot from its eyes, but she understood it knew its doom. It was a bright spot in the dark stormy sky, making the occasional lightning strike seem dim.

Suddenly, the demon exploded, raining gore upon the ground a hundred feet below. It took a few moments for the gore to settle, and once it was over, Kane marveled at Zolmex. With a satisfied nod, he floated out the window and was gone. Cassandra had only a moment to register the events before the vision began to fog.

THE FOG WAS BRIEF AS CASSANDRA WAS QUICKLY HURLED INTO ANOTHER vision of her father's choosing. She understood now how powerful Zolmex was, even though she had no idea how to use it. All Cassandra knew was that she was ready to receive her birthright. She had learned much about her father and Zolmex through these vivid dreams, and for that she was thankful. Still, her patience wore thin as she desired the artifact she'd been chasing for over a year. She wanted to awaken and complete her journey to find it. She knew she had to be close. She appreciated the vivid dreams, but she was ready to move on. The only thing that remained was information about her mother, and she hoped her father would soon reveal that secret to her.

The fog cleared to the sounds of screams, both human and monster, as the ground rumbled beneath her feet, nearly knocking her down. The sky was dark, filled with black smoke from the burning buildings around her. She was in a city, mostly destroyed now, with bodies lying all around her. Most were human, knights in shining armor, the twisted and broken bodies mangled beyond recognition. They had met their deaths at the hands of something other than a human-made weapon. No human weapon could do what had happened to these soldiers.

Other bodies included beasts, the likes of which she had never seen. She could only imagine they were demonic creatures, given that her recent visions had included such. Their bodies smoldered and melted into a tarry substance. In the recesses of Pelesea's library, she had read that demon corpses melted away to nothingness once slain. So, she found herself at the end of what appeared to be a long battle between humans and demons in a city she didn't recognize.

Suddenly, a great cheer arose from what Cassandra could only guess were the surviving humans who fought the deadly demons. Their cheer was eerie, as if on the brink of madness, the desperation thick in their cries. She focused on that and walked toward it. The smoke was heavy in that direction, but she needed to discover the source of the desperate and muted joy that had no place in this setting. The ground rumbled violently then, throwing her to her hands and knees, where she found a river of blood flowing over a cobblestone street. Something was happening, something her father intended for her to see, and she would not miss it.

She stubbornly regained her feet and stumbled toward the location of the dying cheers. The ground still shook violently, and she struggled to maintain her feet. There were no living beings around her, just the dead that littered the street, along with the thick smoke that blinded her. She felt alone amid such an abundance of death.

The smoke cleared momentarily, and Cassandra saw a puzzling scene. To her relief, she found other living soldiers, battered, bruised, and bleeding. They weren't engaged in battle as she thought she would find them. Instead, their swords hung limply at their sides as they watched a giant pool of tar take shape before them. It appeared to be a living mass as it sloshed wildly. The men kept a healthy distance, and she understood why. She felt an evil presence there like nothing before. It was god-like and made her arm hair stand on end.

She knew then that she was in Novafontera, witnessing the banishing of Marnelphion. From what she remembered from her studies, this could be the exact moment the New Order banished the demon lord, and now she was living it! Suddenly, the tar churned violently and was tugged along the street as if being pulled toward hell, which was what she assumed was happening. The puddle of tar moved away from the group of men, tearing the cobblestones and pulling up a mound of dirt and stone behind it to create a spire of earth about ten feet tall in the middle of the street. It slowly stopped as if the force tugging it was losing its fight to pull it away. Eventually, it settled under the spire and bubbled.

A voice rose above it all amid the chaos and quaking earth. It was the voice of a leader, someone the desperate warriors of Novafontera could look up to. She quickly recalled the name of the New Order's leader, Spring Goodwright, and knew it had to be him.

"Quickly, New Order, to my side! We go after the monster. He's injured and near death. Let's finish this!" Spring commanded.

She couldn't find him in the smoke, but she knew he was close, so she continued her trek, using the deep voice as a beacon in the chaos. She carefully dodged bodies, debris, and the occasional warrior who ran past her, ready to give their life for Spring's cause. According to the history books Cassandra had read, they were going to meet their demise. All of them would die in hell trying to slay Marnelphion so that he could never return. She stopped and thought of that for a moment. Soldiers ran past her as she stood calmly, understanding they would die for nothing, and she would ultimately be responsible for his return. The prophecy predicted it, and everything the prophecy foretold was coming true. She suddenly felt ill, and a great sorrow washed over her.

The smoke finally cleared enough for her to witness Spring. He was shorter than she imagined but strong in stature and commanded respect. She could not see his face clearly because of the smoke, but he had long blond hair that matched his golden plate mail. In truth, he exuded magnificence. He stood at the precipice of a gate that shimmered in the air. A nearby wizard was using a wand to hold it open, and Spring was gathering his followers. Dozens of angels were nearby and ready to follow the brave men and women of the New Order.

"Leo! Bring Zolmex. It's the only way to destroy the beast!" Spring called out, then turned and entered the gate.

"No, don't," Cassandra whispered, tears now threatening to spill down her face.

They were all going to die. Cassandra watched as all the angels, the remaining members of the New Order, and even a handful of Novafontera soldiers followed Spring to hell. The gate closed behind them, sealing their doom, but Leo never made it. She was looking for him specifically because he would have Zolmex. Around her, the remaining soldiers were checking their injured or joining in skirmishes with any remaining demons. The battle of Novafontera was over, but the struggle in hell raged on, and she knew that everyone who went through that gate was being slaughtered.

She hoped to catch a glimpse of Leo, but she also knew he had died that day. She didn't know where to look in the middle of the chaos. Before she could decide, a wave of cold air ran across the remainder of the cobblestone road. It was so cold suddenly that she shivered as if caught in a snowstorm. Others around her noticed it, too, stopping what they were doing and looking around, puzzled.

Then there was a sucking sound coming from the tar as if Marnelphion were trying to emerge from the bubbling filth to retake his shape. Instead, Cassandra witnessed the curse as a deep, evil voice whispered through the streets: "I curse you, Spring Goodwright. From this day forward, no man will walk into your city without meeting his doom."

The voice seemed to linger in the air momentarily, and then the presence was gone. The chill Cassandra experienced from the cold air didn't compare to the sensation the voice gave her. She wanted to curl up in the road and die just from the sound of it. She looked around and realized that the soldiers in the area were doing just that. Those unfortunate enough to be in the vicinity of the tar were slain. The curse was so potent that it instantly killed anyone nearby who heard it.

Cassandra looked around helplessly at the fallen dead and knew that if she'd been there that fateful day, she would have died as well. It seemed to her that perhaps thousands of men and women lay dead all around the city proper. Then, a screeching sound came from the tar, and Cassandra was afraid that a horrible demon, perhaps Marnelphion himself, would rise and continue the attack. She was alone; every other mortal in the area was dead. Whatever was about to happen, she would experience it alone.

The awful sound continued to rise in pitch and became so loud that she had to cover her ears. She was petrified and couldn't move. Instead, she watched the tar, hoping whatever emerged couldn't harm her. To her surprise, the terrible sound suddenly stopped. She slowly removed her hands from her ears and watched the bubbling evil residue of Marnelphion. As the gunk churned and hissed, one of the bubbles that rose from it popped and omitted a green gas. The small cloud quickly dissipated into the air, but another bubble followed, and soon, many bubbles were spewing the poison that she knew would eventually fill the streets. Marnelphion's curse was unfolding over the once proud city of Novafontera.

She wanted to tell someone, to warn them that poison would soon cover the city, but there was no one to warn. She felt ill at the thought of the women and children who remained in the city, hiding from the battle, waiting for it to end. They would die as well. She couldn't do anything as the air around the bubbling tar was already turning green. She started slowly backpedaling when she noticed a movement to her right through a break in the thick smoke, and it startled her because everyone around her was dead. It was indistinct and more of a shadow than anything.

She willed her legs to move eventually to find the source of the shadow she'd glimpsed. She didn't have to walk far, and what she ultimately found saddened her. A wizard was lying on the cobblestone street, and she knew it was Leo because he still tightly grasped Zolmex. His eyes were wide and unseeing—he was dead. She thought back to just a few moments before when the brave leader of the New Order called for Leo to follow him. Would he have ventured forth if he'd known Leo was dead? Probably not, and without Zolmex, they were currently being slaughtered in hell. The sadness she felt then for the New Order and anyone else who had bravely ventured to hell was unmatched by any experience she'd previously endured.

Then, she witnessed the source of the movement she'd caught from the corner of her eye. From the black smoke, her father floated toward Leo. She stopped and watched. He floated above the dead wizard briefly, then reached a bony hand toward Zolmex. The artifact floated from Leo's grasp and into his.

"You have done well, Leo. You have helped slay the beast," her father said solemnly.

He looked up and past Cassandra at the approaching cloud of noxious gas. He reached another hand toward the dead wizard, and this time, Leo's lifeless form floated up beside him. "I will spare you this doom and find a place to honor your death."

Her father, the lich known as Kane, turned and floated through the smoke and away from the tar. Leo's body followed, his arms hanging limply in the air. Cassandra knew what kind of burial Leo would have because she'd found his tomb. Her father would put his body in an unadorned, cheap coffin with a scroll inside that she would discover over six centuries later. Her father, although not evil, had changed over the centuries since undeath had taken him. He was a liar and a user. The New Order was dead, and he didn't care. Marnelphion was banished, and that benefited him. Nothing or no one else mattered.

Her anger got the best of her, and she stomped her foot. "Don't leave!"

He disappeared into the smoke, Leo's body with him.

"Father!" she screamed.

She waited for the smoke to clear and for him to return to her. He didn't, and soon, the gas was at her back, eating at her lungs. She coughed. Even in her vision, she felt the burn of the poisonous gas as if she were there. Her father wasn't returning because he hadn't returned on that fateful day. He let the New Order die, as well as anyone left in the city. He could have sent Zolmex to hell with Spring. Another wizard had opened the gate; he could have used the artifact. She couldn't recall if the New Order had a second wizard. Regardless, she knew her father hadn't helped. They were dead, and he didn't care.

The poison seeped into her skin and burned. It filled her lungs, and she clutched her chest at the incredible pain before the vision faded. For that brief moment, she endured just a taste of the torture countless citizens of Novafontera had felt. Again, her father didn't care. The thick smoke and poisonous gas combined around her blurred out her surroundings. This vision was fading away.

THE PAIN IN HER CHEST FROM THE DEADLY GAS SUBSIDED IMMEDIATELY, but not the pain in her heart. She had watched her father unwillingly transform into the creature he had become, but even then, she could sense the goodness in him. Now, however long ago he had succumbed to lichdom, it had taken a toll on his soul. He seemed uncaring, which explained the prophecy she found herself a part of a little better. Did he care about her? Probably not. She was sure there was another motive behind his actions. He tasked her with summoning that beast, Marnelphion, back to the world to kill who knows how many people. And for what? To banish him once more with Zolmex? Was her life the ultimate price for that? She now knew he probably didn't care.

As she pondered the depressing thoughts of the prophecy's true purpose, the vision began to restore once more. She wanted nothing more than to awaken from the awful visions her father insisted she endure. She would then find Zolmex, and as she'd vowed to Cedric all those months ago, she would use it to protect her sister, if Kessi was even alive. That thought crushed her. Was she indeed alone? Would her father show her Kessi's fate? She focused on Binta and how she desperately wanted to reunite with her good friend. Perhaps they could live a happy life away from all the pain and misery. But for now, Cassandra was forced to participate in the realistic dreams her father concocted.

As she recovered from the burning poison in her lungs, the air became clean once more. The smoke was gone, replaced by fresh air and the dawn of a new day. She quickly realized she was in the exact location where her father had met Phylance, the angel in her previous dream. She glanced around, and sure enough, her father was near her, waiting as before, motionless and emotionless. She wanted to confront him over what she'd just experienced, to ask him why he let all of those people die, including the heroes of the New Order. Also, why was she part of the prophecy, and what gain did he expect to receive from it? However, she knew it was a dream, and he wouldn't answer. The scenario was simply a memory he was sharing. So, she sighed and waited.

Soon, the rift appeared just as before as the sun crested the horizon. She wondered if she was reliving the vision from before, especially when Phylance emerged from the bright light. But it wasn't the same; the angel was sad.

"Congratulations, Kane, you have succeeded," Phylance said with no emotion.

"I assured you of this outcome."

The angel nodded and again appeared sad.

"You are unhappy with the results?" her father asked.

"No… and yes. Many of my friends died in hell, chasing the great demon. One was my sister, Olivia. Therefore, I'm sad."

"I understand. I lost my parents to a similar fate."

"You understand nothing, lich," the angel growled back. "Angels are immortal, and she should still be here. We have roamed the heavens for thousands of centuries. What am I to do now?"

It appeared to Cassandra that Phylance would crumple in a heap of misery. He neared tears, and she knew a crying angel was not good. She wondered if Phylance's broken heart bothered her father.

Phylance composed himself and continued, "Still, I have come per our bargain to invite you to the heavens."

The angel stood straighter as if remembering his mission, shaking away the sadness. "There is a gathering of angels on the other side of the rift. They have come to welcome you and to marvel at your accomplishment. Few mortals have ever glimpsed paradise, and fewer still have ever called it home."

Her father looked at the rift and seemed uncertain. Phylance must have sensed his hesitance and touched Kane's shoulder.

"But as you said, this frail body of mine won't survive the transcendence," her father said.

"That is correct, my friend. There is no chance you will survive it."

"Thank you for your honesty," her father said, placing one of his hands on Phylance's shoulder in return.

They both stared into the rift. Heaven was just a few steps away from her father, yet he couldn't take those steps because the experience would destroy him. Suddenly, Phylance began to twitch as his muscles seemed to spasm, yet he remained unmoving.

"I have resolved that problem, my old friend," her father said.

Cassandra could see the angel's eyes go wide, and she knew something was happening between them. Phylance tried to speak, but all that came out was a whispered string of gibberish. She looked on as her father's eyes, which had glowed red for centuries in undeath, slowly dimmed to nothing but dark sockets. She initially didn't understand what was transpiring until she saw Phylance's pupils turn red briefly before returning to their usual blue.

Cassandra understood then what her father was up to. She recalled her conversation with Cedric, and he'd explained how Kane was able to become immortal—through possession! She had just witnessed him possessing the angel. The two separated, and when they did, the angel held Zolmex. The old body of Kane seemed more lifeless then, and the little red dots in the eye sockets were now gone. The skeletal figure weakly held up its hands before its face.

"How?" Phylance's voice whispered from the undead body of her father.

"Possession, dear Phylance. I have finally discovered a way to travel to the heavens safely."

"By betraying me?"

"By surviving," her father said, spreading his new angel wings and admiring them.

Phylance's new body, the ancient vessel her father had used for so long, began to break down. His arms dropped uselessly to his sides, and his fingers curled into his palms.

"Without my powers to keep the body animated, my old body will disintegrate."

"So, betrayal and murder," Phylance said in a weakening voice.

"I'll offer you one favor because I consider you a friend."

"I want nothing from you but my body," Phylance said as one leg folded, and now the proud angel knelt on one knee, refusing to fall.

"I cannot return that, Phylance. As you've told me multiple times, I wouldn't survive the transcendence to the heavens in my old body. Besides, I feel alive again for the first time in many centuries, even more so as an angel."

"You are a false friend and certainly no angel," Phylance said, gasping with each syllable.

"You are correct," her father said, standing before the kneeling angel. "I am no angel, I am a god. More importantly, I am still your friend."

"How… could I call …"

"Call me a friend after this?" Kane finished for him.

Phylance could only nod as his head lolled and his decaying body threatened to collapse.

"Because I offer you an eternity with your sister."

His old body gave out then, and Phylance collapsed face first in the forest understory. Her father knelt beside the dying angel and said, "I can find her, especially after I reach the heavens. She is dead, but I'll collect her essence and pull her from hell. I'm a master at creating extra-dimensional spaces. I have thousands of them across the realms and used them to remain hidden from Marnelphion while he roamed the world. I can make one a paradise for you and your sister to rule forever. I offer this in friendship, but you must decide if this is your fate or if you simply wish to cease existing."

Phylance mustered the energy to turn his decaying head to look her father in the face. He struggled to speak but eventually muttered, "Do it."

Kane held Zolmex before the angel and said, "Look into the gem and let it take you."

Phylance hesitated and struggled to speak but failed. Her father smiled and said, "No, you cannot trust me, I understand that. But you have my word. I can save you and will do what I can to find Olivia."

He held the tip of Zolmex close to Phylance's face, and the angel turned just enough to view the gem, even as his right arm fell from his decaying body. A flash of blue and white light was so bright that Cassandra had to hide her eyes. When she could see again, her father was standing, admiring the gem atop the artifact.

"I promise, Phylance, I will do my best to find Olivia. Either way, you will live on. I have saved you as my first act as a god," he whispered.

Her father turned his attention to the rift and the paradise that waited beyond. He looked at the pile of bones that used to be his body and stepped through. The gate closed behind him, and Cassandra was alone. She walked closer to the skeletal remains of her father, or Phylance, depending on how one viewed the situation. The delayed decay from the years it served her father in undeath now advanced quickly. The body was slowly turning to dust before her eyes.

The vision was failing again, Cassandra could sense it. She stood still and waited for it to take her to the next part of the journey her father was showing her. Cassandra looked back to her father's disintegrating body and lost some of her anger with him. Yes, he'd allowed Marnelphion to massacre many people, but that wasn't his intent or focus. The only thing he was trying to do here was live again, to get back a life stolen from him. Yes, there were casualties along the way, but that wasn't his true purpose. He simply wanted to feel alive. And she'd just witnessed that miracle, an event her father had meticulously planned. He had finally succeeded. She looked up to where the rift had closed and knew from that point forward, her father would be known as Kane, the lich-god, and a god he indeed was.

9

Treesha

GREYSON CALLED TO HIS STAFF AND WAS RELIEVED TO FIND the raw power of Plath within. His god was close, and to battle the vengeful Sebastian and his cronies would take all his holy strength. Alleah and Chloe were also ready, standing near Greyson with their maces. Sebastian smiled and closed confidently, two of his men following. Greyson stepped up to take on all three, which would sorely press him. He wanted to protect Alleah and Chloe at all costs, but Sebastian had other men who quickly surrounded both his friends. Poor Lud couldn't assist, still shaking with fear from the butterflies he called fligs and still in the snevol's grasp.

Greyson squared off against the three, Sebastian in front and the other two flanking him. Sebastian's remaining men used their swords to herd Alleah and Chloe away from Greyson, segregating them into three skir-mishes. A side glance told Greyson that Alleah and Chloe faced four-to-one odds—he knew they were in trouble. Greyson asked Plath to provide a spell to survive such a tremendously lopsided encounter. He knew nothing in his repertoire to help but hoped Plath would answer his desperate plea. He felt the power surge through his staff and into him, and the warmth made him tingle. Greyson sensed a power there to freeze his enemies. They could escape if he could paralyze them, so he focused on that and prepared his staff to release Plath's magic.

"Only subdue the women. We will enjoy them for many days before their usefulness fades. They'll fetch a fine price on the slave market. But they will suffer first for betraying us," Sebastian commanded.

Greyson could only see the two women peripherally, surrounded now and hopelessly outmatched. He estimated the area his spell would cover and focused the staff's power on the eight men surrounding his friends. It would probably cost him dearly in his own battle, but he didn't care. Alleah and Chloe had been through enough.

"Kill this one quick before he can unleash his tricky magic on us again," Sebastian continued, speaking to the two men who flanked Greyson.

He nearly had his spell ready for release when he noticed the strange look on Sebastian's face. The smirk was gone, replaced by abject fear. He wasn't intimidated by Greyson's pending spell or mighty staff but looked over Greyson's shoulder to something behind him. Greyson was too committed to the new spell at that point and couldn't stop for fear of losing it. He had little time to consider the change in Sebastian's demeanor and chose to ignore it. Still, before the pent-up magic of the staff washed over his enemies, Lud screamed horrifically, hinting to Greyson that something terrible was about to happen.

He was suddenly struck hard in the back, which knocked him to the ground at Sebastian's feet. He was now vulnerable, and worse, he lost the special spell that Plath had provided. He managed to maintain his grip on the staff but couldn't catch his breath or begin to defend himself if Sebastian attacked him. He wanted to warn Alleah and Chloe, but words would not form with his breath lost.

Greyson had no idea what had knocked him prone, but it felt like a horse had bumped into him, hinting that a more extraordinary being or a large animal was responsible. He managed to roll a few feet away and struggle to a kneeling position. He brought his staff horizontally before him to defend against a potential attack, but he shouldn't have bothered, for the creature that bumped him out of the way was now engaged with a desperate and backpedaling Sebastian.

He'd never seen anything like it—it was nearly seven feet tall but shaped like a butterfly with a human head. The creature had no arms but six serrated legs, three on each side of its worm-like body. Its face was blue with no mouth and a long proboscis coiled under its chin. Its powdery wings looked fragile and were bright blue, making the strange creature appear delicate, but Greyson understood that it was deceptive when those mighty wings buffeted him. He shielded his eyes from the unexpected attack but could see enough to witness the creature thrashing Sebastian.

The creature was intelligent and understood how to neutralize any attacks. It flew quickly toward Sebastian as the terrified man tried to chop at it with his sword. To Sebastian's credit, he hit one of the legs, but the sword appeared to do minor damage, if any, and the creature enveloped him in a tight hug. Sebastian screamed as the strong butterfly legs dug into his arms, pinning his weapon to his side. Sebastian and his men had chased Greyson and his friends through Sylor Woods without armor, and Greyson was sure he regretted that decision now.

Sebastian soon became overpowered, screaming in agony as the beast's sharp appendages dug into his sides and back. To Greyson's horror, the beast then uncoiled the long feeding tube and felt around Sebastian's face with it, as a blind person might touch someone to understand their appearance. Sebastian's eyes grew wide, and he shook his head, sealing his lips tightly. Again showing its intelligence, the flig squeezed him harder, eliciting a scream of agony as the leg barbs dug deep.

Once Sebastian opened his mouth, the butterfly man jabbed the proboscis into it, cutting off the scream. Sebastian's eyes grew even more expansive, and he gagged and gasped for air as the creature seemed to be feeling and tasting him from the inside. It soon withdrew the appendage and coiled it under its chin once more. Satisfied with whatever it had discovered in Sebastian's insides, it picked the evil man up and quickly flew away with him, giving testament to the strength of the strange butterfly creature.

By then, Greyson had made his feet and stood dumbfounded, watching the creature carry his screaming nemesis over the butterfly field. He briefly witnessed through the thick brush that the many butterflies stirred and swarmed the air. The glimpse of sky seemed painted in many colors from the hundreds of tiny wings, and Greyson could only watch in amazement as the large beast flew Sebastian above the treeline and out of sight.

Screams similar to Sebastian's soon surrounded Greyson, and he snapped out of his trance to see pure chaos around him. Dozens of the butterfly-like creatures were flittering about, grappling and probing the remainder of Sebastian's men. He saw a second one take flight, carrying a screaming man, and it soon lifted him of sight.

A bloodcurdling scream had Greyson turning back toward Lud, only to see the bushes behind the goblin scout shaking from where the fleeing snevol had just run. Lud's eyes were wide, and he was frozen with fear as another of the creatures fluttered toward him.

The goblin managed to yell, "Flig!" once more.

The flig, obviously the adult version of the human-faced butterfly that Chloe had found, grabbed the goblin, its barbed legs digging deep into goblin skin, and easily lifted the creature into the air. Just as the first one had done to Sebastian, the flig uncoiled its proboscis and shoved it down the goblin's gaping mouth. This time, the creature immediately withdrew the feeding tube and shook its head as if Lud tasted awful. Given the goblin's diet, Greyson understood that reaction. Lud never screamed and didn't make a sound at all but instead looked toward Greyson and mouthed, *Flig,* one last time before the creature tightened its grip and sliced the goblin into several pieces with its razor-sharp legs.

Pieces of Lud fell around the area as the battle erupted. The fligs were overpowering them all, even Alleah and Chloe. Luckily, they wore armor, unlike their enemies, and the sharp flig appendages dug into leather instead of skin. One of the things was already carrying Chloe to the butterfly field. They were all going in the same direction, gaining altitude once they reached the field of juvenile fligs. Greyson thought that was a good thing. Being taken to one centralized place might be the only way he would ever see Chloe again.

The larger fligs, equipped with giant butterfly wings, flew quicker, straighter, and more accurately. The baby fligs seemed to flutter around like butterflies with their tiny wings. He watched helplessly as a screaming Chloe was soon out of sight.

Alleah screamed as she, too, witnessed Chloe's disappearance. Greyson turned to her in time to see a flig shove its long feeding tube down her throat, stifling her. Greyson cringed, knowing that the butterfly creature was testing her, and he knew from poor Lud's demise what would happen if she failed that test. He was relieved to see it extract the feeding tube, pick her up, and fly toward the flig field.

"Greyson, help!" Alleah screamed. He could no longer see her as the flig's back was toward him, and she was hidden behind the creature's large body.

Chloe and her flig escort were out of sight, and Alleah would soon follow. Greyson stood and considered using his staff to invoke a powerful spell against the beast carrying Alleah, but he knew that was a bad idea.

Instead, he cupped his hands around his mouth, hoping Alleah would be able to hear him, and yelled, "Alleah, don't struggle. Let it take you where it's going, and hopefully, we'll find Chloe there."

He saw that none of Sebastian's men were doing well against the beasts; all had their weapons pinned to their sides by strong butterfly legs and were being carried away. None of them seemed to be sliced into pieces other than their little goblin scout, and the snevol appeared to be the only one to have escaped.

As those thoughts rushed through his mind, he was struck from behind again, but this time, two strong legs pinned his staff against his side, and another four grabbed hold of him. He was lifted a few feet from the ground as the flig easily snared him. The legs cut deeply, and he tried blotting out the pain. He knew what was coming next, and he hoped the thing wouldn't shred him to pieces because he had to follow his friends. It was his only chance to rescue them, and if the flig decided not to carry him away, he would never see them again.

Sure enough, the proboscis reached from behind him and felt around his face for a moment before moving to his lips. He felt the stout creature hug him tight so its legs would dig into his sides and elicit a scream. Luckily, they couldn't penetrate his armor, but he opened his mouth anyway. It was the only way to get to his friends. The flig forced the proboscis down his throat, and he suddenly couldn't breathe as the invasive feeding tube explored his insides. The flig used the appendage to feel around and test the quality of its catch. To his relief, the creature extracted it quickly and flew him toward the field. He was pleased to have passed the unusual test.

He was one of the last to be abducted from the woods behind two of Sebastian's men. The fligs all seemed to fly the same course, and once Greyson and his flig escort were over the beautiful but dangerous flig field, the butterfly-like creature changed its flight to climb steeply into the sky, far above the trees. Greyson saw all the fligs flying together with their prey, to his relief. At least fifty of them fluttered about the area, and most were unencumbered by a struggling victim. However, he did see Chloe and Alleah far ahead. He was thankful for that, but he had to formulate a plan. After all, the creatures weren't friendly, and he guessed that wherever they were taking them would not be pleasant.

They were far above the tree line of Sylor Woods now. Greyson tried to keep calm, but knowing he was that far in the sky with his arms pinned to his sides did not make him comfortable. He took in the view of the massive woods and saw a mountain range that seemed close from this vantage point. Greyson wondered if it was where he would find his home. He knew he would find Tara at the top of a small mountain and recalled the more prominent peaks beyond it. The mountain range before him fit that description perfectly, and if that was Tara's mountain, they were very close to his home.

He thought back to the last time he was there and his dead friends hung from the trees, gutted by Cerus. He'd never had the chance for closure and longed to revisit the community. But first, he had to find a way to free his friends and himself from these dangerous creatures. The course of the fligs was heading in that general direction. They covered many miles quickly, the flight of the fligs much quicker than he would have guessed, moving over Sylor Woods and closing the distance to Tara.

Greyson was suddenly distracted by the sound of paper rustling in the breeze. He couldn't move much, but he turned his head enough to see Lud's map impaled on one of the legs of the flig that carried him. The brutal creature that held him was the same one that had cut Lud to pieces. As he viewed the parchment, he noticed a river far below, snaking through the woods. It meandered northwesterly, almost precisely toward the mountain range where he thought Tara might be.

The flig carrying him changed its direction slightly to fly toward the east. Greyson looked that way to find the creature's destination: a single mountain peak near the river's edge. It wasn't tall, maybe a few hundred feet above the rushing water, and as the fligs began to descend toward it, he noticed a cave opening at the top. Many smaller fligs congregated there, flying around the area. They were beautiful and probably harmless now, but Greyson knew they would be dangerous once they matured. There was no denying where the fligs were taking them, and he didn't want to enter that mysterious cave.

The fligs lined up in a coordinated approach, each flying their prey into the mouth of the cave and disappearing into the darkness before the next quickly entered behind them. Greyson witnessed the flig carrying Chloe vanish into the cave. His heart raced as he pondered the unknown that awaited them within the darkness. They were all together now. His friends, Sebastian, his men, and Greyson were all prisoners of these strange creatures. He had a bad feeling about the outcome here. How did they hope to escape while held tight in their attackers' spiny grasp?

It seemed to take an eternity for his flig to reach the cave, and as it got closer, he saw Alleah and her captor disappear into the darkness as well. Many anxious moments passed as his flig got in line to enter the unknown. For all he knew, Alleah and Chloe were already dead. Perhaps the fligs sliced their victims to pieces as this one did to Lud once they entered. He closed his eyes and said a silent prayer. He was relieved to find Plath very much with him and holy energy still pulsing within his staff.

He opened his eyes just as they were about to enter. Many smaller holes were located haphazardly around that entrance, and a mix of butterflies and young fligs flew in and out of them, adding a dazzling display of color to the death trap Greyson knew awaited inside. He heard one of Sebastian's men cry out in fear behind him. Again, he knew they all shared the same fate unless they found an escape plan. Yet, what could they do?

His flig flew inside the cave just behind one of Sebastian's men. The light disappeared, and Greyson could see nothing in the noticeably cooler cave. The flig still held him firmly, making his arms useless, and the pain in his punctured arms became almost unbearable. Soon, he felt his feet touch the stone floor and was relieved to stand again. The flig walked him deeper into the place once they touched down and refused to release its death grip on him. All he could do was stand there momentarily and let his eyes adjust to the darkness.

He could see nothing but the light from the outside dimly penetrating the darkness behind him. But he could hear well and made out the sound of several of Sebastian's men crying or moaning in pain. He knew the shock of what had transpired was still settling for many of them. A few moments ago, near a field several miles away, they were ready to engage in combat, and now they were held in darkness within a cave in a mountain peak. Perhaps they were in a lair of the fligs. After all, what else could this be? Either way, no one had time to register what had happened to them.

"Alleah? Chloe? Are you all right?" he yelled.

"I'm here!" Chloe yelled back from somewhere deeper in the cave.

"Me, too!" Alleah answered from his left.

Alleah was closer, but all he made out were unidentifiable shapes, his eyes still adjusting. Shortly after speaking, his flig shook him hard, making the barbs dig further into his arms. He yelled out in pain and soon heard his friends do the same. The beast didn't want them communicating.

Either out of desperation or ignorance, Sebastian yelled, "Use your magic, Lightbringer, and get us out of here!"

Sure enough, that was followed by a painful yelp as Sebastian's flig shook him. He sounded much deeper in the cave than Chloe, and Greyson surmised that that was not a good position to be in.

It took a while for his vision to adjust to his surroundings because there was no light inside the cave other than what spilled in from outside, which fligs continuously broke as they milled around the entrance or flew in and out of the place. As his eyes adjusted, he noticed they were all there: Sebastian, his ten men, Chloe, and Alleah. The women were on the far side of the cave, about thirty yards from where Greyson stood, with Chloe a little deeper within. Sebastian was the first in line, the deepest in the dark place, and Greyson could barely make out his form. Greyson was among the last herded in and stood a mere twenty yards from the entrance.

The fligs divided their prisoners to stand on either side of the entrance and in a line leading deeper into the cavern. They held each of them tightly, and Greyson knew it would take a giant to break free of the iron grips of the fligs. The creatures seemed to be waiting for something, and they all faced the back of the cave. After Greyson had located his friends, he studied the darkness, looking in the direction in which the beasts stared. It was unlit there, and he could barely make out Sebastian and nothing past the vile man.

"Lightbringer! Do something now!" Sebastian suddenly screamed as if he saw something Greyson could not.

His flig captor shook him, digging its barbs into him as punishment for speaking. As Sebastian's screams echoed through the cavernous room, something deeper within caught Greyson's eye—the shadow of something much larger than the adult fligs. He squinted as his vision came into focus at a painfully slow rate.

In the darkness, only a few feet from Sebastian, who had already discovered the cave's inhabitant, was the outline of a prominent figure. Greyson could see movement from the shadow-cloaked behemoth. He still couldn't make it out entirely but realized then that the fligs had lined up each row of prisoners toward it. He finally made out the creature, and what he saw disgusted him: a sizeable caterpillar-like creature sitting on a stone throne!

It had to be at least twelve feet long and was very wide. It sat like a human, and had many tiny arms. Those mini appendages never quit moving, most quietly smacking together anxiously. That was the movement Greyson had detected moments earlier in the darkness. The creature jiggled from the effort and made a peculiar clicking noise followed by cooing. Its face was human-like, with eyes, a small nose, and an enormous mouth with mandibles on either side. It looked like the result of a mad wizard's experiment to cross-breed a caterpillar with a human. Its giant, bloated body was a powdery white, contrasting with the blue-skinned fligs.

It pointed toward the closest prisoner in Greyson's line, one of Sebastian's men, and the flig holding him moved before the giant caterpillar. The man struggled very little, and Greyson could see him grimace when he did move. Blood stained the man's shirt where the flig's legs dug. Sebastian's men had no protection from those vicious appendages. They could hardly move, much less try to break free.

The caterpillar sat up excitedly and clapped its many sets of small hands. Greyson estimated there were at least four dozen lined down its body. Some clapped while others waved for the flig to bring the man closer. The flig held him still while two others moved a large flat rock, long enough for a man to lie on, a testament to the fligs' strength. They held it horizontally between the prisoner and the caterpillar.

Greyson didn't know what would happen next but was sure it would not end well. He tried to think of a possible escape. Plath was with him—he needed a spell or distraction. The flig still pinned his staff to his side, and he couldn't access it entirely, but he could still form a vague connection with Plath through it. He couldn't summon anything significant unless he held it properly and concentrated. Both of those options seemed impossible at the moment.

"Sebastian, do something!" the man standing before the caterpillar creature yelled.

Before Sebastian could answer, the flig holding the man squeezed him with his powerful legs, eliciting a painful scream. When the man opened his mouth, the flig thrust his proboscis down his throat. This time, instead of probing the man's insides for a moment, it kept the tube in place as the man struggled to breathe. The man tried to escape, even though the flig's legs dug deeply and fresh blood gushed from his arms and torso. The man screamed the best he could, which came out as a muffled moan against the proboscis.

The man stopped his struggles and stood motionless, the feeding tube still jammed down his throat. To Greyson's disgust, the feeding tube seemed to pulse, as if the creature were forcing something into the man's body. Greyson knew from experience that the man couldn't breathe with the tube blocking his airway, and his face turned blue from lack of oxygen. Soon, it didn't matter as the man's eyes rolled to the back of his head, and he went limp.

The flig lessened its grip, its barbed legs making a sickening sound as they retracted from the man's chest and abdomen. With surprising gentleness, it retracted its proboscis and turned the man horizontal with its legs, laying him gently on the rock the fligs held. The caterpillar came to life then, sitting up straighter and obnoxiously waving its tiny arms, motioning the fligs to bring the man forward. The creature was so animated that Greyson thought it might fall from its rock seat.

Greyson and the rest of the captives looked on, not understanding the caterpillar's intent. The fligs holding the stone gently took flight and brought the rock slab with the unconscious victim toward the creature. The man's body shook as if in a semi-liquid state. He didn't seem whole, and Greyson was sure his eyes played tricks on him due to the lack of light, but the poor man seemed to slosh about the rock. Greyson was confident the man was dead. The caterpillar sat back and cooed, opened its mouth wide and smacked its many hands together anxiously. The fligs tilted the rock so the man's liquefied remains slid into the creature's mouth.

The caterpillar swallowed him with a few slurps and gulps, then squealed with glee, clapping its dozens of hands once more. The fligs flew off, and another pair took their place with a similar flat stone. The caterpillar creature motioned to the next man in line, whom the flig dragged toward the rock. After seeing the fate of his friend, this man fought hard to escape his captives, and the flig's legs tore him as a result. By the time he arrived at the rock, he had several wounds gushing blood. He was too weak to scream, so the flig prodded his mouth open with its proboscis and quickly forced it down the man's esophagus. The strange liquefying process started again, to the delight of the caterpillar that was obviously a god to the fligs.

Greyson could watch no more; it was time to escape or die. He quickly estimated how many foes had filled the cave and how any of the captives could escape the fligs' firm grip. The chances of an escape were slim, but he had to try something. He desperately tried to call forth the power of his staff. Again, his grip wasn't proper, and as he tried to manipulate his arm, the flig dug its barbs deeper. He stopped with a grimace, and the power of Plath eluded him. He would have to cast a spell he knew and hope his god could amplify it without using the staff. He was a prodigy, and he hoped the fligs were about to learn the hard way.

His concentration was interrupted by Sebastian, who seemed near crying and screamed once more, "Do something, Lightbringer!"

Greyson ignored him and made eye contact with Alleah. She was on the other side of the cave, but he could see her nod to him. She was helpless, as was Chloe, nearer the front of the feeding line. He returned the nod and took a deep breath—it was time to play the hero. None of the others had a chance; even his fellow priests seemed helpless. Greyson was their only hope, and so he would try.

His flig stepped, moving him closer to the bloated caterpillar-like creature as the line moved forward. The next victim was dragged to the rock, screaming hysterically. Greyson realized that Chloe would be next. He had to act fast, so he closed his eyes and prayed quickly to Plath, formulating his trademark light-summoning ability. Greyson coaxed energy from the staff the best he could, hoping it would be enough to blind all in the cave.

He knew Plath had answered his call. "Everyone, listen up," he yelled over the man's screaming. He hoped the fligs couldn't understand him.

The flig tightened its grip, but the armor shielded his body from the attack, although his arms paid the price for his heroics. He tried to put the pain out of his mind and continued, "I want you all to close your eyes tight… for I'm going to… blind these creatures using the holy power of Plath."

His arms screamed at him, and he had to growl away the pain and move it to the recesses of his mind. He conjured the energy to complete his instructions. "Do not open them until… I give the signal. Once I do, free yourselves from these hideous things… and jump off the cliff."

He screamed as the barbs dug through his flesh and knocked against bone. He barely remained conscious and realized then how close he'd come to passing out from the pain. If that happened, they were all dead. The grip loosened, retracting the barbs and tearing more flesh. He yelled in agony once more.

"What? That's suicide, Lightbringer!" Sebastian yelled, then screamed similarly to Greyson.

"River below us!" was all that Greyson dared to say, and he hoped his friends heard him.

He glanced at Alleah, and she gave another nod, but he could tell she wasn't confident in the plan by the look on her face. Honestly, Greyson wasn't either, but the alternative was far worse. To prove that point, the caterpillar creature burped loudly and clapped his hands. Greyson focused on the beast again and estimated it had already consumed four of Sebastian's men.

"I'm not doing that, you fool!" Sebastian argued.

"Close your eyes now!" Greyson yelled to anyone who would listen.

He released his spell, hoping that his friends at least understood what he was doing. He even hoped Sebastian and his men would run for it. The more chaos that ensued, the better the chance everyone would live. He also wouldn't wish death by liquidation on anyone, even his enemies, so he truly hoped the men lived long enough to escape this fate. Greyson felt the staff surge with power and could see the conjured light even though he clenched his eyes tightly shut. The light was so intense that he could even feel the heat of it. The caterpillar monster screamed, and the rock slab hit the floor as there was a buzz about the room. The fligs had no mouths Greyson could see, but he imagined they were screaming on the inside or possibly in a silent language.

His flig released him and must have fluttered away as Greyson felt the wind of those mighty wings. He fell to his knees for a moment as the pain in his torn arms became unbearable. He managed to call off the powerful light and yell, "Now! Run for the cave exit!"

He opened his eyes and was relieved to see most of the fligs had released their captives. Chloe's flig was one of the few that hadn't—it flew straight for the cave opening, still clutching their friend. Blinded fligs flew into each other or the walls. Some even collided with desperate men running for the cave entrance.

"Chloe!" Alleah yelled, reaching out a hand as Chloe flew past her.

The flig still pinned Chloe's arms to her sides, so she couldn't reach for Alleah's hand or do anything else. She smiled defeatedly as the flig flew out of the cave entrance. Greyson's heart sank as Chloe's flig cleared the opening, and a second one carried one of Sebastian's sidekicks. Both fligs were blinded as they circled haphazardly in the air just outside the cave. Chloe remained silent, accepting her fate, but Sebastian's man wailed hysterically, kicking and struggling against the hold. It was just a tiny piece of the utter chaos around them.

Alleah was suddenly beside Greyson, watching in horror as their friend met her doom.

"Chloe!" Alleah yelled again helplessly.

Suddenly, the flig carrying their friend flew toward the cave again, and Greyson thought it would reenter. He tightened the grip on his staff and prepared to fight the beast if it did.

A bloodied Sebastian was there at the lip of the cave, running toward the ledge, ready to jump as Greyson had instructed. He also noticed the close-flying flig and changed the direction of his jump at the last second, so his trajectory took him straight for the creature. Somehow, the creature flew perfectly into the crazed man's path, colliding midair. Chloe screamed in agony from the jostling of the impact, and Sebastian grabbed the flig around the torso, which trapped the wings and made all three plummet out of sight.

"No!" Alleah cried.

A man's head flew past Greyson to smack into the wall with a sickening thud. He looked in the direction from which the macabre missile had come to see fligs blindly flailing, cutting down Sebastian's men and other fligs alike. It was time to go.

Greyson grabbed Alleah's hand and said, "Let's go!"

They raced toward the edge. He had no idea if they were anywhere close to the river, but it was this way or become a liquified snack. Alleah started slowing as they reached the edge, losing her nerve. Greyson pulled her along with all his might, trying to keep her moving before one of the fligs sliced her into pieces. To her credit, she slowed only for a moment and, at his urging, was running again. She didn't scream as they jumped over the ledge hand in hand. Time seemed to stand still for Greyson as he measured their chances of hitting the river that snaked below them. Luckily, they were perfectly on target to hit the water, which looked deep and rough from his vantage point. He briefly considered that if the water was deep enough to cushion their fall, it would quickly rush them away. His plan might work.

He tried to spot Chloe, but there was too much chaos in the sky: falling bodies, flying fligs, agitated juveniles, and butterflies, which seemed to number in the thousands.

The fall took his stomach, and he and Alleah were flailing their arms. He lost her hand immediately but, luckily, held his staff. He didn't see any of Sebastian's men, and Chloe and her flig were nowhere to be found. He couldn't search for long as his attention was on the fast-approaching river. If he and Alleah didn't land in it, they had jumped to their deaths.

He spotted the spiraling flig that carried Chloe and Sebastian out of the corner of his eye just before they splashed forcefully into the water. The river seemed to swallow them up, and all three were gone. He looked to Alleah, who was slightly above him now in their free fall. He wasn't sure if she'd seen Chloe disappear into the water. He didn't have time to ask as they hit the water shortly after.

There were a few rocks where they splashed into the raging river, but the water was deep and they were lucky enough to avoid the obstacles lurking there. The current dragged them deep below the surface. Greyson immediately lost sight of Alleah, and all chaos ensued. He struggled to surface in the deep water, but the undertow had a death grip on him. As he fought to resurface, something splashed into the water beside him, and he could only assume it was one of Sebastian's men or a dead flig. Something from that unidentifiable missile struck his forehead, and his world went black.

TREESHA KNELT BY THE RIVER'S EDGE, EXAMINING THE FLIG'S BODY that had washed ashore. She knew it hadn't been dead for long, and it looked like it had simply drowned. Treesha looked to the southeast, where she knew the flig hive to be nearly sixty miles away. Rarely did she see a flig in her woods, much less a dead one. The poor creature wasn't overly intelligent, but fligs wouldn't fly into a river and drown. Something or someone had done this. She stood and looked up and down the river but saw no other fligs or creatures invading her woods.

The cool morning breeze blew her golden hair, now streaked with grey as she was in her sixth decade. She was a beautiful woman but knew nothing of it, having never seen her reflection before except for a glimpse in the river. Her plain brown dress was nothing spectacular but showed her shapely figure quite nicely. She was also unaware of that because she had worn no clothing for most of her life and had seen few other women to model her clothing after.

Her now-dead husband, Brayland, had taught her how to make clothing. He was the first person she'd ever witnessed wear clothes. He'd insisted she wear something and made many dresses for her. It took her a while to get used to restrictive clothing. However, he'd desired it, so she'd worn clothes ever since on the days she suspected she would see another human, which wasn't often. Even as she stood glancing downstream, she thought of how uncomfortable her dress was, subconsciously pulling at the material hugging her hips. She'd decided to wear it that morning, knowing someone had invaded her woods.

She took a moment to reflect on Brayland. He'd discovered her when she was just a child, maybe ten years old. He was twice her age and happened upon her as he traveled through her woods. She was more animal-like than human the day he found her, but she didn't feel threatened by him, and she soon learned to trust him. It was a long process, but he eventually taught her to speak. He also showed her how to eat with utensils, build a fire, and, most notably, as she became a young woman, how to make love. It took several decades to reach the point where he considered her a "civilized person," but he was patient. Treesha loved and missed him.

With the help of her husband, she had recounted her childhood. She never knew her parents and could only remember living among a pack of wolves during her earliest days. Brayland determined that nature had birthed her because of her unusual story and because she always had a special connection to everything around her—animals, plants, the river, the wind, and the trees. Everything in the woods seemed to be an extension of her. These woods were her part of the world, and nature was her domain.

Of course, other strangers had entered her woods over the years, and typically, she allowed it as long as they passed through and didn't cause trouble. However, in her woods, the death of a living being was a significant crime unless the killer used the carcass for food. A dead flig without explanation troubled her. There were strangers in her woods now, and it was time to discover their intent.

She stuck two fingers in the cool water. She reached out with her mind and felt the abundance of life found within. There were four things that didn't belong there, two of them possibly dead. They were human, not flig, and at least one seemed hostile. They were to the north, close to her home. She ducked into a nearby tree and exited another near where she expected the intruders to be, nearly two miles from the dead flig.

Sure enough, two were at the water's edge, one male and one female. The female lay washed ashore as the male struggled to get to her. He was in the deeper part of the water and just coming out of the strong current that ended at the small beach, less than one hundred yards from the home Brayland had built for her. Treesha remained hidden and watched. She would know the intention of the intruders soon enough.

The man coughed, choked, and finally reached the shallow part of the water, which came to his knees. He was exhausted from fighting the strong current and looked injured. He bent at the waist and coughed up water, breathing heavily, remaining in that position for a long while. Water poured from the ends of his long hair, and his wet clothing clung to him. Treesha didn't think him nearly as handsome as her late husband. Eventually, his gaze rose to see the woman lying on the shore, and the hate she saw plastered on his face told Treesha his intentions.

He staggered toward her. The man had been through an ordeal, and from the wounds to his arms and abdomen, she assumed it was a confrontation with the dead flig. Was he angry at the sight of his female companion, thinking the flig had killed her, or was he hostile to the woman? Treesha guessed the latter and watched intently. He fell to his knees beside her and checked her small wrist for a pulse. At first, Treesha thought she was wrong and that the man cared for the young woman. But he spoke, and she knew her first guess was correct.

"Good, you are still alive. Now let's get you out of those wet clothes so I can collect my fee. Then we'll let the water finish its job, hey?"

Treesha hadn't spoken since Brayland's death, but she remembered words and knew what the man intended. She watched as he lifted the woman under her arms and dragged her out of the water. Treesha reached into her pocket and fingered the wooden bear carving she always carried. The angry man, winded from the effort, sat near the woman and unbuckled her strange clothing. Treesha had never seen it before, other than through some sketches in one of Brayland's books, but she thought the woman wore armor. It was leather with metal reinforcements, which Treesha found pretty. She hadn't seen much metal in her lifetime but found the silver studs beautiful.

She stood and was about to exit her hiding place when the man said, "Ah, a small cottage. I'll check to see if anyone is home. No need to settle our debts out here in the cold if we can have a warm bed, huh?"

He looked around, taking in the sight and maybe suspecting the owner was around. Treesha smiled wickedly. He had finally noticed her home, and she was most assuredly around. She would not allow him entrance. He wasn't a good man, and she had seen enough. She stepped out of her hiding place near where he sat, startling him.

"Whoa, old woman, you scared me!" he said, holding his hand to his chest and smiling.

She couldn't remember some words but knew "old woman" sounded crude. Either way, he wasn't fooling her. She glared at him and didn't advance. She took her closed fist from her pocket, the bear trinket tucked safely inside.

"Is this your home? We were in an accident, my girlfriend and I," he said, pointing to the unconscious woman who stirred with a moan.

He walked back to her and knelt beside her, turning her gently to her side and patting her back. She coughed up water, and he said, "It's all right, dear, there is a nice lady here to help us."

The man had a weapon holder on his side. Brayland had owned a similar sheath, and the weapon inside could cut things, including people. This man's weapon holder was empty, and that relieved her. The woman was semi-conscious now, and she looked panicked as she gained her bearings and saw the man kneeling beside her. She was afraid of him, Treesha knew without a doubt. He didn't notice her; his focus was solely on Treesha.

"Say, is that your home, woman?"

Treesha understood most of what he meant, and she nodded.

"You live alone? You got a husband?"

He asked about Brayland and wanted to know if she was alone. He was trying to figure out if she was a threat. He had no idea just how much of a threat she was. She didn't acknowledge him this time and only stared blankly at him, wanting to draw him away from the woman.

The man smiled and said, "Are you daft, old woman?"

When she didn't answer, he sat on his haunches and laughed. He was so amused by the circumstance that he didn't notice the young woman reaching for a nearby rock. Treesha kept his attention on her for as long as the woman needed.

After the man finally gained control of his laughing fit, he said, "All right, then, you just stay out of my way, and we'll get along fine. I'm going to help my girlfriend here inside, and once I get her settled in, perhaps I'll come back and take care of you."

He looked her up and down, which made her uncomfortable. She had only seen two men up close in her lifetime: one was her husband, and one was a man with wicked thoughts. This man looked at her the same way the bad man had.

He added with a wicked smile, "You look like you've got a lot of years on you, but I have to say, you have curves in all the right places. Plus, your face isn't too hard on the eyes. I feel I can help—"

The woman brought the rock up and hit him in the head. It wasn't a hard strike because she was lying on the ground and still a little out of it, but it was enough to knock the man over. He fell back into the water, holding his temple. Treesha tossed the wooden bear figurine on the ground and whispered her friend's name. Then she walked beside the woman, who was standing on shaking legs, the rock still in her hand. This woman was a fighter.

As the man cussed and struggled to get back to his feet and out of the water while holding his bleeding head, the young woman noticed Treesha. She jumped and brought her rock before her as if to defend herself.

Treesha smiled to let the woman know she meant no harm. The woman was young and very pretty. Treesha liked her immediately. "Treesha," she said, pointing to herself.

The woman lowered her rock and faced the man, just coming to his wits. "I am Chloe, and this piece of filth is Sebastian," she said, nodding to the angry man.

Treesha turned to regard the man again, who was stomping out of the water. Chloe readied her rock, not backing down, and stood between the man and Treesha. The man stopped his approach and looked beside them, his eyes widening. Chloe followed his gaze, and she let out a yelp of surprise and stepped back when she saw what Sebastian was looking at.

"Buster," Treesha said, pointing a thumb toward the grizzly bear now standing on two legs beside her.

Treesha nodded to the massive bear, and it roared in response, rushing toward the man. A few moments later, little remained of him, and the water was crimson. Chloe couldn't watch and turned her back on the massacre. Treesha watched intently as her friend disposed of the evil that plagued her woods. Satisfied that Buster would have no problems disposing of the man, she went to Chloe, who was sitting, turned away from the river, and coughing more water.

Confused, Treesha asked, "You loved?" and pointed to the bloody water.

"What? No, of course not," Chloe said. "The bear attack was just violent, and I've seen enough death since arriving in this godforsaken land never to want to see it again."

"He was bad. I had to," Treesha said, not understanding the woman's hesitance to rid herself of the man.

Chloe stood as if to speak, but Buster's play stole her words. Treesha looked to the water and saw the bear munching on the remains, either a leg or an arm. She turned back to watch Chloe, who didn't look pleased with the scene. Was she secretly in love with the evil man? It didn't seem that way, but her reaction confused Treesha.

Chloe finally pulled her eyes off Buster and said, "My friends are in trouble. I need to find them."

"Two friends?"

"Yes! You've seen them?"

Treesha shook her head and nodded toward Buster's meal. "Are they like him, or like you?"

"They aren't like that man, Treesha. They are my friends. A man and a woman. How did you know of them if you haven't seen them?"

"The water said so."

Chloe looked confused and glanced at the water one last time as Buster munched on the last few pieces of what was once an evil man. She shook her head and said, "Magic?"

Treesha didn't understand her question and turned her attention to

Buster, who was now approaching. The bear shook the excess water away and issued an enormous roar. Pieces of the man clung to the bear's teeth and, along with the red muzzle, confirmed the man's demise. Treesha smiled at her visitor, but Chloe held her hands over her ears, blocking the bear's greeting. Again, Treesha didn't understand her behavior. After the friendly greeting, Buster went sniffing around the immediate area, paying them no mind, which wasn't uncommon after a large kill.

Chloe stepped into her view and said, "Treesha, I must help them. Please let me know if you've seen them or know where they are. I must find them quickly. I saw them last in a flig cave. They were in danger and could still be."

"You stay there," Treesha said, pointing to her small cottage. "Buster and I will find them."

She picked up the bear token and called Buster back. The bear rushed toward her eagerly but began to dissipate before he reached her. Soon, he was nothing but smoke as the wooden token drank him in. Treesha could hear Chloe gasp at the sight, but she didn't have time to explain. She pocketed the token and entered a nearby tree.

She stepped out somewhere further south at the river's edge. She didn't know the exact location of the other two trespassers, but she knew they were in this area of her woods. She wasn't sure if they lived. The river had sucked the life out of them, and they were either dead or close to it. She placed her fingers in the water again and closed her eyes. They were near. She recalled Buster, and they made their way quietly to the south.

It took her nearly an hour to stumble upon the couple, and she hid as she did before to judge their character. Both were out of the river now, one woman, one man. The man was unconscious, but the woman seemed to care about him. She had him lying on his side and was firmly hitting his back. He eventually coughed up water, indicating he was indeed alive.

Was he good? She wasn't sure, but the woman seemed nice, and her mannerisms reminded her of Chloe. Both had wounds on their arms, similar to the other intruders, proving they were together. These had to be the woman's lost friends. She looked over to Buster, who sat patiently and seemed uninterested, his belly full. The bear yawned and lay down on his side to prove the point.

"Yeah, I feel no threat as well, my friend. Let us watch some more," Treesha said.

She observed the two intently, and it looked like the woman was trying to heal the man, who was not only water-logged with injured arms but also bled from a wound to his forehead. He moaned as she whispered something while holding a strange necklace containing an unusual symbol. Her other hand went to the man's head, and Treesha witnessed a slight glow as energy seemed to pour out of the woman's hand and into his wound.

The man stirred, and the woman smiled. Treesha had smiled that way toward Brayland. He had made her happy. The man made this woman happy as well. They were not bad, and Buster didn't need to intervene. She was about to dismiss the bear when she had an idea. She smiled and ventured forth from her hiding spot, summoning the lounging bear to follow her.

The woman noticed her and stood. Her hand went to the hilt of a weapon. It wasn't like Brayland's, but Treesha knew it was a weapon of some kind. It wasn't sharp like the one Brayland once carried, but the end had a lump of iron that looked like it could do enough damage to defend the young woman if attacked. Treesha smiled, and the woman removed her hand from the weapon's handle and relaxed her stance. She eyed the bear nervously but wasn't as unnerved as some who had met Buster. This woman had seen worse.

"Hello. I have a feeling these are your woods, and we are trespassing," the woman said.

Treesha understood then that she was very wise for her young age. She was also stunning. Treesha hadn't seen many women in her lifetime, but this one possessed an exquisite beauty.

"You're a druid, aren't you?" she continued.

That was a word Brayland had used to describe her when they'd first met. It had taken her a while to learn what the word meant, and after she did, she'd embraced the title. She was indeed a druid.

"Yes, I am Treesha, druid of Sylor Woods," she said with a smile.

The woman relaxed and looked to Buster briefly before continuing, "I apologize for the trespass. My friends and I are fleeing the butterfly men. Do you know of them?"

Treesha nodded yet said nothing. She wanted the woman to elaborate. What was her plan now that she was in her woods?

"I am Alleah, and this is my friend, Greyson." She knelt and examined his wound once more before continuing, "We're searching for our friend. We hope to find her safe and be on our way."

"Chloe."

Alleah stood again quickly and took several steps toward her. "Yes! You have met her?"

"Yes, she is safe. I will take you to her," Treesha said, putting together words a little easier now after speaking with the intruders.

Greyson moaned, and Alleah went back to him. The look on her face reminded Treesha of how she looked at Brayland when they were in love. These two were a couple, and it made her heart swell knowing they brought love and not hate to her woods.

"Alleah?" he said, tossing his head back and forth.

"I'm here, Greyson," she said, touching his cheek.

Treesha approached as Buster wandered to the river for a drink. She wanted to watch the interaction; it reminded her of her younger self.

"You saved us again, Greyson, just like that day the men at Port Racip ambushed us. You saved Chloe and me."

Greyson's eyes fluttered open, and he smiled. Alleah returned it, and Treesha saw tears forming in the beautiful woman's eyes.

"Binta?" Greyson whispered and brought his hand up to pluck Alleah's from his cheek and hold it tightly. His smile faded, as did his grasp as he lost consciousness once more.

Alleah smiled weakly at Treesha and said, "He's delirious. Can you help me get him to a bed so I may continue healing him?"

Treesha nodded and didn't address the pain and disappointment that flashed across the young woman's face after he called her the wrong name. She summoned Buster and had the great bear tuck his legs under him so they could drape Greyson's body over his back. Once secure, Buster rose, and they started on their way.

"Wait," Alleah said before they'd taken a few steps.

"What is it, dear girl?"

"His staff. It's missing."

"He owns a staff?"

"Yes, a powerful conduit to his god," Alleah said as she walked up and down the river's edge, looking for it in the water.

After a few minutes, Treesha said, "Come, we will find it later. We have a long walk ahead of us."

Alleah looked doubtfully at her, then back at the river, scanning it one final time. With a sigh and a nod, she finally complied, and the three moved off toward Treesha's home with an unconscious and delirious Greyson in tow.

NEARLY TWO WEEKS HAD PASSED, AND GREYSON WAS STILL UNCON-scious. He had developed a fever, and the cut on his head had worsened. Alleah and Chloe healed him with their spells, and Treesha even had a few herbs and ointments to add. If not for them, his wounds would have proven fatal. Luckily, his fever had broken two days prior, and they felt he would make it through the ordeal. He currently rested in the only bed in her one-room cottage. Treesha hung a sheet to cut off the sleeping young man from the rest of the room, giving him some privacy.

The three women sat at the table in the quaint home, just on the other side of the sheet, sharing a meal. Treesha quickly became friends with them and welcomed their company. Her grasp of the common tongue, which had deteriorated since Brayland had died, returned a little more with each passing day. She was glad for the visitors and the company.

A fire burned in the hearth as the cool fall weather set in across Sylor Woods. A lovely stew of roots and mushrooms boiled in a pot above it. The warmth of a fire and the pleasant aroma of good food filled her small home. Most of all, her company filled it with joy. And since no fligs had invaded her woods looking for her new companions, they had also relaxed.

As Alleah and Chloe laughed at a shared memory, Treesha glanced to the corner of the room where she'd propped their weapons. They had eventually found Greyson's staff, and it was there, along with Alleah's weapon, which Treesha had learned was a mace. Chloe had lost her mace in the daring escape from the fligs, but they'd found Sebastian's sword, which Chloe claimed as her own now, and it leaned beside the other weapons. They didn't carry their weapons because they felt safe in her home, which meant the world to her.

She had learned a lot about the three companions through Alleah and Chloe's stories and from their body actions. The way Alleah doted on Greyson and remained by his side until his fever broke confirmed she cared for the man very much. Chloe was also very concerned, but Alleah's actions indicated she felt more than friendship for Greyson. Equally important was how Chloe carried herself as if she'd recently experienced something awful, but not physically. No, her wounds were more mental and, therefore, more serious in Treesha's opinion. The girl was recovering from something horrible, and Treesha guessed it wasn't from the flig incident.

The most troubling discovery, however, had been the strict tenets of the goddess the two young women worshipped. Treesha had learned a little about gods and goddesses through Brayland but didn't understand them. She witnessed the power of Alleah and Chloe's goddess when they worked their magic on Greyson's injuries. Still, the requirements of their goddess puzzled the druid, who understood Alleah's feelings about her friend wouldn't coincide with sticking to those rules. She didn't want to pry but felt compelled to broach the subject again.

"So, you may never be with a man?" Treesha asked them both, breaking their private conversation.

They seemed slightly surprised by her bluntness but didn't appear offended. Alleah finally shook her head and said, "No. Sex, kissing, or even touching another person in that manner is forbidden."

"So, neither of you have been with Greyson intimately?"

"What? Of course not," Alleah blurted out as if the notion were ridiculous.

Treesha noticed how Chloe stared at her friend accusatorily for a moment. Still, she said nothing and continued to let Alleah lead the conversation.

"But you want to?" Treesha asked.

"Of course not!" Alleah said, her pretty face instantly turning red.

"Strange behavior from someone who will soon have to choose between the man she desires and the goddess she loves."

"That's what I said!" Chloe finally chimed in.

The surprised look Alleah gave her friend spoke volumes.

"What? She knows you like him. We all do. It's written all over your face," Chloe said.

"I find it sad that you cannot enjoy the pleasures of sex. I find that to be very greedy of your goddess," Treesha said.

"Sinnis is all-powerful and asks little of us for the blessings she provides," Chloe retaliated.

Treesha smiled and nodded, letting it go. She made eye contact with Alleah, who immediately diverted her gaze to the table. The young woman seemed torn at that moment, and it was obviously something she and Chloe had already discussed. Treesha pitied Alleah for she didn't understand gods and goddesses, but she knew Sinnis must be vital to her. She also understood it was hard to resist the sexual urges one has when in love. If there was a man who could tempt someone as pure as Alleah, he must be something special. She looked forward to meeting Greyson Kavince.

As he first gained consciousness, a wonderful smell of cooked food bombarded Greyson's senses. He was too tired to open his eyes but could still enjoy the incredible aroma. Soon after, he heard his friends' voices mixed with another he didn't recognize. He lay like that for many minutes, slowly gaining consciousness. Eventually, he found the energy to crack his eyes and take in the strange surroundings. He blinked away the bright light that filtered through the lone window near where he lay. He didn't recognize it and sat with a start. He immediately realized that was a bad idea as a bolt of lightning shot through his forehead. He grimaced and rubbed his throbbing head. A small bandage there made him realize he'd recently suffered a wound.

He thought back, but recent events seemed foggy. How had he ended up in this bed? Where was he? He looked up at the makeshift curtain hung around him and didn't recognize any of it. Then he realized the voices he heard were coming from the other side of the curtain. He rubbed his temple and tried to focus on them. He thought at first he'd dreamed them, but Alleah and Chloe were there; he was not alone.

Then he remembered Swamp Ikma and Port Racip. He recalled the Garden of Sinnis Plath had helped him create and smiled. Then he recalled the fligs! He stood as quickly as his injured head would allow and nearly fell over from the dizziness. He stood there for a long while before finding the energy to open the curtain, almost pulling it free from the hooks holding it to the ceiling as he lost his balance.

He steadied himself with a death grip on the curtain and blinked away the dizzy spell. He took in the house. The place was small, consisting of only one room, hence the makeshift curtain to give him privacy, he surmised. His eyes wandered the cozy place as he gained his bearings. He was relieved to see his staff resting in a far corner, perhaps calling to him. There was also a fire with a pot of food cooking, which was the source of the delicious smell. Finally, his eyes came to rest on the table where the three women sat just a few feet away. They all stared at him now, Alleah and Chloe with their mouths agape, and another woman he found extremely attractive, although older, who smiled warmly. Her hair showed streaks of grey, but even sitting down, he could tell she had a perfect figure.

"Alleah. Chloe," he said with a smile and a nod.

The effort of nodding nearly had him blacking out, and he had to raise a hand to his head once more. They had survived the fligs, and that was a relief to him. These two women had become close to him over the last few months. He didn't want to consider life without them. They were his family now and had survived the impossible, which he credited to Plath. They were lucky to be alive; he felt fortunate to have such excellent allies.

"Greyson," Alleah whispered, slowly standing.

Chloe continued to stare and made no sound, like she was in a trance. As his throbbing head subsided enough for him to focus on the women, he realized again they were all staring at him. He looked down to where their eyes lingered and discovered he was completely naked. His hands went to his crotch to cover himself. It was no small feat as he had to stand without support, which had him nearly toppling to the floor. Once he gained his bearings again, he felt his cheeks flushing and could do nothing more than smile stupidly. Alleah had already seen his manhood when they'd first met. He didn't mind her seeing him again, for he hoped it hinted at the pleasures he could offer.

"Excuse me, ladies," he said as he backed behind the curtain.

As he found his clothes and sat on the bed to pull on his pants, he wondered how he'd become naked in the first place. Perhaps Alleah had seen her fill. A smile crept across his face as he pondered that.

"Greyson, do you need assistance?" Alleah asked from behind the curtain.

"Just a minute. I feel a bit dizzy, is all. I'll be out in a moment."

He took a deep breath and steadied himself. He was dizzy and had apparently taken a hit to the head. He vaguely recalled the dive from the flig cliff but remembered little afterward. The situation had seemed desperate, and he credited Plath for their escape. They were alive, and that was all that mattered. As he pulled on his pants, he considered the older woman. She was probably the cottage's owner, and he wondered if she lived with anyone. There was only one small bed and a table with four chairs, but he felt she lived alone. She was attractive, and he considered the possibilities as he dressed.

"Greyson, are you all right?" Alleah's voice came from behind the curtain, but closer this time.

She had approached the curtain. Was she concerned about his condition, or did she want to see more of him? Greyson decided to open the curtain again before he dressed fully. He was shirtless, which startled her once more, but only momentarily. She pretended to ignore his lack of a shirt, but he could tell it affected her. Alleah checked his bandaged forehead and was satisfied with its condition.

"I think you'll live," she said with a smile.

"Thanks to you and Chloe, I'm sure," he said as Chloe hugged him.

It was awkward for her as her cheek pressed against his naked chest, but she didn't recoil, and he liked how it made her slightly uncomfortable.

"And Treesha," Alleah interrupted his thoughts, waving her hand toward the woman still sitting at the table.

"Treesha?" Greyson said. When he saw her again, he couldn't help but drink in her beauty.

"Yes, she found us at the river's edge," Chloe added, finally breaking the hug.

Greyson walked to the woman, who remained seated and almost looked afraid of him. Could it be arousal that he sensed from the exotic woman? He could only hope. Perhaps their rescue would lead to a plethora of delights for the four of them. Her eyes looked him up and down, and he smiled. Maybe the effect of seeing him naked was too much for her. How long had she lived alone, he wondered. He would need to exploit all the possibilities that this situation offered. He'd focused his desires on Alleah only recently and had never considered Chloe a potential mate. He would gladly welcome her to his bed but would especially enjoy sampling the goods from their host. She possessed a unique beauty and exuded sexuality in a primitive way, as if depraved.

He stopped before her, took her hand, and kissed her knuckles. "And you, Treesha. Thank you for your hospitality."

Alleah was beside him as he rose. It took a moment for the pain in his head to subside from the effort of bending. When it faded, he considered how quickly she'd followed him back to the table. Was she jealous of Treesha? Perhaps this was the perfect setting to break Alleah's will, seduce Chloe, and ravage their beautiful host. Three gorgeous and lonely women surrounded him, an ideal scenario for the young priest to exploit.

He looked to Alleah, who had a puzzled expression. She thrust his shirt into his hands, and he nodded slightly. He knew then that the strange look she gave him was of jealousy. She was falling for him, just as Glime hinted she might. He silently thanked Plath as he put on his shirt.

Chloe explained more about their host. "She saved me from Sebastian and summoned Buster the bear to rescue me."

With his thoughts consumed with the three women and the delights they potentially offered, he'd forgotten about the evil men from Racip who had been chasing them. He looked his friends over, and they seemed uninjured. He was grateful his desperate plan had saved them. It had also saved Sebastian and possibly more of his lackeys, which he considered a good thing despite the fact they were enemies. They were so lucky to be alive and fortunate to have encountered Treesha. Also, had Chloe said that Treesha summoned an ally in the form of a bear? His eyes widened as he finally put the pieces together and understood what Treesha was.

He turned to her and said, "You're a druid?"

The woman smiled and nodded. "Some call me the druid of Sylor Woods."

Even her voice was warm and sexually charged. Greyson would need to pursue this one.

"You must be hungry," she said, standing. "Here, have my seat, and I'll make you some stew."

"Yes, as a matter of fact, I am starving, and whatever you have cooking smells great."

Greyson took her seat as Treesha prepared him a bowl of her stew. He watched her walk the short distance across the small room. Her clothing hugged every perfect curve, and he was mesmerized. A stirring in his groin made him realize she would be his conquest before they returned to the road to Tara. It took many moments before he could tear his eyes from her backside, and once he did, he realized Alleah was in the middle of a sentence.

"—and you sustained a knock to the head from the fall. Luckily, I pulled you from the water before you drowned."

He nodded as if he'd heard the entire story. "And Sebastian is no longer a threat?"

"No, he and his men are gone. Treesha can sense invaders in her woods, and there are none," Chloe confirmed.

He looked appreciatively at Treesha's perfect body again as the druid bent to ladle some stew from the pot. He shook the trance away; he needed to focus on the current situation and their next steps.

"How long have I been unconscious?"

"Nearly two weeks," Chloe said.

"Thank you for taking care of me—the both of you. You saved me," Greyson said, looking between Alleah and Chloe.

"No," Alleah said, shaking her head.

He saw tears in her eyes then, and she looked at him with a new appreciation. Things had changed since the encounter with the fligs. He'd been unconscious for longer than he'd liked, but it appeared that his friends had done some reflecting during that time.

"You have saved the two of us multiple times, Greyson," Alleah continued. "Once from Jessica at Port Racip, once in Ikma, and then from the fligs. We owe you, the way I look at it."

She smiled and squeezed his hand, and he realized that he'd rarely felt her touch since he'd known her. It made him tingle. He was vaguely aware of Chloe nodding in agreement with Alleah, but his focus was the look in Alleah's eyes. Had his desperate plan to save them from the fligs been the final act to push her feelings for him to the forefront? He was glad for whatever it was and returned the squeeze.

Treesha returned to the table with his food and smiled. He looked her up and down as Alleah released his hand. He didn't mean to be so distracted, and he could see the hint of jealousy on Alleah's face as his attention shifted to the druid. She was old enough to be his grandmother, and he desired her all the more for it. He knew from experience what an older woman offered in bed.

As if reading his thoughts, Treesha moved behind the curtain to give them privacy. Once more, he appreciated how her clothing hugged her hips and he licked his lips in response. He knew Alleah could see the lust in his eyes, and he hoped it wouldn't dampen her new feelings for him or whatever was churning inside her. How long had it been since he'd enjoyed the company of a woman? He couldn't recall but knew it was in Pelesea with Binta. That was long ago, and he vowed to change that soon.

The friends talked for the next few hours, and he listened to the tale of their daring escape and subsequent rescue. Treesha left the cottage at some point, which he was thankful for, so he could focus entirely on his friends. He enjoyed hearing of Sebastian's final demise, and the fact that Treesha was powerful and dangerous made him desire her even more. They'd also been lucky enough to make it to the northern tip of the woods, thanks to the flight of the fligs as well as the current of the river. So, Tara was close. However, he had unfinished business here, and Tara could wait a little longer.

Two days passed, and Greyson fully recovered from his injuries. There was no infection, and he felt like his old self again. During that time, thoughts of Tara were constantly on his mind, but they needed the reprieve. Alleah and Chloe were enjoying the time at the cottage after such a grueling adventure. The sexual tension had only grown during that time. He felt it mostly from Alleah, as she'd touched him more during those two days than the entire time he'd known her. Not sexually, but she would dress his wound, touching his head soothingly, or touch his shoulder as she laughed if he said something funny. He knew she was ripe for the taking. And as much as it pained him to come between her and her goddess, he knew she would fit just fine with the tenets of Plath. Sinnis be damned, he would have her and convert her to a follower of Plath at the same time.

Chloe, on the other hand, had become more standoffish. It was almost as if she suspected the inevitable. That gave credence to the hints Greyson was picking up from Alleah. He didn't imagine it; she was falling for him. He had also lusted after Treesha during those few days of recovery, appreciating her walk and tight clothing. He caught glimpses of her when Alleah wasn't looking, for he didn't want to be disrespectful if Alleah was finally willing to give herself to him. He knew they would leave soon to find Tara, and if he were going to bed Treesha, he needed to act fast while simultaneously seducing Alleah from her goddess. The time to act was upon him. He called forth the charm spell he'd used on Cassandra over a year ago and felt its strength gather within the staff. It was far more potent than the first one, and he was confident it would work on his dear friend. The staff teemed with the energy of the spell, waiting for release.

He delayed releasing it, hoping to catch the sexy Treesha within its powerful scope as well. However, she was out in the woods that morning, and he knew he would have to release the spell soon or lose it. He would have Alleah and hopefully Chloe that night and then use his natural charms to take Treesha before they left the cottage.

After he'd first awakened from his slumber, the three had decided to depart the comfortable confines of Treesha's home and head for Tara as soon as Greyson regained his strength. That had been two days ago, and he was physically ready. Treesha was hunting for food for their journey, giving testament to her character. She was still a mystery to him, having kept her distance from the group of friends as they made their plans. Over the last two days, the druid had wandered the woods more than she'd stayed in her home. It made it hard for him to find an opportunity to seduce her, which annoyed him.

As sexually frustrated as he felt, and despite the desire he had to charm all three of them and use the cottage to fornicate for the next few days, he knew they had to complete their quest. They needed to reach Tara before winter and would need to leave soon. But he would enjoy a long-awaited conquest or three before they did.

They had recovered Lud's map earlier in the day, the one Greyson had last seen stuck to the flig's leg that had captured him. It washed up on the river bank, and Treesha sensed it more than found it because they would never have discovered it in the thicket it had become stuck in without her uncanny senses. Ultimately, the map was just a portrait of a horse patty, Lud's favorite food. The three passed it around the table again, ensuring their eyes didn't deceive them.

"The corners are washed away and blurred, but it is a horse pile," Chloe said, passing it to Alleah.

She nodded and tossed it back to the center of the table. "So, all those times Lud sat and studied his map while we patiently waited, he was just admiring this picture?" Alleah said.

"Evidently," Greyson answered.

"Goblins are gross," Chloe said.

"Agreed," Greyson and Alleah said simultaneously.

Alleah then looked at him, a look he'd grown familiar with the last few days, a look that showed she felt more than just friendship for him, a look that promised him many sexual delights, and giggled. He locked gazes with her from across the table, and her giggling quickly subsided. As her smile faded, her face flushed, and she absently bit her lower lip. He couldn't wait to see her pretty face in the throes of sexual enlightenment.

Chloe elbowed her, and she snapped out of her trance.

"What?"

Chloe whispered sternly, "You're doing it again."

"No, I'm not."

Greyson heard every word they said but decided to ignore it and continue with their current conversation. "So, Treesha says that about three days on foot following the river will lead to a road spanning east to west, where I think we'll find a road to Attins. Once we find Attins, we find Tara."

"Fall has set in. It will be cold," Alleah said.

"Yes, but if we can reach Attins before the first snowfall, that farming community will have plenty of warm beds and good food. They will also welcome me with open arms since I am a prodigy from Tara."

"Prodigy?" Chloe asked.

"Yes, prodigies from Tara were supposed to promise sexual delights to the young women of Attins."

He could tell that his story aroused Alleah at least a bit. She swallowed hard as he spoke and seemed to gain a dreamy look as if imagining something. He had an idea of what that might be. Chloe crossed her arms over her chest and sat back in her chair. She wasn't happy with him or the least bit tempted by his story. Nothing a little charm couldn't fix, he decided.

"Well, if you'll excuse me, ladies, I wish to go for a short walk alone to commune with Plath."

He walked to the door and felt the energy sizzling inside his staff's stone, almost as if it had grown in potency since Plath gifted it to him.

There would be no further delaying the powerful charm spell contained within. He would need to either use it or lose it. He decided on the former.

"I shall return in a few hours," he said as he opened the door, and the cold fall wind battered him.

He thought back to Pelesea and the warmth spell he'd used to coax Cass into walking close to him. He would need a similar spell to stay out in this cold. He briefly wondered how Treesha fared since she'd been in it for several hours. He stopped before stepping over the threshold, making a circling motion with his shoulder, and grimaced slightly.

He turned to his friends and said, "I think the fall and subsequent journey through the rough rapids has aggravated my old injury. Is there any chance you could massage it tonight, Alleah?"

Chloe's eyes became as wide as saucers, and her mouth gaped. She looked to Alleah, who ignored her.

With a smile, his beautiful friend said, "Of course, I'd be glad to."

He smiled back and shut the door before Chloe could offer a rebuttal. As soon as it closed, he heard Chloe lecturing Alleah. It was a perfect distraction for the charm spell. He peeked through the window, and although he couldn't hear what was said, he could tell they were having a heated discussion. He closed his eyes, prayed to Plath, and tightly grabbed his staff. He pointed it toward the window and gently released the powerful charm. Invisible and potent energy washed through the cottage, enveloping his friends. The spell was so holy and mighty that his eyes watered. Neither would be able to resist. His goal was Alleah, but he would not deny Chloe if she felt compelled to participate in what he had planned.

A single tear eventually rolled down his cheek as the spell subsided. Alleah and Chloe continued their discussion as if nothing had happened.

"Perfect," he whispered.

He felt sexually charged and ready to dominate the two this very night. He thought of Treesha and wanted to have her before they left. He would see to it. He looked through the window again. The two seemed unfazed, Chloe becoming animated and swinging her hands this way and that as she spoke. He smiled and wiped the tear from his face. Now, he'd let the charm simmer.

He cast a warming spell to protect him from the biting wind and whistled as he walked through Treesha's forest. It was beautiful this time of year as the deciduous trees had lost most of their leaves, littering the ground with orange, yellow, and red leaves. He hardly noticed their beautiful collage, his thoughts solely on his three prizes. He whistled all the more happily and used his magnificent staff as a walking stick to trek into the woods.

LATER THAT NIGHT, AS THE FOUR SAT AROUND THE FIRE PIT JUST OUT-side the cottage, letting their dinner settle, Greyson boiled a large pot of water. Their mood had been mostly sour as Chloe and Alleah hardly spoke. They had argued, and he knew it was about him. He wasn't sure if the spell had persuaded either of them, and he didn't want to push his luck, so he let them stew in their foul moods.

Instead, he focused on Treesha, who wore the same tight-fitting dress that showed all her incredible curves. He assumed she didn't get cold, and he believed it was because of her druid powers. Her nipples were evident through the thin material, so he wondered how warm she was. He wished at that moment that he'd charmed her instead. The anger of his charmed friends wasn't setting the mood.

He stood and brushed the seat of his pants. He turned to Treesha and said, "Thank you for the conies. They were delicious."

"My pleasure, Greyson."

Greyson paused momentarily, and it seemed to him as if she'd empha-sized the word "pleasure" as she spoke.

He shook the thought away, grabbed a thick towel, and took up the pot of hot water. "Well, if you ladies will excuse me, I must wash up if Alleah will treat my shoulder tonight. I don't want to be dirty or odiferous," he said with a smile.

"Treesha, perhaps you and Chloe could join us. The more the merrier, I always say," Greyson teased to test the waters.

Chloe sat back and crossed her arms once again. The charm hadn't affected her and seemed to make her hostile toward him. Alleah smiled, but he could tell she forced it. He would have to work a little on her to loosen her up and win her over. He turned to Treesha to measure her reaction, but she had her back to him now. She was tying her boots, and he found her backside mesmerizing. He stood still and watched the spectacle, unable to turn away. When she rose and brushed her beautiful greying hair behind her ears, he nearly dropped the pot of water.

"No, I must hunt this night as well. I want to send you off from my woods with as much food as possible, just in case this Attins place is not as hospitable as you remember. I'll return by morning. Please don't wait up."

"Be careful," Alleah said as Treesha grabbed her staff and walked into the thick brush.

Greyson was disappointed she was leaving and shook his head once the exotic druid was gone. At least he could have his way with Alleah, which had been his priority for the last few months. His time of conquest had come. He looked to Alleah, who smiled warmly at him.

He returned the smile and said, "I will be back soon if you want to get the bed set up for the massage."

"Bed?" Chloe asked.

"Yes, probably the best way to massage the joint," Greyson said.

Alleah, obviously still angry, said, "Yes, it's the best way. I'll prepare some balms and a few spells."

She got up and walked inside, leaving an angry Chloe to stare at him. He watched Alleah go, her hips doing a fine job of charming him as well. Once she was inside, he looked at Chloe, and her icy glare melted the smile on his face.

"I do not approve of this, Greyson," she said sourly.

"Don't worry, Chloe. Alleah has worked on my shoulder since I injured it. I'm in capable hands," he said, playing it off.

"I'm not worried about your shoulder," she said, getting up and tossing more logs on the fire. "I'm worried about Sinnis and what you have planned for my friend."

"Chloe, I assure you, my intentions are honorable," he lied as he began to walk to the back of the cottage and the small tub that awaited his cooling bath water.

"She likes you, Greyson, and this is a test for her. Please help her pass it and keep her faith in Sinnis," Chloe said, coming close with eyes filled with hope.

It was her last-ditch effort to thwart what all three knew was coming. Greyson smiled and said, "Please join us, Chloe. Any feelings we have for each other are genuine. I consider the two of you dear friends, especially after what we've been through together."

Chloe's eyes darted back and forth, trying to read his face. Finally, with a sigh, she said, "I know. I just know she's vulnerable, and you are a sex fiend."

"Me?" Greyson asked with feigned surprise.

"Just go take your bath," she said, and she plopped back down and started poking the logs in the fire with a stick.

He was disappointed that she wasn't affected by his charm, but she didn't matter as much as Alleah, who was the real prize. He shrugged and went to the back of the cottage. He summoned a light and bathed, the warm water soothing him. What he had told Chloe was true; he considered them both very good friends, but Alleah would be much more after tonight. She would be his new Binta.

He dressed quickly and made his way back to Chloe, who remained hypnotized by the fire but had obviously surrendered to the idea her friend would soon lose her virginity. He decided not to disturb her and snuck back into the cottage.

True to her word, Alleah had the bed ready, along with some balms. She sat on the bed, one leg curled under her, and patted the bed in front of her.

"Come, take your shirt off and sit before me," she bade him.

She tried to sound like that confident healer he'd always known, with no other intentions but to heal him. However, he heard the quiver in her voice. He smiled and undid his shirt slowly. She swallowed hard. She was nervous, but he knew she would comply. She wanted this to happen. Greyson thanked Plath for the wonderful gift.

He sat on the bed in front of her, shirtless and ready, step one of her seduction. He thought briefly of Binta but put her out of his mind. He could rekindle that relationship when he returned to Pelesea, assuming she hadn't moved on by then. He wondered again about possibly recruiting female followers of Plath, beginning with Binta and Alleah and using them to start a harem. The thought pleased him.

"Please hand me that balm, Greyson," Alleah said, pointing to a small container.

He reached over, grabbed it, and handed it to her. She took it, and her finger brushed him, something she would never have done a few months ago. She uncapped the balm, took a gob of the healing ointment, and rubbed it in her hands. He waited patiently until she was ready to begin her treatment. The first touch made him smile as she briefly rubbed his shoulder.

"Does this hurt?" she whispered.

"No."

"Good. Raise your arm straight up."

He complied, and her fingers ran along the scar in his armpit where Cerus had stabbed him with that awful spear and shattered his shoulder. There was no pain there now, but it was the perfect excuse to have a timid Alleah on the bed and touching him. Alleah had reconstructed and healed his shoulder, and he'd forgotten how much he owed her. A pang of guilt washed over him as the charm did its work. Glime had warned him that Alleah might cave at some point, that she had feelings for him, but the charm ensured things progressed.

"Your scar has healed nicely," she said, her breath hot on his ear.

She was close, and he could feel her body against his back as one hand ran slowly over his old wound and the other wrapped around and landed on his chest, pushing him gently back toward her. He let her guide him and leaned against her, aware of her breasts now pressed against him.

"You thought of me when you slept with Zeva," she said, her mouth inches from his ear.

"Of course. You're the sexiest woman I have ever known," he said, slightly turning his head so their faces were just inches apart.

"You could have thought of Binta or any other woman but me. I feel honored that you wanted it to be me, Greyson."

"I would like to try the real thing," he said, testing the waters.

She didn't respond but released him and resumed attending to his arm. The sexual tension was thick in the air, but he'd pushed his luck a little. She had retreated, but he was confident the charm had done enough. She scooped up another handful of the balm and rubbed it in, working his shoulder in various directions and asking him at different intervals how his pain level was. He answered but couldn't remember what he said; he focused on the pending embrace just moments away.

Soon she pressed against him once more, and he was sure he could feel her nipples poking his back. She was his.

"Greyson, will you do me the honor of being the last person I ever heal with the power of Sinnis?" she whispered in his ear.

"The last? Why?"

"You know why."

"Are you sure?" he asked, playing the nice-guy card one last time before he devoured her. He turned his head toward her, and she took his chin and moved his face closer to hers, a kiss imminent.

The curtain suddenly moved aside, and Chloe was there. They both jumped at the intrusion, Greyson quickly standing and Alleah turning to dangle both legs over the edge of the bed. Chloe had his staff in one hand and her newfound sword in the other, albeit pointing toward the floor. Greyson's eyes widened at the sight.

"Greyson, I want you to go outside and cool off," Chloe said.

"What?"

"Chloe, you don't need to do this," Alleah said.

"Yes, I do, and it's for your own good!"

She was in complete control; she wasn't emotional or frantic. She meant what she was saying, and it made Greyson nervous.

"Chloe, please give me my staff," Greyson said, extending a hand her way.

"No," she said with a shake of her head. "I love you, Greyson, but I need you to listen. Go outside and cool off. Let me talk to Alleah one last time. If the two of you so badly want to entwine with each other after that, then I won't stand in your way."

Greyson looked to Alleah, who was nearing tears and hugging her arms. The moment was quickly passing, and the wet blanket known as Chloe had ruined his opportunity. He grabbed his shirt and walked out. He was angry, but worse than that, he needed a sexual release.

He stood outside the door, his breath cloudy puffs as the cool night air quickly took the remaining bit of sexual arousal from him. He promptly put on his shirt and walked to the fire.

"Great!" he said, throwing a stick into the blaze, and sat on a nearby log.

He ran his hands through his hair in frustration and stared into the flames, becoming lost in their dance. His chance was gone, and he would have to try again when Chloe wasn't around or perhaps as she slept. He'd been so close to having that which he desired so badly. Alleah had been ready. Would Chloe talk her out of it?

A splash in the nearby river startled him from his thoughts. He imagined that one of Sebastian's men or a flig had come to seek revenge. He heard the splash again, and he knew something was there.

"I could use my staff, Chloe," he said bitterly.

He picked up a stick the size of a torch and used his powers to make the end glow brightly. It illuminated the area as well as a torch or lantern might. He heard the splash again and made his way toward the river. When he was at the edge, he noticed Treesha's dress hanging in a nearby tree. His heart raced at the thought of one of those butterfly things liquidating her or one of Sebastian's cronies hurting her.

"Hello?" he called out. "Treesha, are you all right?"

His words garnered the attention of something far from shore, and it swam toward him. He couldn't determine what was heading for him, even with his magical illumination. It approached quickly, just under the water's surface. He suddenly felt vulnerable without his friends or a weapon and took several steps back. To his relief, Treesha surfaced near the shore where the water shallowed. She stood in knee-deep water, naked and stunning. Water cascaded from her shimmering figure as she stood there, running her hands through her soaked hair, guiding it behind and out of her face.

"I'm fine, Greyson. Why are you here?" she asked.

"I heard you splashing. It's cold out here. How can you stand the water? It must be freezing," he said, staring at her perfect body and drinking in her nakedness.

"I'm communing with nature, my dear boy. I do this each night when the human world sleeps. That's when nature really comes alive. I can sense every fish swimming beside me, the birds flying through the night sky, and the forest animals scurrying about. It's the best time to swim."

She walked closer, and it was his turn to swallow hard as Alleah had done before him earlier. He was nervous but sexually charged again. Perhaps the sexy druid would make an acceptable substitution for Alleah.

"I'm never cold, Greyson. I've lived in the forest all my life and for many years without the luxury of clothing."

She continued her trek out of the water, and he felt as if in a spell. He could only watch as she approached slowly and seductively. He decided that she had the most perfect figure he'd ever seen. Her silvery-blond hair dripped with water, and her naked body shone in the moonlight. She walked up to him as he stood petrified.

When she finally stood before him, she said, "Do you like what you see?"

He could only nod, thoughts of Alleah far in the recesses of his mind. He wanted this woman, and he would do anything to sample her perfect body.

"You are such a handsome boy. I want to play with you. Is that all right?"

He nodded again, and she smiled. His heart raced as she put both hands on his face and moved his head toward hers. He felt made of clay, and the druid had the power to mold him in any position she desired. She kissed him hard, and he kissed her back. Their tongues danced for many moments, and she moaned into his mouth.

She eventually broke the kiss and said, "I haven't been kissed in many years, Greyson. Thank you for that."

He only nodded again, unsure of what he should do next. He'd been with many older women before, and they made excellent lovers. However, he froze before Treesha, where he would usually take the lead and dominate his lover. He felt like a child and couldn't move, unsure what to do to please her. It was an odd feeling, and he had no choice but to await her next move.

She put her hands on his shoulders, gently pushing him to his knees. Soon, he was at eye level with her most intimate parts, and they looked so inviting. She retook both sides of his head and craned his neck to look her in the eyes.

"Keep your eyes on me, Greyson. I want to see those pretty eyes as you pleasure me."

He could only follow her commands. He gladly did as he was told, and his groin began to tingle as Treesha leaned over to stick a nipple in his mouth. His instincts took over then, and he sucked one breast into his mouth, then the other, giving each an equal amount of attention. He kept his eyes on her face, even when she gasped and closed her eyes in ecstasy.

She grabbed a handful of his hair and took over which breast she wanted to be suckled, moving his head to either one as she wished. He gladly let her. He was aroused now and ready to take her but continued to let her control his actions, something he'd never done before. He felt like putty in her hands, but he never expected her next words.

***

TREESHA SAID, "YOU HAVE BEEN A NAUGHTY BOY, HAVEN'T YOU?"

She knew he couldn't answer; he was entirely under her spell now. He mumbled a reply, and she smiled. He had a talented mouth, and she loved the feeling of his tongue on her breasts. He was young but knew how to please a woman. She felt an orgasm approaching. It had been so long since she had someone to ravage her body. He kept his eyes on her as he did his work, and she easily manipulated his head from one breast to the other. The feeling of playing with him was magnificent, but she also needed to teach him a lesson that both could benefit from.

"I saw you try to use your magical staff to seduce your friends. I took your spell and used it against you. I made sure I protected them from the sexual predator you are. Do you understand?"

His eyes were more expansive now, and he mumbled his understanding as he fed on her nipple.

"Do you also understand that you must do exactly as I say? All the things you meant to do to your friends, I will do to you. Do you understand? You are completely under my power now."

She moved his head from her breast and made him answer. "Say that you understand, my young toy."

"Yes," he whimpered, and his eyes filled with tears.

He didn't like being the one who was used. As sexual as the young man was, he didn't enjoy her dominating and using him. She hoped this would teach him a valuable lesson. She would also enjoy administering the lesson, assuming the young man was as good as she thought he might be. She rose so that his face was level with her crotch, a place no man had been for so very long. As tempting as she knew that had to be for him, he didn't deviate his gaze, keeping his eyes locked on hers as ordered.

She slowly turned to face the river, her backside now in his face. She said over her shoulder, "Now you will use that talented tongue to lick everything I offer you, do you understand?"

"Yes," he said quietly, tears rolling down his cheeks.

She spread her stance and bent over, touching the ground before her. She looked back to the young man and said, "Begin, and be sure you lick everything, and I mean everything, Greyson."

He didn't hesitate to service her as ordered. Pleasing her orally was something that Brayland had enjoyed when he was alive. She loved the feeling and closed her eyes and gasped as Greyson did his best to follow her commands. As expected, he was way more talented with his tongue than Brayland. He even licked her in places Brayland wouldn't dare. She lost some of her control as an intense orgasm wracked her body. She tried hard to suppress her moaning but with little success. She hoped to take the young man before his friends knew of her actions, so she needed to be quiet.

"Stop, my young servant," she finally whispered as her climax subsided.

He obliged and sat back on his heels, awaiting her next command. She turned to him, and his gaze was toward the ground, almost shamefully. Her lesson was working beautifully. With a finger on his chin, she brought his gaze up to meet hers once more.

"Remember this feeling, Greyson, and never do this to a woman. I'm going to take you now on my terms. You are my servant until I release you, understand?"

"Yes," he muttered once more.

"It isn't a good feeling for someone to use you, just as you're about to find out. I know that we could have done this without the spell, that you would have willingly given yourself to me. But I wanted you to feel it this way, the same degrading way you tried with your friends. This is your spell I manipulate, and these are the effects of your creation. Remember them well."

She waved her hands, summoning a strong wind that picked up the fallen leaves and piled them in one place behind her, creating a cushioned bed for their lovemaking. She lay back and motioned for her slave to climb atop her.

Before he entered her, she said, "You know what to do. Do it well, and I'll release you soon. Perform badly, Greyson, and I might keep you here long after your friends have left my woods. Understand?"

He nodded this time, and several tears dropped from his cheeks. Treesha needn't have worried. The young man was an excellent lover, and he entered her quickly and took little time bringing her to another climax. It had been so long since she'd experienced a man, and the feeling of him inside her was terrific.

"Yes, Greyson, yes!" she whispered in his ear.

He was a machine and kept his rhythm, bringing her closer and closer to release once again.

"Don't stop… my young servant. Don't dare stop," she breathed, her words coming out in short gasps.

How long had it been since she last slept with Brayland? It didn't matter;

Greyson was a far superior lover. Again, she didn't want to alarm Alleah and Chloe, but she couldn't suppress her screams.

"Yes, Greyson!" she whispered, and he increased his thrusting, taking her over the edge.

She wrapped her legs around his haunches and dug her fingernails into his back. Then, to suppress her cries of pleasure, she bit hard enough into his shoulder that his blood trickled into her mouth. She moaned for so very long, and her charmed lover only worked all the harder to please her, feeling no pain nor weariness. Her orgasms were intense, decades in the making, and her body quivered under her young lover. As her body rolled with waves of unmatched ecstasy, the forest responded in kind. The trees rustled, the animals scurried, and the fish jumped. Nature shuddered. Eventually, she took his seed, and he collapsed beside her, both spent.

She didn't know how long she would have her guests, but Treesha knew she would never forget the finest lover to walk in her woods—Greyson Kavince! She wished she could have made love to the boy under different circumstances, but she felt confident he'd learned his lesson. Greyson would now have more respect for the women he tried to seduce.

She released him from her spell, and without a word, he used his god-given powers to heal his wounded shoulder where she'd bitten him. He returned like a whipped pup to the house. In many ways, he was, and for a moment, she envied Alleah for the potential relationship the two shared. He would respect her more now. She sighed and returned to the cooling waters to clean up, a delighted woman.

GREYSON ENTERED THE COTTAGE TO FIND HIS FRIENDS DRINKING TEA at the table. Alleah locked gazes with him for just a moment, then looked down at her drink, obviously embarrassed by her actions. Chloe looked at him sternly but nervously.

Greyson absently plucked a dried leaf from his hair and said, "Get some rest; we leave in the morning."

"What?" Chloe said.

"Why the change of plans? Is it because of my actions this night?" Alleah added.

He smiled, sat across from the two, and reached for their hands. Alleah took his hand immediately, and it took Chloe a few moments before she followed suit.

"No, my dear friend, neither of you have done anything wrong. I'm honored that you would consider breaking your oath with your goddess to be with me. It was the wrong decision, and neither of us should be so tempted again."

Alleah looked more relieved than hurt, and that made him happy. They squeezed hands, and he looked at Chloe.

"And you, Chloe, acted as a good friend to Alleah, and I love you for it."

That broke the tension in the young woman's eyes, and she released his hand, rushed over to him, and hugged him tight. Alleah joined shortly after, and once more, everything was right with their little party. Greyson silently vowed never to charm another woman for his sexual desires.

10

THE ULTIMATE ORDER

NEBROSH GEENS, OR "NEB" AS HIS BROTHERS AND SISTERS OF the Mecca-Loraine monastery called him, gazed out the window of the meeting room he currently found himself in. It looked like the snowy contents of the dark clouds hanging over the small town of Oldorburg would soon bury the place. However, that wasn't what drew his attention outside. Across the street, blowing in the strong fall air, six bodies swung from the gallows pole—all four members of the merchant guild that had formerly controlled the sheriff and the town, Magistrate Sams, and a lone woman, Prudence Palence, the administrator of the Oldorburg orphanage.

Neb shifted his eyes to the grand structure that housed the orphans at the highest point in Oldorburg, atop a hill that overlooked the entire town. The architecture was stunning, and he appreciated the apparent work it had taken to construct the magnificent building.

He regarded the bodies once more as they were lined up at the center of the town for all to witness. Two of the gallows had been raised at the time of Oldorburg's founding to deter crime. The other four gallows were recent additions, creating a line of six hanged corpses for all to see. The reason for the executions? He wasn't sure, but their host was about to enlighten them.

He turned back to the meeting where his mentor, Boz, listened to a young, slimy man named Dorin McVale. He wore a dull grey uniform with a black skull emblazoned on his right shoulder. It seemed to Neb that the man was trying to give the impression that he was a high-ranking military officer. The man gushed over his religion and accomplishments in Pelesea so hard that Neb thought he would sprain a wrist patting himself on the back. He didn't like or trust the man. Sitting at the same table with him felt uncomfortable, yet Boz seemed perfectly at ease.

Boz was one of the higher-ranking carofex in the monastery of Mecca-Loraine, approximately one hundred miles southwest of Oldorburg. Neb had been assigned to Boz's teachings when he arrived in the town about two years ago. He had learned much from the deadly carofex and had become quite a powerful fighter. Like Boz, he was a fire carofex, deadly in hand-to-hand combat, and a master of fire. They each wore a loose-fitting robe, and Boz wore his hood, exposing only his strong chin as he typically did. Neb didn't have a hood because he hadn't yet earned one within the monastery's hierarchy. Reserved for the highest ranking carofex, he wasn't allowed to travel with one yet. However, he and Boz each had their heads shaved smooth, and each sported a large flame tattoo on their back, typical of the monastery's members.

Dorin had requested an audience with the monastery a month prior, and the leaders had sent Boz and Neb in response. Neb was a protégé of the mighty Boz and felt honored to make the journey to Oldorburg and be included on any mission with his powerful and dangerous master. This trip was his first visit to the small neighboring town, and thus far, he was not impressed. Neb felt honored to be there because Boz preferred working alone, but this wasn't work—this was politics, and Boz didn't find enjoyment or humor in such excursions. He sat at the large table and stewed as Dorin sat at the end with a greasy smile splayed across his face.

Their host was waiting for another person to join them, but he wouldn't elaborate as to who it was. The table sat six and was generally used for meetings by the merchant guild, making important town decisions. Dorin and his men had killed them all and taken over as the new authority of Oldorburg. When Neb made eye contact with Dorin again, a smirk greeted him. Typically, meeting with carofex made humans uneasy, but not this strange man. It was safe to say Neb wanted to throttle him, and he was certain Boz felt the same. Though Neb didn't fear Dorin, he knew he was dangerous. He locked stares, deciding not to let the man intimidate him.

"Like our decorations?" Dorin said, nodding to the corpses swinging in the breeze.

Neb continued to stare at him stone-faced, and Boz made no reply. The silence was palpable, but that didn't hamper Dorin's mirth. Neb wanted to say something insulting, anything to wipe the smile off the man's face, but the monastery's hierarchy demanded his master answer first. So, he sat, unblinking, waiting for Boz's response.

"I understand that the view can be disturbing for those not accustomed to such displays of dominance," Dorin said, reaching for the bottle of brandy, the only thing on the table besides six small glasses. "Drink?" he asked, holding up the bottle.

When neither answered, he shrugged and poured one for himself. He brought the glass to his lips, but before he could drink, Boz spoke, giving him pause because when Boz spoke, people knew to listen.

"Where is the sheriff?" Boz asked.

Dorin only smiled, then downed his drink in one gulp.

"Dead," was his simple answer. "All of them," he added cryptically.

Before he could elaborate, there was a quick rap on the door, and it opened before Dorin could reply. Two armed guards wearing plate mail, painted as black as night, entered and stood on either side of the door. Neb sensed a presence then, powerful and evil. What entered the room was as puzzling as it was disturbing.

The creature, because Neb could tell it was most certainly not a human, was nearly seven feet tall and dressed similarly to Boz, with a hood hiding most of his face. His mouth was visible, and the creature wore a perpetual grin with long, serrated teeth spilling from its black lips. The skin of the thing's chin was a sickly grey, which matched the creature's hands. The beast's robe covered everything else, and Neb didn't want to see the rest. Dorin rose quickly and knelt, bowing to the monster as it approached.

It placed a sickly hand on his head and said, "Rise, my general," then took the seat that Dorin had been using.

Neb expected a response from Boz, especially when the strange figure seated before them referred to the cowardly Dorin as "general." Boz didn't say anything, so the creature sat as still as a statue, except for the rapping of its long black fingernails on the table. Neb found it unnerving, the very presence of the strange creature almost unbearable. He looked to Boz to see that although he showed no emotion as usual, his demeanor had shifted slightly, telling Neb his master was on guard and that he should be as well. Dorin now stood confidently beside the strange creature. He seemed more infatuated with the thing than nervous.

"May I introduce to you our leader, the mighty Knom."

Neither carofex moved, and after a few moments, the rhythmic striking of the long nails stopped, and the room was utterly silent. Dorin's smile finally faded, and the man shifted uncomfortably.

"It is customary for guests to bow in his presence," he said, watching nervously for Knom's reaction.

Knom raised his hand to halt Dorin's lecturing. "Why, General, these are our guests. I overlook any infractions this day," Knom hissed, his voice reminding Neb of a seething child spitting his words. Black spittle fell on his chin as he spoke.

The creature's implication that Boz and Neb were breaking etiquette and should have indeed bowed did not go unnoticed by Neb. A glance at Boz indicated his master's patience was growing thin.

"Explain to our guests who I am and why they are here," Knom said, spitting his words again.

"Gladly, Master," Dorin said.

He sat beside Boz, unaware of how dangerous sitting with an agitated carofex truly was. Neb watched intently for Knom's reaction. The creature sat unmoving.

"We have invited the lords of the monastery to hear the good news we have to offer at Oldorburg. We expect to count on the carofex as allies during the coming conflict," Dorin began.

"Conflict?" Boz said.

"Yes, Marnelphion is coming, and we hope the carofex will find themselves on the correct side of the conflict."

"The carofex are on no one's side," Boz said.

Knom suddenly spoke up. "That is unfortunate."

Dorin bowed slightly and moved away so Knom could look Boz in the face. Knom continued, "Let me introduce myself and tell you exactly what we're doing here, dear carofex. First, like yourselves, I am also of carofex blood. Unlike you, however, I am a flesh carofex and the only one of my kind. I am also the leader of a special group of followers of Marnelphion that will work alongside him on his conquest. Fill in the details, my general."

"As you wish, Master." Dorin complied, moving back into Boz's view. "As the great Knom has explained, he is an all-powerful flesh carofex. His mastery of martial arts and power over the flesh is unmatched."

"Is that a challenge?" Boz asked.

Dorin smiled as Knom remained expressionless. Neb was entirely on edge now, with Boz agitated and ready for a conflict. Neb had never heard of a flesh carofex, as all carofex were masters over various elements. How could one master flesh? Neb didn't trust the creature's words and doubted he was a true carofex.

"Of course not. As stated, we hope to call the carofex of Mecca-Loraine allies. The last thing we want is a conflict with your kind. This meeting aims to inform you of our intentions and invite you to side with us. When the time comes, we need to know where the carofex stand.

"As the powerful Knom has informed you, Marnelphion is coming to set things right once more. Knom is heading up a group of powerful individuals to lead the humans to the correct side of this conflict."

"Marnelphion is a demon, is he not?" Neb, having heard enough, finally blurted out. Boz had spoken, and he hoped he wouldn't be out of line by following suit. "Why would humans want to side with him? Demons are known for their torture of the human race and nothing more, that I'm aware of."

Dorin's expression became serious, and he leaned over the table toward Neb and said, "There are thousands of us gathered in the east, marching this way as we speak, all humans and suppressed by the laws of man, not Marnelphion. These people are the downtrodden and misunderstood that our society shuns. Criminals, the entire lot. The human world as we know it has been unfair to us. A world led by Marnelphion promises a higher station for us all.

"We will also have privileges to exercise our desired behaviors. Marnelphion will allow the rapists to rape, the murderers to murder, and the arsonists to arson. We will be granted the non-believers as our playthings. He has promised these things and a better life for all of us."

"Demons promise much," Boz said. "He will betray and kill you all."

Ignoring Boz, Dorin continued his crazed speech, his words growing in volume and pitch. "Our new society, comprised of the world's current outcasts, will be called 'Paralisium,' an old demonic word meaning 'paradise.' Furthermore, he will call his people 'The Belamorti.'"

Dorin stood as he shouted the final few words, a finger pointed angrily toward the ceiling and his face reddening in anger. A sudden scratching sound had them all turning to the flesh carofex, who dug his unnaturally sharp nails into the table. Knom didn't speak, but all three understood his displeasure with Boz's words. Dorin composed himself and sat once more as if nothing unusual had happened.

Eventually, Dorin turned back and said calmly, "We will prevail, and there is nothing the world can do to stop us. It is written, and it will come to pass. I know you've heard of the New Order, correct?"

Neither carofex responded, but both knew of the New Order, especially Boz, who had told Neb of his latest mission to kidnap Cassandra Rho. He did it right under the noses of the king and queen of Pelesea, who just happened to be members of that organization.

"I can tell you now that the group of fools will not prevent the summoning we have planned. I have seen to that personally," Dorin continued with a smirk.

"Explain," Boz said.

Dorin leaned in close, unaware that Boz shifted slightly, signaling Neb that the time had come to defend themselves if necessary.

"The New Order, which has recently recruited new members, including the good sheriff of Oldorburg you asked about, now rests comfortably at the bottom of the ocean. They are dead and gone, and the world is ripe for Marnelphion's triumphant return. The human heroes prophesied to prevent his summoning are no more."

Boz had warned Neb of the mighty queen of Pelesea, who had unnerved the powerful carofex, which was a challenging feat. This fool was stating that he'd murdered Penelope as well as all the members of the influential group. He knew that pleased Boz on some level. Still, how would the monastery react to such a claim and the knowledge that Oldorburg was now a base for the despicable criminals to which Dorin referred?

"The New Order no longer matters and is being replaced by a more potent group led by Knom. This group will lead the humans who seek freedom from the harsh rules of the world. It is known simply as the Ultimate Order," Dorin said.

The crazed lunatic sat back, satisfied he had delivered the grand news of the coming war and resurrection of his demon lord. Neb wanted to throttle the ignorant man, but Knom gave him pause. That one was as evil as Dorin was fanatical.

"And now we celebrate the good news that the New Order has perished," Knom added, Dorin again growing obediently silent. "You are invited to partake in our hospitality, which includes a meal like nothing you've tasted before."

"And what do worshippers of a demon eat? People?" Boz dared to ask.

Neb sucked in his breath, awaiting the evil creature's response.

"Yes," Knom answered without hesitation. "Explain to them, General, the wonderful meal that will soon adorn our table."

"Gladly, Master. We will eat the flesh of the children," Dorin said with a wild look in his eyes.

"Children?" Neb asked.

"Of course. What better place to find a plethora of available stock than at an orphanage?" Dorin said, nodding to the building on the hill.

Neb took in the magnificent building again, realizing it was nothing more than a food storage for these crazed people.

"There will also be a special event before the meal, where we will behead the sheriff's wife in his absence," Knom said.

"Yes, the Ultimate Order claims Oldorburg as our headquarters, and the former law no longer applies. There is no longer a sheriff and, therefore, no need for a sheriff's wife," Dorin added.

Knom leaned in a little closer, his nails digging into the table. "As a special treat, we will boil the sheriff's daughter alive in front of her mother, making her death more antagonizing, which Marnelphion appreciates. And by doing so, the babe's flesh will become tender and juicy. It is a perfect meal to honor our god. Do you have the good sense to join us in breaking bread to celebrate our god's return?"

If there was to be a conflict between Boz and Knom, it would occur at that moment. The two dark guards stood fully armed and armored at the door. Neb didn't know Dorin's fighting prowess, but if he was single-handedly responsible for the demise of the New Order, he must be dangerous.

And he didn't want ever to find out what a flesh carofex was capable of. Still, everything hinged on Boz's response.

There were a few tense moments before Boz finally said, "I speak for the carofex of Mecca-Loraine. I can tell you that we do not side with humans on most political issues. However, your tale has piqued my interest and, therefore, the interest of the carofex. We don't eat humans, so we will not partake in your meal. However, we will not interfere with your plans, and you can count on the monastery not to be an enemy in the time of your god's coming."

There was silence for many moments as Boz and Knom had a stare-down. Neither moved, and Boz's breathing became shallow. He had hedged the question, not giving Knom a straight answer. Would that invoke the wrath of the strange carofex? As the moments ticked away, it became evident that a battle wasn't in their immediate future, and Knom finally nodded.

Boz returned the nod and said, "We will take our leave at once for Mecca-Loraine. Enjoy the celebration for your god."

Knom only smiled as the carofex stood, and Dorin summoned guards to escort them away. It seemed to Neb that the whole town watched their trek down the main street, which eventually spilled onto the road leading home. Soon after, Boz and Neb were on horseback, heading for Mecca-Loraine. As soon as they were out of sight, Boz stopped and lowered his hood. The night was cold and his breath was evident in cold puffs in the full moonlight.

"What is it, Master?" Neb asked.

"You will ride hard for Pelesea and deliver the news of the New Order's demise. I will return home and inform our brothers and sisters of the goings-on in Oldorburg. Once in Pelesea, stay as long as you need to glean information. If this Marnelphion beast is coming, we'll need to prepare. We must also know if the New Order is truly dead."

Neb nodded and headed the opposite way to Boz, who had raised his hood once more and made haste toward Mecca-Loraine. As Neb came to the junction leading back to Oldorburg, he stopped his horse. It breathed heavily, snorting large clouds into the air as Neb pondered his next move. He could follow orders and proceed to Pelesea, which his brotherhood required, or he could return to the nasty little town known as Oldorburg. He cared little for the town's citizens, but eating a baby did not sit well with him. He planned on ruining dinner and maybe feeding Dorin his fist if the opportunity arose. Neb would head to Pelesea, but not immediately. What Boz didn't know wouldn't hurt him, and he turned his horse toward Oldorburg.

It was cold, too cold for most, but to Sasha, it felt like she was in a comfortable bed, stirring from a wonderful dream. She slipped back into the darkness, but the pinpoint of light that was consciousness would not relent. She tried to ignore it as comfortable as she was, but something kept tugging at her to awaken. With a frustrated sigh, she tried to open her eyes, but they wouldn't open. To her horror, she tried to move and realized she couldn't. Her muscles betrayed her and didn't answer her call.

Her heart pounded in her chest, accelerating her blood flow and defeating any weariness. She was awake now—it wasn't a dream! She couldn't use her eyes, so she used her other senses. It was so very cold that only an ice carofex could hope to survive. She could hear nothing but a faint sound that reminded her of a muffled wind. After many moments, she tried to understand her body's orientation. She was standing but paralyzed. She didn't understand that. She felt a sensation in her right hand and realized it was the origin of the pinpoint of consciousness, the reason she was even aware of her surroundings now.

She tried to move that arm to no avail. She slowly realized it was reaching her left hip, grasping the hilt of her magnificent blade, Iustia. It remained sheathed, and only a few fingers touched the top of the hilt. She'd been frozen that way while drawing it. But that brief contact allowed Iustia to communicate with her, to wake her from this slumber.

What had led to this strange stasis? Her mind began to slowly piece together the events that had brought her to this point, and she recalled the New Order's predicament! Their boat, *Hope*, and everyone on board had been about to sink. Baxter had blown the magical device, a horn shaped like a conch shell, desperately attempting to save the crew. She vaguely remembered a thick fog answering its call, and things had quickly grown deathly cold. If this frozen state was the destiny of her friends and fellow crewmates, none of them could survive it. Only her carofexian blood allowed her to live.

She called upon the powers of Iustia. She cleared her troubled mind and reached out to the mighty sword, asking for assistance. Once she opened her thoughts to it, she had no problem developing a link of empathy. Energy surged through her and around her. Iustia sensed her condition and imparted to her that a thick layer of ice encased her, strong and magical. The ice could have kept her in suspended hibernation for an eternity, and only the sword's intrusion into her thoughts had awakened her.

The sword was constructed of ice and had an uncanny power over it. Sasha called to that power, commanding Iustia to reach out through the ice that encased her. It took a while to gain synergy with the sword so she could feel every inch of it. She was trapped in an icy tomb, and it stood to reason that if she was, then so were all her friends. Did that mean they were dead? She was an ice carofex, but they were not. Sasha had to escape this and free them. She focused and fell deeper into the sword's powers.

It wasn't easy to fully use the sword's properties with the slight touch that connected them. However, after many hours, Sasha felt Iustia's progress, and the ice casing began to crack. It finally started to fall away, and Sasha could move once more. As large chunks of ice tumbled to the floor, she shook her golden locks, still heavily encased in ice, and entirely withdrew her sword, holding it at the ready, not knowing what evil she might find before her.

The cold, howling wind was her first opponent, cold enough to freeze a person in seconds. To her, it was just slightly uncomfortable. As Sasha found her bearings, she discovered she stood in the same spot on the ship's deck where she was when the fog had settled around them. It took her some time to unfreeze her boots from the icy deck. With Iustia firmly in her grasp, she managed to will the ice to release her. The light was dim, but her eyes adjusted quickly, and she gasped as she took in her surroundings.

"No," she whispered.

There were no enemies before her, as Baxter warned could be the case after blowing the unpredictable horn. But what she saw broke her heart: her friends were encased in ice and standing around her, precisely in the same positions as when Baxter had activated the horn. They stood petrified, most with weapons at the ready. She walked to each nearby sailor or fellow New Order member, and they were all the same: shrouded in thick ice and possibly dead. She saw no signs of life, movement, sound, or hint otherwise that they lived.

When she reached Daro, her heart sank. Her friend stood before her, his swords in hand and his cloak blowing behind him. Even through the thick ice, he was handsome, and his eyes remained wide and unblinking. She ran a hand over his face, looking for a trace of life. She could feel through the sensation of her sword that he was alive, and she sighed in relief. That meant that, in all likelihood, her friends and crew members were alive. Sasha surmised that whatever vile magic this was, killing them wasn't the intent.

"But why?" she whispered to Daro, wishing he could respond.

She had survived, and she could only hope that her friends would as well. First, she would free them all. She brought Iustia up between her and Daro and almost busted the ice encasing him. She stopped when the wind howled around her. She lowered her sword and thought better of that route. If she freed him or any of her friends, they would die from this unnatural cold. The better option was to leave them as they were and hope the ice preserved them.

She took a few steps back to see more of the crew and her friends. They were all there, even Kringus and Penelope on the captain's deck, hand in hand, but frozen like the rest. Nearly a hundred yards to her right was a cave opening, allowing the dim light source as weak sun rays poured into the entrance. She walked to the bow opposite where Kringus and Penelope stood and closer to the cave entrance. The deck wore a thick layer of ice that few could hope to gain traction on. It was easy for Sasha, especially with Iustia, so she moved quickly to the bow, moving between the frozen crew. It was foggy beyond the cave, but Sasha could see and hear the ocean there. Small waves broke against the icy river leading into the cave, the one in which *Hope* now floated.

The wind blew hard through that opening, creating a perpetual howling sound. The wind was cold enough to freeze the river, which was large enough to hold the massive ship. *Hope* was far above the water line, and Sasha peered over the rail to discover it was frozen to the spot more than truly afloat. She could only imagine that ice now filled the ship's hull instead of water. All was frozen, everything and everyone.

She studied the rest of the cave, which consisted of large stalactites and stalagmites of snow and ice stretching around. The enormous cave led deeper into whatever strange place this was. She reached the captain's deck to better look deeper into the place, stopping long enough to regard Kringus and Penelope. They seemed frozen safely like the rest, and she was about to move past them and to the higher railing when she noticed Baxter frozen in place. His lips were pursed into a blow, but the conch was gone, and only his curved hand remained. It was as if someone had plucked it from his grasp when he activated the magical item.

"Where is the device?" she asked no one in particular.

She shrugged away the troubling thought and went to the stern's rail. As she assumed, the river continued deeper into the cave, winding into the eventual darkness, too far for the dull light to illuminate. Her mouth fell open, and she gasped when she saw the many vessels lining the river behind *Hope*. She counted a dozen before losing them in the cave's black heart. The vessels were of various sizes, a few even more significant than the galleon on which she now stood. The *Hope* was the latest addition to the collection and was closest to the cave entrance, where the river magically thawed and spilled into the ocean.

All the ships were similarly frozen to the river, with their crews encased in the thick ice. Sasha could make out the crew members of the nearest ships, all frozen in time. How long had they been here? A shiver ran down her spine despite her being an ice carofex and immune to such discomfort.

"What kind of hell is this?" Sasha murmured.

"Hello?" she yelled into the cave, the echo lasting many moments.

She didn't expect an answer, so she wasn't disappointed when none came. She watched for signs of life from the frozen crew among the closest ships. There were none; she was alone. Who collected the boats and gave false hope to the desperate sailors among them? She knew that whoever it was didn't expect her to break free from the icy curse. So, what did that mean for her? Would she starve to death? She looked around the void that surrounded her. The dark cavern loomed large, and the only true route was the one deeper into the place. The other option was the ocean, which didn't appear inviting.

She went to Kringus, who stood proudly with the magnificent ship frozen in time. Penelope stood beside him, and they held their swords in one hand and each other's hands in the other. They were frozen together for all eternity unless Sasha did something about it.

She bowed before the royal couple and said, "I take my leave now, not to abandon you but to find a solution. To the best of my ability, I will return to free all of you."

Sasha then went to Daro and peered into his bright eyes. He was her friend, the one who had helped her defeat the demon Vasheba and obtain Iustia; the one who helped her defeat her uncle and avoid imprisonment; the one who gave her apples and kisses.

She leaned close to his face and said, "I will return for you, dear friend, and pay you back for all the help you've given me over the short time we've known each other."

She kissed his frozen lips, letting her mouth linger, something inside her telling her to savor this one for it might be their last. She thought again of freeing Daro for a few moments so she would have company for whatever awaited her. She knew that was selfish and would probably kill the wonderful person she had come to love and trust. In the end, she left the ship with a sigh. Iustia helped her navigate the ice that formed on the side of the boat, and she quickly climbed down to the snowy ground next to the river.

Sasha looked up toward the ship's railing but could no longer see her friends. She would have to go it alone. With one last glance at the opening that led to the ocean and possibly freedom, she turned and ventured deeper into the cave, hopefully to find a way to save her friends.

NEB HAD REENTERED OLDORBURG, AND THE GUARDS MET HIM WITH a lukewarm response this time. He stabled his horse, and the guards escorted him to the Blue's Edge tavern, supposedly named after an old merchant named Blue. It was one of the older establishments in the town in one of the original buildings. They directed him to a table, and although he was unguarded, he felt like many eyes were on him. Evidently, Boz's response to sharing a meal didn't go over well with Knom. He second-guessed his decision to come back.

He was the only patron in the place, and no one entered as he sat there, which unnerved him. He momentarily wished Boz were there with him, but he refocused his energy and tucked that desire far away in the recesses of his mind. Now was the time to use Boz's training, not the time to panic. He would never have returned to the town if he didn't think he could defend himself. As his struggle played out in his mind, he caught sight of a barmaid on her way over to his table. She had dark curly hair and big brown eyes to match. She wore a friendly smile, which appeared too friendly and a bit fake to his trained eyes.

"Hello, stranger, and welcome to Blue's Edge," she greeted him. "What will it be?"

"Where are the other patrons?"

"We're closed. You are our special guest, so Dorin has made an exception for you."

"Where is Dorin?"

"Indisposed of meeting with Knom to discuss the carofex declining our invitation to our grand celebration."

"Sorry, I don't eat children."

"You should, they're delicious," the friendly woman said.

She sat and said, "I'm Annabella, Dorin's wife, and you are Neb, the carofex. Now that we have the introductions out of the way, we can speak frankly."

"You're Dorin's wife?"

"Does that surprise you?" she asked, playing with one of her many curls and smiling wide for him.

"No," he simply said.

That stole some of her bluster, and she released her hair, and the smile faded.

"All right, I see there's no small talk with you, Neb. I must warn you that your brother—"

"Master," Neb corrected.

She smiled at his continued confrontational nature and said, "Your friend, whatever you want to call him, may have made a big mistake. If Knom decides his actions were offensive, your people could suffer."

"I came back."

"Yes, a most curious action and one I need to discover the reason for. Care to elaborate?"

"I have come to learn more of your feast. It intrigues me."

"That's not the only reason you've come, I'm sure, and you play a dangerous game, carofex. If Knom suspects you're interfering in any way, you'll join the sheriff's wife on the chopping block. I don't want you to lose that perfect head of yours," she said, reaching to rub his bald head.

He grabbed her wrist with the speed of a striking snake long before she touched him. She was startled by his actions at first, but soon, her shocked expression gave way to a big smile.

"Careful, Neb, Dorin finds me valuable, and you should cooperate as much as—"

Her smile was quickly replaced with a grimace as Neb tightened his grip. She raised her free hand to pry his fingers open but couldn't free herself from his iron grip.

"You scream, I break it."

She tried to compose herself but was obviously in a lot of discomfort.

"What do you want, foolish—"

He applied even more pressure, and she nearly fell from her chair.

"All right, what do you want?"

"Where are they?"

"Who?"

"You know," Neb said, tired of the game.

"They are at the sheriff's office. You have no hope of freeing them. You should reconsider," she said between painful breaths.

With lightning speed, his right arm struck her in the exact spot Boz had taught him: the jaw, to knock an opponent unconscious. His strike was true, and she hadn't expected it, so the effect was devastating for the woman as she crumpled to the floor, unconscious.

Neb was up and running for the kitchen as soon as she dropped. He knew guards watched the front, so he headed for the back door, hoping there was an exit. Once he entered the kitchen area, he thankfully discovered a door and was quickly through it. He heard a commotion in the tavern and knew pursuit followed.

Once outside, he found the merchant guild building where he and Boz had met Dorin and Knom. It was next to the tavern, and he knew the sheriff's office was on the other side. He took a deep breath and used the skills taught him at the monastery to climb sheer surfaces. Like the tavern, the merchant guild was one of the oldest buildings in Oldorburg, and he quickly found handholds and footholds. He went like a speeding arachnid up the side of the building.

Before he could reach the top, three men in chain mail came storming out the back door of the tavern. Neb stopped his climb halfway up and held perfectly still, just as Boz had trained him. Sure enough, his pursuers ran by, thinking he was still fleeing on foot. When they were gone, he finished his climb.

Once atop the building, he took in the surrounding perimeter. Hundreds of men seemed to be milling around now, obviously looking for him. Many gathered around the jail, ensuring no one could enter. He knew what to do, and Boz would be most displeased. What he'd done already had doomed the monastery, and his subsequent actions would be considered an act of war. But Neb was determined to finish what he came to Oldorburg to do.

He pulled out the fire stones he'd taken from the monastery stores. He was forbidden to carry them as he wasn't a high-ranking carofex. Still, he knew how to use them proficiently, and considering the unusual circumstances of Oldorburg's call, he'd decided to pocket them in case of trouble. They felt good in his hands, and he could work them to summon a freld.

Frelds were fire minions from the world of fire and loyal to the carofex. These particular stones could call to Zeliz, a particularly nasty freld that loved to cause havoc among the humans. The creature was an expert in the art of fire gates, and Neb believed it could get him far from Oldorburg in the blink of an eye.

It was too early to call the creature. First, Neb needed to reach the roof of the sheriff's office, which he hoped would include the jail. If Annabella had lied, he was out of luck; if she spoke the truth, he would hopefully have the sheriff's wife and child in a few moments. He could make his mark on the celebration if he stole the grand sacrifice and meal. Neb glanced at the orphanage and knew there was no hope in trying to free all the children. He would save one child and anger the fanatical followers of Marnelphion. That's all he wanted to do anyway: make a point—you don't eat babies!

Luckily, it was night, so the town had already lit the lanterns along the main street. Neb focused on one particular lantern across the street and used all his willpower to call to the flame within. He would need a lot of luck and to use all the tricks he knew for this to succeed. The chances were slim, but he continued his plan because there was no turning back. The flame danced, unnoticed by the many men gathered in the streets now, searching for him. His head began to ache as the flame stubbornly refused his call.

He steadied himself and reached deeper into his core, summoning the knowledge Boz had imparted. Suddenly, the lantern, the subject of his concentration, shattered, and the flame spread along the porch and banisters to which it was attached. The men ducked in surprise, then spread out like ants, trying to discern the source of the attack. Neb took the moment of chaos to jump to the roof of the sheriff's office. He rolled and lay still, listening intently to see if they'd spotted him. All he heard were shouts from across the street to douse the flames.

He was up and running to the back half of the building, where he thought the jail would be. He took out the rocks and began his summoning. Soon, a large fire roared before him, but it wouldn't burn the structure. Instead, it was a gate to summon Zeliz. He spoke the command words, and before long, a four-foot flame was before him. He knew the light it emitted might cause him to be spotted, but there was no other way. He called Zeliz, and luckily, the freld answered.

He backed away as the creature stepped through the flaming gate. It was red-skinned with horns and a wicked smile. Neb had heard of people confusing the frelds with demons, and he understood that error as the creature before him looked like a demon straight from the bowels of hell. The frelds weren't nearly as powerful as demons, but the purpose of this one was to flee, not fight. It looked at him, recognizing Neb, but then looked around for Boz, who was always present during these exercises.

"It's just me, Zeliz, and the carofex need your services," Neb said, trying to focus the creature on the task at hand.

The beast looked at him doubtfully but stood ready for Neb's orders.

"There is a woman and a child jailed below. Use your powers to enter a light source within the building and bring them to this spot. I need them unharmed, so protect them from the flames before you drag them through."

The freld reluctantly nodded and backed once more into the gate. Neb didn't know what the creature would do if there was more than one woman or child in the cells. All he could do was wait and hope the ploy worked. The flames changed hues as the freld used its gating power to establish a link with a fire within the jail.

That was when he first saw the fleshy appendages grasping the roof's edge. They looked like tentacles with hooked ends. He watched in horror as the strange tentacles pulled a seething Knom to the top of the roof. With a snap of those peculiar, elongated appendages, the flesh carofex flew above the rooftop and landed near Neb. Ropy membranes extended from Knom's palms. The tentacles retracted into the flesh carofex, and he stood unmoving before Neb with that wicked smile.

"You shouldn't have returned, monk of Mecca-Loraine," the creature hissed, the black spittle plentiful this time as it dripped down its chin. "You have doomed your people."

Neb heard a woman's scream from below, indicating Zeliz had found a target. A small child's cry only reassured him that the freld had found the correct person to rescue. He had to give his ally time to return, hopefully producing a large gate for them to flee.

Both carofex stood facing each other, flesh versus fire. Neb still didn't know what the creature was capable of, but he knew he didn't want anything to do with those strangely hooked tentacles. Both dropped their robes, and what stood before Neb was enough to distract him. The creature wore only pants now, similar to Neb, but the skin on his torso and arms was a sickly grey, just like his hands. His face and head were bald, and the same grey skin covered them. The most startling thing about seeing Knom's face was the empty eye sockets where his eyes should have been.

"I will flay your perfect flesh from your bones, monk," Knom hissed.

He held his palms up, and Neb watched as they split open, the tentacles flying at him. He managed to dodge aside, but the attack had him off balance, and Knom took advantage. The flesh carofex wrapped one of the appendages around Neb's ankle. It was intense, and the end of that tentacle ended in a single sharp talon about two inches long. That strange tip began to dig into his calf.

Desperate, he stifled a scream and commanded the flames from Zeliz's summoning fire to shoot forth and burn the ropy extension. It didn't do much damage, but it hurt Knom enough for him to release his grasp, bringing the two ropes to his sides. He smiled widely and looked in Neb's general direction.

"You cannot beat me," he spat, just as Zeliz stepped back through the gate with a woman and a young girl.

Although Knom couldn't see, he could hear the arrival, and his grin turned to a frown as if he knew precisely what Neb was doing. "How dare you," he said hatefully. "This will spell doom for your monastery. He tolerates no betrayals."

Neb ignored Knom and focused on the freld. "We need to be far from here, toward Pelesea if possible," he whispered quickly to the creature, who dropped the woman and the child to the floor.

He bent to the terrified mother and daughter, the infant crying hysterically with her face buried in her mother's shoulder. "Don't be afraid. I'm trying to save you," he told the woman, who nodded and held her child's head tighter to herself.

He helped her up and turned to Zeliz, only to find the creature shaking his head, with no gate visible to take them safely away. The freld wanted to be released from servitude to live free in the human world. Although not usually done, if the task were important enough, the carofex would occasionally release frelds into the world as a reward for their service. Rarely did a freld deny its master and demand release. Neb had little choice but to agree if he hoped to succeed here.

Suddenly, Knom had his rope-like extensions wrapped around the freld's neck. Neb continued coaxing the freld into summoning a gate. However, the creature could do little other than struggle to maintain his balance as the flesh carofex pulled hard. Neb ran toward Knom, wanting to engage the flesh carofex while Zeliz created a gate for their escape. Knom picked the freld up by its throat and slammed it onto the roof, making the structure crack in many places. Zeliz was stunned but not hurt badly. Knom released the freld and focused his attacks on Neb.

"I'll take your eyes, fool," Knom said.

Neb ignored the threat and engaged. Knom used the ropes as whips, striking at Neb as he closed. One stuck in his back, digging deeply. He ignored the fiery pain and continued to close. Soon, he was face to face with the evil that was Knom. He began a barrage of attacks that would have stunned most of his opponents, but Knom was far superior to anyone he had fought and quickly blocked all his attacks. Neb's barrage forced Knom to sever the tentacles and engage with him.

Their fists were a blur, each attacking and defending perfectly. However, Knom still held the advantage as the ropy appendages moved independently. The one on Neb's back began to dig into his flesh. Neb cried in pain and arched his back, giving Knom a free shot. The chop was aimed at Neb's throat, and he narrowly avoided having his throat crushed. He turned enough so the attack hit the side of his head and didn't crush his windpipe. The strike was powerful, and Neb was thrown on his back and nearly off the roof.

He moved to pull the digging vine from his back. It was dying, so he pulled it out easily and tossed it over the roof. He glanced over and saw many men looking up, waiting for a victor. They were as good as dead if the freld didn't open the gate. Neb gained his feet, and the freld was there, the new gate burning brightly to his relief.

"Freedom," Zeliz said, crossing his hands over his chest and blocking the exit.

Neb knew the freld wouldn't allow them to pass unless he freed him. Neb felt the blood trickle down the side of his face from Knom's vicious attack. He was about to offer the freld his freedom when Knom's new tentacles thrust deeply into the back of Zeliz's head with a sickening splat. The flesh carofex easily lifted the freld from the ground, its legs and arms jerking involuntarily. Neb knew right away that the creature was dead.

"Move through the gate, now!" Neb yelled to the woman, who didn't hesitate to comply.

Soon, the woman and child were gone, having stepped through the flames. Neb turned toward the freld, which lay motionless on the roof, and Knom stood triumphantly over him. He retrieved his tentacles from the freld's body, and to Neb's horror, Zeliz's eyes were at the end of each sharpened stalk. The flesh carofex placed the eyes in his empty sockets with a sickening plop. He eased the ropy appendages away from his face, leaving the freld's eyes embedded and fully functional. Somehow, Knom blinked those transplanted eyes and soon focused on Neb, using the new organs as his own.

"I see you!" Knom said, then started his approach, his tentacles waving menacingly and his freld eyes glaring.

Neb turned toward the gate to find it closing fast now that Zeliz was dead. He was thankful for that as he might make it through without Knom following him. He ran for it, but his sixth sense had him diving to the side before he made it. The sharpened tentacles struck the roof and embedded deeply, narrowly missing him. Knom growled in frustration as Neb made his feet and went to the closing gate. He glanced back at Knom, realizing the creature had released the stuck tentacles, surrendering pursuit. The flesh carofex knew he couldn't catch Neb in time or follow him through.

He looked at Neb hatefully through his new freld eyes and said, "I will find you, and you will discover the hard way what it means to betray Marnelphion."

Neb stared momentarily at the hideous sight. The evil carofex stood over the detached and deadly tentacles, as they rotted. The freld eyes stared hatefully. With a snap of his wrists, new tentacles shot forth in a last-ditch effort to snare him, and Neb stepped through the gate long before they reached him. The last thing Neb heard was Knom roaring in defiance as the gate closed behind him.

CALYNDA

THE NEXT PART OF CASSANDRA'S DREAM JOURNEY BEGAN, AND she found herself in a beautiful forest. She had never felt like she belonged as much as she did in those woods. Something about them fit her; they seemed like the home she'd never had. She was at peace here, wherever this was. For the first time since she began these vivid dreams, she didn't dread this one. There was a sense of goodness about it before it ever began.

The sun shone brightly, and the large deciduous trees loomed over her, their canopy creating a cool and pleasant shade for her. Many flowers blossomed all around, giving vibrant colors to the forest understory, their pleasant scents filling the air. Bees, birds, and butterflies swarmed around her, busy with their duties as part of the ecosystem. There was something about this particular forest that made her feel almost giddy.

She smiled and spun around, her arms out beside her like a small child. The setting was a storybook, and she felt compelled to act like it. She closed her eyes and laughed as she spun, the dizziness eventually overtaking her. She fell to the ground and waited patiently for the dizzy spell to fade. Once the world stopped spinning, she stood again.

She understood this was a vision from her father, but where was he? She looked all around, but no one was there but her. She then realized that her clothes were different and her scimitars weren't comfortably strapped on her hips. Instead, she wore a dress, something she wasn't accustomed to. She tried to remember when she'd last worn one but couldn't. She held up the edges of the simple but pretty white dress and liked it. She then vowed that if she survived whatever darkness awaited her, she would find a nice wood like this one and live there. She would wear a white dress if she did.

Faint music from her left made her stop and stare in that direction. It was nice, joyful music that spoke to her heart. She followed the sound, and she soon discovered a path and followed it. It was narrow but well used, as if travelers on foot had recently passed there. Cassandra knew from the narrow size that no horses or wagons had traversed this trail. She soon discovered many more paths as they intermingled and journeyed in different directions into the thick woods. She continued following the music and saw that many of the trails led to various homes, which looked similar in design to the magical cottage Cedric had possessed.

She didn't see anyone, but the music was much louder, and she could hear people laughing and conversing. She followed the wonderful sounds, and the path eventually spilled into a large clearing. There, she found the source of all the commotion: a gathering of people. The women were dressed similarly to her, all wearing dresses of different colors, and the men wore shirts and pants, most accented by a colorful vest. They were joyful, something she wasn't used to.

Musicians played their lyres and sang, dancers were abundant, and the smell of food permeated the air to compete with the fragrant flowers. There was a pond with swimmers splashing and laughing. At first, she thought perhaps her father was showing her a piece of the heavens. That was when she spotted him. He appeared as he did in her dreams of Zolmex and the changing mural in Victoria's tower: dark-haired with matching eyes and his chin sporting a goatee. He was very handsome and not nearly as dark as he appeared in her dreams. His face wasn't of Phylance, the angel, and certainly not the one he was born with. She understood then that he'd taken someone's body to use as his own and had liked it so much that he considered it his true self. She'd seen him in this version in every dream she'd had.

Seeing him that close and in a natural setting made him look gentle, and the change in demeanor startled her. He seemed almost happy, which was an emotion she'd not seen him have since he was young before his adoptive parents were murdered. She was glad to see him happy again, although it made her feel uneasy to know the body he wore so naturally wasn't his own. He was walking straight toward her, using the path on which she currently stood. She wanted to avoid him, as his presence made her nervous. She knew the powerful lich he indeed was. Her legs wouldn't respond to her command to run.

She couldn't move, so her only option was to wait for him to reach her. She knew he wanted her to see something, just as he had in the other dreams. He talked and laughed with someone, but Cassandra couldn't see his travel companion due to the thick vegetation. So, she waited, and her nervousness grew, but when the couple cleared the dense vines and flowers, Cassandra's heart filled with joy.

There, hand in hand, walked her father with a beautiful woman, her golden locks blowing in the breeze. They laughed, and she occasionally laid her head on his shoulder as they walked. She was young, maybe in her twenties, while this version of her father appeared to be slightly older. They looked like a couple in love.

The woman looked directly at Cassandra. It was only briefly, and Cassandra knew she wasn't there for the woman to see her, but her heart melted when she looked into those blue eyes for just a moment. They were familiar—they were Cassandra's! The woman's curly hair was similar to Cassandra's as well. She felt as if she looked into a mirror. The woman was a few years older but looked exactly like her in many ways.

"Mother," she whispered.

The couple laughed, flirted, and moved right past her as if she weren't there, which she knew she wasn't. She watched her father pick a flower and put it in her mother's hair. They stopped and kissed, and Cassandra's heart filled with joy. Her eyes watered at the sight; they were a normal couple, and her father wasn't some monster, regardless of being a lich-god. She had a newfound appreciation for what her father was. He wasn't some evil creature of undeath; he was just a kid who'd lost his parents and adjusted the best he could. He had made himself a god, and Cassandra knew he'd done what he needed to survive. He was her hero and, in all appearances, just a man in love. His hands roamed the woman's body, and she giggled, which sounded angelic.

"Mortemus, stop," she whispered, her voice soft and soothing.

"Why? I can no longer resist you, Calynda, my love," her father said and nibbled her neck.

The woman gasped and closed her eyes. Her neck was sensitive, just like Cassandra's, and she quickly lost her inhibitions as Cassandra's father began to peel off her dress.

"Someone might see," she whispered in a half-hearted attempt to stop his advances.

He fell over her, and they began their lovemaking. Cassandra couldn't see them, but she knew what was transpiring. Her eyes watered as she found the scene pure and innocent. Her father and Calynda were in love.

"Calynda." She whispered her mother's name.

It was the most beautiful name she'd ever heard. She wiped a tear as the couple made love nearby. The vision began to cloud and fade; she didn't want it to. Her perfect world and the beautiful vision of her mother and father were melting away.

"No," she whispered, and just before the image was entirely gone, she thought she saw ravens gathering in the trees above her parents.

WHEN HER DREAM CLEARED, SHE FOUND HERSELF IN A SMALL HOUSE, standing near a window and watching the birds fly about a clearing. A white rabbit caught her attention, and she watched it for a bit. It hopped about the area seemingly without a care in the world. Again, it felt like she was experiencing a little piece of the heavens. The same flowery smells assaulted her, and she knew she was in the same forest. That fact relieved her because she didn't want the wonderful dream to end. She loved the woods, and she wanted to see her mother again.

"Calynda," she said with a smile.

She turned from the window to take in the interior of the home in which she found herself. The decorations were simple, and the place was immaculately clean. Colorful flowers adorned every corner, and viny plants filled most nooks that didn't contain blossoming plants. It was stunning, and Cassandra fell in love with the house immediately. There was one bed, a small table, a fireplace, and a few chests. Cassandra thought it was the perfect home and longed to have something like it.

She was shaken from her trance by the sound of someone conversing outside. She turned to the window once more and saw her father walking a path that led to the home she was in. Calynda walked with him, and she had changed. She was still beautiful, but her face was fuller, and she waddled more than she walked. She was pregnant, and Cassandra felt she would soon witness her birth. Her mother's belly was immense, and she seemed uncomfortable.

She had a hard time catching her breath as the sight overwhelmed her. They still seemed very much in love, and her father doted on her mother as he helped her up the two steps to the cottage door. Cassandra no longer saw the lich in her father; instead, she saw a loving husband and soon-to-be father. They entered the small room, and Cassandra saw that Calynda was too big for a normal pregnancy. Her father helped her reach a chair, and she struggled to sit. Her mother was out of breath and appeared exhausted. Her hair hung in strands down her face, and she seemed to be in pain.

"What can I get you, my love?" Mortemus said.

"A drink, please," she said with a hand to the small of her back.

Cassandra watched the interaction intently, slowly understanding that something was wrong. Her father fetched a glass of water as her mother struggled to breathe. Cassandra approached her and knelt before her, taking in her beauty. She wanted to comfort her mother, as her father seemed not to understand the severity of the situation. Cassandra reached to take her mother's hand but couldn't grasp it through the dream. It reminded her again that she was seeing something that happened years ago.

"Here you are, honey," her father said, handing her the glass.

"Thank you, my love," Calynda said, taking a large gulp of water. "I feel horrible. I don't mean to complain, but I don't know if I can carry twins to full term without it killing me."

Cassandra's eyes widened at the mention of twins. "Kessi?" she whispered.

After meeting Cedric, she'd learned that Kessi wasn't her biological sister, so it surprised her to discover she might actually be a twin. It didn't make sense, and she was confused by the revelation.

"You are an amazing woman, Calynda, and you will be fine," Mortemus said lovingly.

She smiled weakly and said, "You give me more credit than you should, my love."

Her father knelt before her and held her hand as she drank. He looked lovingly at her, and Cassandra admired how her father acted around Calynda. They were the perfect couple. But there was a sadness between them, as if they both understood that certain doom was waiting for them and their unborn babies.

She didn't know how much time passed as events accelerated unnaturally. Cassandra stood in the same spot in the corner of the house as days passed within a few seconds. She saw blurs of her parents coming and going, the sun rising and setting, and as the days turned to weeks, her mother left her bed less and less. When it slowed down, her mother was bedridden with her father standing by her side, holding her hand. A man, obviously a healer, looked her over and felt her engorged tummy. Calynda was unconscious, and when the healer gave her father a slight shake of his head, Cassandra knew it was serious.

Tears formed in Cassandra's eyes. Was her mother going to die? Was she going to die during childbirth? Did Cassandra have a twin? There were too many questions that made her anxious and made her dread the next part of the vision. Her mother was the most beautiful woman she'd ever met, yet the glimpse of Calynda offered by her father was too brief. Cassandra knew she would never see her mother awake again or hear her beautifully soft voice.

The healer went outside, and she vaguely heard him addressing a group of people gathered there. Cassandra didn't bother to look to see who he was speaking to because she was so engrossed with her dying mother. Her father did something that she didn't expect—he wept openly, holding her mother's hand to his face, washing it in his tears. He was losing another person close to him, and it was breaking his heart. The sight made her cry for both of her parents.

Cassandra didn't know how much time had passed since she'd witnessed her father transcending to the heavens. Apparently, he'd explored the heavens as a god and then returned to live as a normal man among the mortals. Had her father experienced love with another woman, or was this

his first? She knew it wasn't his first heartbreak as he'd lost his parents at a young age. Cassandra's father had experienced as much tragedy as she had.

The speaker outside the home gained her attention when he referred to ravens. She wiped the tears from her cheeks and peered out the window. The healer was standing on the steps of the home, addressing the gathered people. Cassandra was amazed at how many concerned people were there. They were packed into the small clearing around the home and extended deep into the woods. Some even sat on the tree branches to better view the speaker.

"My fellow ravenkin, I have sad news to announce on this eve of such a grand event. First, some good news: I feel the children will be born before tomorrow's sunrise."

There was some murmuring among those gathered, a slight feeling of happiness temporarily overriding the pending doom they all dreaded.

"However, I don't think our precious Calynda will survive the night."

There was a hush over the crowd, and things were so quiet that all Cassandra could hear was her father sobbing behind her. Her tears flowed heavier then. From what she could gather, the ravenkin were a group of people living in a community in a beautifully wooded area. They seemed peaceful and self-sufficient. And most importantly, her mother had some vital status among them.

Cassandra was confused as to why they called themselves ravenkin. The reference gave a clue as to her control over ravens, but nothing indicated how. She could hear people crying softly in the crowd, breaking her heart.

"The good news is, I believe we can save the babies," the healer continued.

"Are they still going to be raven mothers?" one man asked.

"Raven mothers?" Cassandra whispered to herself.

"I believe that is the case. We know that the fullest moon we've had in decades blessed Calynda on the night of her pregnancy. She and Mortemus witnessed the ravens gathered in the trees above them as they conceived. All signs point to the children being raven mothers. We will know at the moment of birth because the ravens will come. They will bless them, and we can safely assume they are both female. Time will tell."

These people referred to themselves as ravenkin but looked human. They desired the birth of raven mothers, but what was a raven mother? Was Cassandra one? She understood that her father had given her this particular dream so that she would know her mother and understand her strange control over ravens. She'd wondered about that unusual ability since her surrogate mother had died at the hands of the wolves outside of Oldorburg.

Time moved forward again in her dream, but only for a few hours as she watched the moon ascend high in the sky, and then things slowed once more. Cassandra's heart missed a beat. Was her father about to show her birth or her mother's death? The gathering of people remained outside, filling the clearing, and quiet fires sprang up in several places. They stayed in honor of her mother, filling Cassandra with a great sense of pride and sorrow. She turned at some point to see her father sitting by Calynda's side, stroking her hair. She moaned occasionally but never gained consciousness. Her father continued to wipe her sweat-matted hair from her forehead. He whispered continuously to her as the inevitable end was nearing.

As Cassandra watched, a familiar feeling washed over her, similar to when the strange priest of Marnelphion turned him into a lich. She sensed power in him, an uneasy, almost arrogant rawness that she'd not sensed since he killed all the Marnelphion priests on that fateful night. Her mind wandered, trying to determine what kind of tragedy she was about to witness related to her birth.

At some point, the healer was beside her father, praying over Calynda. Her father was distraught and continued to whisper in her mother's ear. The healer put a firm hand on her father's shoulder. Mortemus looked up, his tear-streaked face glowing from the fire in the small fireplace. It was early fall, so the night air blowing through the window was cool. With incredible sadness, Cassandra realized it was her birthday.

"She is gone, my friend," the healer said.

Her father cried all the harder, his shoulders shuddering against the deep sobs. He buried his face in Calynda's neck. Her still form looked like an angel to Cassandra. Tears streaked down her face as she watched the spectacle. Cassandra sobbed with her father, and the healer let it play out, patting Mortemus gently.

"We must save the children," the healer said.

Mortemus could only nod but never looked up.

The healer solemnly said, "I will call the midwives in."

He went to the door and summoned the two women in. One carried blankets, and one held a long, clean knife. As the healer turned, her father was suddenly before him, startling the man. Cassandra hadn't even seen him move; the action was so fast, and it also surprised her. That feeling of unbridled power came to her once more. Her mother had just died, yet she was terrified more than sad. Her father was about to do something to her and her sister, but what?

"I will do it," he said in such a way the healer couldn't deny him.

Cassandra could tell the healer wanted to help, that Mortemus was in no condition to cut the babies out, and that the healer was the only one proficient enough to remove them safely.

"At least keep the midwives to help," the healer pleaded.

Mortemus shook his head and said, "No, please leave so I can save my daughters."

The healer nodded finally and motioned for the midwives to give Mortemus the knife and blankets. Her father took the knife and let the blankets fall to the floor. He had a strange look on his face, and it scared Cassandra. What was he about to do?

Once alone, he shut the door and locked it. He tossed the knife on the blankets and went to the window. He looked out among the gathered people, his tears gone. It was almost dawn, the first hints of light peeking through the dark sky. All eyes were on the home as she watched her father's demeanor change from sadness to anger. He stood right beside Cassandra now, looking out into the breaking day. She saw the tears drying on his cheeks, and he gritted his teeth. Cassandra's heart raced. What was her father doing?

"We find ourselves here, Marnelphion. You cursed me as much as Novafontera the day we banished you. You vowed that I would fall in love, and you would take that woman from me as punishment for assisting the New Order. You have succeeded, but I know your plan for my daughter. What you didn't count on was me having twins. I accept your challenge and curse you all the more. Assuming you can find her, I offer you my first-born, but my second-born will be your demise, sending you back to where you belong."

He punched the wall next to Cassandra, making her jump and yell in surprise. She knew no one could hear her, but she covered her mouth quickly to stifle it. The people outside were muttering. The healer and midwives waited on the steps, an air of nervousness spreading through them like a wave crashing on a beach.

That was when Cassandra felt the ravens. They were there, and they were coming! They started landing in the trees, and hundreds of wonderful birds arrived to welcome her into the world. The ravenkin looked around in astonishment, some crying their thanks and some weeping uncontrollably.

"The raven mothers have arrived!" one woman shouted before fainting.

Cassandra was distracted by her father reaching into the hole in the wall where his powerful punch had splintered the wood. His hand emerged, holding a dagger, one much bigger than the knife the midwife had given him. The blade was serrated and blood red. The carved handle depicted the face of a grinning demon. There was something evil about the blade, and it made no sense for her father to possess and hide such a device. He knew one day he would need it to cut open his dead wife, but why use a terrible knife such as that?

And what had he mumbled about a second curse? Cassandra knew of Novafontera's curse, as did anyone who looked upon the dead city, but had Marnelphion cursed her father somehow? Was her beautiful mother dead because of Marnelphion? She wondered how the evil knife played into it.

He turned to Calynda and began a strange chant. The fire was immediately extinguished with a loud pop, making Cassandra jump again. Her father started the grim task of cutting open her mother. Cassandra looked on helplessly, rooted to her spot near the window. Soon, he had a screaming baby in his hands and lifted it toward the window. The early-morning light showed Cassandra that it was indeed a girl. She smiled in between her sobs.

"Behold, my first-born, Marnelphion," he whispered.

The ravens cawed as the baby cried, and the crowd grew more restless. He laid the newborn on the bed beside her mother and soon removed the second one.

"Behold, my second-born child, demon, and your bane."

The ravens cawed even louder, and they seemed to grow in number. Cassandra peered outside, and they were everywhere. The ravenkin stood in shock as the birds they shared an affinity with landed on their shoulders and heads once the trees were full. The people stood perfectly still, smiling at the abundant blessing the ravens offered the newborns. Their raven mothers had arrived.

Cassandra was so engrossed in the scene that she didn't notice at first that the babies were no longer crying. She was aware of a commotion outside and saw the healer pounding on the door, several strong men working to open it. The healer rushed to the window and peered in, right past Cassandra, not seeing her because she wasn't truly there. His surprised look spoke volumes, and he gasped and covered his mouth.

Fear gripped her heart, but Cassandra slowly turned, unsure what she would find. The last few moments had been a plethora of emotions, and her heart pounded in her chest as she moved to face the room. Her mother lay peacefully on the bed, with her hands resting on her chest. Mortemus had covered her to hide her open belly. However, her father and both babies were gone, including the wicked knife her father had used to cut them from the womb.

She walked up to the bed and silently wept as she took in the sight of her lifeless mother. A fleeting thought occurred to her: this was definitely her mother lying before her because she looked just like Cassandra. Her hair, eyes, and mouth made Cassandra feel like she was looking into a mirror. There was no doubt this was her mother, and she'd just witnessed her birth. She found her mother beautiful, even in death, and she began to cry once more, falling to her knees and releasing her grief.

The door burst open, and several men rushed in, followed by the healer, to find her dead mother and nothing more. The vision began to fade as the ravenkin searched the small room. Cassandra turned back to her mother one last time and smiled. She studied her face, burning it to memory as the world blurred.

"Goodbye, Mother," she said quietly as everything went dark.

WHEN CASSANDRA CAME TO, IT TOOK HER QUITE SOME TIME TO REALIZE where she was and even longer to understand she was no longer in one of her father's visions. He had shown her everything he wanted her to know. She found herself lying on the floor in the cave where the dreams had begun. She sat up and moved so her back was against the wall. She didn't know how long she'd been dreaming but remembered every vivid detail. She felt exhausted, as if she'd lived all those experiences shown to her in the visions.

She put her head in her hands and cried. Her father wasn't the monster she thought he might be. Yes, he did some unscrupulous things, but usually out of revenge or in response to a great wrong done to him. He wanted her to know him better, so he'd shown her. She understood he probably withheld many things he didn't want her to see. However, she believed what he showed her were actual events.

She'd witnessed her birth and met her mother, although not officially. She was a beautiful and kind woman, revered for birthing two raven mothers, whatever that meant. Some things remained unresolved, such as who her sister was. Sadly, she didn't think it was Kessi because she didn't influence ravens like Cassandra. Besides, Cedric believed Kessi was just a decoy and not her real sister.

Also, the prophecy still didn't make sense. Cedric had told her that she was a sacrifice that would be responsible for Marnelphion entering the world once more. He also told her that she would destroy him, sending him back to hell. Her father cut two babies from her mother's womb. Her father had said one would bring Marnelphion back, and the other would banish him. Either she or her twin would be the sacrifice. The other one would be the hero. But which one was Cassandra?

And who was her twin if it wasn't Kessi, and where was she? Were they identical? Was it someone she knew? She thought briefly of Binta. They had connected quickly, and in a way Cassandra had never experienced. Of course, the kiss was also a new experience, and it made her wonder if their attraction to each other was because they were twins. Their backgrounds were similar, though Binta had told Cassandra about her parents.

Either way, she was excited and sad at the same time about the prospect that Binta could be her sister. On the one hand, if Binta was indeed her sister, they could beat the prophecy together. On the other hand, Cassandra loved Binta romantically and wanted more of what they'd started so long ago in Cassandra's room at Victoria's School of Magic.

She dried her tears and sat there for a long time, the events of her father's visions running through her head, along with images of her mother. What had her father done with her twin, and how could Cassandra find her, assuming it wasn't Binta? And what did the title of raven mother mean? It meant something to the ravenkin people from her vision. It was an important event, and Cassandra and her sister had been blessed by the ravens, truly becoming raven mothers.

She noticed for the first time that a second doorway had appeared during her visions on the far wall near the entrance to the cozy study she'd visited earlier. She gasped when she saw it and slowly gained her feet. She still had her weapons and holy symbol. She reached the door and saw stairs ascending higher into the cave.

She stopped at the entrance and looked at the flight of stairs. They climbed a short distance, only twenty feet, before reaching a hallway. She couldn't see much from her vantage point, and she knew to discover what truly lay at the top of the steps, she would have to climb them. The familiar blue-flamed torches lined the stairwell, and it appeared that more were burning in the hallway above. She knew the next stage of her adventure was upon her.

"Zolmex," she whispered.

Her birthright would be the next piece to the puzzle, the next clue as to where her journey was taking her and how it would end. These steps were the next cog in her father's plan and the reason she had eventually searched out the cave. Her birthright was up there, she was sure. She only needed to walk up the steps and take it. With a nervous sigh, Cassandra began the climb to her destiny.

BIRTHRIGHT

"It's time to make a move," Bale said.

He, Matilda, Ronnis, and Cass met in the magical cottage. Of course, Binta was on the floor, barely dressed in tiny underwear. Her hands were tied behind her back, and she was lying in a fetal position, trying to sleep. Bale found it amusing that her binds had rubbed her wrists raw and that the scar from Matilda's attack on the poor girl's arm was an angry red. Ronnis and Cass had continued their sexual domination over the wretch but had obeyed his orders to keep her bound, and Binta had paid the price. He cared nothing for Binta and had decided she would help draw out the troublesome Rho girl from hiding, not as Matilda had tried by attempting to kill her, but in a way that he believed would work.

"What do you suggest?" Matilda asked.

"The whore will serve as a decoy."

"In what way?" Matilda asked curiously.

"We will parade her from here to the dead city known as Larual, announcing her as the Rho girl. We'll spread the word here and there about the good news of her capture. She will be our fake sacrifice, and if those fools that call themselves the New Order try to interfere, that will lead them straight to Larual, the grand city of undeath.

"We will tell the whores of Prailic that Cassandra is being held in the dangerous and deadly city, and they, in turn, will spread the word to their clients as quickly as they spread their sexual diseases. We will inform the Lividans of Malofese and even the agents of the great goblin king, Repat, to the south. They will all know our plans, but none will know they are false."

"This helps us in what way, Bale?" Matilda prodded.

He flashed a metal smile to his companions. His teeth flickered in the light of the fireplace. He knew Matilda would follow his lead here, and Ronnis had torn the left side of his face in the hopes of catching Cassandra so he wouldn't cause a fit. However, Cass was the key. The young demoness claimed ownership over Binta, and since this plan included her death, she wouldn't be so willing to proceed. However, he would kill Cass if she opposed him, which would be unfortunate. He enjoyed having the girl around; she had an evil streak he found entertaining. He glanced at Binta's wounds and smiled once more.

"We take her, put a hood over her head, tie her to one of our wagons, then parade her to Larual. Then, as the attention is focused on her, Neclesious and the four of us hide here. If it appears to the Rho girl that we have pulled our army off the mountain, she will crawl out of her hole."

"Then what?"

"Then we five take the real Cassandra Rho to my fortress for torture and safekeeping until the Great Summoning, which is only eleven months away, may I remind you."

"So, we pull your grand army of priests? Is that wise?" Matilda asked.

"We have sat here too long, and a radical move needs to happen for us to be successful. Time is of the essence, and I'm no longer interested in playing games with the Rho girl."

"What of Binta?" Cass finally chimed in.

He'd expected that response, so he only smiled when she finally asked. "She dies," he said coldly.

"I want to keep her as part of the torture of Cassandra," Cass said desperately.

Bale leaned in close, and his smile evaporated. "No, you want her for your carnal pleasures and aren't interested in the bigger picture. You see, we want Cassandra, and I couldn't care less about this whore that you've grown attached to. I support your planned tortures of the Rho girl, but you will need to do it without Binta."

Cass sat back, and he could see the displeasure on her face. He didn't care; she would conform to his decision or die. She crossed her arms over her chest but bit back a reply. He took that as a positive indication she would follow his plans.

"So, has Neclesious given you any indication that this plan will work?" Matilda asked.

"No, but he agrees with me on the details, and therefore, Marnelphion approves it."

"Cassandra is a manipulative coward, and she will crawl out of her hole if we give the illusion that we've left," Ronnis said.

Bale looked to the strange man, who wore his porcelain mask almost constantly now that both sides of his face were shredded. He was more loyal to the cause than Cass, but neither were followers of Marnelphion. Both would require close monitoring from this point forward. Bale's decision to sacrifice Binta was a big test for Cass.

Bale smiled at the masked man and said, "I appreciate your confidence in my plan."

Ronnis nodded, but Cass's arms remained crossed as she stewed. She wasn't happy, but she wasn't opposing the plan. That was as good a sign as Bale could have hoped for.

"So, when are you expecting to execute this risky plan?" Matilda asked.

"There is nothing risky about it. I feel it will work; therefore, we will execute it immediately."

Bale stood and looked at Binta's pathetic form curled on the floor. "Use her tonight and get it out of your system. Tomorrow, we send her to Larual. Ensure you don't kill her. She's an important part of our victory now."

Bale exited the cottage and relayed the new plans to his men. Despite the short notice, they were efficient travelers and would be ready to break camp in the morning. He looked to the drop-off where Matilda insisted the Rho girl was hiding. He could see nothing but sharp rocks far below. If she was there, she was well hidden and magically so. With a smirk, he turned and began his preparations for traveling. He knew without a doubt they would have their prey soon enough.

THE FOLLOWING DAY, THE PRIESTS OF MARNELPHION STOOD AT THE foot of Witch's Rise. Their two wagons, one covered for supplies and one caged to haul their catch, were stocked and ready. The priests were all gathered and awaiting the trek to the west. The plan was for Bale and his group to take the covered wagon to the swamp, carrying Cassandra inside. Matilda, Cass, and Ronnis would join him, and he felt confident it would be enough to watch over the Rho girl.

The priests would take the caged wagon, nothing more than a jail cell on wheels. They were eager to serve Bale and, more importantly, Marnelphion. They were in formation, waiting for their prize to come down the ridge. The caged wagon was too clunky to make it up the mountainside, so they brought Binta to it instead. Cass held her leash and escorted her down, Ronnis on the other side of the abused girl. Her hands were still bound behind her back, and a small vial of milk hung from a chain around her neck.

Binta was a pathetic sight, as she looked to be drunk, staggering this way and that as Cass roughly pulled her along. She was dressed precisely how she had been the entire time since Bale had joined the small group: naked except for tiny underwear that hid nothing. It was appropriate attire for her travels, he thought. Bale had considered her a useless whore since his arrival and had indulged Cass and Ronnis, who wished to keep and torture her, but now she served a real purpose, and he was glad that Marnelphion had allowed her healing. Bale smiled as he watched Cass drag the tormented girl down the trail. She was the key to everything.

She was roughly the same height as Cassandra and the same age, and, to make it more pleasing, she was Cassandra's love interest. She was a perfect decoy. Her dark hair would require her to wear a sack over her head since Matilda told him Cassandra had golden locks. There was a risk of the desert air suffocating Binta if she wore the hood for very long, but it was a risk he was willing to take.

They escorted her into the waiting wagon, followed by two priests with specific instructions. One carried a length of rope and a knife, while the other had the sack to hide her pretty face. As she got closer, Bale could see her lustful expression as she bit her lower lip. She would stray toward Ronnis occasionally, and Cass would pull her back. That gave the illusion at a distance that she was staggering, but all she wanted was more sex from the buffoon, Ronnis. Bale found it astounding that Binta's spirit was fully broken at such a young age. Marnelphion so enjoyed such tragedies of the innocent. Bale considered how much he could appreciate the girl after the summoning. Having a wretch such as Binta on call to satisfy his sexual needs seemed appealing. But, there was no chance of that, for he expected the girl to be dead soon. She was just a distraction for now, but that was about to change. Exposure to Larual would kill her if the journey there didn't.

The priests took over her care, but Cass continued to hold the leash so they could do their work. Bale could see the struggle within Cass. She couldn't bring herself to undo the leash and let the priests fully take Binta from her, but she wasn't stopping the plan, which pleased him. Now that two men were handling Binta, Bale wondered if the whore's animal instincts would take over and she would try to attack them sexually. She seemed to have little control over her desires, especially with the demon milk contained in the vial that hung between her perfect breasts.

The priests cut her binds, and she didn't even seem to notice the rawness of her wrists. She was in a state of ecstasy and didn't feel the pain. He understood the powerful effects of the milk, and this one had consumed too much. He assumed she would never be sane enough to function again.

As he suspected, she immediately used her free hand to fondle the closest priest while biting her lower lip lustfully. He pried it away from his crotch, and with the help of the other priest, who had to tear her other hand away from between her legs, they managed to get her arms above her head. To make the process easier, one priest held her hands high, near the top of the cage, while he suckled her breasts and kissed her deeply. That caused enough distraction for the poor girl to stop attacking crotches. Binta didn't even notice the new rope the second priest used to bind her raw wrists to a bar at the top of the cage-like wagon.

She squirmed to get to the men as the first priest broke the kiss and stepped away. She was a wild animal of lust, and the vial of milk kept her under a sexual trance. Bale admired her perfect figure for the first time since his arrival as he stood beside the cage Binta now called home. He wished now that he'd taken a turn with her, but he was satisfied. This little tart was bait, and that was all right by him.

Ronnis was suddenly beside him, the porcelain mask hiding his disfigured face. Bale secretly liked the man. Ronnis rarely spoke and only when there was something important to say, so Bale understood the man needed to talk with him.

"What is it, Lord Ronnis?" he said, electing to keep his eyes on the delectable body belonging to Binta Mulay instead of turning toward him.

"If you want her to resemble Cassandra, there is another step in the process," Ronnis answered, his eyes also on Binta.

The priests placed the hood over Binta's head, and she moaned and squeezed her legs together. Bale saw her shining thighs and didn't know if the juices were hers or Ronnis's. He couldn't help but laugh at the lord's good fortune.

He turned to him and said, "What do you speak of?"

"The last time I had Cassandra Rho in my clutches, I had her bound to a table and at my disposal. It was like a table set for a meal, and I was a famished man, ready to partake. Unfortunately, my arrogance got the best of me, but fortunately for your cause. Instead of raping her innocent and unspoiled body, I decided to brand her and let her ponder the upcoming events of the following day."

"Brand?" Bale asked curiously.

"Yes, I branded her ass with the end of my sword," Ronnis said, moving the hilt so Bale could see the perfect craftsmanship of the snake eating its tail.

"Interesting."

"Yes, and if anyone has seen the brand and then sees this one without it, they will know she is a decoy. The chance is small but still a risk for you."

"Indeed," Bale agreed. "And so, you propose we brand Binta the same way?"

"Yes."

Bale smiled and smacked Ronnis hard on the shoulder. The hit didn't jostle the large man much, and his expression was impossible to read due to the mask, so Bale wasn't sure if Ronnis felt the same comradery over the need for branding Binta. He hoped so, and perhaps the unusual masked man would take any pent-up anger out on Binta with the forthcoming brand.

"Gedlor, bring me a torch," Bale demanded of the priest leading the expedition to the west, holding out a hand while keeping his smiling face on Ronnis.

Bale understood his metal teeth unnerved anyone around him that he cared to show them to. Again, he couldn't measure Ronnis's reaction to them because of the mask, but the lord's body language told Bale he wasn't the least bit unnerved.

Soon, a lit torch was in Bale's hand, and he offered it to Ronnis. "A parting gift for your plaything," he cooed.

Ronnis nodded, took the torch, and entered the cage. It was empty now, except for Binta and Cass, who still held Binta's leash. Bale moved closer to hear the interaction between the two. Gedlor joined him, seemingly concerned as well.

Cass pinched Binta's nipple and twisted it to elicit a moan when she saw Ronnis enter.

"I do not want to lose her," Cass said to Ronnis when he arrived.

"I know, neither do I."

"Should we use her once more before we fully release her?" Cass asked, smacking Binta's breast and enjoying the subsequent moan.

Ronnis stood motionless momentarily, the torch burning in one hand as he considered the offer. Eventually, he shook his head. "No, the time has passed for such pleasures. We need to focus on Cassandra and her tortures now."

Bale was satisfied with that response and smiled at Gedlor, who nodded.

"Fine," Cass said with a pout. She unfastened the leash and whispered in Binta's ear, "I release you, little whore. Go off into the world and offer sex to all you encounter. I wish I were there to arrange it for you. Just know that Cassandra will be dead before you ever find yourself sexually fulfilled. I have promised to defeat both of you, and today is the first day of your demise. One down, one to go."

"Cassandra," Binta whispered, briefly becoming aware of her surroundings before growing quiet behind the hood.

Cass laughed at the spectacle and left the cage, finding Bale to stand beside him. He liked the cruel girl and would perhaps pursue sex with her at some point. She wasn't a true nepalin but was close enough to offer many pleasures, Bale was sure. He flashed Cass his metal smile, and her disgusted look made him smile all the wider. He intimidated her, and she had given up her prize. She would follow orders, and that pleased him. Things were quickly falling into place.

Bale focused on Ronnis again and watched intently. The lord drew that magnificent black blade and held the torch to the handle. He stared at Binta's writhing form as he did. He was like a statue, void of emotion and there to do one job. Bale liked his focus.

Ronnis reached up and tore the sack from Binta's head. This startled Bale for a moment, unsure of what Ronnis intended. He wrapped part of the blade with it to keep his hand from burning, and Bale relaxed, now understanding the purpose of the bold move. Bale noticed Binta's hair was sweaty from the brief time under the sack. She would most likely die in that thick sack. He thought the idea was wonderfully pleasing. She just needed to live long enough to serve as their decoy.

Finally, the blade handle was red hot, and Ronnis tossed the torch through the bars. He then tore Binta's underwear down to her knees and knelt. He was at eye level with her perfect hips and took the opportunity to kiss them through the mask before proceeding.

He turned her so he was behind her, pressing one firm hand on her left hip and bringing the blade up to her right hip. It looked as if Ronnis estimated the position of the brand to match Cassandra's. Once he thought it was correct, he pushed his hands toward each other, and the familiar sizzle of burning flesh filled the air. The hilt burned into Binta's hip. Oddly enough, she didn't thrash and scream as Bale expected, and she seemed to get a sexual thrill out of the experience, moaning with pleasure.

Ronnis held it there for a few more moments before removing the hot blade from her delicate skin. The bright red brand looked more like a disfigured scar than a snake's face. Bale knew it would heal properly, and he might have to use his priestly magic to help progress it. He'd done that once already, he recalled, looking toward the nasty scar on the girl's arm, one that would be there the rest of her short life.

BINTA BRIEFLY FOUGHT OFF THE DELIRIUM BY CALLING OUT HER friend's name. Someone had mentioned Cassandra, and Binta had held on to that recognition and the accompanying blissful reprieve from her lustful tortures. She couldn't focus for long, her powerful mind lost to her desires. It was the demon milk, and she was aware of it. She couldn't feel anything else besides the beautiful milk hanging around her neck and dangling on her chest. The container's thin glass separated her from the liquid, and she wished it would seep through and into her body. She needed more of it and would do anything for it.

She felt someone removing her panties, and from the ox-like method that she knew all too well, she readied herself for Ronnis to enter her. She needed him then and hoped he wouldn't be gentle. In truth, he never was. There was a delay, which made her anticipate him even more. He didn't enter her, and instead, she felt an exquisite pain on her hip, which only fueled her pending orgasm.

Ronnis held something hot to her skin. The awful smell that followed confirmed what she already knew: he was branding her. It took her mind back to a time long ago when Kima and her friends held her down, jabbing the sharp studs through her nose and nipples. The pain had overwhelmed her and aroused her all at once. She could faintly smell burned flesh, though the pain was dull. That and the recollection of Cassandra faded away as her climax took her mind deeper into her troubled state.

Cassandra reached the top of the short stairwell and expected to find the skull room there, complete with Zolmex lying on the table for her to retrieve. Again, she was disappointed. At the top was an open doorway to a large, rectangular room. The hairs on her neck stood on end. Danger hung heavily in the air, and the room resembled a trap from the first cave her father had tortured her with. Either way, a sixth sense somewhere deep inside told her that Zolmex was near.

She put her hands on the hilts of her scimitars, finding comfort in their familiar grips. Caution was her guide as she examined the room, not daring to enter. Another doorway was on the far side, with a heavy slab of stone sealing it tight. She had a strong feeling that Zolmex was beyond that door.

Also in the room was one more item—a set of full plate armor standing to attention, complete with a helm and a battle-axe propped in its arm. It stood eerily in the corner, silently watching over the empty space. She watched it for many moments, expecting it to move or give her some indication that a person wore the armor. To her relief, it didn't move. A dozen blue-flamed torches lined the walls, giving her a full view of the area. She watched intently, waiting for a sign of things to come with this latest puzzle from her father. With a sigh, she finally stepped into the room.

As expected, she heard the familiar gears and pullies within the walls closing her inside. The door from which she entered was slowly closing. She'd seen many of these triggers in that deadly cave she and her friends had adventured in a year ago. That adventure had not turned out well, and she felt uncomfortable waiting for the stone to seal her inside. She glanced at the far door, hoping it would rise simultaneously. It did not.

She wasn't about to turn and leave, so she waited as the stone door finally sealed her in. It was deadly silent in the room, reminding Cassandra of the golem encounter in the first cave. Her legs ached at the recollection as the golems had nearly torn her in two, trapped in that deadly room. She stayed on high alert, ready to defend herself at the first sign of danger.

After a few minutes of nothing, she relaxed and said, "What now, Father?"

The answer came shortly after when six blue flames from the dozen torches lining the walls flew from the sconces toward the armor, darkening the room slightly. The armor absorbed the magical flames, which seemed to give it a life of its own. Blue light now shone through the eyeholes of the great helm, and it peeked out of the various ridges and seams in the immaculate suit of armor.

As she expected, a few moments after the strange phenomenon, the helm turned in her direction as if suddenly alive and aware of her presence. Its stiff arms grabbed the battle-axe up in a ready stance. Its legs followed suit, stiffly turning and walking toward her. The first few steps were awkward, but it eventually moved smoothly and quickly, the battle-axe swinging freely and proficiently as it advanced.

"Great," Cassandra whispered, drawing her scimitars and taking a defensive pose.

The magical guardian seemed to gain speed as it got closer. It was as if the enchantment used to bring it to life took a few moments to make it move properly. Cassandra had her knowledge of combat thanks to Vixa, and that had saved her life. The magical knight was quicker than she could have imagined, and she realized she would require every bit of Vixa's skills to defend herself.

She barely brought her scimitars up to block the attack and nearly lost her weapons from the decisive strike. She found herself on the defensive during the battle's early stages, managing to dodge or parry the exact and deadly attacks. One slip and she would be in trouble. She tried to find an offensive maneuver, but it took all her skills to maintain an even footing.

They danced around the room, Cassandra dodging and slipping in some strikes as she could. None of those were strong enough to penetrate the armor of the magical being, but she was finding her rhythm and learning her opponent's fighting techniques. Many minutes passed, and she felt fatigued from the battle while the animated suit of armor didn't tire. She needed to do something or she would lose, and only a few yards from her objective, she guessed.

"What do you want from me, Father?" she screamed in frustration.

What else did she have to prove to him? Why was obtaining her birthright, which she knew he wanted her to have, so difficult? Even with her enhanced combat skills, she couldn't find a weakness in the mystical guardian she battled. She focused on the arcane symbols in the room as she fought. She had forgotten how the blue-flamed torches had sprung to life when she first entered and searched for a way to use that magic.

"It's my magic," she whispered.

It was true. The cave had come to life after it had taken her spell and absorbed it into the walls. The torches sprang to life shortly after, and she felt one with the magical place. That was true in this room, as the torches were thick with the symbols and offered her magic if needed. The beast was also comprised of her magic, having absorbed six of the torches. It was a heavy concentration that she might be able to command, and she began contemplating that option. Perhaps she could control the magical beast? Was that it? Did her father want to see if she could wrestle control of the mystical being away from him?

Her contemplations nearly cost her life as a quick swipe from the battle-axe almost cleaved her in two. She ducked at the last moment, and sparks flew over her as the giant blade struck the wall above. She had played this game long enough, and the warrior's instinct welled inside her. With a growl, she pushed her attacks, temporarily gaining the offensive. She knew it wouldn't last long because of the fatigue setting in, but she had to try something.

Her hair was matted to her face from the sweat of such a long duel, and her arms shook from fatigue, but her blades were a whirlwind, and the mystical armor had to go on the defensive. It didn't retreat as she'd hoped, but it couldn't attack her due to the flurry of strikes—she had the advantage. She knew this one attempt was all she had, so she went all in with the effort, dropping the scimitar in her left hand and pointing to the nearest torch.

She couldn't focus on her magic long, so she peripherally gathered the arcane symbols around the torch. She pulled as many as possible to form a lethal ball of magical energy. The mystical guardian was recovering from her barrage, and she needed to act fast. With a scream of rage and denial, she moved her left arm forward and toward her opponent, pulling the mighty mass of magical energy with it.

A sizzling ball of energy formed in the air, pulling the symbols comprising several nearby torches and snuffing them out in the process. The ball slammed into the animated helm, finally knocking it off balance. It wasn't much of a distraction, but it was the best she could do. She summoned her fighting instincts, the warrior's heart instilled in her from Vixa, and lunged behind the magical barrage.

She quickly leaped and wrapped her legs around the creature's neck as she would typically do to pull her victim to the ground. She knew better than to try that move against the magical being and instead she plunged her remaining scimitar deep into the eyehole of the helm so that the hilt smashed against the visor. Her sword punctured the back of the helm, most of the blade visible. She had no choice but to release it as she fell behind the creature. She now had no scimitars to defend herself, but she knew she'd won. The strike was deadly perfect, and the skirmish was over.

She was relieved the attack was a success, and she managed a beleaguered smile as she crouched behind the suit of armor. She had done it; she had completed the impossible challenge. She expected the armor to fall or the magical energy that comprised it to flow free of it and the contraption to topple over. Instead, the monster reached up and pulled the sword slowly from its eye. Her smile faded as she watched the scimitar easily extracted from the helm.

Once free, it tossed the sword to the corner of the room and turned to face her again. She couldn't see a face, but she knew if it had one it wore an expression of confidence. It advanced, and she knew her doom.

"Impossible," she whispered, her smile melting away.

She rolled at the last moment as a huge overhead chop of the great axe came at her with surprising speed. It hit the stone floor where she'd crouched moments before, missing her by inches. She ended her roll near her discarded sword and rose with it in her hand, just in time to knock aside a mighty swipe. Her weary arm tingled from the strike. The creature became more potent as the moments passed, and she grew tired.

She had to go into a defensive posture, which spelled doom for her. The thing was enraged, swinging powerfully and accurately. She was quickly losing hope. Her parries were weak, and her arms felt like rubber. It promptly backed her into a corner with its powerful blows. Her other sword was hopelessly lost to her, lying in the far corner, and even if she could retrieve it, she knew there was no hope of defeating the magical being before her.

She had no time to focus on her magic. A strong swipe nicked the wall beside her head, and only the corner of the walls prevented a killing blow. Chips from the wall sprayed across her face, temporarily blinding her. The mystical being reached down, pulled the sword from her grasp, and tossed it across the room. It landed with a clang next to its mate.

She was doomed. She had no weapons, could not focus on her magic, which seemed to have no effect anyway, and had scored a killing blow on the beast, yet it had shaken that off like swatting away a fly. She could only continue to dodge the attacks, but her body was failing; exhaustion was setting in.

She rolled again, barely dodging an attack, but as she gained her feet, the monster did something she hadn't seen and didn't expect: it maneuvered a quick backhanded swing that she couldn't hope to avoid. She sucked in her gut, or it would have cut her into two pieces. Still, the razor-sharp axe dug deep into her belly, eliciting a scream of pain.

She held her stomach tight and felt the blood pour from the wound. She fell back on her wobbly legs and sat hard against the wall. The jolt nearly had her passing out, and the pain in her abdomen was excruciating. She summoned the courage to look down and removed her hand to see a very deep cut across her midsection. It had severed several core muscles, and she couldn't hope to continue the fight. She was relieved she didn't see her guts spilling onto the floor, but that mattered little with the pending doom before her.

The animated creature approached and raised its axe for a powerful downward chop. Cassandra couldn't move and wouldn't try—it was over. In her final moments, she thought of all the events that had landed her in this room, only to die by herself while her father looked on like a spectator at a gladiator pit. That made her think of the impossible odds she'd faced fighting in the Queen's Tournament with the barbarians. Winning that was a fluke; she wasn't a strong fighter and had no business engaging in gladiator-like battles. Why did her father think she could defeat such a creature as the one before her?

She thought of her mothers, Unis and Sera; her sister, Kessi; Binta, her true love; and even Laryn, the young woman she'd befriended at the barbarian training complex who'd been senselessly murdered. All these people were lost to her, which wasn't fair. She looked up at the creature, tears spilling down her cheeks, and her anger came to the forefront of her thoughts.

"I hate you," she whispered as her ordinarily blue eyes turned a brighter, unnatural blue.

She focused more clearly now, this close to death. She'd been going about this wrong, battling something unbeatable. But the energy that swirled in the suit of armor, giving it life, was her creation. She gave it life with her magic, and now she would take it back.

She saw the powerful arcane symbols that comprised the beast. She barely noticed the axe chopping down for the killing blow. Instead, she saw how the magic was structured. Her father had used her magic against her, creating something complex and nearly indestructible. However, now, albeit a little too late, she could see the life force for what it was.

"No!" she shouted, raising her hand and summoning her waning strength to pull at the energy binding the beast.

It flew back, dropping the giant battle-axe at Cassandra's feet. The armor crashed to the ground in many pieces and flew across the room. The powerful energy that had been its life force, a cloud of blue vapors, hung in the air before Cassandra, entirely in her control. She kept one hand holding her mortal wound, and with the other, she waved above her head. The energy followed her movement and flew around the room circularly, relighting the eight torches that had grown dark. Everything was back in place, and Cassandra's eyes slowly turned back to their natural blue.

She attempted to stand but knew that was a bad idea before she even tried. She yelled out in pain and sank back to the floor. She used the wall to slowly guide herself back to a sitting position. She thought of her mother then and how her father had cut her sister and her out of her mother's dead body. She felt closer to her mother at that moment and understood it was because she was probably dying.

Tears continued to stream down her cheeks, not just from the immense pain but from the awful memories of her life. It had been a terrible existence for a person who only wished to be left alone. Cassandra only wanted to live peacefully with her few friends and her sister. She never bothered anyone during her brief life. She never bullied people like Cass, tried to get them in her bed like Greyson, or tried to murder anyone like those who chased her. She wanted to live a simple life with her family, alone and happy. She wanted to be a powerful wizard, witch, or whatever the hell they called her, but she only wanted to protect those she loved. She never really had a chance.

The armor still lay across the room, indicating that she had defeated the magical being. However, neither door opened upon its demise as she'd hoped. There was more to this test, and her father wouldn't even let her glimpse Zolmex before she died. She cried hysterically then, letting all of her emotions out. Her blood soaked her shirt and hand, and she could feel her lifeblood pooling on the floor around her. She thought of her beautiful mother again, thankful that her father had at least given her a glimpse of her. It took her a long time to regain her control and cease the sobbing. There was no sense in self-pity. She would rise above that and die with dignity. She felt dizzy as the blood continued to pool.

She remembered her amulet hanging from her neck, the holy symbol of Gella. She grasped it with one bloody hand and recalled how the symbol had already saved her life. The very necklace she wore was the one she had found when near death at the barbarian burial ground, not far from where she currently sat. She kissed it and began a prayer. Perhaps Gella would assist her once more. She didn't think she could heal such a vicious wound, but she would try. If Gella didn't answer her call, she would succumb to death, understanding she had done everything she could to defeat the prophecy that chased her.

She prayed hard and made it personal. "Thank you, Gella, for saving a wretch like me and allowing me to serve as your acolyte—no, priestess. You saved me from the barbarian burial grounds and created food to keep me from starving in the dead of winter.

"You saved more than my life. You saved my very soul during my time at the temple in Pelesea. You took me in as an acolyte when no one would have me, and my troubles washed away. I owe you everything: my thanks, my health, my faith, and my life."

Cassandra thought back to those early days in the temple when she'd accepted Gella into her heart and how peace had found a home there. She hadn't repaid the goddess for that enlightening, and guilt washed over her. Tears began again as Cassandra realized her goddess had been with her daily since then. She felt unworthy of calling herself a priestess, just as she always did when she needed Gella.

However, when she sensed the incredible warmth that bathed her body, she knew her goddess was with her. Cassandra didn't deserve her, but she was there. Her hand fell from her injured stomach, and she lost consciousness, losing her grip on the holy symbol. It didn't matter; Gella took over, healing her grievous wound and restoring her faith.

Cassandra was only unconscious momentarily, snapping out of her trance almost immediately. She blinked to help refocus and realized there was no longer a burning pain in her abdomen. She looked down and saw the wound had healed, leaving a red scar running across her midsection. It appeared months old and even itched as the advanced healing process was fully underway. It wasn't pretty, but it was no longer mortal. Gella ensured she would survive, and hope began to rekindle in her broken heart. A smile formed on her face as she kissed her symbol and said a long and silent, heartfelt prayer, thanking her goddess.

She stood on legs that no longer trembled. Her body felt as if it had been through some extreme physical ordeal, but oddly, it wasn't the least bit fatigued. She walked past the scattered pieces of armor and collected her scimitars. Neither standing, walking, nor bending was painful. Cassandra knew she would always have a nasty scar as a reminder of this day.

Once her swords were comfortably on her hips, she looked at the doors, sealed with no clue how to open them. She ran a hand over the door that she thought would lead to Zolmex. She could find no way to open it. She'd assumed if she defeated the magically animated armor, it would open of its own accord. She was missing something. She rubbed the itchy scar on her belly. She would live, and that was the most important thing. She grasped her holy symbol tightly and smiled, knowing her goddess had saved her.

Then she heard the metal scraping behind her and saw the various pieces of armor slowly sliding across the floor to collect in one pile. Her heart raced at the idea the magical beast was re-forming. If it did, how could she defeat it? What was she missing? Perhaps she needed to leave the room before the creature re-formed.

She turned quickly to the door and said, "Notel X."

Nothing happened, and the door didn't magically open with the command. Cassandra glanced back to the armor, which was now collectively forming a full suit once more. It was a pile of metal but was slowly rising from the floor, the helm first, so it would soon look like a standing suit of armor as she'd first found it.

"Calynda," she said, desperately hoping her mother's name would be the correct password to open the door.

Nothing happened, and soon, the armor was fully formed, standing at attention again. The battle-axe slowly moved toward the armor, making an eerie scraping sound. She couldn't let that happen. She needed to figure this out. She turned toward the guardian and steeled her resolve. She recalled her father's instructions as she focused: obtaining Zolmex would require both a physical and a mental test.

The physical test was her ability to stave off the magical being's attacks. What was the mental part of this test? She thought of all the things she'd learned from when she first discovered who her father was, from Cedric to the many visions her father had recently shared with her. There had to be a clue there on how to defeat this.

She closed her eyes and meditated, trying to ignore the unnerving sound of the large axe that had already cut deeply into her making its way across the floor. Her father liked games, riddles, puzzles, and traps. He was also a creator of many powerful things, including Zolmex. He was god-like and could possess people and travel into the heavens if desired. He could also appear as a normal man and have relationships as a mortal, as he'd had with her mother.

She opened her eyes just in time to see the torches all flicker in unison, and then the flames jumped from their tops and flew to the armor, bringing it to life once more. This time, all torches snuffed out, and the only light in the room was the bright blue light shining through the eyes of the great helm and peeking out through the various seams in the armor. This time, the creature would be mighty, and she would be unable to control it. She didn't bother unsheathing her scimitars—she wouldn't need them. She had to figure out the riddle her father had left her before the thing cut her to pieces.

"Notel X," she said once more with no effect.

The creature brought its battle-axe to bear.

"Calynda," she commanded.

Still nothing.

"Kessi," she tried, now becoming desperate.

Still, the door didn't respond.

She thought of her brief training with Sitra in the art of blind fighting as the monster began its approach. She was beside the door that she felt would lead to Zolmex and her freedom. She backed away from the advancing plate mail until her back hit the wall. The door was to her left. If she could find a way to open it, she would duck out of the room before the thing attacked.

"Phylance," she said, speaking the name of the angel her father had possessed.

The door remained silent and unmoving, and the creature was upon her. Then, as the battle-axe swept toward her head, she thought of Cedric's words: "*Your father was good at making such pockets in space. He also chose his activation phrases carefully, usually using a normal saying, but backward.*"

She ducked the attack and deftly moved to the side. This time, she expected the quick backhand that had cut her open, and she was already out of range by the time the attack came. The creature was faster now and was ready for another swipe. However, she felt like she was on to something, recalling Cedric's words concerning the activation code for the magical cottage her father had created. The cottage password had been Red Rowen, which was backward for New Order.

She quickly processed that information and blurted out, "X Leton," backward for Notel X.

The door didn't move, and her efforts were met with a fake swing that stopped short and was followed by an unexpected backhand. The stiff metal glove of the armor didn't connect solidly, or it would have killed her. Yet, the force of the glancing blow was so strong, she flew back against the wall and into a sitting position once more. She tasted coppery blood in her mouth and knew the hit had done some damage. The thing was above her, just as before when it had nearly killed her.

As the mystical being advanced on her again, she desperately searched for an answer. It dawned on her that "X Leton" sounded familiar. She thought of the crypt where she'd found "Notel X" scribbled on an old scroll. Leo's old skeletal remains held the key to this puzzle. Her mind processed the information quickly as if a great revelation had come over her. "X" needed to be spelled out to solve the riddle! "X" spelled out was "Eks," and if you said it backward with the rest of the clue, you had the solution!

The image of Leo's bearded remains flashed in her mind as she screamed out the obvious password, "Skeleton!"

The door didn't open as she hoped, but the magical being stopped its advance. She couldn't see the axe but knew it loomed over its head, the ridges in the armor allowing small amounts of light, enough to show its arms were pulled back, ready for a killing blow. She still sat by the door, dazed and spitting blood from the backhand she'd endured.

Despite her injuries and close calls with death since entering the room, a wave of relief washed over her. The guardian ambled back to where the armor first stood when she entered the room. Once there, it assumed the same pose and stood very still. Cassandra began to laugh and shake her head. She had defeated the guardian of her birthright, and the emotional stress was too much. All she could do was laugh uncontrollably.

The armor released the blue energy back into the room, and each flame found its spot on the end of a torch. The room was well lit once more, and everything reset to the condition it started in. She laughed nervously and ran a shaking hand through her sweaty hair. She felt the vibrations in the wall before she heard the familiar sound of gears and pullies. Soon, the door beside her opened, and hot desert air mixed with bright natural light filled the room.

Her heart raced, and her nervous laughter quickly turned into sobbing. She knew from her dreams that her birthright awaited her through that door. She had finally made it. She remained seated next to the door, afraid to stand and look inside. She put her head in her hands and cried for a long while.

AFTER SOME LIGHT HEALING TO BINTA'S BRAND TO MAKE IT LOOK older than a fresh wound, the priests covered her head once more and locked the portal cell. They took up their formation and began the trek to the west. They would encounter several information outlets along the way, and Bale knew word would spread fast, especially when they reached Prailic. Bale's men would spread the word that they held Cassandra Rho, and all unwanted attention would be directed toward Binta Mulay, a simple whore.

He smiled at the thought and turned to the two remaining allies, Cass and Ronnis. Cass still had her arms crossed and wasn't pleased with losing her toy. Ronnis stood with his strange and unsettling mask and said nothing. Bale knew neither was pleased, but he was happy with their willingness to obey his commands. He would tolerate nothing less.

"This better work, Bale," Cass said, then stormed off with a huff before he could respond.

The two men watched her go, both appreciating the sway of her hips.

"A fine replacement for Binta, wouldn't you say?" Bale asked.

Ronnis turned to him, the creepy mask hiding his expression. He removed it after a moment to reveal his torn face, which was just as blank as the mask. He laid it gently on a nearby rock, then took out his honey brandy. His eyes never left Cass as he took a long draw.

"Yes," he finally agreed.

"Well, if she can't see the big picture of what we're doing here, she might become just that," Bale said, smacking Ronnis hard on the shoulder and laughing.

The three allies climbed Witch's Rise to join Matilda and Neclesious in hiding at the top. The next step would be to lie in wait and nab Cassandra when she came scurrying out of her hole. Bale had a feeling that would be very soon.

⟆

GEDLOR LED THE FANATICAL PRIESTS, DRIVING THE WAGON THAT HELD Binta. The priests sang loudly to their god to draw as much attention to their prize as possible. Binta stood out among the strange procession. From a distance, she could easily be mistaken for Cassandra Rho. The group of powerful worshippers of Marnelphion turned west and headed for their first stop along their journey. Prailic was nearly two hundred miles to the southwest. The place was a regular stop for travelers in that part of the world. Many prostitutes called the place home, and what better way to spread gossip than by prostitution?

They passed by an outcropping of cacti, and no one noticed the hidden little fairy. After they'd passed, Gophia flew out of the cluster and back to Mateon and Sitra. It had taken them months to heal, and Sitra's eyes were still a little puffy, while Mateon's neck would never be the same, but he was well enough to travel. They refused to wait any longer and were determined to help Cassandra and Binta.

They'd heard the procession, guessed the cargo and had sent Gophia to spy on them. They needed to know who the prisoner was and where the other could be. So, they nervously waited until Gophia returned. When she finally did, she was hysterical.

"Bad people have Cassandra!" she yelled in her tiny fairy voice.

"Are you sure that was Cassandra?" Sitra asked.

"Yes, yes!" Gophia said, wringing her hands and flitting all about.

"What about Binta?" Mateon asked.

Gophia shrugged, not remembering that Mateon was blind and Sitra was blindfolded. However, her silence spoke volumes to the couple, and they understood the fairy had only spotted one of the young women.

Gophia landed on Sitra's shoulder and said, "Help Cassandra?"

Without hesitation, Sitra said, "Yes," and they headed off after the caravan of priests carrying who they thought to be Cassandra.

CASSANDRA EVENTUALLY GAINED CONTROL OF HER CRYING ENOUGH to pull herself together and stand. She took a deep breath and walked toward the doorway. Cassandra had pursued the scene for so long, and she had dreamed about it so many times, that it felt like she was experiencing the dream once more. She took a deep breath as she peered inside.

The thick desert air poured out of the opening, and she had to squint from the bright light until her eyes adjusted. She first noticed the two windows, shaped like eye sockets, just like in her dream. Light poured into the room from those two windows. Then her eyes adjusted, and she saw the table, and there, lying atop it, was Zolmex! She gasped at the sight and froze in place, not believing that this could be real. Her muscles wouldn't answer her call as she stood paralyzed at the magnificent sight.

She looked to the spot where she'd always seen her father in her dreams, but he wasn't there. Cassandra felt a great sense of relief at his absence. What would she say to him, and how would he react to her? Luckily, she wouldn't find out. She scanned the room for traps or other hazards that could prevent her from picking up her birthright. She had longed for this moment but didn't trust her father to let her obtain the artifact and be on her way.

She started to enter the room, hoping there were no more tests or traps, but paused to consider her actions. Why did she desire the device so much? Cedric had informed her that obtaining it was part of the prophecy. So, why was she doing it? Cassandra had told herself that she wanted it to protect Kessi and her mother before Sera's murder. That was true, and she did desire it to defend herself and Kessi and to use it to have the peaceful life she always wanted. But was there a part of her that wanted to be powerful? According to Cedric, Zolmex would do that. Was she dooming the world by being selfish? She knew it didn't matter; she had come this far and was not about to turn back now. She finally entered the room.

The heat was thick within it, just like her dream. The table was before her, and just being near Zolmex, she could sense its power. She adjusted her eyes to see the arcane symbols that might be in the air, and she was nearly overwhelmed—they were so abundant around the artifact. She shifted her gaze from the arcane symbols to the wondrous item. It appeared to be silver, with intricate etchings along the two-foot handle. At the tip was a beautiful oval topaz. The blue stone sparkled in the desert sunbeams that spilled into the room.

She approached the table and soon stood over the amazing rod of power. She noticed that beside the artifact, the words from her dreams were etched into the table: *To Find a King.* She absently ran her fingers over the carved lettering, inching them closer to Zolmex. She looked out the windows but saw nothing but the sky from her vantage point. She knew if she approached them, she would have a perfect view of the empty barbarian burial ground. She also knew that every time she reached for Zolmex in her dream, she was denied it and instead teleported to the edge of the burial ground.

She took a deep breath and, with one last look around her, reached for her birthright. Holding Zolmex was the moment of truth: had she finally won the right to carry her birthright, or would her father have more games for her to play? Her fingers curled around the metal handle, to her delight and surprise, finally feeling the tangible item. A surge of energy flowed through her arm and into her body, and she gasped at the power it offered. She lifted it from the table and held it before her, marveling at the beauty.

The craftsmanship was like nothing she'd ever seen, the fantastic details etched into its length and the flawless stone. She could vaguely hear the first door in the room behind her opening, the chains and pullies activated once more, offering her freedom. It was time to exit the cave and show the world her power.

She remembered when Cedric first told her of the birthright, and they discussed her destiny while far beneath Pelesea's temple. That seemed like an eternity ago, and now she'd finally realized her destiny. Cassandra thought of her father's visions showing the early days of Zolmex, and the age of the device overwhelmed her. The fact that Leo the wizard had wielded it against Marnelphion all those years ago humbled her. A sense of pride and wonder washed over Cassandra as she stood there, mesmerized and in awe, holding it before her. Cassandra could feel her senses expand, and her awareness of her magical abilities became enhanced. She felt magnificent! A smile creased her pretty face as she finally felt immense with her birthright in hand.

Her next step was crucial. Her father supported the prophecy, and Cedric had told her how it required her sacrifice to Marnelphion, but she would also be the one to defeat the demon. It made no sense to Cassandra, and she vowed to ignore it and find Kessi and Binta. Then, she would find a home in the woods, similar to the one her parents had lived in. They would live happily and peacefully there, and Cassandra would protect them with the magnificent artifact. That was her plan, and who could stop her now that she wielded Zolmex? She didn't understand the artifact's functions, but she could feel its power as if it were an extension of herself. Many spells ran through her head, most of which she had never cast, but Zolmex showed her the secret to each of them. They seemed elementary. She was truly powerful while Zolmex was in her possession. She felt god-like!

She slowly began to feel something else. It was an awkward feeling and very uncomfortable. A wave of nausea washed over her, and she grew warm. Something was wrong, and Cassandra looked accusingly at Zolmex. There was a pulling deep within her, almost like her very essence was being drawn from her body. Cassandra grew increasingly uncomfortable as the moments passed, and she used the table to support herself. Another bout of nausea gripped her, and she began to sweat. She wanted to release Zolmex, but she couldn't. To her horror, she realized the artifact was controlling her.

The tugging within her became more intense, painfully so. She panicked, helpless to stop whatever change was coming over her.

"Father, please," she whimpered.

Then, she felt like she was being ripped in half. She couldn't catch her breath, and the room began to glow with a bright blue light. The light's intensity grew, as did her discomfort, and she momentarily thought that the wound on her abdomen would split open and Zolmex would pull her soul free of her body. The light became so bright that it blinded her, and the pain was so intense that she screamed in agony and finally fell to her knees. Still, she grasped Zolmex tightly, unable to release it. Blue light flooded the room as Cassandra lay crumpled on the floor, a death grip on the birthright she had longed to obtain.

When the blinding light subsided and eventually disappeared, Cassandra awakened. She had changed. Her golden locks were now black, and her ripped and dirty outfit that Sitra had given her, with the tear across the abdomen, was gone, replaced with a long black dress with a slit up one leg, reaching to her mid-thigh. She wore black boots to match. Her scimitars remained belted around her hips.

She blinked away the light, revealing her eyes were now brown instead of blue. She looked around in confusion, trying to determine where she was. She realized she held Zolmex and brought it up before her to examine it closely. A smile spread across her face as she took in the beauty of the artifact.

"Finally," she whispered.

Without thinking, she reached down and undid her belt that held her scimitars, letting it drop to the floor, all the while keeping her focus on her birthright. Then she reached up to her holy symbol, still comfortably around her neck, and jerked it free, breaking the chain. She tossed the symbol, the same one she'd found in the barbarian burial ground, to the floor. She took the end of Zolmex and touched it to the table, and the tip glowed brightly for a moment. When she removed it, the inscribed wording had changed slightly from *To Find a King* to now read *To Find Cassandra*.

She walked out of the room confidently and went to the cave exit. The torches that now sported dark magical flames, almost black instead of blue when first lit by Cassandra's spell, snuffed out as she moved past them. The cave had served its purpose, and now was the time to introduce the world to Zolmex.

MATILDA'S TRAP

HE FOUR COMPANIONS NOW SAT IN THE MAGICAL COTTAGE ATOP Witch's Rise, waiting for Cassandra to appear. Bale had insisted they move the cottage down the trail just a bit in case Cassandra could see the hidden pocket of space. It was out of view from the spot where Matilda had seen her disappear. Matilda had also sent Neclesious out, and he remained perched high on one of the peaks above the area, out of sight of Cassandra just in case she was watching from her hiding spot.

Matilda hoped Bale was right about his plan. She was glad to have the dangerous Binta creature out of her camp, but she also wanted to ensure they could capture the elusive Cassandra Rho when the time came. She hoped Cassandra would quickly make an appearance now that the gathering of priests no longer guarded her escape.

They all sat silently in the cottage, and Matilda held her skull-like symbol of Marnelphion in her hand, her eyes closed, and in deep meditation. She wanted to be close to her god at this moment of their glory. Cass's anger with Bale had subsided a bit as he'd reassured her that the loss of Binta was a necessary step in their plans. Matilda had also reminded her of the coming tortures of Cassandra that Cass would oversee. All four had grown restless, and the wait wasn't easy, especially for Matilda, who was desperate to find her prey with only eleven months until the Great Summoning. Fortunately, they didn't have to wait long.

Matilda could almost sense something in the air as if their moment to catch Cassandra was upon them. A sixth sense washed over her, and she opened her eyes, breaking her meditation. She took in the sight of her companions, and everything seemed normal. They sat silently, with Ronnis drinking, the group's only activity. Cass sat on the small couch next to Ronnis, a look of pure boredom on her face as she played with one of her curls. Bale just stared straight ahead, seeming to be in a trance. Matilda knew that the imp, Neclesious, had established a mental link with him to alert him of Cassandra's presence if she appeared. Perhaps Bale was focused solely on the imp's activity, giving him the illusion of being entranced.

Gedlor had left nearly six hours earlier with that wretched creature, Binta Mulay, in tow. Now, the trap was in place and needed springing. Hopefully, they could coax their little prey out from hiding and end the maddening wait.

Matilda sensed it as much as if someone had nudged her—something stirred on the mountain's top. Perhaps Marnelphion was trying to alert her, or maybe it was the imp's telepathy with Bale that she sensed. Whatever the reason, she knew their moment of glory was upon them. Matilda stood and was about to venture a peek from their hiding spot when Bale stirred from his trance. She turned to him, and he wore a devious smile.

"She is here," he said.

Matilda smiled, her premonition confirmed. Cass sat up with a grin, and Ronnis took another long sip of brandy before closing the flask and donning his mask.

"Everyone remembers the plan?" Bale asked.

Matilda had to bite her tongue, understanding that Bale was there, not to steal her role as executioner and summoner of their god, but to ensure they successfully captured Cassandra. Still, he would not play babysitter for them. Matilda, Cass, and Ronnis had waited for this moment and would embrace it. She would not let Bale interfere or give the impression he had anything to do with Cassandra's capture.

"You instigated the plan to clear the area of allies to entice Cassandra to leave her hiding spot. You were wise in making that move. However, the trap is my idea, and we have had plenty of time to rehearse this scenario. Watch and enjoy this moment of our victory," Matilda said.

Bale smiled, allowing Matilda to have this moment, and she was grateful for it. She nodded to Cass and Ronnis, who returned it, indicating their readiness. They had waited for an eternity on the mountain it seemed, hoping for this moment. Bale only sat in silence as they left the cottage. Matilda was glad he didn't argue the point, as she wanted to prove what she could do without him. He eventually rose to follow, but she was confident he wouldn't interfere.

Cass and Ronnis led the small troop up the trail to approach Cassandra as Matilda walked behind them. Her anxiety raced as she thought of the rumored powers of the artifact Cassandra sought. If the girl possessed it, capturing her could be a challenge. Matilda had a plan for that instance and carried the item in a small lead box. Her nervousness rose as they came around the bend. Soon, Cassandra would be in sight. All her plans hinged on the girl's capture, and she wanted to do it without Bale's help.

She produced the tiny lead box from a pocket and opened it to verify the item was there. Sure enough, nestled comfortably within was the null stone she had taken from Emiline. It dangled from the end of a simple chain, and Matilda immediately felt its weight, both physically and magically. It would negate all magical properties within its proximity.

She had stolen Emiline's powerful stone when she first met the vampire lord, Heinsvick, on that fateful day in Novafontera. His favorite bride, Emiline, wore the device to defeat magical attacks made against her. That was the whole purpose of this formation, with Matilda marching behind the other two: to give Cassandra the ability to use her magic. When she needed it the most, Matilda would take it away, and she would be left vulnerable. Once Cassandra realized she was helpless, it would be too late to crawl back into her hole. Matilda returned the necklace to its lead case, not wanting to affect the battlefield quite yet. She would wait for Cassandra to play her hand, then spring the trap. With a deep breath, she quickened her pace.

Ronnis moved off to a side trail to climb above their prey, just as they had practiced. He would soon change into his snake form and drop onto Cassandra from above. Cass would be the first to engage Cassandra, and the young girl was confident that her demon abilities could easily handle any petty magics Cassandra could summon. Matilda followed behind, the null stone at the ready.

Soon, Cassandra was within sight. Only Cass and Matilda approached now, Ronnis slithering in the rocks above. Cassandra had her back to them as Neclesious distracted her with half-hearted swoops from the cliff face. Cassandra stood unmoving, unafraid, and confident. That pose struck Matilda as odd, as anyone witnessing an imp was usually anything but calm. The imp hovered between the girl and where Matilda had seen her disappear, effectively cutting off her retreat.

"Smart," Matilda whispered to herself.

As they closed, Matilda spotted the artifact in Cassandra's grasp! She absently put a hand on the lead box, to confirm once more that the null stone was available. Cassandra held the artifact between her and the imp but surely didn't panic. To Matilda's surprise, Cassandra didn't seem startled by the presence of the imp but almost seemed to expect it. Why would she suspect anything, especially if she thought they had all left? That did not sit well with Matilda. Also, as they closed, Matilda noticed other differences in the girl. When she chased her weeks earlier, Matilda had taken special care in memorizing how Cassandra looked. Her golden locks, blue eyes, and farmer's attire were burned into Matilda's brain. The girl before them had black hair and wore a dress to match. This girl seemed to have a sexy way about her, different from what Matilda remembered. Still, she carried the legendary Zolmex, so this had to be the Rho girl.

They closed ground quickly, and Neclesious kept Cassandra's attention. The girl had no idea they approached. Matilda focused on the silvery rod. Was there a chance this was not Zolmex, and Matilda's mind was just running wild? After all, Cass had never mentioned the artifact, but Matilda knew it well and always expected Cassandra to carry it if they ever met. Why would she not? The prophecy predicted its use by the Rho girl.

Still, Matilda hadn't seen Cassandra carrying the rod when she disappeared into her hole weeks earlier. Had she obtained it while hiding? Had the cowardly Kane gifted her the wonder? It matched the description of the artifact and the pictures she'd seen in multiple tomes. Matilda wondered at that awful moment if the null stone could prevent the powerful magic of the artifact. She was suddenly not as confident in her plan, but there was no turning back now.

They were only twenty yards away now, and Cassandra still appeared oblivious to their presence. Neclesious kept his attacks close, and the girl raised her rod to defend several times. The imp was wise enough not to get too near the hateful artifact. The creature did its job so well that it looked like Cassandra's capture would be easy. So far, everything was going as planned. Cass strolled confidently toward their prey. There was still no sign of Ronnis, but Matilda expected that; it wasn't yet time for his appearance. Matilda hurried to catch up with Cass, wanting Cassandra in the null stone's radius once she released it from its prison.

Then Cass stopped her approach, and studied Cassandra's changed appearance. If Cass, who knew her better than Matilda, was confused by what she saw, perhaps this wasn't Cassandra. The thought broke her heart. Matilda considered that perhaps Kane had also used a decoy, and the real Cassandra was fleeing. Panic gripped Matilda, and she struggled to breathe, the hot desert air suddenly too thick.

"Cassandra?" a not-so-confident Cass asked.

They were roughly ten yards away, and the girl turned around to face her old tormentor. The imp flew off to hide in the rocks above. Matilda looked on nervously as even Cass was unsure of who it was before her. The girl didn't seem like the same person to Matilda, though her face was similar. It was hard for her to tell since the only peek she'd had of the girl came at nighttime. Matilda looked to Cass, who studied the girl intently.

"Cass," the girl breathed as a confident smile formed.

"I like what you've done to your… everything," Cass said with a chuckle, holding her hands to encompass Cassandra.

"You should because I'm an improved version of Cassandra, as you're about to find out."

"This is not Cassandra?" Matilda asked.

"Oh, it's her. She's just trying to disguise herself," Cass said a little too unsurely.

"You've always been a fool, Cass. I am Ardna, and I am everything Cassandra is not. I am strong, powerful, and, as you ladies are about to find out, not in the mood for fools," the girl spat.

"If you aren't Cassandra, how do you know me?" Cass asked.

"I know everything about you, Cass. Do not think I don't remember everything you've done to me. You are a bully, nothing more."

"My point exactly. You are indeed Cassandra if you remember all the wonderful things I've done to you, right?"

"I—" the girl who called herself Ardna but who was Cassandra in disguise began.

A puzzled look came across her face as she tried to sort out the conflicting information. She finally smiled and raised the rod in her hand. "I found Zolmex," she whispered.

"Good, I look forward to taking it from you. Perhaps it will help in my sexual domination of Binta," Cass said, either not understanding the significance of the weapon or not believing the girl.

The anger that flashed across the girl's face had Matilda taking a step back. Cass had pushed her buttons, and the mention of Binta immediately enraged her.

"Where is Binta?" she growled.

"Safe," Matilda said, before Cass could say something stupid.

"Who are you?"

"I am Matilda, the person most concerned with your well-being, Cassandra."

"You lie, and that is not my name."

"I tortured Binta while you were away," Cass teased. "I broke her spirit and gave her demon milk. She is my sex slave now."

"You lie!" Cassandra spat.

"Oh no, I assure you, she is quite submissive to me and has an incredibly talented tongue," Cass teased. "I see why you're attracted to her now," she added with a demonic laugh.

"You better pray that you're lying and that she's unharmed."

Matilda knew these two would come to blows soon. Cass was too unruly, and perhaps that would cost them everything. Matilda recalled that Bale wanted Cass and Ronnis killed when he first arrived and that Matilda had argued for their inclusion. Now, she second-guessed the wisdom in that. Matilda scouted the rocks above them, looking for a sign from Ronnis. She wouldn't be able to conceal the null stone much longer.

"You are a loser, Cassandra, and always will be. Why don't you hand that over before things get messy?" Cass said, pointing to Zolmex. "If you are a good girl, perhaps I'll have Binta pleasure you. I assure you, she's quite good at it."

That was all the Rho girl could handle, and her hand suddenly became engulfed with green energy that crackled with power. "Face the wrath of Zolmex, Cass!" she screamed.

Cassandra, or Ardna as she called herself, fed the ball of energy to the rod's tip, and Zolmex quickly absorbed it. Matilda reached for the null stone, suspecting that things were about to get ugly. Before she could unfasten the lead box, Cassandra pointed Zolmex at Cass, and it shot forth an amplified magic sphere from its tip. The artifact had taken Cassandra's spell and created something much more devastating.

Cass had little time to react and tensed up as the magical energy struck her. Cass and Matilda were familiar with the spell and knew what damage it could do. Ronnis's face was a testament of what Cassandra was capable of, and that was without the help of a legendary artifact. The energy expanded and created a bubble just before it struck its target, enveloping Cass fully.

Cass was as surprised at her new prison as anyone else. She patted and prodded the edges, but it wouldn't give. Electricity colored blue and green ran the diameter of the energy sphere, hinting at a tremendous power, and just like that, Cass was caught. The bubble rose off the ground, and with a flick of Cassandra's wrist, the energy sphere moved swiftly off the cliff face and hovered just out of reach of the ledge. Matilda stood mesmerized, the lead case in hand.

"Tell me where Binta is," Cassandra demanded.

Cass ceased her struggles and stared hatefully at her enemy. Now, Matilda couldn't release the null stone because it would mean Cass would plummet down the cliff face. She knew about Cass's ability to release her hidden demonic traits, but she didn't know if she could transform before she hit the rocky bottom at the foot of the cliff.

"Fine, then die," the girl said, then the sphere disappeared with a wave of her hand.

Cass's surprised look was genuine, but Matilda only saw it briefly as the girl fell out of sight. As Cassandra turned slowly to face her, Matilda struggled to open the lead case holding her special surprise.

"I don't think so," the girl said when she saw Matilda fumbling with it.

A dart of powerful magic slammed into the case, knocking it from Matilda's hands. It landed about thirty feet away, and Matilda's fingers burned and throbbed from the effect. She brought a hand to her mouth, sucking an injured finger, and the girl advanced.

"I know who you are. You are the person trying to sacrifice me to your evil god. If I kill you, my troubles are over," she said, pointing Zolmex her way.

Matilda saw peripherally that Neclesious had returned and picked up the smoking lead case. Matilda knew the null stone was their only hope. This girl, whether Cassandra or someone named Ardna, was too dangerous with the artifact in hand. She had to keep the powerful girl's attention long enough for the imp to open it. Unfortunately, the girl noticed the creature as well, and with a flick of her wrist, the powerful energy enveloped her hand once more.

"Cassandra, you cannot change your destiny," Matilda said, trying to keep her attention.

"Shut up! I'm tired of everyone telling me of my destiny."

She never turned to Matilda; instead, she focused on the imp struggling to open the damaged case. She released her energy again, using the rod to modify it. She pointed the rod toward the imp, whose eyes widened with fear, and the creature, an inhabitant of hell and witness to many horrific deeds, flew away. Cassandra didn't use the rod as she had against Cass, who was now probably dead. Instead, she pointed the deadly device toward the imp, and the energy glowing in her opposite hand snuffed out. It blasted through the top of the rod a moment later, once more modified and deadly.

The imp had no chance, and the effect was devastating when the energy hit Neclesious just as he was flying away. There was an explosion on impact, followed by raining guts and blood—so much blood! Matilda witnessed the case holding the null stone drop over the lip of the cliff and out of sight, and with it, her hope of defeating this young woman who had so easily disposed of two demonic beings. Cass was gone, and Neclesious was no more.

The trap wasn't working as Matilda had planned. With two allies quickly dispatched and the null stone now lost, her hope dwindled. She had never seen such raw power before, and she wasn't sure they could have taken Cassandra, even with all the priests they once had. She saw a large black snake fall harmlessly behind Cassandra, which was another missed attack. Ronnis was supposed to fall directly on her as a distraction. The lord didn't seem hurt and was soon slithering toward Cassandra.

"Only now do you see your error," Cassandra began with a smirk. "I am far more powerful than you. Did your pathetic demon lord foresee this ending to your life's work? I know you planned to torture me and ultimately sacrifice me to the filth you worship. I think perhaps I'll torture you instead. Go to sleep, old woman," Cassandra said, waving a hand at Matilda.

Matilda felt an immense wave of magical energy roll over her, and she could barely resist the urge to sleep. Her grogginess made her lose focus on the spell she was summoning, and it fizzled out as she blinked her tired eyes. She didn't want to fall asleep because then she would be vulnerable to the crazed and powerful girl. And Matilda did not doubt the girl's threats of torture. She had to get Zolmex from her grasp, or they would all die.

She fell to her knees, then to her face, before knowing what was happening. She could will herself to remain awake, but her spell was gone, and her connection with Marnelphion was minimal. The spell was unlike anything she'd ever experienced. Matilda was a seasoned priestess of a mighty demon, yet Cassandra toyed with her, quickly taking her out of the fight. She was not out of the battle but knew the delay could cost her dearly. And if she did succumb entirely to the spell, what tortures would the powerful girl exact on her?

Then Bale was there, and Matilda had never been so thankful to see him. He used his powers of Marnelphion to attack the girl. Black energy shot forth from his hands as he presented them before her. The ropes of energy engulfed Cassandra, wrapping her in the black, sickly strands. Matilda fought the effects of the sleep spell and sat up, shaking her head with a yawn. She knew the strands of black magic would hold the girl and drain her energy, making it easy to take Zolmex from her before she killed them all. She hated that Bale would finally be the one to neutralize the girl, but she was glad he was there.

The sticky binds wrapped around Cassandra and she ceased to move, appearing as a mummy wrapped in tar-like strands of cloth. Matilda breathed a sigh of relief, thinking their prey was finally contained. Bale walked over to her and helped her stand. His firm grasp was the only thing that kept her from falling back to the ground. He chuckled and held her up. She hated him.

"There, your dangerous prey has been caught. Now, let's disarm and shackle the girl," Bale said.

It took Matilda many moments to shake off the spell's effects, but she only truly snapped out of it when Bale offered her lizard jelly. He held it under her nose, and Matilda recoiled. Bale held her head and made her breathe in. The stench was dreadful, but it cleared her senses. He put the foul substance away when Matilda refocused.

With a metallic smile, he patted her on the shoulder and looked around, only then realizing none of their allies remained. "Where is Neclesious?"

Bale hadn't seen the entire encounter nor the imp's demise and probably had no idea how potent their foe was. She was about to enlighten him when Cassandra began to shake underneath her binds. They watched dumbfounded as the black, sticky bands slipped away from the girl and melted into the rocky ground. Matilda and Bale watched, then looked to Cassandra, who stared hatefully at Bale. Neither she nor her tight-fitting dress showed any residue from the spell. Suddenly, Bale didn't seem so confident. The gem atop the artifact glowed brightly, but before she could bring Zolmex to bear, Ronnis, in snake form, wrapped himself around Cassandra's legs, finally making her topple over.

With a growl, the girl sat up and came face to face with the snake form of Ronnis. He was wrapped tightly around her legs, and his head was eye level with her. Matilda knew his bite was venomous, so he didn't strike. Cassandra pointed Zolmex at his face and smiled. Bale was running, probably knowing his priestly magic was useless and he would need to overpower the girl physically.

Matilda knew it would be too late, and Ronnis would be the third victim to fall to their strange foe who claimed to be someone other than Cassandra. If they faced these kinds of losses against someone who wasn't even Cassandra, they couldn't ever hope to catch or defeat the actual spawn of Kane. But Matilda knew better. None other than Kane's child could wield Zolmex to its maximum potential. The girl was Cassandra, whether she admitted it or not.

However, the artifact did nothing, and the girl looked at the rod, a puzzled expression on her pretty face. That was when Matilda saw Cass flying over the lip of the cliff, the amulet holding the null stone hanging from a chain in her hand. Matilda felt the residual effects of Cassandra's spell melt away, and Ronnis involuntarily turned to human form. He was still atop Cassandra's legs, now holding them with his arms.

"Ronnis!" the girl said in surprise, recognizing the masked man immediately.

Her expression was one of repulsion as she finally recognized her enemy. Bale was there then, finally jerking the rod from the girl's hand. "I'll take that!"

"No!" she screamed as Bale tossed the artifact to Matilda.

Fueled by rage at being disarmed of her birthright, Cassandra somehow pulled a leg free from Ronnis and kicked him hard in the face. His mask flew away, and the large man rolled off her with a groan. Cassandra jumped to her feet with incredible speed and ran toward Zolmex. Matilda was studying the magnificent artifact she now held before her and didn't see the attack until it was too late. She closed her eyes, expecting Cassandra's tackle, but it never came.

"Let me go!" she heard Cassandra yell.

Matilda opened her eyes to see that Bale held Cassandra from behind as she struggled to break free. She was like a wild animal, and Matilda knew they had to restrain her quickly. She produced the shackles and tossed them to Ronnis, who sat holding his bloodied nose.

"Put these on her. Do *not* let her escape!" she ordered.

Cass flew in to join the mix, her demon form on display. She hovered before Cassandra as Bale held the struggling girl's arms behind her. When Cassandra noticed Cass, the crazed girl stopped and stared wide-eyed. Cass smiled evilly and gently placed the necklace around Cassandra's neck. Cassandra didn't move or even struggle against the effort, she was so shocked at the sight of a demonic Cass.

"Cass?" Cassandra said with amazement.

"That's right. You cannot best me, Cassandra. I have defeated you once more. Now, you are mine," Cass purred.

"Ours," Matilda added, now standing beside the hovering demon.

Cass nodded with a smile. Ronnis was soon beside Matilda, his face smeared with blood and the shackles at the ready. It looked to Matilda that they'd narrowly avoided a disaster. They'd lost Neclesious, and Bale would make Cassandra pay for that, but Matilda could handle that if it meant her prized catch was now hers.

"You… were always a demon?" Cassandra stammered.

"Of course not, you idiot."

"But how?"

"Your simple mind would never understand, but I have you to thank for my glorious rebirth," Cass said, finally folding her wings and landing gracefully in front of Cassandra.

"Secure her," Matilda said with a nod to Ronnis.

"Gladly," the lord said, and he approached their captive.

Cassandra, who had been completely subdued and limp in Bale's grasp since the reappearance of Cass, suddenly came to life. The look in her eyes had Matilda taking a step behind Cass and Ronnis. She was not about to let the girl regain possession of Zolmex, as improbable as that seemed.

Ronnis stood before Cassandra, either ignorant of her change or too angry to notice. His bloody nose was just another humiliation at the hands of the girl, and Matilda knew he wanted revenge. She was about to warn him when Cassandra's foot kicked out and connected solidly with Ronnis's groin. He doubled over and fell to his knees. Before that motion could register in Matilda's mind, Cassandra used Ronnis's back as a stepping stool. She took a quick step and jumped, flinging herself backward. In the process, her right foot connected with Cass's chin, sending the demon sprawling. The move broke Bale's hold, and she landed softly behind him.

Matilda felt as if she were watching a dream unfold before her. All the pieces were moving too fast for her mind to comprehend. If what Cass told her of Cassandra was true, there was no way she could perform such a move. What happened next was beyond anything Matilda could comprehend, and she could not believe the skill set of this young woman.

As Bale turned to face Cassandra, she had already removed the null stone from her neck and, with the snap of her wrist, stabbed four stiff fingers into his neck. He stumbled backward a few steps and nearly fell over Ronnis, grabbing at his throat. Cassandra stayed with him and slammed the null stone in his gaping mouth. She followed that up with an uppercut that smashed his metal teeth together with such force that the null stone fractured, and Matilda felt the heavy veil it offered diminish.

Matilda could feel Zolmex hum in her hands as the magic negated by the stone began to fill the artifact once more. Bale's strong bite didn't destroy the null stone because Matilda still felt the magical void it offered, but she knew they were in trouble if they couldn't get Cassandra under control.

"Subdue her," Bale said hatefully, tossing the null stone away.

He remained on one knee after the vicious uppercut, blood pouring from his mouth. Matilda knew Cass was probably their only hope, as the stone wouldn't cancel her demonic powers since they were natural and not magical. Cass was gaining her feet from the powerful kick that had knocked her down. The young woman was furious, and Matilda was happy for the rage, as long as Cass used it to subdue and not kill their prey.

Suddenly, Zolmex was nearly torn from her grasp, and Matilda looked to see Cassandra holding her hand toward the artifact. The two had a bond, and the artifact wanted its master. Matilda held tight with both hands as lightning arched between the rod and Cassandra's hand. The light was blinding, and the energy burned her hands. It lasted only a moment, but Matilda had to drop Zolmex when it became too hot.

Cassandra gathered that little bit of lightning magic into her fist and struck Bale again before he could fully rise. The force of the blow, which included a deadly dose of lightning, sent the priest flying back against the stone wall. He smashed into it with a sickening crunch and fell lifelessly to the ground. Smoke wafted from his head due to Cassandra's pent-up energy she'd coaxed from the artifact.

Matilda didn't know if Bale was dead, and she couldn't care less if he was. However, as she pondered that, Cassandra unleashed a deadly kick to Ronnis's chin just as he was gaining a kneeling position. The kick had him sprawling and his body jerking from the vicious attack. He was no longer a threat to Cassandra, leaving only two.

Luckily, Cass was stalking in, and Cassandra's attention was on her. Matilda knew the hate between those two was unmatched, and she took the opportunity to rid herself of Zolmex. Matilda ran as fast as she could toward the cliff face, picking up the fractured null stone along the way. Cassandra had lost track of her, or Matilda suspected she never would have been able to do what she did next: toss Zolmex and the stone over the cliff.

She watched them fall, satisfied that Zolmex was no longer available to Cassandra and that the null stone no longer hampered her spells. She knew Cassandra could cast as well, but she liked her odds better now with her repertoire of spells and Cass's natural abilities. She stalked back toward Cassandra and Cass as they circled each other.

"Tell me where Binta is, and I'll let you walk away, Cass," Cassandra said.

Cass chuckled at the absurd demand, and Cassandra added, "Otherwise, you'll end up like your boyfriend," pointing toward Ronnis's unconscious form.

Cass's face reddened, and she unfolded her demon wings. "I will so enjoy torturing you from this day forward until your death, which is not far off."

"We'll see," Cassandra said, then reached her hand toward Matilda again to draw forth more magic, but her eyes widened when she realized Matilda no longer held Zolmex.

Cass used the distraction to grab her whip from her belt and lash out at her opponent. Matilda knew that Cass wasn't proficient with it but had been practicing for the last few weeks as they staked out the top of Witch's Rise. The end wrapped around Cassandra's arm, and Cass used her enhanced strength to pull her toward her. Cassandra fell forward, and Cass attempted to kick her, but Cassandra rolled away and was out of reach of the wild attack.

Cassandra freed herself and gained her feet when Matilda said, "There's no need to resist. We have you and our magic is functioning normally."

Matilda meant her words for Cass in case the girl had something magical she wished to use on their prey. Cassandra gave Matilda a hateful look but didn't see Cass unsheathe a golden dagger shaped like a large tooth. As Cass readied herself for another attack, Matilda used one of her most potent spells to hold Cassandra still. Invisible waves of energy flew toward Cassandra, but the girl did something that Matilda never expected: she dodged the attack as if she could see the magic before her.

Cassandra stepped aside but then seemed to pull the magic back with a few gestures from her hands and directed the spell toward Matilda. Unable to react quickly enough, Matilda felt the energy wash over her as her spell froze her muscles, and she became paralyzed. She never expected to have to defend herself from one of her own spells, and being caught unaware resulted in her failure. Matilda could only watch now as their last hope to capture Cassandra fell on Cass's shoulders.

"You remember this, don't you?" Cass asked Cassandra, holding up the Tooth of Leo, the dagger she had stabbed Cassandra in the back with nearly a year ago.

"Cass, your taunts mean nothing. Look around. I have defeated your entire group of friends, and now I will beat you once and for all. Soon, your toy will belong to me."

"You're very confident for someone who has never beaten me at anything," Cass retorted as the girls circled.

"You have a distorted view of things or possibly a bad memory. Do you remember when you tried to drown me in the caves?"

Cass laughed and said, "Yes, those are good memories."

"How's your chest?"

Cass quit laughing, and the smile quickly faded from her face, soon replaced by a frown, which transformed into a scowl. With a scream, Cass bounded forward, and Cassandra did the same, the two crashing into each other and locking in a tangle of arms, each jockeying for position. Cass had Tooth aimed at Cassandra's ribs, and Cassandra had a tight grasp on Cass's wrist, trying to stay the blade. Cass's free hand had a fistful of Cassandra's hair, tugging her off balance while Cassandra punched Cass hard on the side with quick, efficient strikes.

Matilda was amazed at Cassandra's fighting prowess. She'd assumed from what Cass had told her of the young woman she would be helpless in combat. If Cass didn't possess demonic strength, Cassandra would have overpowered her easily. As it was, Cass was slowly gaining the advantage as the dagger came dangerously close to Cassandra's ribs.

Cassandra switched tactics and summoned a sphere of magic in the hand holding Cass's wrist. Her skin burned and dark smoke rose in the air. Cass uttered a small scream and released Tooth, which clanged to the rock floor. Cass slung Cassandra forcefully by the hair, making her fall. Amazingly, she rolled with the motion and came up to her feet as if she'd never left them. But now she held the Tooth of Leo.

"You bitch!" Cass yelled, holding her wrist as the last wafts of smoke dissipated from the wound.

Matilda tried desperately to break free but failed. She had just witnessed the girl create, use, and manipulate spells without using components! Matilda had to put this in perspective: Cassandra was a demi-god, and with Zolmex, Cassandra was unbeatable. Even without the artifact, she was formidable. Her faith in Cass waned.

The sworn enemies circled once more. Matilda noticed that Bale stirred then, trying to rise. Cass wisely stopped the circling so that Cassandra had her back to him. Cass summoned two small magical missiles from her fingertips toward Cassandra to distract her further. The spell was one Matilda knew, the same one Cassandra had supposedly used against Ronnis. The magic was powerful, required no components, and was difficult to dodge. It was the most potent of the basic spells taught to students.

Cassandra also knew this, and her eyes widened briefly before she dropped the dagger and formed a magical shield the missiles crashed into. She gave a small grunt and fell to one knee from the impact. Bale was up and approaching, his face red and blistered from Cassandra's earlier attack. He looked enraged, and Matilda knew this did not bode well for Cassandra. She had managed to block Cass's attack somehow, but she did not realize Bale approached.

Cass laughed again—Matilda thought it was to distract her opponent once more—and said, "You can't win, Cassandra. Beg for my forgiveness, and I'll go easy on you and perhaps Binta."

Cassandra remained kneeling and balled her fists. "I hate you!" she growled. "And my name is Ardna!"

Cass only laughed at the remark as Bale pulled out his serrated dagger. Matilda panicked at the sight of an angered Bale holding his dagger threateningly. Perhaps he or any of her other allies might be unable to restrain themselves as they fought the powerful girl. What if one of them killed her? Matilda had to break free. She struggled and managed to move her right pinky slightly. It wasn't enough—Bale was ready to strike!

As if sensing the attack, Cassandra quickly picked up the dagger, turned, and threw it at her new attacker. Tooth buried in his shoulder to the hilt. Bale screamed in pain and surprise, but only briefly. To Matilda's amazement, he froze in place, just like Matilda's current predicament. His wound poured blood, but Bale couldn't move, which Cass had told her was a property of the blade. He fell backward, hitting his head hard on the sheet of rock comprising the mountaintop floor.

Cass used the distraction to strike with her whip. It wrapped around Cassandra's arm tightly. The whip snap must have hurt her, and she yelled in pain. Cass yanked hard on the whip, and with Cassandra already off balance, she stumbled awkwardly toward Cass, which cost her dearly. Cass connected with a right hook to Cassandra's jaw, making the girl's legs buckle. Cassandra was dazed but had enough bearings to fall flat as Cass attempted to kick her in the face. Cassandra used the momentum to pull her off balance using the whip.

Cass would have fallen but took flight instead, dragging Cassandra with her. The half-demon quickly lifted a struggling Cassandra off her feet and into the air. Cassandra stopped fighting once she was twenty feet off the ground and held on to the whip like a lifeline.

The fight was getting out of control, and Matilda needed to break the spell. She managed to make a fist, then wiggle the fingers of her right hand. Soon, she would be free.

Cass drove Cassandra straight into one of the surrounding rock walls. Matilda expected the impact to shake the girl and have her dropping twenty feet to quickly end the fight. Instead, she clung to the wall, untangled herself from the whip, and promptly climbed down it like a spider! Matilda had seen such spells from advanced wizards, but always with spell components, which usually consisted of eating a spider. Cassandra was excellent and a worthwhile sacrifice for her god.

The sight caught Cass off guard, and Matilda could see her confused look as she watched Cassandra quickly scale down the rock wall. The distraction cost her as Cassandra took the initiative once she reached the ground. She summoned a large ball of energy and threw it at Cass, who couldn't hope to dodge it. Cass turned her back and folded her wings to protect herself. The energy loudly sizzled as it dug into those delicate wings, and Cass screamed in agony.

She plummeted to the ground, spreading her wings as much as the pain allowed to help break her fall. The demon appendages smoked, and a thick, black trail followed her to the ground, where she landed harder than Matilda liked. She would have grimaced at the sight if she weren't paralyzed. The feeling finally returned to her legs, and she took one step. The spell was finally waning.

Cassandra stood before a kneeling Cass, whose wings still smoked. The half-demon was injured, and the fall had done as much damage as the attack on her burned wings. Two glowing spheres of magic enveloped each of Cassandra's hands, teeming with power. The smirk on Cassandra's face indicated that the fight was over, and Matilda was about to witness Cass's demise. She focused on breaking the paralyzing spell. If she could free herself, she could possibly avoid the pending disaster.

"You are a terrible person, Cass, and a bully. You have plagued me far too long, and now I will free the world of your curse. Go back to hell or wherever you crawled from," Cassandra said, preparing to release her magic.

Cass, beaten and defeated, looked up at her nemesis and whispered the words Cassandra had used many times toward those who mistreated her: "I hate you."

Cassandra smiled and said, "I hate you too, bitch."

Cass's end was near. Matilda's heart raced as she remained helpless. Although her legs answered her call now and her arms moved once more, they were sluggish, and she couldn't help her fallen ally. Matilda would have to deal with Cassandra on her own. She prayed that Marnelphion would see to Cassandra's capture. This encounter had not gone as planned.

Then, something happened that no one expected. Cass called for her dagger, and the golden-bladed artifact disappeared from Bale's shoulder and reappeared in her hand. Cass was quick enough to stab the blade through the top of Cassandra's right boot, impaling the top of the girl's foot. Cass threw up her arms afterward, still expecting Cassandra's attack. Matilda understood that reaction as Cassandra had defeated everything they'd thrown at her thus far. But not this time.

No counterattack came, and Cass slowly lowered her arms in shock. Matilda was walking toward them and could see the look on Cassandra's face. It was the expression someone wore when seriously injured, but it was the shock before the pain registered. Her eyes were wide, and her mouth slightly opened as if to scream in pain or denial. The blade had frozen her muscles before she ever felt the bite of the dagger.

Cass stood slowly with a grimace and attempted unsuccessfully to stretch out her damaged wings. She didn't get far and, with a yelp, folded them gently. Matilda was beside her then, and they both looked to Cassandra, who stood motionless and helpless before them. Her fists' pent-up energy slowly dwindled and eventually faded to nothingness. They had finally defeated the mysterious girl—she was Matilda's prisoner!

"Bitch!" Cass yelled suddenly and grabbed two fistfuls of Cassandra's hair. She brought her face close to hers and whispered, "You will pay for everything you've done to me. I am your torturer, and I can't think of a better way to spend the next year than inflicting pain on you and listening to your screams of anguish."

Matilda gently pulled Cass back, who reluctantly released Cassandra's hair. The girl didn't respond to Cass's words or any pain she might have felt from Cass's hold.

"Amazing," Matilda whispered as she waved a hand in front of Cassandra's face. There was still no reaction from their captive. "How long will the blade hold?"

"As long as I leave it in her stinking foot," Cass spat.

"Excellent," Matilda said with a wide smile. "Let's regroup and secure our prisoner."

Matilda checked on Bale, and none of his injuries were severe, but combined, they had taken a toll on him. His face was red and blistered from Cassandra's electrical punch; he'd banged his head on the stone several times during the scuffle; and he'd lost a lot of blood from the dagger wound. Matilda healed him enough to stand and function again, and it was the only time Matilda had ever seen the dangerous priest timid, if not a bit humiliated. She smiled on the inside at his discomfort.

Ronnis had been knocked cold, and his most significant injury was to his pride. Dried blood still caked his face from his busted nose, and he said nothing as he collected his mask and sword and gathered himself. Matilda took the shackles from him. She wanted to secure Cassandra before she found a way to break free from the dagger's hold. Soon, all four stood before their prey, each battered and bruised, except for Matilda, who had avoided Cassandra's wrath during the melee.

Matilda was about to shackle the girl, but she couldn't help but doubt this was the true Cassandra. She looked her over. The dark hair and eyes didn't match Cass's description, and the tight, sexy dress seemed out of place. She paused, shackles in hand, and stared at the frozen girl.

"Why the delay, Matilda? Shackle her before she causes more trouble," Bale said, and Matilda detected a hint of fear in his voice.

"I wonder if this is Cassandra," Matilda replied.

"Of course it is!" Cass yelled. "Shackle the bitch."

"She said her name was Ardna, and this doesn't look like the Cassandra you described."

"It's a disguise, nothing more. She has all of Cassandra's memories, and I know it's her," Cass said confidently.

"A decoy fooled me once before, and I will not tolerate it again," Matilda said.

"Ronnis, do you agree with me?" Cass asked.

They all turned to the masked man, who had remained silent thus far. He stood before their captive and was quiet for many moments. Finally, he said, "This is Cassandra, I do not doubt, and my trusty sword confirms my belief."

"I must be sure this time," Matilda whispered as doubts still crept through her mind.

"There is a way," Ronnis said. They all turned to him again, and he held up his black-bladed sword. "I branded her with this, remember?"

"And I stabbed her in the back with Tooth. Surely there would be a scar," Cass added excitedly.

"Strip her," Bale said with a toothy smile.

Cass moved forward and reached for Cassandra, but Ronnis caught her by the wrist. The half-demon seemed surprised by the move, and she looked at Ronnis incredulously. "I'll do it," he said firmly.

Cass nodded and withdrew her hand. Ronnis sheathed his sword and moved closer to Cassandra so they were face to face. He stayed that way for many moments, and Matilda knew what anger and humiliation he must feel inside. He hated Cassandra, but she was sure his feelings had doubled with this latest encounter.

Ronnis calmly removed his mask, showing his torn face, then leaned and whispered something into her ear. Matilda couldn't hear what was said, but a chill ran down her spine at the thought of what he might have told their captive. His message took many moments to deliver, and Matilda almost interrupted him so they could strip the girl and discover the information she desperately needed.

He moved away before she could and roughly pulled the straps of Cassandra's dress down her shoulders. He gritted his teeth as he took handfuls of the front of her dress and ripped it roughly, exposing her breasts. The view seemed to fuel his anger as he eagerly tore and pulled so hard at the dress that the poor girl almost toppled over several times during the attack. Eventually, the dress fell to her ankles, and she was naked, except for black underwear and her black boots. By that point, Ronnis was breathing heavily and stood just inches before her, fistfuls of the dress in each hand. He stood there for a few moments, admiring her nakedness, and eventually backed out of the way.

Matilda quickly moved so she could see Cassandra's right hip. There, just below her underwear, was the brand of a snake's face. The delight Matilda felt at the sight was overwhelming. She smiled and moved to examine the girl's back, and sure enough, there was a small scar on Cassandra's lower back, right where Cass expected it to be. Matilda continued her walk around the girl, admiring her young body and delighted that it had been so thoroughly scarred. She noticed as she came to stand in front of her that a newer, red scar ran across her abdomen.

"So, what do you think caused this?" Matilda asked, rubbing a finger along its length. She watched Cassandra's face for any reaction, but there remained none.

Bale shrugged and said, "Perhaps this has something to do with her change in appearance?"

"Either way, this is Cassandra Rho," Cass added.

"Perhaps the girl has a split personality that you never knew about," Matilda said, and Cass only shrugged.

"Either way, we have her. Let's bind her and get her to the wagon," Bale said, taking the metal shackles from Matilda and finally binding her hands.

Once they had her properly restrained, Matilda examined her injured foot. Blood had now filled the boot and leaked to the stone floor. The wound could become fatal, but not soon. She would let the girl suffer a bit longer.

Matilda stood and said, "Before we remove the dagger, I want to secure Zolmex and the null stone. Cass, can you fly?"

Cass shook her head, not even attempting to unfold her wings. At the mention of it, she retracted her demon traits, the wings disappearing, and the young woman appeared human once more.

"We wouldn't need her to if Neclesious was still here," Bale said, examining many tiny pools of smoking tar that were once the imp.

Bale offered to carry their captive, but Cass quickly lifted the small woman over her shoulder, her demonic strength easily capable of the task. They still had to stop several times during their descent from Witch's Rise for Cass to rest, but they finally made it to the bottom of the mountain and the waiting covered wagon. They loaded Cassandra into the wagon and drove it to where they thought Zolmex might be.

Matilda had hoped that the artifact would stand out in the rocks at the base of the cliff, but it took them many hours of searching to even find what they believed was the correct cliff face. It took hours more searching, but with the help of various magic detection spells from Matilda, Bale, and Cass, they finally found Zolmex jutting from some rocks. Luckily, the null stone wasn't far, and although cracks ran through the emerald, it negated their detection spells soon after they spotted Zolmex, so Matilda knew it still functioned. She sighed and counted her blessings.

Soon, they had the necklace around Cassandra's neck again and Zolmex safely tucked inside the magical cottage. Matilda insisted on carrying the tiny magical device that summoned the cottage. Cass seemed not to mind, as she was caught up in the excitement of having Cassandra as a plaything.

After checking Cassandra's binds and confident she couldn't escape, Matilda decided it was time to interrogate their new prisoner. Bale started the wagon on its way toward Malikai's stronghold, deep within the Yaddaton Desert, as Matilda sat across from Cassandra, who was flanked by Cass and Ronnis, the lord's Black Adder drawn and held to her ribs. Once Matilda was ready, she nodded to Cass, who withdrew her dagger and quickly had the dangerous tip to Cassandra's other side.

Cassandra was finally able to scream in agony from the wound on her foot that Matilda decided should bleed out a little more to teach her spirited prisoner a lesson. She gave the wagon's interior a cursory look and didn't question her near nakedness. She had obviously been aware of her surroundings while under Tooth's spell, and would have heard every word of whatever Ronnis whispered to her before stripping her. She looked hatefully at Cass and struggled with her bindings. Cass only smiled, and the shackles didn't give. After a prod from Ronnis's sword, Cassandra seemed to understand she was caught. She sat back and closed her eyes.

"Tell me your name, girl," Matilda finally asked.

Cassandra opened her eyes and glared. She offered no response, so Matilda moved forward and leaned over the girl. Instead of trying to coax answers from her with feigned niceties like she had Kessi, she tried to be intimidating here. The two glared at each other briefly as Cass and Ronnis looked on eagerly. After a long while, the only sound the jostling of the wagon, the girl spat in Matilda's face. Matilda recalled Kessi spitting in her face when questioned similarly, indicating that this really might be Cassandra Rho.

Matilda smiled, and as she'd done with Kessi, she wiped a finger along her cheek and pushed it into her mouth, where she sucked it dry. Oddly, this girl gave the same response that Kessi had given: "You're gross."

Matilda smiled, slowly understanding that this was her prized catch. She backhanded her hard, making her lean toward Ronnis, who pushed her upright. Blood pooled in her mouth from the solid hit as she ran her tongue over her busted lip.

"Tell me your name," Matilda repeated, still standing over their captive.

The girl answered the question similarly: she spat in her face. Blood comprised most of the mess that ran down her cheek this time. Matilda didn't flinch and did the same thing as before, cleaning the blood and spit from her face by sucking it off her finger. The girl looked disgusted, and Matilda even saw the same look from Cass who watched the exchange. She couldn't read Ronnis as he wore his mask. Matilda suddenly stomped on Cassandra's injured foot. That had the girl crying out in pain as she rocked back and forth, her face locked in a grimace of exquisite pain.

"I grow tired of your games, girl. Unless you want more of that, you will tell me your name," Matilda said. "Do you understand?"

"Yes," the girl said, still rocking slowly and trying to regulate her breathing.

"Good. Then what is your name?" Matilda asked.

Several streams of blood ran down Cassandra's chin from Matilda's strike. Although she didn't spit this time, she wouldn't answer.

"Don't answer, bitch," Cass encouraged, eagerly waiting for Matilda to strike her again.

Matilda waved off the volatile girl and asked again, "Name?"

"I told you, I am Ardna."

"If that's true, where is Cassandra, and why do you know everything she does? And by all means, why did you carry her birthright?"

"Because I'm her, only much, much better."

"So, you are Cassandra Rho, then?" Matilda asked, confused.

"No, you old fool, I've told you who I am."

Matilda, done with the girl's sassy replies and frustrated by the lack of information, stomped at Cassandra's foot again, this time intentionally missing it. The girl sucked in her breath and closed her eyes tightly, expecting the agonizing pain to wash over her once more. Instead, Matilda only smiled, and as the girl slowly opened her eyes, Matilda finally retook her seat.

"You see, girl, I don't want to torture you, and I will gladly heal your wounded foot if you only cooperate," Matilda said gently. "Do we understand each other?"

"Of course, you are a nasty woman who has taken my things and chained me because you are afraid of what I would do to you and your stupid cronies should I ever retake Zolmex."

Matilda saw Cass grind her teeth as Cassandra spoke, and she knew that the three of them were on edge. Perhaps a different type of threat would alleviate the tension.

"You know I've captured your sister and your lover, Binta. Both are in good hands for now, but depending on how you behave in my care, their treatment may worsen," Matilda said, smiling.

"I doubt that, you old hag. You couldn't catch me for the longest time."

Matilda's smile melted from her face as her anger boiled. This one had to be Cassandra, but she would never confirm it. She gave in to the idea that they would assume her identity and then have Malikai use more potent magic on her to read her thoughts once they arrived at his stronghold. For now, they would watch her closely. She thought of Cerus and how this girl had cost her so much, including her mighty husband.

"Hold her," she calmly told Cass and Ronnis, and she stood again.

Cass smiled as she and Ronnis sheathed their weapons and grabbed Cassandra roughly, each taking an arm. Matilda stood over the girl, who only stared at her hatefully. She needed to break this one's spirit, so Matilda began to punch Cassandra violently, paying the sassy girl back for Cerus's death. Matilda only thought of him as she administered the beating, drawing more blood and closing one of Cassandra's eyes. When the girl nearly lost consciousness, she lifted her head by the hair to punch her face some more. The beating continued for quite a while, and the vicious Cass enjoyed every strike, giggling like a child.

Blood covered Matilda's hands when she was through administering her lesson. Ronnis and Cass released Cassandra, and she fell unconscious to the seat. The three stood around her, and much blood covered the inside of the wagon.

"Should you heal her?" Cass asked, concerned now that the fun was over and the amount of damage Matilda had done to Cassandra sank in.

Matilda took her seat, grabbed a cloth, and began wiping her hands.

She shook her head and said, "Not yet. Let her suffer. She is too mouthy. It will only worsen if we don't stop that nasty habit now."

Cass looked at Cassandra doubtfully, and Matilda had to admit that she'd taken quite the beating, but it was well deserved for the trouble she'd caused them all.

"Don't fret, Cass. I won't let her die unless I discover she's but another decoy."

Cass nodded and seemed satisfied with that reasoning. She and Ronnis sat at the far end of the wagon where the waning light of the desert sun streaked inside. They spoke in hushed tones, probably planning Cassandra's many tortures. Matilda sighed and looked at her prisoner. The girl had to be her prized catch; no one else could have fought the way she did. She was the catalyst for the Great Summoning because she was special. Marnelphion demanded only the best. Matilda closed her eyes and smiled.

They would reach Malikai's stronghold, and the mighty wizard would teleport them to Bale's swampy lair. There, they could administer their tortures and hide from the pesky New Order or anyone else who tried to hamper the Great Summoning. Of course, Matilda would have to pay the steep price for Malikai's services, but she was happy to pay to get Cassandra safely into Bale's lair. Matilda was not letting her go.

And so the wagon moved through Yaddaton, the four powerful friends intent on getting Cassandra to a secluded place for tortures well earned. Matilda was content, and Marnelphion was pleased. Things were going as planned, and the outlook for humanity became bleak.

Epilogue

Amison met with the carofexian monk from Mecca-Loraine to discuss an urgent matter concerning the New Order. Sloan first met with him to read his mind and understand his true intentions. She found no malice within him, and the fact that he traveled with the sheriff of Oldorburg's wife and child only made his story more credible. Jamison elected to meet the young man in his study, where he'd grown accustomed to holding important meetings. He knew the throne room was probably more appropriate, but he already felt pretentious enough trying to fill the king and queen's shoes, so he elected not to use it.

Four sat around a comfortable fire, sipping tea or mead, depending on the individual's preference. Sloan, Neb, the carofex, and Max's wife, Tanna, joined Jamison. The three travelers, including Tanna's toddler daughter, Sade, were staying in the castle and had been in Pelesea for less than a day. Jamison was happy to meet with them, given the urgency of their visit.

The monk wore his robes without a hood, which Jamison appreciated. His bald head was on display, and Jamison understood it was customary for Mecca-Loraine monks to shave their heads. Tanna was a beautiful woman, and Jamison, who had met Max before the New Order departed, was incredibly anxious to hear from the young mother.

"So, please tell me, how is your daughter?" Jamison asked first to make his guests comfortable.

"She is tired, and your hospitality is greatly appreciated. She is sleeping now in the cozy room you offered us," Tanna answered.

"So, the three of you traveled from Oldorburg?"

"Kind of," Tanna answered, looking to Neb for assistance.

The monk sat still and emotionless and nodded his agreement. "A freld assisted us, so we didn't have to travel the full distance by foot."

"A freld?" Jamison asked Sloan.

"A creature of fire, Steward. They are known for their cruelty but also serve as allies to the fire carofex," the wizard answered. The carofex didn't disagree and nodded his agreement.

"So, why have you come?" Jamison asked, beginning to understand caution was probably necessary when dealing with the carofex.

Tanna looked to Neb, who spoke blandly. "The New Order is dead."

"What?" Jamison asked, sitting up in his chair.

"That's impossible," Sloan added with a nervous smile.

"Is it?" the monk asked, again with no emotion.

"Why do you believe this?" Jamison asked.

"Let me elaborate, if I may," Tanna said.

"Please," Jamison said with a wave of his hand.

"Oldorburg is overrun. The important people of the town are dead," Tanna explained.

"What? Baxter was there recently to bring Max to Pelesea, and all was peaceful then," Jamison argued.

"Yes, and Knom would have killed my husband if he hadn't left with Baxter. Sade and I would also be dead if it weren't for Neb," Tanna said, tearing up.

Jamison noticed that Neb sat still and emotionless but nodded again to Jamison to verify Tanna's story.

"Who has done such a thing?" Sloan asked.

"The same people who claim to have murdered the New Order, including Max," Tanna said, putting her head in her hands and sobbing.

Sloan comforted the woman and offered a kerchief as Neb remained stone-faced. He glanced at Jamison, and based on the look on the carofex's face, the steward knew that the story was true.

"A man named Dorin McVale, who brags that he worked in Pelesea for a long while with other evil men, intent on harming the New Order, claims to have sabotaged the ship *Hope*," Neb explained.

"That's impossible. The dockhands who prepared and stocked the New Order's galleon were honorable and trusted workers. They would have had to be in Pelesea for a long while, probably years, to earn that trust," Jamison argued.

"These people are a serious threat and not only claim to have sunk the ship the New Order used to cross the Nepress Sea but have formed a following of thousands of people to the east. Knom, a flesh carofex, leads a group called the Ultimate Order, which this mass of people follows," Neb said.

"Ultimate Order?" Sloan asked.

"Yes, they call themselves the Ultimate Order, I believe, as an insult to the New Order," Neb said.

Jamison let the words sink in, not wanting to believe them but understanding that what his guests said was true. "Who are these people?" he asked.

Tanna had regained her composure by this point but held on to the kerchief as Sloan retook her seat beside Jamison. The carofex answered, undeterred by the interactions of the women. "Murderers, thieves, and other villains, so Dorin claims."

Jamison sat back in his chair and pondered the information. First, he had received information from Inuentas that confirmed his true love, Binta Mulay, was probably dead. Second, these good people were telling him that the New Order members were dead. And lastly, what was this group of lawbreakers planning on doing? They had overtaken Oldorburg, but to what gain?

"So, what does this Ultimate Order desire?" he asked.

"They worship the demon Marnelphion, so they want what he wants. They support the summoning."

"And they are human?" Sloan asked.

"I don't know. I've only met their leader, Knom, who is a flesh carofex."

"What is a flesh carofex?" Jamison asked Sloan more than he directed the question to Neb.

However, for the first time during the meeting, Neb showed some emotion, his breathing becoming more labored as he leaned closer. "There is no such thing as a flesh carofex. Our race has an affinity for the various elements, never flesh. This abomination is the only one I know exists, and I don't know its origin. I can tell you this, however: it's dangerous. It killed my freld."

Jamison smiled uneasily as the monk returned to his unanimated form. After contemplating, he said, "The two of you and your child, Tanna, may remain here as guests for as long as you like. I will send scouts to the east to verify your tale."

He then took Tanna's hand and added, "Sloan and I will also work on verifying the fate of the New Order. I've known Kringus a long while, and I assure you he's not easy to kill."

"Yes, please don't assume the New Order is dead. We have no proof," Sloan added.

"But you have no proof they aren't," Neb said.

"Not yet, but we'll work on that. Sloan has some scrying abilities that may help us find the answer," Jamison said, but the bluntness of the monk's words had Tanna crying all over again.

GRESS SAT ON HIS THRONE IN THE CULIEM TRIBE, WITH HIS STRONGEST warriors and shamans gathered nearby. They were at the remains of their tribe's former home that Maltor's men had burned to the ground months ago. Maltor and Jak stood before the king, the few hundred remaining members of the Serpent Tribe behind them. Also gathered around them were the remaining thousands of the Culiem Tribe. Hundreds of culiem fairies flitted about the area, most near the throne. Maltor's four wives lay at the foot of the throne, now Gress's property. They all watched the unprecedented ceremony that Gress undertook to exile Maltor from the Yaddaton Desert and officially dissolve the Serpent Tribe.

Maltor, now healed from his grievous wounds, stood proudly before the young king. His right ear was missing, and the wound in his back would always cause him pain but wouldn't prove fatal, thanks to the burning touch of the wraith that inadvertently closed it. His damaged hip from his battle with Boskel, the former king of the Culiem Tribe whom he'd defeated in the challenge circle, had him standing slightly crookedly. Regardless of those wounds, Maltor felt great and lucky to be alive.

"And now, proud Maltor, I formally banish you from the Yaddaton Desert. From this point forward, if you are seen in our homeland again, my warriors will kill you on sight," Gress announced.

There was a great hush among those gathered. The members of the former Serpent Tribe already knew their king's sentence, so Gress's words didn't shock them. However, hearing the words was hard for them, especially those who had lived most of their lives under Maltor's rule.

"Furthermore," Gress continued, "your tribe is hereby dissolved from this moment forward, never to resurface. All those gathered before me from that former tribe are now my subjects and will pledge allegiance to the Culiem Tribe.

"Anyone who wishes to join you in your banishment may do so, and we will not judge them, but they will face the same harsh punishment as their king—they will be forever banned from Yaddaton. Let those who wish to join their king step forward to join him now."

There was a murmuring from his people, and Maltor knew that only a few hundred people remained of his tribe, and he could no longer be their king. They were loyal and would join him now that Gress allowed them. He appreciated their undying loyalty but couldn't allow them to leave Yaddaton.

He stepped up before the king, separating himself from the rest of the people. Gress's men bristled at Maltor's proximity to their king; armed with his mighty sword, he was a real threat. Gress waved them off. Maltor knelt, his head bowed in respect to the young king. His hip ached in that position, but he would hold it as long as it took.

"Maltor, do you have something to say to your people?" Gress asked.

Maltor raised his head and nodded. "Yes, good king, if I may."

Gress nodded, and Maltor stood and turned toward the remaining members of his tribe. They all looked at him hopefully, and he hated to quench that hope, but he needed to shift their allegiance to Gress. Where he was going, he couldn't rule people or provide for them outside the desert. He had no idea how he would fend for himself, much less others.

"My loyal people. I leave the Yaddaton now, not in shame, but with my head held high. I am and always will be Maltor, son of Gron, King of the Serpent Tribe."

There was a strong, unified cheer from his people. It was brief but powerful. They still believed in him even after he had single-handedly decimated the tribe. He nodded in recognition.

"However, I ask that you pledge your allegiance to the Culiem Tribe and Gress, their king. He is honorable and will rule you well. The fact that I stand before you, healed and armed, is a testament to his character. He will rule you with as much conviction as I have and take you in without judgment.

"I was wrong to challenge Boskel and destroy the structures of the Culiem Tribe, but I was not of sound mind. Because of that and the ensuing battle with the interlopers that took us all by surprise with their black magic, I have failed you. I am honored to have served as your king and will always rule here in my heart.

"Today, however, as I stand before you, I ask that you let me leave alone. To join me is folly, for my road is dangerous and amongst interlopers."

He pointed to the south, where his trail would lead him, and his people were somber. Tears streaked the cheeks of some of them, and it warmed his heart that they still believed in him after everything.

He turned to Gress and his former wives, whom Maltor had greatly mistreated in the short time they were members of his tribe. He had briefly taken them as his own after the battle with Boskel and knew each of them intimately. His lovemaking hadn't been kind, for his poisoned mind believed at the time that Cassandra was dead. They shied away as he grew near, and he couldn't make eye contact with them. It was time to move on to the next phase of his life. He had only known life in the Yaddaton and didn't know what to expect outside its boundaries.

He stood before Gress and offered a hand. Gress watched him intently, and his men were ready to defend if Maltor tried to draw his weapon. Gress stood and faced him. Although a bit shorter, he stood as proudly as any king Maltor had met. He knew that his people were in good hands.

Gress took Maltor's offered hand, and they shook firmly, sealing the pact. Gress moved beside Maltor, turning him with his firm grasp so the two kings could stand side by side and face the gathering. Gress took Maltor's hand and raised it above their heads. The former members of the defunct Serpent Tribe cheered loudly.

Maltor stood proudly for several moments, his hand raised high until Gress released it. Then, with a nod from the young king, Maltor knew he was free to begin his trek. Maltor looked briefly at his former brides, but they refused to look him in the eye. That was his former life. He turned from them for the last time and found Jak in the small crowd of former subjects. He made his way to his faithful friend and hugged the man tightly. Maltor had learned that Jak had come back to save him, and if he hadn't, Maltor would already be dead. He owed the man his life, and he hated to say goodbye.

"I owe you everything, my faithful friend," Maltor said. "Watch over my people and live out your days loyal to Gress."

Jak smiled, shook his head, and said, "No."

Maltor cocked his head and furrowed his brow, not understanding the defiance at this crucial point.

"My journey lies with you, my king," Jak clarified.

Maltor shook his head and began to speak, but Jak cut him off. "You are going to find Cassandra, I know. Like you, there is nothing for me here now. Besides, I know where Cassandra is."

Maltor's eyes widened at that proclamation. "You've seen her?"

"She lives."

Maltor grabbed Jak's shoulders and laughed loudly for the first time since Cassandra's disappearance. The two turned toward the remnants of Maltor's tribe, who parted so they could pass. Maltor walked first, Jak following. The people wept and touched Maltor as he walked through, and he acknowledged them all. Tears formed in his eyes as an emotion he had long locked away inside himself when he first became king threatened to spill forth.

He made it through, and soon Jak stood beside him. His people stood together once more behind them and awaited his next move. The Culiem Tribe looked on as well. The path ahead promised nothing but unknown challenges and possibly Cassandra Rho. Without looking back or to the sides, Maltor and Jak walked away from their people, no longer members of the Yaddaton.

TREESHA STOOD AT THE EDGE OF HER WOODS, SAYING GOODBYE TO her new friends. She had experienced many emotions over the last few days, having them in her home, and the familiar feeling of loneliness began to creep back into her. She was a loner and always would be, but these people before her were good souls, just as good as Brayland had been, and she would allow them to stay as long as they wanted. However, they had an important agenda to attend to. She went to each one separately to say her goodbyes.

She approached Alleah first and hugged the young woman. "You are strength personified and the natural leader of this small band. Take care of them and yourself, and do not be tempted by the desires all of us face. Be strong and true, and your goddess will shine through you."

Alleah smiled and nodded. "You are an amazing person, Treesha, and I will never forget you. Thank you for your hospitality."

She went to the shorter girl then. Chloe was as strong as Alleah but had been through something terrible that had changed her. She was a good person, and Treesha hoped she would overcome whatever demons she faced. She hugged the young girl tight.

"And you, Chloe, are an inspiration to the group. You have been through something that has made you stronger. You may not know it yet, but you are better for it. And from what I can tell, you are a loyal friend. Good luck to you on your quest. May your goddess bless you," Treesha said.

It looked as if the girl neared tears, and she hugged Treesha back. It took a while for her to release the hold. When she did, there were tears she needed to wipe away. "Thank you for saving me. I'll never forget you," Chloe said.

That left the most difficult of the three. Greyson had said little to her since she forced him to pleasure her sexually and, even now, would not look her in the eye as she approached him. She couldn't blame the proud young man; she had taken his seed and dignity.

"Greyson, these women need your wisdom and guidance. Work together to overcome any obstacles you face. I have faith you will please your god with your efforts."

He nodded but kept his gaze to the ground. Treesha hugged him, and even though he tried to keep it brief and quickly pull away, she held him tight. "Remember, women are gifts, not playthings for your personal use, right?" she whispered in his ear.

He broke the hug and nodded. Treesha could sense his embarrassment in how he moved and see the anger slightly etched on his face. She smiled warmly, and he gave her the briefest of smiles.

She stood back and looked at the three adventurers. They were ready to go on whatever quest awaited them. She had never asked what that was but knew they were searching for someplace called Tara.

"So, you are ready to leave me as you found me. I have enjoyed our time together and will miss your company. Remember—you are always welcome here if you cannot find this Tara place. I will sense you as soon as you enter my woods. Either way, you are all three welcome here anytime.

"My woods end here, and the forest breaks a few miles north. There is a road you will find as long as you follow the river. Hopefully, that will lead you to Tara. Goodbye, my new friends."

They waved one last time and then took to the north, following the river as Treesha had instructed. She watched them until she could see them no more. That familiar feeling of loneliness started to set in. She would be all right; she had Buster and her other forest animals. She held a hand to her belly and smiled. In nine months, she would no longer be alone.

KESSI AWAKENED TO RAYS OF SUNSHINE SPILLING ON HER FACE. IT TOOK her a few moments to gain her bearings, and when she did, she found herself in a large bed. There were several windows, one open and letting the cool fall air blow in. She blinked away the sleep and noticed Kody curled in a big chair beside her. She tried to recall the events that had led to her waking in a strange bed. She didn't recognize the room or remember exactly what had happened.

"Kody," she whispered.

The young man's eyes flew open, and he nearly fell off the chair.

"Kessi!" he said, rushing up beside her. He smiled at her and grabbed her hand. "I thought you would never wake up."

"What happened to me? Where am I?"

"You don't remember? You fought against the werewolves to save Emiline, and you went into some trance, and we could all hear music. Then you collapsed, and we carried you here to my house, where you've slept for nearly three weeks."

"Emiline, how is she?" Kessi asked, struggling to sit up.

Before Kody could answer, Sabrina burst through the door. "I heard voices!" she said before she saw Kessi, and her eyes widened.

Kody stepped back so the two friends could embrace. Sabrina flung herself on Kessi, and the two hugged for a long while. When Sabrina finally broke the hug and sat back, wiping strands of hair from Kessi's face, she said, "We've been worried."

"Sorry, I—" Kessi began, but Sabrina wouldn't let her get the words out.

"You were spectacular! We wouldn't have won the day without you and your god, Kessi! Your powerful trance was the second time you've shown this special power. You're amazing, and your god has blessed us all."

"The others, are they here?" Kessi asked, referring to her friends and former cellmates of Nesin.

"Every single one of them," Sabrina said with a smile. "They refused to leave without you, so we've decided to stay until the spring and continue our journey to Attins then. This place is as safe as anywhere else, and I feel that these people are now friends."

Kessi glanced at Kody. He had a stupid look on his face. He smiled at her when she made eye contact, and she couldn't help but chuckle. He was going to be trouble for her, she knew. His dark eyes and curly hair only enhanced his boyish appearance. She was attracted to him and hoped that she could continue building on the small foundation they already had.

However, Cassandra was at the forefront of her thoughts, and she knew she wouldn't stay in Sylor until spring. Time was of the essence, and her sister was in trouble. There was no need to discuss that now, but she knew she could convince her friends to travel to Attins earlier if she quickly recovered her strength. What she would do about Kody remained a mystery.

When she and Kody shared their awkward moment, Sabrina smiled and said, "And Kody has been by your side, neglecting his chores and not letting the rest of us have a turn sitting with you since you were bedridden weeks ago."

Kessi reached out her hand to the boy, and he took it. "Thank you, Kody," she said.

"Oh, it was nothing. I was just worried about you," he replied, his face flushing.

Kessi squeezed his hand in appreciation, but then she saw something that made her heart jump in her chest. Two figures appeared at the door. Galish, the vampire, was there, along with Emiline.

"Emiline!" Kessi shouted and struggled to get out of bed.

Her friend looked different, more beautiful somehow, and more at peace. Kody and Sabrina helped her out of bed, and on wobbly legs, she made her way over to the door to stand before the vampires. She nodded to Galish, who returned the nod and stepped aside.

"Emiline, you look so different," Kessi breathed.

"That's because I am, thanks to you," the vampire said.

Emiline walked past Kessi to the sun's rays pouring into the room. She smiled and stuck a hand into them. Emiline closed her eyes and sighed. "I have missed this," she said.

"The sun doesn't affect you?" Kessi asked in amazement.

Kessi's mind drifted back to the fight against the werewolves. She had witnessed Emiline's transformation then and understood she had much to do with it. Adlesk had healed Emiline of her affliction. Not entirely, but enough so she no longer had to be afraid or alone.

"She's been prancing through the woods, enjoying her rebirth," Galish said, and Kessi caught just a glimpse of the vampire's smile.

"I have sun carofex blood in my veins, thanks to Galish, and I'm permanently immune to the sun now, thanks to you, Kessi, my dearest friend," Emiline said.

The two embraced, and Kessi's heart filled with joy. She looked around the room at her friends, and she understood how lucky they all were to have survived Nesin and escaped it. All seemed right in the world. But as her gaze roamed to the open window, she thought of Cassandra. She was out there somewhere and needed help. Kessi would find her sister, and once she was safe, she would stop and enjoy her good fortunes. She vowed to find her, and the slight hint of a song she heard and felt in her soul told her that Adlesk was with her and nothing would stop her.

About the Author

A fan of fantasy and science fiction from a young age, Phillip Martin dreamed about writing stories. He's used that desire to run roleplaying games and even develop them. His roleplaying stories have created countless adventures and worlds for the benefit of his closest friends. Finally, some of his vivid imaginings have been immortalized in print for others to enjoy. Phillip lives in Christiansburg, Virginia, and can be found at www.cassandra-rho.com.